John Adams, Hugh Farmer

A Dissertation on Miracles

designed to shew, that they are arguments of a divine interposition, and absolute

proofs of the mission and doctrine of a prophet

John Adams, Hugh Farmer

A Dissertation on Miracles
designed to shew, that they are arguments of a divine interposition, and absolute proofs of the mission and doctrine of a prophet

ISBN/EAN: 9783337780500

Printed in Europe, USA, Canada, Australia, Japan

Cover: Foto ©Andreas Hilbeck / pixelio.de

More available books at **www.hansebooks.com**

A

DISSERTATION

ON

MIRACLES;

DESIGNED TO SHEW,

That they are ARGUMENTS of a
DIVINE INTERPOSITION,

AND

Abfolute PROOFS of the Miffion and
Doctrine of a PROPHET.

Believe me for the very Works fake. JOHN xiv. 11.

A NEW EDITION, CORRECTED.

By HUGH FARMER.

EDINBURGH :

Printed for J. DICKSON, J. FAIRBAIRN,
and J. OGLE.

1798.

PREFACE.

THE Chriſtian revelation well deſerves the eſteem of mankind, on account of its intrinſic excellence ; neverthelefs, the proper proof of its divine original is, that miraculous teſtimony which was borne to thoſe who firſt publiſhed it to the world. But, unhappily for the intereſts of the Goſpel, its moſt learned advocates have greatly impaired, if not deſtroyed, the force of this teſtimony, by aſſerting the power of inviſible beings, of different and oppoſite charaſters, to work miracles.

This opinion (than which fcarce any has been more generally inculcated) has occaſioned much perplexity to many fincere Chriſtians. When they ſurvey the miracles of the Goſpel, they can fcarce help *feeling* the force of the argument ariſing from them in favour of its divinity : but, when they recur to their ſpeculative opinions concerning the power of evil fpirits, their minds are in the fame fituation with that of the moſt learned of all the Jews *, when

a 2   he

---

* Maimonides, de Fund. leg. c. 8. feſt. 1. Compare the paſſage frcm Dr. Clarke, cited ch. 2. feſt. 6. p. 84.

he confeſſed " a fufpicion, that all miracles may be
" wrought by the power of magic or incantation."

What has ſerved to perplex the friends of revelation, has emboldened others to rejeᶜt it. From the
earlieſt ages of Chriſtianity, down to the preſent
day, unbelievers have treated the argument from miracles (as it is commonly ſtated) not only as an improper means of conviᶜtion, but as an affront to their
underſtandings. Celſus, (in a paſſage we ſhall have
occaſion to cite *,) not without an equal mixture of
ſcorn and indignation, upbraids Chriſtians with their
abſurdity, in making uſe of the ſame works, to prove
one perſon to be a divine meſſenger, and to diſgrace
another as a magician and impoſtor. And a late celebrated writer, when arguing againſt thoſe who allow the
devil a power of performing miracles, and who, (according to his conception,) after proving the doᶜtrine
by the miracle, are reduced to prove the miracle by
the doᶜtrine; aſks and reſolves the following queſtion : " Now, what is to be done in this caſe ? There
" is but one ſtep to be taken, to recur to reaſon, and
" leave miracles to themſelves : better indeed had it
" been never to have had recourſe to them, nor to
" have perplexed good ſenſe with ſuch a number of
" ſubtle diſtinᶜtions †."

It may, perhaps, be ſaid, " That could deiſts be
" perſuaded of the *truth* of the Scripture miracles,
" they would not deny their *divinity*." But the
　　　　　　　　　　　　　　　　　　　　ſame

* Ch. 2. ſeᶜt. 6. p. 83.

† Rouſſeau, in his Emilius, V. 3. p. 113.

fame opinion concerning the miraculous power of wicked fpirits, which furnifhes them with an objection againft the divinity of the miracles of Scripture, fupplies them with the ftrongeft argument againft their truth. For they cannot perfuade themfelves, that God, when he fees fit to give proofs of his own extraordinary interpofition, will chufe fuch as are deceitful or ambiguous. And whatever their own fentiments may be with refpect to the power of evil beings to work miracles; yet, as long as they are taught to believe that the Scripture afcribes to them this power, they will think themfelves warranted by the Scripture itfelf to reject or difregard its miracles.

. The more I reflect upon this fubject, the more fully am I convinced, that it is entirely owing to *the natural impreffion* which miracles make upon the human mind, and not to thofe fpeculative opinions which have been moft commonly entertained concerning them, that Chriftianity has maintained its ground in the world. And to thefe natural impreffions we might fafely truft the caufe of revelation; were they not liable to be effaced by the power of fuperftition, and the fophiftry of fcience, falfely fo called. In other inftances, as well as in this, the natural fenfe of mankind may be in fome meafure fubdued by the force of oppofite principles. And whenever this is the cafe, it becomes neceffary to fhew that thofe principles are ill founded.

What is attempted in the following fheets, is, to refute thofe principles of demonifm, which have done fo much difcredit to the argument drawn from miracles in favour of the Jewifh and Chriftian revelations.

a 3 Without

Without entering into an examination of the peculiar nature and circumſtances of the Scripture miracles, I conſider only *the general queſtion,* Whether
miracles are, in themſelves, evidences of a divine in-
terpoſiticn; and conſequently (when properly applied) certain proofs of the divine original of a ſupernatural revelation ?   Nor is it merely the credit
of revelation that is concerned in this queſtion; but
the honour alſo of the general adminiſtration of divine providence, and the common intereſts of piety
and virtue.   And one would imagine, that all men
would wiſh to ſee the affirmative of this queſtion fully
proved : for what can contribute more to our happineſs, than the belief that the world is under the government of God alone; and that no created ſpirits,
much leſs ſuch as oppoſe his benevolent and wiſe
deſigns, can diſturb that courſe and order of things
which he has eſtabliſhed?   With reſpect to the
friends of revelation, there is this additional reaſon
to diſpoſe them in favour of this principle, that they
muſt allow, that (at leaſt) it facilitates the proof of
revelation, and reduces it within a narrow compaſs ;
leaving them only the eaſy taſk of proving the truth
of the miracles of the Goſpel, in order to their fully
eſtabliſhing its divine original.

   Notwithſtanding many recommendations of this
principle, I am ſenſible it muſt meet with oppoſition
from the prejudices of mankind, which inſenſibly
bias even upright enquirers after truth.   Many are
ready to acknowledge, that an opinion is not therefore
falſe, becauſe it contradicts received notions; and
yet but few are duly ſenſible how exceeding difficult

it

it is to get rid of falfe opinions, early entertained, conftantly inculcated, and ftamped with the authority of thofe who are moft refpe&ed for their learning and abilities. Habits have as great an influence over the judgments, as over the a&ions of mankind.

The fubje& before us certainly deferves an impar-tial and attentive examination. And though the manner in which it is here handled may be liable to feveral obje&ions; yet the author hopes for fome in-dulgence from thofe who are acquainted with the difficulties with which the fubje& was embarraffed, and confider the compafs neceffary to be taken in treating it. One obje&ion it may be proper here to obviate, viz. " that by maintaining, that miracles, " if they are not works peculiar to God, form no " conclufive proof of a divine revelation; I give an " advantage to infidelity." To perfons accuftomed to follow truth wherever it leads, fuch language will feem rather to require a rebuke, than to deferve an anfwer. It is not the language of probity, but of policy, which has ever difcouraged all enquiries after truth, and ftill continues to ftop its progrefs in the world. This language betrays an unworthy fufpicion of the Chriftian revelation, which, nobly confcious of the validity of its credentials, demands a rigorous examination, and muft in the end be a gainer by it. If the tenets advanced in the following fheets are falfe, it is fit they fhould be dete&ed; and if they are true, we may embrace them with fafety: becaufe truth will be always found confiftent with itfelf. It is not however the do&rine which we affert that gives advantage to infidelity, but that which we op-

a 4

pofe,

pofe, viz. " the power of other beings befides God
" to work miracles, even in oppofition to heaven."
While this principle is maintained, and maintained
upon the credit of thofe very Scriptures whofe authority it fubverts; unbelievers, if we may judge by
the experience of near two thoufand years, will always reject the evidence of miracles as inconclufive.
If they are to be convinced, it muft be done, I apprehend, in the method here attempted, by fhewing
them, that this principle is as contrary to the fenfe
of revelation, as it is to the genuine dictates of reafon; and confequently that miracles, being appropriate to God, conftitute a certain proof of a divine
miffion, and are the moft proper means of confirming and propagating a new revelation.

I will only add, that it was never more neceffary
to do juftice to revelation on this fubject, than in the
prefent age; which is every day making fuch quick
advances in the knowledge of nature. For hereby
we are daily furnifhed with new proofs, that in the
fyftem of nature there is no combat of oppofite
powers; that all the parts of which that fyftem is
compofed, though infinitely various, act by uniform
laws, and confpire together in carrying on the fame
defign; and confequently that they are under the
conftant direction of *One* almighty Ruler. Will not
the prejudices of unbelievers therefore be every day
increafing, while men mifreprefent revelation as
teaching the contrary doctrine?

CON-

CONTENTS.

SECT.

SECT. III.

The laws of nature being the immediate ordinance or operation of God, the rule of his government, and effential to the order and happinefs of the world; it is impoffible that God fhould delegate to any of his creatures a power of working miracles, by which thofe divine eftablifhments may be fuperfeded and controuled, p. 57.

SECT. IV.

The afcribing to any fuperior beings, befides God, and thofe immediately commiffioned by him, the power of working miracles, deftroys the evidence of the exiftence and providence of God, p. 63; is hurtful to true piety, p. 64; and a fruitful fource of idolatry and fuperftition, p. 65. Chriftians too nearly refemble the Pagans, who deified the principle of evil, p. 66.

SECT. V.

If miracles were performed in favour of falfe doctrires; mankind would be expofed to frequent and unavoidable delufion, p. 69. Of the natural impreffion of miracles, when performed in atteftation of a profeffed miffion, p. 70. Whether miracles may accompany a falfe doctrine, *for the trial of mankind*, p. 72. Whether, in this cafe, the nature of the doctrine would univerfally fecure mankind from deception, p. 75. What confequences might be expected to follow from miracles wrought in fupport of idolatry, p. 76; or vice, p. 78. God will not fubject mankind to neceffary delufion, p. 80.

SECT. VI.

If miracles may be performed without a divine interpofition, and in fupport of falfehood; they cannot be, in themfelves, authentic credentials of a divine miffion, and criterions of truth, p. 81. Whether, in cafe of a conteft between two oppofite parties working miracles for victory, the party that works *the moft* and *greateft* miracles, is efpoufed by God, p. 83.

CHAP. III.

Arguments from *Revelation*, to prove, that Miracles
are, in themfelves, certain Evidences of a Divine
Interpofition, p. 94.

SECT. I.

SECT.

SECT. II.

SECT. III.

SECT. IV.

SECT. V.

SECT. VI.

CHAP. IV.

SECT. I.

as

b   CHAP.

CHAP. V.

A

DISSERTATION

ON

M I R A C L E S.

CHAP. I.

PRELIMINARY CONSIDERATIONS.

BEFORE we enquire, whether miracles are the peculiar works of God, and *in themselves* proper evidences of a divine interpofition, and confequently of a fupernatural revelation; it will be neceffary to prepare the way by feveral preliminary confiderations. I fhall begin with

SECT. I.

Explaining the Nature of Miracles.

THAT the vifible world is governed by ftated general rules, commonly called the laws of nature; or that there is an order of caufes and effects eftablifhed in every part of the fyftem of nature, fo far as it falls under our obfervation; is a point which none can controvert. Effects produced by the

1   A   regular

regular operation of the laws of nature, or that are
conformable to its eftablifhed courfe, are called *natural*. Effects contrary to this fettled conftitution and
courfe of things, I efteem *miraculous*. Were the conftant motion of the planets to be fufpended, or a
dead man to return to life; each of thefe would be a
miracle; becaufe repugnant to thofe general rules,
by which this world is governed at all other times.

All miracles pre-fuppofe an eftablifhed fyftem of
nature, within the limits of which they operate, and
with the order of which they difagree. The creation
of the world at firft, therefore, though an immediate
effect of divine omnipotence, would not come under
this denomination. It was different from, but not
contrary to, that courfe of nature, which had not hitherto taken place. And miracles may be faid to
difagree with, or to be contrary to, the general rules
and order of the natural fyftem, not only when they
change the former qualities of any of the conftituent
parts of nature, (as when water, for example, is converted into wine:) or when they *controul* their ufual
operation and effects, (as when fire, without lofing
its properties, does not burn combuftible materials;
or a river is divided in its courfe, the water ftill pre-
ferving its gravity:) but alfo when they *fuperfede* (as
they always do) the ufual operation of natural caufes.
For effects produced in the pre-eftablifhed fyftem of
nature, without the affiftance of natural caufes, are
manifeft variations from, or contradictions to, the order and ufual courfe of things in that fyftem. That
a man fhould be enabled to fpeak a new language,
which he never learnt in a natural way, and that his

body

body fhould· be fupported without food ; are events evidently contrary to the ord:nary courfe of things, and to that conftitution of divine providence, which renders mankind dependent upon their own ftudy and application for the knowledge of languages, and upon food for fuftenance. We do not affirm, that miracles do univerfally and neceffarily imply a proper *fuf-penfion* of the laws of the natural world, fo as that they fhould ceafe to produce their ufual effeēts : the human mind may receive new knowledge in a fuper-natural manner, without any fufpenfion of its prefent powers. Neverthelefs, the fupernatural communication of new knowledge to the human mind, is contrary to the general rules by which the human fyftem is governed, or to that connexion which God has eftablifhed between our acquifition of knowledge, and the proper exercife of our rational faculties.

To this account of miracles it has been objeēted,

1*ft ;* " That miracles may be performed, whete " there is no difagreement with any law of nature, " nor any variation from its eftablifhed courfe : be- " caufe many things which exceed the power of man, " may be performed by fuperior beings." This ob- jeētion has been illuftrated and fupported in the fol- lowing manner : " *A fpirit* may have a natural power " of lifting up a ftone from the earth ; and therefore " if he does fo, there is no law of nature contra- " diēted, any more than when *a man* lifts it up. " Were a man to walk upon the water, upheld by " fome *invifible power,* the law of gravitation would " no more be violated or fufpended, than if he was " upheld by fome *vifible power.* What departure is

A 2 " there

" there from the laws and conftitution of the uni-
" verfe, when a difeafe is cured by a fuperior being,
" any more than when it is cured by the force of
" fome powerful medicine; unlefs there be a law of
" nature or conftitution of the univerfe forbidding
" the-occafional interpofition of fuperior beings in
" this lower world? a point which ought not to be
" taken for granted, and affumed into the definition
" of miracles."

In anfwer to this objection, we may obferve, that
it is built on a mifapprehenfion of what I here intend
by the laws of nature. For though the word, *nature*,
may be fometimes ufed for the whole compafs of exiftence, created and uncreated; (in which fenfe of
the word, no effect can ever be produced contrary to
the laws of nature, that is, to the natural powers of
all orders of exiftence;) yet this is not the moft common acceptation of the word, nor that in which it is
here ufed. Neither do I apply this term to the conftitution of the univerfe, and comprehend under it the
invifible worlds, and thofe fuperior beings that inhabit them. By the laws of nature, I here mean,
thofe rules by which the vifible world is ftatedly governed, or the ordinary courfe of events in it, as
fixed and afcertained by obfervation and experience;
and particularly the order of that fyftem to which
we belong *. Now according to the ufual courfe of
events

---

* Thus, for example, that there is a force impreffed upon
all bodies whereby they mutually attract, or tend towards each
other, according to the quantity of matter they contain, and in
a certain

events in this fyftem, a ftone which lies upon the ground, will reft there, till it is removed by fome *corporeal force*, fuperior to that by which it gravitates towards the earth : all bodies fpecifically heavier than water, will fink in it, when no *bodily fubftance* interpofes to prevent it : and the difeafes of our animal frame will continue, till the conftitution, either by its own efforts, or by the affiftance of material caufes, returns to its original ftate. And therefore there is a real tranfgreffion of thefe feveral laws of matter and motion, when a ftone is raifed up in the air, or

A 3 . fupported

a certain proportion to their diftances : that every body perfeveres in the fame ftate, either of reft, or uniform rectilinear motion, except fo far as it is compelled to change that ftate by fome foreign force : that the change of motion is ever proportioned to the moving force whereby it is effected, and in the direction of the right line wherein that force is impreffed : and that the actions of two bodies on one another are always mutually equal, and directed contrary ways : thefe are laws of nature, or general rules obferved by natural bodies in their actions on one another, and in all the changes which befal them in their natural ftate. It may be faid, that the general laws of nature denote only the *phænomena* or objects of nature. To me they feem to exprefs fomewhat more, viz. that the phænomena are connected together in a certain order, and fucceed one another in an invariable train, according to fome general rules, fixed by divine wifdom. Nor does it appear, that any part of the natural fyftem, (not even the fmalleft particle of matter, any more than the vaft body of the fun or earth,) is ever moved ; but according to thefe ftated rules. The more nature is ftudied, and the better it is underftood ; the more reafon have we to believe, that its laws are ftrictly and inviolably obferved.

supported on the surface of the water *, without the
application of any corporeal force; or when a disease
is cured, without the assistance of the springs and
powers belonging to the human frame, or the application of any suitable medicine.

In affirming all miracles to be deviations from or
contradictions to the laws and order established in all
the parts of the creation, which fall under human
cognizance; it is not supposed or taken for granted,
that there is a law or constitution of the universe preventing the occasional interposition of all superior beings in this visible world, for the purpose of working
miracles. Whether there are *any;* and if any, *what*
other beings there are in the universe, who have a
power of interposing for any such purpose; is left
undetermined by our definition, and is the point
which is to fall under future examination. All that
our definition implies as a thing allowed, is, that, as
far as our observation reaches, there is an established
disposition and course of things, or that certain cau-
ses uniformly produce certain effects, according to
fixed laws or rules. Every contradiction to this constitution of the natural system, and the correspondent
course of events in it, I call a miracle, by *whatever*
                                                    spiritual

---

* If in this and the foregoing instance the law of gravitation be not suspended, but only overcome by the interposition
of some spiritual agent: yet on this supposition, a real miracle
is performed; because the operation and effects of the law of
gravitation are controuled, in a manner repugnant to the general rules by which the natural world is governed.

fpiritual beings it is apprehended to be effected, whether created agents, or the Creator himfelf.

Thofe who have oppofed this notion of miracles,
have not attended to the obvious diftinction between
the ufual courfe of nature in this vifible world, and *the*
(fuppofed) *natural powers of invifible agents :* and they
will not allow, that the former is changed, if the effect produced does not exceed the latter. But fuppofe an angel to be as able to carry a man through
the air, as a man is to carry a child in his arms ; ne-
verthclefs the former would be contrary, and the latter conformable to thofe general laws or rules of motion obferved by bodies in our fyftem in their actions
on one another. And if no effect can be faid to be
repugnant to the courfe of nature, unlefs when it fur-
paffes the natural power of the agent ; then, till the
utmoft power of the agent is known, it can never be
determined whether the operation agrees with the
courfe of nature or not. Nay, it would follow, from
this principle, that the courfe of nature can never be
changed : for fuch a change cannot be effected, but
by an agent who has power equal to the work ; and
yet if the agent has power equal to the work, then
the courfe of nature is not changed. On this principle, the courfe of nature cannot be changed by God
himfelf, merely becaufe he has a natural power of
doing it. And yet who does not perceive, that his
caufing the fun to ftand ftill for twenty-four hours
though it lies within the compafs of his omnipotence,
would be a variation from the order of nature, or the
common courfe of events in the natural world ?

2*dly ;* As fome will not allow, that *the order of na-*

ture is contradicted, fo others deny, that *any miracle is performed;* unlefs the action exceeds the utmoft capacities of the agent. Accordingly they maintain *, that the fame action may be or not be miraculous, according to the different abilities of the performer. Were *a man,* fay they, to ftop the courfe of the heavenly bodies, which is above the reach of all the powers of his nature; this would be a miraculous operation: but were *a fuperior being,* who had power equal to fuch a work, to fufpend the motion of the heavenly bodies; this would be no miracle at all. But this opinion is liable to many of the fame difficulties with the other. For from hence will it not follow, that while the agent is unknown, it will be impoffible to determine whether the operation is or is not miraculous? and likewife that God himfelf can never work miracles, becaufe he is naturally able to work them? Nay, as, according to the former opinion, no law of nature can ever be fuperfeded or controuled; fo, according to the latter, no miracle can ever be performed: it being impoffible that any action fhould exceed the power of the real agent. Every effect muft neceffarily have an adequate caufe. An effect, therefore, which is beyond the ability of the perfon who produces it, feems rather an abfurdity, than a miracle.

Should it be alledged, " that what the man himfelf has no power of performing, he may do by " the affiftance of a fuperior being:" it would be

eafy

* Dr. Chandler in particular, in his difcourfe of the nature and ufe of miracles, p. 17, maintains this opinion.

eafy to reply, that this fuperior being is the only proper agent, the work being accomplifhed by his power
alone. When we fpeak of a prophet as the *performer*
of his miracles, nothing more is to be underflood by
this popular language, than that they *take place* agreeably to his declaration, and are defigned as a teftimony to his miffion. He is not, in flrictnefs of
fpeech, the proper agent; the works are not done
by him, but *for* him, by that invifible being who interpofes in his behalf. If the works did not exceed his own ability, they could be no atteftation to
his character, nor proofs of the interpofition of any
fuperior being whatever. And the fame works would
be equally miraculous, were they to be performed for
any other purpofe, than that of bearing teftimony to
a prophet, or even without his intervention. The
refurrection of Chrift, and that of thofe who came
out of their graves at the fame time, though accomplifhed *immediately by God;* were as real miracles, as
if they had been effected, as many others were, *at the
voice,* or *by the inftrumentality of man.* When miracles are performed *at the inftance or with the intervention of man;* this circumftance ferves to point out *the
relation* they bear to him, not to prove their being
done by his *power.* The cafe mentioned above, and
which is framed with a view to fhew, that a miracle
is an operation beyond the ability of the agent; feems
very incapable of anfwering the purpofe. To ftop
the courfe of the celeftial bodies, is faid to be either
fupernatural or not, according as the agent wants or
poffeffes power equal to the work. But how could
this (or any other) operation be performed by a
power-

power unequal to it? It could be deemed miraculous on no other account, than its contrariety to the
general courfe of nature. If it was performed at the
prayer of a prophet; this would better ferve the purpofe of attefting his chara&er, but would make no
alteration in the nature of the work itfelf.

Moft writers, in defining a miracle, feem to place
it, not in *the effect produced*, but in the *caufe*, or at
leaft include the latter in their definition.   A *miraculous effect*, like every *common appearance*, has its
own proper fpecific nature, diftiи.guifhing it from all
others of a different kind, feparate from the confideration of its caufe.   And it is the operation or ef-
fe& alone, which is affirmed to be contrary to that
eftablifhed order and difpofition of things, commonly
called the courfe of nature : the real invifible agent
by whom the effe& is produced, though he a&s out
of his ufual fphere, exerts only his natural powers.
The contrariety or conformity of the event itfelf to
thofe laws by which this world is governed in the
courfe of God's general providence, is that alone
which denominates and conftitutes it a proper miracle
or not.   In this light, at leaft, the fubje& appears to
me; though, confidering the many different views
taken of it by our ableft writers, it becomes me to
propofe my fentiments upon it, with a juft deference to the judgment of others *.

From

* The greater part of our lateft writers upon this fubje&,
define miracles, *effects unufual, above human power, and manifefting the interpofition of fuperior power*. The following reafons
prevented me from adopting this definition.   1. The term *uu-
ufual*

From the account here given of miracles, as operations contrary to the courfe of nature, the following conclufions are fairly deducible.

1ft; No

ufu does not diftinguifh real miracles from many things which
are not miraculous, fuch as the *rare* and *uncommon* appearances
and productions of nature. 2. Nor does the calling a miracle,
an *effect above human power*, diftinguifh it from all other effects
equally above human power, produced by fuperior beings when
acting *within their ufual fphere*, which for that reafon cannot be
miraculous. 3. As this definition comprehends many things
which are not miraculous, and to which no perfons apply the
term; fo it excludes many things which are allowed by all to
be proper miracles. For there feems to be a difference between
effects *above* human power, or which argue a higher degree'of
power; and effects which argue a power barely *different* from
human, and in no manner fuperior to it. If a ftone of a pound
weight were fufpended in the air by *an angel;* all would admit
this to be a miracle. But does this argue a greater power than
is exerted, when a ftone of the fame weight, or one 50 times
heavier, is fufpended by *a man?* To make a piece of iron to
fwim, (a miracle afcribed to Elifha, 2 Kings vi. 6.) may not
abfolutely require more power, than men exert every day in
different methods, though it requires a power which *does not
belong* to their nature. 4. According to this definition, beafts
and birds may work miracles; for they do many things that are
above the power of man. 5. This definition, inftead of defcribing miracles by *the nature of the works themfelves*, defcribes
them by their *author*, and *the degree of power* fuppofed neceffary
to their performance. 6. Works which argue only a power
more than human, can be no abfolute proofs of a divine interpofition. 7. The laft part of the definition, *manifefting the interpofition of fuperior power*, is fuperfluous. It is only faying,
effects *above* human power, muft be produced by a power
above it.

1ft ; No event, however *unufual* or *ftrange,* however *wonderful* and *unaccountable,* can on thefe accounts alone be deemed- miraculous, or contrary to nature ; fince it may be only the lefs known or the. lefs common effect of its eftablifhed laws and order. Comets, eclipfes, monftrous births, prodigies, the peculiar properties of particular bodies, and all the rare appearances of nature, however they may raife mens wonder, efpecially in the more ignorant ages of the world ; are as regular effects of the laws of the natural world, as any of thofe with which we are moft familiar. Under certain circumftances the *monfter* is nature's genuine iffue ; and in the fame circumftances there would always be the fame kind of production *. Where nature proceeds regularly in her courfe, without being fubject to any adventitious influence ; there no miracle is performed.

2dly ; In order to determine whether any operation be truly miraculous ; it is not neceffary to inquire into the powers of fuperior created intelligences, and to fhew how far they do or do not extend. Such inquiries are wholly relative to the *caufe* or *author* of miracles, and are of no ufe in fettling their proper fpecific *nature,* as deviations from or contradictions to the ordinary courfe. of things. They do, indeed, neceffarily argue the interpofition of fome fpiritual agent, who is equal to fuch works ; but their nature is the fame, whether that agent be God, or an angel, or an evil demon.

3dly ; Before we can pronounce with certainty any effect

---

* Wollafton's Religion of Nature, p. 151. 7th ed. 8vo.

effect to be a true miracle, it is neceffary, (and nothing more is neceflary, than) that the common courfe
of nature be in fome degree firft underftood. In all
thofe cafes in which we are *ignorant* of nature; it is
impoffible to determine what is or is not a deviation
from it, or to diftinguifh between miracles and natural effects. Even a real miracle cannot be admitted
as fuch, or carry any conviction, to thofe who are
not affured that the event is contradictory to the
courfe of nature. On the other hand, in all cafes
in which the courfe of nature is *underftood;* it will
be eafy to determine whether any particular event be
contrary or conformable to it, that is, whether it be
a real miracle *. Miracles therefore are not, what
fome reprefent them, appeals to our ignorance; they
fuppofe fome antecedent knowledge of nature; *without* which, it is owned, no proper judgment can be
formed concerning them; though *with* it, their reality may be fo apparent as to prevent all difpute or
hefitation. *Every fenfible deviation from or contradiction to the known laws of nature, muft be an evident
and inconteftible miracle.*

4thly; Thofe who maintain, that both miracles
and the courfe of nature are equally the operation of
the divine power, have not fufficient ground to affert,
" that what *diftinguifhes* miracles from common e-
" vents, is, that, with regard to the former, the in-
" fluence of the divine power is obvious and fenfi-
" ble." For in both cafes, the influence (that is,
the actual exertion or exercife) of the divine power
is

* This fubject is purfued farther, ch. i. fec. iii.

is fecret and invifible; and the evidence and effects
of it may in both be alike fenfible and obvious. Nor
is it neceffary that all miracles fhould anfwer this defcription, but fuch only as are defigned for the conviction of mankind. The proper diftinction, therefore, between the miraculous and ordinary effects of
the divine power, confifts in this, that, in the former
cafe, God acts according to general laws; in the latter, he departs from them.

SECT. II.

*Miracles not impoffible to the power of God, nor neceffarily re-
pugnant to our ideas of his wifdom and immutability. Neither
do they imply any inconfiftency in the divine conduct, or a defect
or difturbance of the laws of nature.*

IT would at beft be a point of ufelefs fpeculation,
to inquire what purpofes might be ferved by miracles, if from the general nature of all fuch works,
there arifes a full proof againft their exiftence. And
fuch proof would arife, in cafe they were, what fome
reprefent them, abfurd and impoffible.

But to deny the poffibility of miracles, is to contradict a principle the moft certain and evident of all the
deductions of reafon, allowed even by the adverfaries
of fupernatural revelation; the being of a God. For
if there exifts an all-perfect mind, who made and governs the world, his omnipotence is a caufe adequate
to thefe marvellous operations. Infinite power, though
it does not extend to contradictions, performs with
eafe

eafe whatever is poffible in its nature. And fo far are miraculous works from being impoffible, that they are fimilar to what we fee actually effected in the common courfe of divine providence. I will endeavour to illuftrate this by the following example: to caufe water to be both water and wine at the fame time, is a manifeft abfurdity and contradiction; and therefore cannot be the object of any power: but to turn water into wine, or to change one liquid into another fpecifically different, is certainly within the reach of divine omnipotence; inafmuch as there is nothing contradictory in the idea of fuch transformation, and we obferve continual changes of a like kind in many parts of the creation. Thus the moifture of the earth, by a common but admirable operation in the natural world, is converted into the juice of the grape, and numberlefs other juices, differing in kind from each other, according to the different nature of the plant or tree which imbibes it.

This obfervation might be extended farther, and applied to other inftances. Revelation is itfelf a miracle; but wherefore fhould it be thought impoffible with God? To his infpiration we owe our underftandings, with all their powers; from him we derive the noble faculty of fpeech, by which we communicate our ideas to each other: and has the father of our fpirits no accefs to them, no ability of imparting immediately and directly the knowledge of his will, and of affording fufficient evidence of his own extraordinary prefence and operation? Is there any thing in this more inexplicable, than in the common action of mind on body, or of body on mind? Will any

affert,

affert, that the almighty author of our frame is unable
to repair the diforders of it? that he, who with fuch
exquifite fkill formed the feeing eye and the hearing
ear, cannot reftore fight to the blind and hearing to
the deaf? or that it is impoffible for *him* to raife the
dead, who every year renews the face of nature, and
revives the feed fown in the earth, and every day a-
wakens mankind from the death of fleep to new life;
in a manner as incomprehenfible by us as the greateft
miracle?   He gave being to every living thing, to
innumerable kinds of animals, and to a great diver-
fity of rational creatures; continually does he call into exiftence ten thoufand new individuals: and is a
fecond gift of life more difficult than the firft?   The
analogy between miracles, and the common operations of God in the fettled courfe of nature, is a
convincing demonftration of the poffibility of the
former.

Nothing can lead men to controvert a point fo obvious as this, but their not confidering, that the
courfe of nature, which denotes only the ftated laws
by which the world is governed, is certainly the voluntary appointment of God, if not the immediate
operation of his power.   For if it be admitted, that
nature is the operation or conftitution of God; it
cannot be denied, that the power exerted in producing natural, may alfo produce preternatural effects;
there being no other difference between them than
this, that in the former cafe, the operations are regular, uniform, and conftant; in the latter, occafional, uncommon, and out of the ordinary tract of
God's adminiftration.   Upon what grounds can it
be

be concluded, that God is limited to a fettled courfe of acting, and to the prefent laws of nature? Is he not a free agent? Did he not act without the intervention of natural caufes, when he created the world at firft, and fettled the prefent conftitution and courfe of things? It muft folely depend on the will of the Deity, in what manner he fhall exercife his own power; whether in continuing or controuling the courfe of nature, which is his own appointment; that is, whether he fhall work miracles or not. Thus, for example, it is owing either to his original law, or immediate agency, that the planets move round a centre, and keep in their refpective orbits: but the fame omnipotent hand which guides them in their prefent courfe, could eafily arreft them, or give them a new direction. To deny this, is to deny that God is at liberty to act as he fees fit, that he has any power over his own creation, and laws which derive all their authority from his fovereign will. The poffibility of miracles, therefore, cannot reafonably be difputed by thofe, who believe the exiftence of the all-perfect Divinity, the great Author and Lord of nature. And this is a principle which ought to be admitted, before we engage in inquiries into the truth of any fuppofed difcoveries of his will. For if there be no God, it is obvious to all, there can be no divine revelation *.

B.   As

---

* Miracles, indeed, which are the evidences of a fupernatural revelation, may be ufeful to convince men of the exiftence and perfections of the true God. Neverthelefs, we find St. Paul, with perfect propriety, firft inftructing idolaters in this fundamental point, before he opened to them the peculiar doctrines of the Gofpel. Acts xiv. 15. xvii. 22—31.

As miracles are not impoffible to the *power* of God,
fo neither are they neceffarily repugnant to our ideas
of his *wifdom* and *immutability*. Frequent miraculous
interpofitions might, indeed, argue a defect in thofe
general laws by which the world is governed; to the
regular execution of which laws, we owe our ideas
of order and harmony, our rational expectations of
fuccefs in all our undertakings, and our ftrongeft
convictions of wife council in the frame and government of the univerfe*. And confequently, it muft
appear highly improbable, that variations from thofe
laws fhould take place, unlefs upon fome fpecial and
urgent occafions. Yet whoever reflects on the boundlefs extent and duration of the divine government,
will eafily perceive, that nothing can be more abfurd
as well as arrogant, than for a man, a creature whofe
faculties are fo limited, and who is but of yefterday,
to prefume to determine, that no fit occafion for extraordinary interpofals can ever occur in that adminiftration, the plan of which tranfcends his compre-
henfion. By what principles of reafon can it be demonftrated, that he who reigns from eternity to eternity, never formed any defigns, except fuch as may
be accomplifhed by the prefent eftablifhment and
ftructure of the univerfe? In the *natural* world new
phænomena have been obferved; new luminaries in
the heavens have fuddenly fhone out, and as fuddenly
vanifhed. And notwithftanding the great appearing
regularity, with which the heavenly bodies perform
their revolutions; yet thofe which belong to our fyftem

---

* This argument is farther illuftrated below, ch. ii. fect. iii.

tem are fubject to fuch diforders, as may in a fucceffion of ages require redrefs from the immediate hand
of its creator *. And if the *natural* world may admit or demand extraordinary exertions of the divine
power; much more may the *moral;* becaufe more
liable to *diforder,* and at the fame-time capable of the
moft divine *improvements.* May not God then interpofe in an extraordinary manner, to atteft a divine
miffion, and communicate fome important inftruction
to his rational creatures, which they could not gather
from the common operations of his providence; or to
raife them to a fublimer pitch of piety and virtue, than
they could otherwife attain ? If they are frail and liable
to fall into fin, and are, either as a check upon the
exorbitance of paffion, or on other accounts, wifely
and juftly fubjected to all the miferies of a mortal
ftate ; may not the divine Being erect a new difpenfation to reform them from wickednefs, to redeem
them from death, and to advance them to a nobler
ftate of exiftence? Such occafional interpofitions
might be farther ferviceable, by obviating the inconveniences of governing by fixed and general laws.
For extraordinary interpofitions of the divine omnipotence in controuling the courfe of nature, befides

B 2 anfwering

---

* " While comets move in very excentric orbs in all man-
" ner of pofitions, blind fate could never make all the planets
" move one and the fame way in orbs concentric ; fome incon-
" fiderable *irregularities* excepted, which may have arifen from
" the mutual actions of comets and planets upon one another ;
" and which will be apt to *increafe* till this fyftem wants a re-
" *formation.*" Sir *If. Newton's* Opt. p. 378. 4th edit.

anfwering the ends to which they are more immediately directed, are well adapted to banifh from the
world the notions of neceffity and fate, (which owe
their rife to the uniformity and eftablifhed order of
the divine adminiftration;) to awaken intelligent beings to a fenfe of their duty and dependence; and to
give them a new conviction, and a deeper impreffion
of God's governing power and juftiçe. And if in
fuch inftances, and for fuch valuable purpofes as
thefe, (and there may be many others of a fimilar
kind far beyond the reach of our faculties,) the Deity
fhould diverfify his operations; would not fuch operations difplay, rather than obfcure, his wifdom, benevolence, and other attributes? It would be difficult to prove, that God may not, in certain circumftances, have *greater reafons* for varying from his
ftated rules of acting, than for adhering to them.
And whenever this is the cafe, and the end propofed
is proportionable to the means of accomplifhing it;
the miracles are *worthy* of a divine interpofition.

With regard to the *immutability* of God in particular; that cannot be reproached or impeached on
account of occafional interpofitions; fince they might
be defigned from the beginning, upon the forefight
of a juft occafion for them; and, inftead of arguing
any change in the Almighty, be only the execution,
at the fore-appointed feafon, of his eternal and immutable councils. Nor is it by purfuing invariably the
fame methods of providence, but by conftantly adapt-
ing them to every different occafion, that God difplays his unalterable and impartial rectitude. It will
not therefore follow from the fuppofition of God's

miraculoufly

miraculoufly interpofing his power in fome circumftances, that he muft neceffarily do it in all others,
however different; becaufe in the one cafe they may
be expedient or neceffary to anfwer the wife defigns
of providence, and not fo in the other.

Nor do miracles imply any inconfiftency in the divine conduct, or any defect or difturbance of the laws
of nature. When the Deity occafionally controuls or
fuperfedes them, he does not hereby contradict or defeat his intention in their firft eftablifhment : he propofes a defign different from it, but not inconfiftent
with it. The laws of nature, being the laws of God,
are certainly perfect, that is, perfectly adapted to anfwer all the ufes for which they are defigned : but miracles derogate not from this perfection ; becaufe they
aim at an end which the laws of nature were not intended to anfwer, and indeed could not poffibly anfwer,—the marking a fpecial divine interpofition, and
authorizing the miffion of him at whofe inftance they
are performed. Nor do occafional interpofitions of
the divine power difturb the order of nature in the
common courfe of things. The operation of nature
may be controuled in particular inftances, without
affecting the general fyftem. Not to plead, that fome
miracles feem only to fuperfede the operation of natural caufes, without controuling it ; or to produce
new effects without the affiftance of nature, but without interrupting it in its ufual courfe.

There is nothing then in the general idea of miracles, confidered as variations from the common courfe
of nature, to furnifh a certain univerfal proof againft
their exiftence ; and there is a power fuperior to na-

B 3   ture,

 turc, who is ever able, and who in certain circumftances may fee ample reafon, to over-rule what he
at firft eſtabliſhed.

S E C T. III.

*Of the different caufes to which miracles have been aſcribed.
The point undertaken to be proved, is, that miracles are never effected without a divine interpofition.*

AS fome have afferted the impoffibility of miracles, even to the power of God; others, on
the contrary, have reprefented them as works which
may be performed without any difficulty, either by a
ſkilful application of the fecret powers of nature; or
by the affiftance of invifible beings, who may be at
liberty to produce fuch effects without the immediate
order-of the Lord of nature. While there are fome
who allowing their poffibility, yet confider them as
performable by God alone, or as the works of infinite power.

I. That miracles are not the effects of the hidden properties of matter, the laws of motion, and
the art of man; or in other words, that they are not
owing to a fuperior knowledge and ſkilful application
of the fecret powers of nature; a few words will be
fufficient to evince. I readily grant, what fome fo
earneftly contend for, viz. " that we are not ac-
" quainted with all the powers of nature; that many
" ftrange properties of matter are now difcovered,
" which were not formerly known; and therefore
                                        " that

" that there may be others equally furprizing,
" yet undifcovered; that fome perfons having a
" greater knowledge of thefe properties than others,
" may, by a dextrous application of natural caufes
" only, perform fuch things as would amaze igno-
" rant. fpectators, and be by them too haftily mif-
" taken for real miracles; and that, fince we cannot
" univerfally determine the bounds of another's know-
" ledge, it is impoffible to afcertain the limits of that
" power which in fome degree increafes with his
" knowledge." All this may be fafely admitted;
for whatever men may be able to do *with* the affiftance of natural caufes, it is certain that they can do
nothing *without* that affiftance; and confequently cannot work miracles, which fuperfede the operation of
natural caufes *. Befides, though we do not know *all*
the laws of nature, yet we are acquainted with *many*
of them. It has been obferved already †, that in order to determine what operations are miraculous, an
antecedent knowledge of nature is requifite. And it
is a juft inference from hence, nor are we under any
concern to deny it, that, inafmuch as our knowledge
of nature is *partial*, and we cannot univerfally determine how far its powers may extend; it may be
equally impoffible for us to determine univerfally,
what operations are miraculous. But, on the other
hand, our ignorance of nature is not *total;* the common courfe of it is in very many inftances perfectly
underftood by all, by the illiterate as well as the philofopher; their own obfervation and experience im-

B 4 parting

---

* Sect. i. p. 2.   † Sect. i. p. 7.

parting to them very clear and fatisfactory inftruction
concerning it; fuch as is moft fully confirmed by the
obfervation and united teftimony of others, in the feveral ages of the world.   In this knowledge of the
laws of nature, all our reafonings, both in the fcien-
ces and in the conduct of human life, and all our
ideas, are founded. Conftant, never-failing experience
farther inftructs mankind in the uniformity and conftancy of the laws of nature: it informs us, that although men may difcover new properties of matter,
and find that natural caufes under a fkilful direction
are capable of producing very wonderful effects; yet
that they cannot fubvert, controul, or fufpend any of
the eftablifhed laws of nature *. No change in thefe
fixed

* Mr. Rouffeau, who has lately revived the objection to
miracles we are here confidering, affirms, " that it might be
" in the power of one unknown law in certain cafes to change
" the effects of fuch as were known." But what reafon can
this celebrated writer affign in fupport of this affertion ? Is it
agreeable to our ideas of the divine wifdom, to fuppofe, that
there is a perfect contradiction between the different parts of
the fame fyftem; that, for example, the operation of the known
laws which regulate the motions of the heavenly bodies, may
be defeated hereafter by fome other law yet unknown ? Do
the new difcoveries which are daily making in the hiftory and
operations of nature, give any ground for fuch a fufpicion ?
And even fuppofing that by the difcovery of fome law yet unknown, the effects of thofe already known might be defeated;
this could not affect the credit of evident miracles, works feen
and known to fuperfede the operation of all natural caufes, and
performed without their inftrumentality. Were we to allow
Mr. Rouffeau, that by a farther acquaintance with the powers
of natnre, men may hereafter be able to raife the dead; it would
ftill

fixed rules of the divine government, can be effected by human power; notwithftanding, in certain other refpects, human power may increafe in proportion to our knowledge. From hence it will follow, that miracles, which are effects repugnant to the fettled laws and courfe of nature, cannot poffibly be produced by natural caufes, though under the moft fkilful direction; nor be otherwife accounted for, than by allowing the interpofition of fome being fuperior to nature, and capable of controuling its eftablifhed order. And in all cafes in which the laws eftablifhed in the natural world are underftood, and the effects produced are contradictory to them; we may conclude, that thofe effects are fupernatural. In fuch cafes, the knowledge

of

---

ftill be a real and evident miracle to raife the dead, without the ufe and affiftance of thofe powers of nature. It has been faid, " That what, in one age, has been deemed a miracle, " has been found in another, more enlightened by philofophy, " to be produced by the powers of nature." This is not true with refpect to the miracles of Scripture. There is not one fact there reprefented as miraculous, which does not ftill appear to be fuch, notwithftanding all our improvements in natural knowledge. And how will the adverfaries of revelation account for this fact? The Greek and Roman hiftorians relate as prodigies many events now known to be perfectly natural: while the writers of the Old and New Teftament, who relate a greater number and variety of miracles, have not mentioned one, but what appears to furpafs the powers of nature now, as much as it did formerly. I only add, that if the Scripture miracles are eafily diftinguifhed from natural events; it is of no moment to inquire, how far ignorance or inconfideration may lead men in other cafes to miftake the wonders of nature for real miracles.

of the miracle is as eafy and certain as that of the laws.
To heal all forts of difeafes, even the moft inveterate,
in an inftant, and without the ufe of natural remedies; to perform thefe cures in numberlefs inftances,
without ever failing in any one, and upon perfons ab-
fent as well as prefent; all men muft acknowledge,
that thefe things far furpafs the bounds of human
power. An uniform, unvaried experience convinces
us, that they do not happen according to the fettled
conftitution of nature, and that a bare volition of the
human mind cannot in any degree contribute towards
their accomplifhment. Nor indeed did any man, in
any age or country of the world, ever lay claim to a
natural and inherent power of performing them.

Real and inconteftible miracles are eafily diftinguifhed from the artifices of impofture, and from curious experiments in natural philofophy; which,
however unaccountable they may appear to the ignorant, can never be pronounced by them to be miraculous; becaufe they do not know them to be deviations from the courfe of nature. Nay, from the vifible natural means ufed in producing them, they
have juft reafon to believe, that they are the effects
of the powers of nature. For thefe reafons, the motions of a crucifix, the pretended liquefaction of
blood, cures gradually effected in the ufe of natural
remedies, but afcribed to the interceffion of faints,
and the like juggles of popery, ought not to pafs
for miracles, even with thofe who cannot detect their
impofture: nor fhould the fkill of an Archimedes in
raifing an immenfe weight, with the affiftance of a
machine which himfelf alone underftood, be judged
fupernatural,

fupernatural, how furprizing foever the effects of it might appear to one ignorant in mechanics : in this laft cafe, the vifible application of mechanical powers; and in the former, the ftrong fufpicion of fraud arifing from the circumftances of the facts, and the covered manner of performing them ; and in both cafes an abfolute ignorance, at leaft, whether the effects might not be produced by natural caufes, fhould prevent any from pronouncing them miraculous : a fentence which fhould be always founded on fuch a clear knowledge of nature, as enables us to determine with certainty, that the effect in queftion is a contradiction to its eftablifhed courfe.

II. There are many who admit, that real miracles exceed the utmoft power of natural caufes and of mankind, who neverthelefs do not afcribe them to God as their author.

" There are or may be in the univerfe," it is alledged, " invifible agents, placed in a higher order " than men, and endowed with fuperior abilities, " fuch as are equal to the greateft wonders; and " God may not fee fit to reftrain them from exer- " cifing thofe abilities. Miracles, therefore, are " proofs only of the interpofition of fome fuperior " beings, not of God more than any other." In this manner unbelievers argue, in order to difcredit the evidence of the Jewifh and Chriftian revelations. " Were we to allow," fay they, " the reality of the " miracles to which thofe revelations appeal ; this " alone would not eftablifh their divine original ; " becaufe the works might be performed by other " powers lower than the divine." Nor is this the
                                                    language

language only of the avowed adverfaries of all fupernatural revelation, but even of very many of its fincere and zealous advocates, not excepting thofe moft
diftinguifhed by their learning and abilities, whofe
high reputation is fufficient to procure a general deference to all their opinions. Dr. Clarke * in particular affirms, " that it is by no means poffible for us
" to determine what degrees of power God may rea-
" fonably be fuppofed to have communicated to cre-
" ated beings, to fubordinate intelligences, to *good*
" or *evil* angels." And " that (unlefs we knew the
" limit of *communicable* and *incommunicable* power) we
" can hardly affirm with any certainty, that any par-
" ticular effect, how great or miraculous foever it
" may feem to us, is beyond the power of all created
" beings in the univerfe to have produced." Without any defire to detract from the juft merit of thofe
great writers, who affert the power of fuperior beings, both good and evil, to work miracles ; we fhall
freely and candidly examine the doctrine they advance ; than which none appears to me more groundlefs, or more dangerous. But before we enter on
this examination, it will be proper to obferve,

III. That thofe advocates of the Chriftian revelation who reject this account of miracles, have generally embraced another as hard to be maintained.
They allow, that fpirits, both *good* and *evil*, by " the
" greater extent of their intellectual abilities, may
" difcover to men a great many *fecrets ;* and that
" their fubtlety, agility, invifibility, and mighty force,
            " may

* V. ii. p. 697. fol. ed.

" may enable them to do moſt *aſtoniſhing things*, and
" enable them alſo to aſſiſt men in performing many
" *great and marvellous works*, ſuch as are far beyond
" the reach of human capacities: while at the ſame
" time they maintain, that a *real miracle* cannot be
" performed by any power which is not ſtrictly *infi-*
" *nite*, or otherwiſe than by the immediate exertion
" of *divine omnipotence.*"

Though this ſcheme be deſigned to ſave the credit
of real miracles, yet it can never anſwer this end, till
the abettors of it enable us to diſtinguiſh between the
great and marvellous works which created ſpirits may
perform, and thoſe which are peculiar to the Almighty. What purpoſe can it ſerve to call them by
different *names*, while we are left in ignorance concerning their reſpective ſpecific *natures*, and are liable to miſtake the one for the other? When the
learned biſhop Fleetwood allows, " that ſpirits may
" perform moſt *ſtrange and aſtoniſhing things, may*
" *convey men through the air, or throw a mountain two*
" *miles at a caſt ;* becauſe their natural powers may
" ſuffice for ſuch purpoſes*:" in what, beſides words,
does he differ from thoſe who allow them the ability
of performing real miracles? If he will not call any
effect a true miracle, which might be produced by the
natural powers of created intelligences; we can never determine what is truly miraculous, without firſt
knowing

---

* See p. 99, 100, 108, 109, 113, 114, of his moſt ingenious
Eſſay upon Miracles ; to which the public is indebted for many excellent reflections upon this ſubject; notwithſtanding the
dangerous conceſſions which he has here made to his adverſaries.

knowing the extent of the abilities of all created agents *. If they can remove a mountain; who fhall fay, that they cannot remove the earth from its orbit ?   And if they can go fo far; why may they not remove the fun from its centre ?   It can never be affirmed concerning this (nor perhaps concerning any other) miraculous effect, that it neceffarily argues the higheft pôffible degrees, or a ftrict *infinity* of power; fuch as cannot be exceeded.   Much lefs can it be proved, that no invifible power which is not infinite, could fupport a human body on the water, or raife it into the air; which neverthelefs are real and evident miracles, becaufe contrary to the known and ufual courfe of nature.

   " But *evil fpirits*," it is faid, " have not only the
" power of working the like wonders, which *good*
" *fpirits* do, but alfo another, which *good fpirits* will
" never make ufe of; that is, by delufion and deceit
" to imitate thofe true miracles, which none but God
" himfelf can really effect."   " The devil," it is faid,
" can deceive the fenfes of mankind, or place falfe
" appearances before them, fo as to make them be-
". lieve, fuch works are really performed as exceed
" the power of all created agents."   Thofe who hold this language do not duly confider, that fuch a deception of the human fenfes would be itfelf a miracle; a miracle multiplied according to the number and different organs of the fpectators; and which muft have the fame effect upon them, as if the work, however miraculous, was truly and really performed.

_ 1   For

* Contrary to what is proved, fect. i. p. 12.

For how could they diftinguifh, when an outward miracle is performed, and when it is that their own fight only is altered? Could they forbear doubting equally concerning all miracles, nay, concerning all the objects of fenfe, if they once firmly believed that their fenfes, the only judges of them, were liable to be thus deceived? If the delufion of Satan confifts, not in affecting the organs of fight, but in placing falfe appearances before them, fuch as are perfect imitations of divine miracles; this is liable to the very fame objections as the former. To be able to make things appear what they are not, and to impofe upon the fpectators beyond their capacity of detecting the cheat, would be equivalent to a power of performing the greateft miracles.

It will now, perhaps, be inquired,—" If miracles " are neither the effects of natural caufes; nor of " fuperior created intelligences, acting from them- " felves alone ; and if it cannot be proved, that they " do univerfally and necessarily require the exertion " of infinite power; to what caufe are they to be " afcribed ?" I anfwer, they are always to be afcribed to *a divine interpofition :* by which I mean, that they are never wrought, but either immediately by God himfelf, or by fuch other beings as he commiffions and empowers to perform them. Miracles may not require a degree of power abfolutely *incom- municable* to any created agent; and yet God may never *actually communicate* a miraculous power to any creature, or do it only where he directly authorizes its ufe. Now, whether God works the miracles himfelf alone, or whether he enables and commiffions

others

others to work them ; there is equally a divine interpofition. And in either cafe every purpofe of religion
will be fecured : for whatever God authorizes and
empowers another to do, is, in effect, done by God ;
and is as manifeftly a declaration of his will, as what
he does immediately himfelf. He can no more au-
thorize another to act, than he can himfelf act, in
oppofition to his own nature, or in confirmation of
impofture.

The point, then, which I fhall undertake to eftablifh, is this, " that miracles are the peculiar works
" of God, or fuch as can never be effected without
" *a divine interpofition,*" in the fenfe of the phrafe already explained. This point we fhall endeavour to
eftablifh both by reafon and revelation. And fhould
we fucceed in this attempt, there will then be no difficulty in fhewing, that miracles are, in themfelves,
certain proofs of the divinity of the miffion and doctrine of the performer, and the moft effectual methods of recommending him to the regard of mankind.

C H A P.

CHAP. II.

ARGUMENTS FROM REASON, TO PROVE THAT MI-
RACLES ARE NEVER EFFECTED WITHOUT A DI-
VINE INTERPOSITION.

MIRACLES, confidered as means of conviction,
or as proofs of an extraordinary divine revelation, pre-fuppofe an ability of judging, whether
God be the author of them, and they can be fitly regarded as his immediate declaration and teftimony in
favour of their performer. The appeal in this cafe
is plainly made to *natural reafon;* which muft firft be
fatisfied with the *evidence* of any fupernatural revelation, before we acknowledge its *authority,* or fubmit
to any of its *decifions.* And, therefore, before we
examine the fenfe of the Jewifh and Chriftian revelations, with regard to the authority of miracles; we
will confider what may be advanced from REASON,
to prove that they can never be performed without
the immediate interpofition of God.

We fhall begin with examining the idea which
reafon teaches us to form of fuperior created intelligences: and in the next place, endeavour to fhew,
that the fuppofition of their power to work miracles
is contrary to fact and experience: and laftly, point
out fome of the numerous abfurdities, which would
follow from their poffeffing a miraculous power.

C   SECT.

SECT. I.

The same arguments which prove the existence of superior created intelligences, do much more strongly conclude against their acting out of their proper sphere. The objection from their spiritual and invisible nature, answered.

WE are far from denying, that there are in the universe beings of a higher order than mankind, such as surpass us far both in natural and moral excellencies. All that we here undertake to shew, is, that reason is so far from clearly informing us of the power of any superior beings, besides God, to work miracles; that the best arguments it can employ, to prove the existence of creatures of a higher order than man, do much more more strongly prove, that they can act only within a certain limited sphere. Those arguments are chiefly the two following.

1*st* ; From the *diversity* of creatures, and the *gradual ascent* from the lowest to the highest order of existence, observable here on earth ; it has been inferred, that the scale of beings is continued upwards above man, and that there are numberless species of creatures superior to him, as we know there are of such as are inferior to him. "Is it not very un-
" likely," we are asked, " that the gradation of be-
" ing should stop just at man, the lowest order of
" reasonable creatures? Is the immense space be-
" tween man and the Deity quite empty, at the same
" time that there is not the least chasm between man
" and

" and nothing ?" In anfwer to this reafoning *,
I obferve,

Firft, That it has not, perhaps, all that force in
it, which its having been uncontroverted might lead
us to fuppofe. We may allow, indeed, that the *infinite number* of living beings with which the earth is
ftocked, affords ground to conclude, that the other
regions of the univerfe are equally furnifhed with inhabitants, adapted to their refpective fituations. We
may allow farther, that the *gradation* of being from
lower to higher, which we obferve in *our* fyftem, furnifhes a proof, that the like gradation obtains in *other*
fyftems, and that their inhabitants differ from one
another in degrees of excellence, and rife one above
another in beautiful order. But whether they rife
above us in perfection, the argument from analogy
alone, as I apprehend, cannot determine. For that
only enables us to judge, by God's manner of acting
in one cafe, how he will act in another; and of what
we do not fee and know of his ways, by what we do.
But all that we obferve in the fyftem to which we belong, is an innumerable variety, and a gradation of
beings. By the rule of analogy therefore fome fimilar œconomy may take place in other fyftems, and

C 2   they

---

* It is hardly neceffary to take notice of the great impro-
priety there would be in fuppofing, that the chafm between
man and his maker can poffibly be filled up. Were the chain
of intelligence continued upwards from man, through as many
orders of created beings as you can imagine; yet the uppermoft
link of this chain would be at an infinite diftance from the
throne of God.

they may contain numberlefs orders of creatures rifing one above another till we come to the higheft of
them *.   Beyond this, the argument from analogy
will not carry us, fuppofing it to carry us fo far †.

Secondly, Let us however fuppofe, that the fcale
of beings in our planet is a conclufive proof, not only of a like gradation of being elfewhere, but alfo of
there

---

* This may likewife ferve as an anfwer to another objection.
From the clofe *connexion* between the different orders of beings
in our fyftem, and *their mutual dependence;* it has been inferred
by fome, that we may be equally related to and dependent upon the inhabitants of fome other fyftem.   All that the argument from analogy proves, is, that in each fyftem of the univerfe, the different orders of creatures are or may be dependent on each other : but it does not prove, that the inhabitants
of one fyftem have a dependence on thofe of another : for of
this we have no example. Befides, if the argument from analogy proved a *mutual* dependence between the inhabitants of
different fyftems ; it would conclude as ftrongly in favour of
the dependence of the inhabitants of other fyftems upon us, as
of our dependence upon them.   There may be a relation between all thofe numberlefs worlds, and fyftems of worlds, of
which the univerfe is compofed, as between various parts of one
ftupendous whole : but the point that ftill wants to be proved,
is, that the inhabitants of other fyftems and worlds have more
power over us, than we have over them.

† Thofe who have fo often made ufe of the argument from
analogy on the point in queftion, will perhaps have a lefs opinion of its force, if they confider farther, that in another view
it militates againft their own principles : for were this argument conclufive, it would prove, that inafmuch as our fyftem
is inhabited by *corporeal* intelligent creatures, other fyftems
are fo likewife ; and thus lead them to deny a world of *fpirits.*

there being in the univerfe creatures as much fuperior
to man, as man is to the meaneft reptile: ftill the
fame kind of reafoning which proves there are fuch
beings, proves at the fame time, that they have a certain limited fphere of action appointed them by God.
For how various foever the powers of different fpecies
of creatures here on earth may be; they are all under
particular laws, and have bounds circumfcribed to
their activity, which they are not able to tranfgrefs.
The rule of analogy teaches us to conclude the fame
concerning all other beings. If we may judge of the
conduct of Providence in unknown inftances, by thofe
which fall under our obfervation ; " HE, who has fet
" bounds to the fea, which it cannot pafs, and fays
" to its proud waves, Hitherto fhall ye come, but no
" farther *," has bounded the power, and fixed the
ftate, of all the creatures which he hath made, not
excepting thofe of the nobleft order. And therefore
whatever their natural powers may be, and however
freely they may be allowed to ufe them ; they are limited and determined to fuch purpofes as God has
appointed, and cannot poffibly be extended beyond
the fphere affigned them by the Creator. And yet
no fooner is it proved, (or thought to be fo) that probably there are, in *fome* portion of the univerfe, beings fuperior to man ; than it feems to be taken for
granted, that they have the liberty of an unbounded
range over the whole creation, that their influence extends over this earthly globe in particular, and that

C 3 they

---

* Job xxxviii. 11. Jerem. v. 22.

they ftand in the fame relation to man, as man himfelf does to inferior creatures.   But though there be
a ftrict connexion between the different orders of creatures on this earth, who all belong to the fame fyftem;
yet none of them have any poffible communication
from this lower world with the inhabitants of different
fyftems; none of them are able to traverfe the univerfe, or to pafs the bounds of their proper dwelling.
And this muft be the cafe in other fyftems, fuppofing
them to be regulated by the fame laws which take
place in our own.   Their inhabitants may have larger capacities than mankind, and a wider province
affigned them; and yet have no more power over us,
than we have over them; they may have no communication with us, nor any influence beyond the limits
of their own globe.

   2dly; If we wave the argument from what is called
the fcale of being, and appeal to the unbounded power
and goodnefs of God, or to the aftonifhing magnificence of the univerfe, in proof of the exiftence of
creatures of a higher order than man : ftill thefe arguments, however conclufive, will not prove, that they
are not under the continual government and controul
of God, or that they have not all their proper depart-
ment.   For not to alledge, that the power and goodnefs of God, though ftrictly infinite, and though they
have (without doubt) difplayed themfelves in the production of more noble orders of beings than mankind; are not, however, exerted to the utmoft in
every, or in *any,* fingle effect; it is certain, they are
never exercifed but under the direction of unerring
wifdom, by which all things are framed in the moft

1   exact

exact proportions: and as to the universe, it is no less distinguished by its perfect order and harmony, than by its grandeur and extent. To what purpose then is it to plead, that we know not what degrees of power God may have communicated to created beings? Can it be shewn, that they are subject to no laws, that their influence is unconfined, and reaches to all the systems of the universe?

But it is the opinion of a justly celebrated writer *, that to deny created spirits the *natural* power of working miracles, is saying, " they have no power natu-
" rally to do any thing at all." He had before explained ·his meaning more fully, in the following terms † : " Supposing (which is very unreasonable to
" suppose) that the natural powers of the highest an-
" gels were no greater than the natural powers of
" men; yet since thereby an angel would be enabled
" to do all that invisibly, which a man can do visi-
" bly; he would even, on this supposition, be natu-
" rally able to do numberless things, which we should
" esteem the greatest of miracles ‡." Angels, ac-
C 4 cording

---

* Dr. Clarke's sermons, vol. ii. p. 700. fol. ed. or his Boyle's lectures on the Truth and Certainty of the Christian Revelation, prop. 14.

† P. 697.

‡ The doctor does not confine this reasoning to *good* angels, but extends it to *evil* ones, p. 699. " If the *devil* has any na-
" tural power of doing any thing at all; even but so much as
" the meanest of men; and be not restrained by God from ex-
" ercising that natural power; it is evident he will be able, by
" reason of his invisibility, to work *true and real miracles*."

The

cording to this learned writer, could not be equal to
men in dignity and power, much lefs fuperior to them;
nor could they even poffefs any power at all; unlefs
they are able to work miracles upon this earthly globe:
and nothing feems to him more unreafonable, than to
deny angels the power of doing all which a man can
do; which alone, he acknowledges, would be equi-
valent to a power of performing the greateft miracles,
on account of the invifible manner of their operation.
This reafoning proceeds upon thefe two principles,
that fuperior natures have the *fame fphere of action* affigned them with thofe inferior to them; and that
they enjoy the very *fame powers and privileges.* The
former of thefe is deftitute of proof, and the latter is
contradicted by the wife order and œconomy of Providence. Has man the ftrength or fwiftnefs of brute
animals? Can he fly in the air, or dive into the
ocean? How much foever man may excel the brutes,
he has not the fame organs and powers of action;
and his operations muft therefore be quite different
from theirs. The fame may be true of *angels* compared with men. Their capacities may be more noble

The ancients alfo, as well as our learned moderns, built their
opinion of the vaft powers of demons, upon the fubtlety and
finenefs of their make, and their *fpiritual nature.* Tertullian in
particular, after fpeaking of their power to inflict difeafes upon
mens *bodies*, aad to caufe a fudden diftraction of *foul*, adds,
" Suppetit illis ad utramque fubftantiam hominis adeundam
" fubtilitas et tenuitas fua. Multum fpiritalibus viribus licet
" ut invifibiles in effectu potius quam in actu fuo appareant."
Apol. c. 22.

ble than ours; and they may move in a much more
exalted fphere, without being able to do every thing
which man is capable of doing. ·

It is a point that hitherto has rather been taken for
granted, than proved, that a power of moving matter is effential to all fpiritual beings. It is difficult to
difcern any neceffary connexion between their imma-
teriality and a power over matter *. If they are not
united

* The late ingenious Dr. Ifaac Watts, in the 6th of his
Philofophical Effays on various fubjeEts, (p. 132. 1ft edit. 8vo.)
attempts to fhew, that though the almighty fpirit who called
the material univerfe into exiftence, can put the feveral parts
of it into motion as he pleafes, no created fpirit has any innate
power in itfelf to move any part of matter; that the world of
bodies, and the world of *minds*, are fo entirely different and feparate in their whole nature, fubftance, and fpecial properties,
that they cannot poffibly have any communication with each
other, except by a particular appointment of God. Spirits being void of all folidity, cannot move matter by *impulfe*, becaufe
there can be no contaĉt. Nor can they (without a divine commiffion) excite motion in bodies by *volition*, there being no natural connexion between their volition and the motion of material beings. The power which the human fpirit has over its
own body, (and thereby over other portions of matter,) is no
proof that a fpirit has in itfelf a native power to move matter
indefinitely : for the human fpirit, by all its volitions, can move
only thofe particular parts of the body which God has fubjeĉted
to voluntary motion, and for which proper mufcles are provided, together with the nervous powers which are neceffary
to move thofe mufcular parts. This limitation of its power
fhews, that it is not effential to its nature, but owing to the
fpecial ordination and conftitution of God, who by uniting fuch
a body to fuch a fpirit, has given to man that degree of power
over matter which he poffeffes. It does not therefore appear,

that

united to fuch organized fyftems of matter, as the fpirit of man is; upon what grounds fhall we afcribe to them, that capacity for human actions and enjoyments, which is the fole effect of our union to thofe particular fyftems of matter? As reafonably may we fuppofe, that light and darknefs dwell together; or that caufes the moft oppofite to each other, fhould all produce the fame effects; as that *fpiritual* beings fhould have the fame natural powers with *corporeal* ones. To the abfurdity of this principle, we may add its tendency to countenance the moft flagrant immorality. That *polluted* intercourfe which was thought to be carried on between the human race and celeftial beings *, of which we read in the lying legends

of

that any immaterial created fpirit can operate upon matter, unlefs firft united to a body. Whether there are any created fpirits who are entirely unembodied, I do not here enquire: all I mean, is to fhew, that their being *fpirits* does not prove their power of acting upon matter, and of working miracles.

* We learn from *Socrates*, (apud *Platon. Cratyl.*) that the *heroes* (who, in the Pagan theology, are ranked next after demons,) " were all of them born from Love, either of a god " with a mortal woman, or of mortal men with goddeffes." Dionyfius Halicarnaffenfis, (Ant. Rom. l. 1. c. 77. p. 61. ed. Oxon.) after relating the rape of Ilia, explains more fully this doctrine of the Pagans. The Jews, in our Saviour's time, endeavoured to approach as near as poffible to Paganifm; for Jofephus fpeaks of *the angels of God mixing with women, and begetting a moft wicked offspring,* Antiq. l. 1. c. 4. The fame opinion was alfo embraced by Philo. And what is yet more to be lamented, many *Chriftian* writers, Juftin Martyr, (Apol. 1. p. 10 & 33. ed. Thirlbii.) Tertullian, (Apol. c. 22.) Athenagoras,

of Jewifh rabbis, and Gentile poets and philofophers, gained credit upon the pretence, (and was indeed no unnatural confequence from it), that fuperior beings poffefs the fame powers with mankind, and could at pleafure affume a human form. This maxim has ferved as a cover for the luft of mankind, in Popifh as well as pagan countries; though, perhaps, it was at firft invented to fupport the credit of a falfe theology. What the heathen priefts once incorporated into their religion, that the philofophers undertook to juftify. And too many Chriftians (in the true fpirit of the Jews before them) have ever been more fond of the fouleft dregs of Paganifm, than of that holy religion which came down from heaven.

If we fet afide the wild fables of antiquity, (however dignified with the pompous title of *philofophy*,) and form our judgment of fuperior beings by the fober rule of analogy; we fhall be under no temptation *to reduce the natural powers of created beings to a low degree;* (a liberty which a learned writer * is pleafed

---

rns, Clemens Alexandrinus, Cyprian and others, maintained that demons, in the fhape of the heathen gods, had commerce with women, and defiled boys; and they endeavoured to father thefe fentiments upon a paffage of facred fcripture, Gen. vi. 2. I would not take notice of a circumftance which reflects no fmall difhonour upon fo many of the primitive Chriftians, did it not appear to be a matter of great importance to be continually recollected, that when they embraced Chriftianity, they, at the fame time, defiled it with the groffeft doctrines of Paganifm.

* Dr. Clarke's Serm. Vol. 2. p. 697.

pleafed to allow us :) the confideration of their poffeffing powers fuperior to mankind, will not create
any proof, or even the loweft degree of prefumption,
that they have any power over this earthly globe, or
are capable of difturbing the laws by which it is governed.   Reafon does indeed make known to us one
almighty, omniprefent Being, who is at liberty to act
every where, and in what manner he pleafes ; and his
omnipotence is the only adequate caufe, we are capable of difcovering in the whole compafs of exiftence,
of thofe effects which are called miraculous : to him
therefore it is moft natural to afcribe them. With regard to all other beings, it is not pretended that they
exift neceffarily ; and that it is impoffible for them to
be excluded from any place, or confined to any : they
may therefore, nay, they muft have fome limits circumfcribed to their agency. The very fame kind of
reafoning which is thought to prove their exiftence,
does much more clearly fhew, that all their powers
are bounded, and their ftation fixed by their omnipotent creator, and that they cannot act beyond their
proper fphere. Should it be faid, " That allowing that
" fuperior created beings have only a limited fphere
" of action affigned them ; yet how does it appear,
" that this lower world itfelf is not their appointed
" fphere, and that they have not a power of inter-
" pofing to work miracles upon this earthly globe ?"
The anfwer will be contained in the following fection.

SECT.

SECT. II.

The fuppofition of the power of any created agents to work miracles of themfelves in this lower world, is contradicted by the obferva-tion and experience of all ages : there being, in fact, no proper evidence of the truth of any miracles, but fuch as may fitly be a-fcribed to the Deity. The objection, that God may lay created fpi-rits under a general, but not an univerfal reftraint, confidered.

THIS being a queftion *of fact*; it is manifeftly incumbent upon thofe who affirm, that mira-cles have been performed by evil beings acting with-out the order of God, to produce the facts upon which they chufe to reft their caufe, and to eftablifh them by an evidence which cannot be overturned *.

In the mean time, if we confult *our own obfervation and experience;* we find that God governs the world by fixed and eftablifhed laws. The more we improve in the knowledge of nature, the more regular does it appear in all its productions. Even the minuteft parts of it obey the laws of God as conftantly as the moft magnificent bodies in the firmament, and co-operate
with

* To prevent miftakes, it may not be improper to obferve, that it is not here intended to prove, that no fuperior beings ftand in any relation to our fyftem, or that they never operate within its limits in a manner imperceptible by the human fen-fes ; but merely that they do not interpofe fenfibly, and in a miraculous manner. We are not fo well acquainted with the regulations of the *fpiritual*, as with thofe of the *material* world.

with them in their proper fphere for the prefervation and benefit of the whole. And this regularity of the courfe of nature is an argument, that it is not difturbed by any miraculous interpofitions. Now if evil fpirits do not work miracles *at prefent;* why fhould we believe they *ever* have ? Indeed, our not having *feen* any miracles ourfelves, is a fufficient reafon for rejecting thofe that are *reported* by others; unlefs it can be fhewn, that they were expedient in the times and places, in which they are faid to have been performed, to anfwer fome extraordinary purpofes of divine providence; or that they are attended by an evidence of their certainty, fuperior to the natural prefumption of their falfehood, and to the proofs which fatisfy us with regard to the common events of life.

But this is far from being the cafe, with regard to the generality of thofe miracles which are related in *hiftory.* Amongft them all, we fhall find none which on any account deferve credit; except fuch as in their nature, intention, and circumftances, are worthy of God; and which therefore, allowing their reality, may reafonably be fuppofed to have him for their author. Of this kind are the miracles of the Jewifh and Chriftian difpenfations. But we are here inquiring into the reality of fuch miracles, as are thought to have been performed by fome evil agent. With regard to thefe; fuch of them as are beft fupported, have been feverally weighed in the balance of reafon, and been found wanting *. It has been
                                                      fhewn,

---

* Cicero in his fecond book of *divination,* (in which he confutes the arguments advanced in favour of it in the firft,) and
                                                      Fontenelle

fhewn, that they are deftitute of every effential character of truth, and bear all the diftinguifhing fea-
tures of *human impoftures;* that they are trifling, lu-
dicrous and abfurd in their own nature; or deftitute
of all rational intention, and manifeftly calculated to
anfwer fome low or worldly purpofe; that they are
related by incompetent witneffes, againft whofe fkill
and integrity there are the ftrongeft exceptions; and
that they never gained credit amongft any, but thofe
whofe ignorance and fuperftition expofed them to the
groffeft delufions *. In all thofe cafes in which the
facts cannot be denied, their miraculous nature may
juftly be called in queftion. The ancient prodigies,
fuch of them, I mean, as were not mere fictions,
were natural accidents, interpreted arbitrarily, and
which

Fontenelle in his *Hiftory of Oracles,* (which is an elegant a-
bridgement of Vandale's larger work on the fame fubject;)
have fufficiently difcredited the feveral modes of Pagan *prophecy.* And Dr. Douglafs in his *Criterion,* and many other excellent writers, have very fuccefsfully expofed the falfehood of
the beft attefted *miracles,* both amongft Papifts and Pagans.

* Some learned perfons, fenfible that the devil does not manifeft a miraculous power in all countries and in all ages, though
they imagine he fometimes does; maintain, " that the world of
" fpirits may undergo many variations, and be fubject to different
" reftraints and regulations in different ages, fo as to interfere
" more or lefs or not at all in human affairs." Dr Taylor's fcheme
of Scripture-Divinity, p. 266. But thefe (fuppofed) revolutions
in the world of fpirits, correfpond to the known and certain revolutions of learning and fcience here on earth. Now whether
is it moft reafonable to believe, that human knowledge con-
tracts, and human ignorance and credulity enlarge, the empire
of

which created terror only as their caufes were unknown. It is merely in thofe ages and countries in
which nature was little underftood, that prodigies
have abounded. Laftly, Very many cafes fuppofed
miraculous, may be refolved by confidering how nature and art may have acted in conjunction *. In
a word, all the facts appealed to, in proof of the miraculous agency of evil fpirits, are èither *not fupernatural*, or *not real.* I will not defcend into particulars,
that I may not repeat what has been fo well urged by
others ; but only add a few general obfervations,
which feem to affect the credit of all thofe miracles, which, in cafe they had been really performed,
could not have God for their author.

1*ft* ; None have ever yet attempted to fhew, that
any of the miracles in 'queftion, are fupported by an
evidence fuperior to the natural improbability or abfurdity of the facts themfelves. How far they are im-
probablé or abfurd, will appear from what occurs in
the fequel. In the mean time all muft admit, that
the more improbable any fact is, the more unexcep-
tionable

---

of fpirits who belong to the other world ; or, that it is not
their real *power*, but mens *belief* concerning it, which is thus
affected by the progrefs or declenfion of human knowledge ?
What Livy fays of the prodigies which were reported to have
happened at Rome at a particular period, is applicable to demoniacal miracles : " Prodigia eo anno multa nuntiata funt,
" quæ-quo magis credebant fimplices ac religiofi homines, eo
" plura nuntiabantur." Lib. 24. c. 10.

* The curious may find this obfervation very well illuftrated
in Dr. Hutchinfon on Witchcraft.

tionable fhould the evidence be by which it is fupported: and if it be abfurd, no teftimony in favour
of it can be worthy of credit.

2*dly;* It is univerfally allowed, that *moft* of thefe miracles were the mere effects of human artifice and fraud.
Now, if *moft* were fo, why not *all?* The principles
upon which all men condemn fo large a *part,* if carried to their juft extent, would oblige them to condemn the *whole.* At leaft, it muft be allowed to be
incumbent on thofe who make a diftinction, to point
out the difference between thofe demoniacal miracles
which they reject, and thofe which they receive: a
tafk which they have hitherto prudently declined *.

3*dly;* The reafon affigned for not allowing all of
them to be human frauds, viz. " Left, if out of fo ma-
" ny facts alledged, none of them are true, we fhould
" deftroy the credit of all human teftimony, even
" that upon which the miracles of Scripture are
" built;" is both inconclufive in itfelf, and difhon-

              D   ourable

---

* We might add, that the behaviour of the perfons, who
are thought to have performed miracles and delivered oracles
by the affiftance of evil fpirits, is exactly fuch as agrees with
the fuppofition of their being deftitute of that affiftance, and
having no other dependence than human artifice and fraud.
Now if their miracles were real, why did they always act as
if they had been fictitious? Why were not the works performed in fuch a manner, as clearly to manifeft the interpofition of fome fuperior being? And why did the conductors of
the ancient oracles, in order to maintain their credit, take
fuch pains to procure early and univerfal intelligence, if fecret,
diftant, and future events were fupernaturally revealed? See
Lucian's Alexand. feu Pfeudomant.

ourable to true religion. Notwithstanding these, and
ten thousand other instances of the deceitfulness of
human testimony; yet has it ever been allowed and
found, under proper circumstances, to be a very safe
and reasonable ground of reliance. The numerous
frauds of every kind which have obtained in the
world, are a ground of caution, not of universal scep-
ticism. Though many miracles have been forged,
it will not from thence follow, that no real miracles
have ever been performed. Nay, " how can we ac-
" count for a practice so universal of forging mira-
" cles for the support of false religions, if on some
" occasions they had not actually been wrought for
" the confirmation of a true one ? Or how is it
" possible, that so many spurious copies should pass
" upon the world, without some genuine original
" from which they were drawn ; whose known exist-
" ence and tried success might give an appearance of
" probability to the counterfeit * ?" It would be
unreasonable, either to receive or reject all miracles
alike ; in case there be a just distinction between some
and others. Now the miracles of Scripture are more
credible in their own nature than any others, being
performed for ends of the highest importance, such
as are suitable to the character of an infinitely perfect
Being, and which could not be accomplished in any
other method. Their truth is confirmed, by wit-
nesses of the most unsuspected credit ; by the public
revolutions

* Dr. Middleton's Prefatory Discourse to a letter from
Rome, p. 86—88.

revolutions and events which they produced, (fuch as the converfion of the world to the Chriftian faith *,) and which cannot poffibly be accounted for, but up- on the fuppofition of their truth ; by the clear pro- phecies delivered by the authors of thefe works, of the completion of which diftant ages are witneffes ; and by a variety of other arguments peculiar to thefe miracles, and which ferve to detect and expofe the falfehood of all others. Thofe feem to me but ill to confult the credit of the Gofpel miracles, who place them on a level with grofs impoftures, inftead of pointing out the wide difference between them ; and who have no other way of fupporting the Chriftian faith, than by countenancing lies and popular errors, which in all ages has created the ftrongeft prejudice againft it, and given occafion to boundlefs fufpi- cions †.

4thly ; Many even of thofe miracles, which of all others feemed to have the faireft pretenfions to credit, have been *undeniably proved* to be mere impoftures. Amongft thefe I reckon many of the miracles of

D 2

popery,

---

* The miracles of Chriftianity confirmed a doctrine contrary to mens ftrongeft prejudices, and could not be believed without danger : other miracles, for the moft part, cannot be rejected without danger, and are defigned to eftablifh popular and pro- fitable errors.

† " Dum per mendacium tenditur, ut fides doceatur, id " demum agitur, ut nulli habetur fides." St. Auguft. ad Confentium.

popery *, and thofe of witchcraft †, both of them attefted upon oath by pretended eye-witneffes, and the
latter examined into with all the accuracy and authority of a court of juftice, and yet both afterwards found
to be the offspring of fraud and delufion. Amongft
all thofe which have efcaped detection, there is no
ground to prefume, that there is one either more credible in itfelf, or more ftrongly attefted, than thofe
in which the impofture has been difcovered. And
therefore. without troubling ourfelves to account for every particular relation; is there not the higheft reafon
to believe, that, had they all been equally fubject to
examination, and undergone a rigorous inquiry, the
impofture muft have been difcovered in all?

Now, if there be no fufficient reafon to believe, that
any fuperior fpirits acting without the order of God,
have ever, from the beginning of the world to this
day, performed a fingle miracle upon our earthly
globe; how void of all foundation, muft be the a-
fcribing to them a miraculous power? Were they
poffeffed of fuch a power, it is natural to fuppofe they
would have exerted it *frequently*; efpecially as it may
be fo eafily made fubfervient to the purpofes of malevolence and impiety? What miferies of every kind
might not wicked fpirits, from a principle of envy
and hatred, introduce amongft mankind? And if
good

---

* Several remarkable conceffions of Papifts themfelves upon this head, are cited below, ch. 3. fect. 4. art. 5.

† See Hutchinfon on Witchcraft, ch. 1.

good fpirits enjoyed an equal liberty of doing good offices to men ; what a theatre of contention would our globe have been between fpirits of fuch oppofite difpofitions and defigns ? And therefore, if in a long fucceffion of ages, there has been no appearance of any fuch conteft between virtuous and wicked fpirits; if no motives whatever have excited the one or the other to exert a miraculous power, fo much as *once* ; is it not a natural inference, that they do not poffefs it ? With regard to God, indeed ; reafon informs us, that he who eftablifhed the courfe of nature, can change it at pleafure, even whether he has already done fo or not. But the cafe is different as to other beings, whofe powers and operations are only to be known (in a natural way) by obfervation and expe- rience. God is manifeft in every part of nature ; but who can point out the effects of other fpirits, and their operations on the univerfe ? And if we fee no effects of their agency on this earthly globe, if no fuch effects have ever been feen ; there can be no ground from reafon to afcribe it to them. It is as repugnant to the obfervation and experience of all ages, to afcribe to evil fpirits a miraculous power, as it is to afcribe life to the inanimate, or fpeech to the brute creation.

To deftroy the force of this argument, fome have pleaded, " that fuperior created intelligences, evil as " well as good, do not want the *natural power* of " working miracles, but only the *liberty* of exerting " it : and notwithftanding they may be reftrained " from ufing it *frequently* or *commonly* ; yet that it

" can never be proved, (as a great * writer expreſſes
" it) that they are under ſuch reſtraints, *univerſally*,
" *perpetually*, and *without exception*." There is evidently, I acknowledge, a real difference between *having the power* of performing miracles or of producing
any other effects, and the actual *exerciſe* of that power;
and thoſe perſons may have the power, who do not
exerciſe it, provided their not exerciſing it be the
matter of their own choice. But I ſcarce underſtand
the propriety of repreſenting any perſons as having a
power, which they are *reſtrained* from exerciſing by
others. As far as they loſe their *liberty* of exerting
it, their *power* is abridged. The malefactor confined
in a dungeon, and the ſlave chained to a galley, by
loſing the liberty, loſes the power of going beyond
the limits of his dungeon, and the length of his
chain. Not, however, to infiſt upon this; I would
obſerve, in anſwer to this objection, Firſt, That were
the Deity to lay ſuperior beings under ſuch a *general
reſtraint* as is here ſuppoſed; the removal of that reſtraint, and the ſetting them at liberty on any *particular occaſion*, on purpoſe that they might work particular miracles, and with no other view; would be
giving them more than a bare *permiſſion*, (as ſome repreſent it;) it would be giving them both a *power*
and a *commiſſion* to perform thoſe particular miracles
on that ſpecial occaſion. The miraculous works in
this caſe could not be confidered in the ſame light as
the ordinary actions of free agents, to whom God in-

dulges

* Dr. Clarke, V. 2. p. 697. fol. ed.

dulges the ufe of their natural powers ; but would argue a fpecial licence, and even the exprefs appointment of the Deity. Now, we are not contending,
that God may not commiffion and empower whom
he pleafes to work miracles ; this being, in effect, the
fame thing as performing them himfelf. And he can
never give his fanction to impofture. So that the objection we are confidering, were it well grounded, can
never ferve the main caufe of thofe by whom it is
urged, or enable them to fhew that miracles may accompany a falfe doctrine. Secondly, There is, however, no manner of foundation for the objection. For
our judgments are to be guided by facts, not by arbitrary hypothefes : and therefore, unlefs it can be
fhewn, that there is full and fufficient evidence of the
truth of fome miracles, which cannot fitly be afcribed
to God ; there is juft the fame reafon to believe, that
fuperior created intelligences are *univerfally* and *per-*
petually reftrained from working miracles, as that they
are *generally* fo. The very fame obfervation and experience which convince us that there are any laws
of nature at all, demonftrate that thofe laws are univerfally and invariably executed. Thirdly, The objection proceeds upon a fuppofition not only groundlefs, but abfurd : it fuppofes, that God communicates
and continues to his creatures, powers which he has
hitherto, through an unknown length of ages paft, almoft totally reftrained them from exerting, and which
he will equally reftrain them from exerting through
all future generations. Indeed, as it cannot be fhewn,
that he has *in any fingle inftance hitherto* permitted, fo
there is all imaginable reafon to believe he never will
hereafter

hereafter in any single inftance permit, them to exercife that miraculous power which they are fuppofed
to poffefs. And can there be a ftronger reflection
upon the wifdom of God, than to maintain that he
conftantly denies his creatures the ufe of thofe natural powers which he beftows and preferves? He has
indeed fixed the bounds, beyond which they cannot
act; neverthelefs, it is a flagrant contradiction to all
that we know of the works of God, to fuppofe that
within thofe bounds they are not allowed freely to exert themfelves. And therefore what fome are pleafed
to call a *reftraint upon the liberty* of fuperior beings,
is more properly a *natural inability* of working miracles *; and the argument againft their poffeffing a
miraculous power, from their never having made ufe
of it, remains in its full force.

To what purpofe is it to plead, " that we do not
" know the *other* world?" We are not unacquainted
with *this*, to which the prefent inquiry refers. In the
foregoing fection we have endeavoured to fhew, that
if we reafon from analogy, and that view which we
are able to take of the works of God; the various
orders of beings fuperior to the human kind *act only
within a certain limited fphere*. And if what we have
advanced farther in the prefent fection be juft, *this
                                                    lower*

---

* If this reafoning appears to any to be inconclufive, my
main argument will not be affected: for that equally holds
good, whether God by *a perpetual law reftrains* all invifible
agents from interpofing at any time to alter the regular courfe
of things in this lower world; or whether they *want a natural
power* of interpofing for any fuch purpofe.

lower world is not their appointed fphere of action; and confequently they are prevented from working miracles by the very law of their nature, without a fpecial divine affiftance and commiffion. Now, if there are no other beings capable of performing miracles; to whom fhall we afcribe them but to God? Upon this principle, they muft be confidered as the immediate operation of the divine power.

S E C T. III.

The laws of nature being ordained by God, and effential to the order and happinefs of the world; it is impoffible God fhould delegate to any of his creatures a power of working miracles, by which thofe divine eftablifhments may be fuperfeded and controuled.

BY the laws of nature, I do not mean thofe laws to which fuperior invifible agents are fubjected, but the rules by which this vifible world is governed, and more efpecially the ufual courfe and order of things in the fyftem to which we belong *. When miracles are performed, thefe laws are fuperfeded, and may be fufpended and controuled. I am here to fhew, that the idea of miracles, as contradictions to the laws and courfe of nature, contains a proof of their never being performed without the immediate agency or order of the fovereign Author and Lord of nature. Confider the defign of thefe laws, and

* See ch. 1. fect. 1. p. 3.

and the authority by which they were enacted. The
laws of nature were at firft ordained, and are continually preferved by God; they are the rules by which
he exercifes his dominion over the world. His wifdom did not, and indeed could not, fee fit to leave
the world without laws; or (which would have been
much the fame thing) leave thofe laws to be controuled at the will of his creatures, to the ftrict and
conftant obfervance of which we owe, the regularity
and uniformity of the natural world; the fettled order of caufes and effects in the moral; and the continued harmony of the univerfe, all the parts of which
are related to each other, and confpire together to
carry on one common defign, and thus demonftrate
that all things are under the fteady and conftant direction of *one* ruling counfel. Nothing gives fo much
force to the argument from the natural world in favour of true theifm, or enables us fo effectually to
anfwer the principal objections againft it, as the fta-
bility and invariable permanency of the courfe of nature. The conftancy of it conftitutes its beauty. And
what would be the confequence of God's departing
from the rules which he has fettled in the world, but
the violation and difparagement of his own majefty
and wifdom, and, the perplexity, confufion and diftrefs of his creatures, inftead of that order which
now reigns every where? If God did not govern the
world by fteady meafures *, no room would be given

us

* See above, ch. 1. fect. 2. p. 12. and Berkley's Treatife
concerning the principles of human knowledge, part 1. fect.
31, 151.

us for the exertion and improvement of our faculties,
nor any affiftance afforded us for the direction of our
conduct; a grown man would no more know how
to manage himfelf in the affairs of life, than an in-
fant juft born: which one confideration abundantly
over-balances whatever particular inconveniences may
thence arife. The laws of nature being ordained for
the general good, are not violated or fuperfeded even
by the great ruler, of the world himfelf, to prevent
partial evil, or on any occafion whatever, unlefs when
the moft important ends of his government neceffarily
require a miraculous interpofition. What probability
then is there, that any other beings fhould be able to
difpofe of the laws of nature, and interrupt them at
their pleafure, or (which is the fame thing) prevent
them from producing their ufual effects? Nay, there
feems to be a neceffity, that natural caufes fhould operate in the moft uniform and fteady manner. For
were God to grant to fuperior beings, fome of them
good, others evil, all of them finite and imperfect,
a power of working miracles at pleafure, fuch as
might fuperfede and controul the operation of nature;
there could be no law of nature, no fettlement or fixed
conftitution of things at all; every appointment of
God for our benefit might be defeated, and the order of this lower world be deftroyed. If fpirits, according to the doctrine of the Platonic philofophers,
are naturally able to move matter, or any particular
parts of it, not only in our fyftem, but in every other
throughout the univerfe; what a boundlefs empire
would they enjoy? and with what extenfive defola-
tion might they overfpread the face of the whole creation?

tion? But is it credible, that God has subjected the
universe to the power of every single spirit superior
to mankind, however malignant in his disposition?
The order * of the world seems to make it necessary,
that all created agents should be effectually restrained
or disabled from disturbing that order, in the manner they might do, did they possess the power of miracles. And there must be a divine law or constitution, preventing the interposition of superior beings
in this manner upon our earthly globe in particular.
Unable as we might have been to determine by spe-
culative reasonings, or arguments *a priori*, what constitution of the universe it became God to establish ;
yet we may discern the wisdom, the fitness, and in
some degree the necessity, of that constitution which
we see he has actually established, and consequently
the impossibility of its being subjected to the arbitrary
will of any of his creatures, from whose dominion
and controul we find it in fact to be exempted. The
laws which the wisdom of God ordained for the general good, his omnipotence carries into certain execution, without the least danger of being checked or
controuled by any opposing power. Hence arises the
impossibility of miracles being ever performed without
the

---

* Should it be here objected, that the order of the world
does not forbid *rare* and *occasional*, but only *frequent* and *common* disturbances of the course of nature : I answer, that we
have already proved, ch. 2. sect. 2. p. 54. that there is no foundation for this distinction, as it respects superior created agents,
who appear to be not only *generally*, but *universally* restrained
from working miracles.

the order of God. Not that the works themselves, abstractedly considered, require the exertion of an infinite power *; but the course of nature being a divine settlement, it cannot, in any instance whatever, be overturned by any finite power, without God's express appointment. · This is affirming nothing more, than that there is no being in the universe capable of opposing the Deity with success.

The most eminent philosophers and divines have maintained, that the law of nature is not only the *ordinance*, but the *operation* of God, and denotes the rule by which his energy is unceasingly exerted in the government of the world; and that natural effects are as much the operation of God as even miracles themselves. This doctrine is strenuously maintained by Dr. Clarke in particular, in many of his writings †.

And

* See above, ch. 1. sect. 3. p. 28—30.

† Sermons, V. 1. p. 620, 621. V. 2. p. 287, 296, 297, 697, 698, fol. ed. In some of the passages here referred to, I acknowledge, the Doctor, in speaking of God's acting upon matter continually and every moment, distinguishes between his doing it *immediately by himself*, and his doing it *mediately by some created intelligent beings*; and the latter seems to him most probable. On this supposition, indeed, it might be as easy for created intelligences to *alter*, as to *continue* the course of nature. But if matter be (as this very eminent philosopher affirms) incapable of any *powers* whatsoever; excepting only this one *negative power*, that every part of it will, of itself, always and necessarily continue in that state, whether of rest or motion, wherein it at present is : and if all those things which we commonly say are the effects of the *natural powers of matter*, are the effects of some intelligent being's acting upon matter continually

And therefore, if his doctrine be true, by contending for the power of evil spirits to work miracles;
does he not contend for their power to suspend and
controul the operations of divine omnipotence? But
whether you consider the course of nature as the regular and continued operation of God, or as his constitution only, and the fixed rule and plan of his government; it cannot be controuled at any time, but by
the same authority by which it was at first *established*, and
is continually *preserved*. And consequently miracles,
which supersede the laws of nature and providence,
and display a sovereign dominion over them, do not
only most naturally bespeak, but necessarily argue,
the immediate interposition and authority of the Lord
of nature, the omnipotent creator and governor of the
world, who reigns without any rival. If it be true
in fact, that God governs the world by general laws,
and

nually and every moment: to whom is it so reasonable to ascribe
this universal and perpetual agency on matter, and every particle of it, throughout the unbounded universe, as to the eternal
and omnipresent Deity? We are sure that matter cannot re-
sist the unremitted and almighty energy of his sovereign will,
who only speaks, and it is done; who commands, and it stands
fast for ever. But how does it appear, that created spirits have
any power to move matter of themselves, and without the spe-
cial commission of God? (See above, ch. 2. sect. 1. p. 41.)
And is it not more reasonable to believe, that the Deity maintains his sovereignty in a more immediate manner over his own
world, and those laws of motion on which its order depends;
than that he has subjected them to the inclinations and volition of any of his creatures, who are necessarily finite and imperfect?

and it be neceſſary that he ſhould do ſo ; he has not delegated, he cannot delegate, to any of his creatures any power over them. To do this, would be to re-ſign the reigns of government. Bu' the neceſſity of God's preſerving the laws of nature inviolate, will more fully appear, as we proceed in conſidering the farther abſurdities which attend the contrary doctrine.

S E C T. IV.

The aſcribing to any ſuperior beings, beſides God, and thoſe imme-diately commiſſioned by him, the power of working miracles, ſubverts the foundation of natural piety, and is a fruitful ſource of idolatry and ſuperſtition.

IT is evident, that prior to all ſupernatural revela-tion, we have no other way of knowing God, than by the works of nature. From theſe we infer the exiſtence, and attributes, and providence of their almighty Author : principles which are the baſis both of all religion, and of all our happineſs. But if ſu-perior beings acting without the order of God, can work miracles ; ſhall we not loſe our proof of the ex-iſtence and perfections of God from the works of na-ture ? For ſome miracles, ſuch as turning inanimate rods into living beings, and raiſing the dead, are ſo perfectly ſimilar to the works of creation, and the ori-ginal gift of life, as not eaſily to be diſtinguiſhed from them ; and afford juſt reaſon to conclude, that any of the authors of ſuch miracles might be the creators of the world : which would leave it doubtful, to whom

we

we were indebted for our exiftence, amongft the numerous beings equally capable of conferring upon us
that important favour *.

If others befides God could change the order of
nature; what evidence fhould we have of his wifdom
and providence in the continual government of the
world? For this evidence arifes from that regularity
and uniformity, which we obferve in the courfe of nature, proceeding on from age to age without interruption. Could others change the order of nature,
even when acting in oppofition to nature's Lord;
what reafon would there be to fear, that there were
other gods in the univerfe befides him, fuch as were
independent upon him, and as oppofite to him in their
natures and defigns, as they were in their operations?
Nay, on this fuppofition, there would be juft ground
to apprehend, that he who had given laws to nature,
had himfelf a *fuperior* lord, who could controul his
appointments, and fubvert his empire.

Even if it could be proved upon the principles of
our adverfaries, that the author of nature had no fuperior or equal, and that it was by his permiffion that
others fhared with him the government of the world;
this alone would be deftructive to all true piety. If
the

* Even without fuch an inducement as miracles, many a-
mongft the heathens have afcribed the creation of ferpents and
other noxious animals, and even of the whole vifible world, to
an evil being, in oppofition to the divine intention. Nay, fome
learned advocates of the Chriftian revelation, in this enlightened age, feem to think, that invifible beings may be poffeffed
of powers equal to the making and governing of worlds.

the courfe of nature be not under the fole direction of God'; what foundation can there be for our worfhip of God alone, and for the continual exercifes of gratitude and fubmiffion to him, in every condition? If we believe, that other invifible beings can interpofe in our affairs at their own pleafure, and either inflict punifhments or beftow bleffings upon us, fuch as are quite out of the ordinary courfe of nature, and contrary to it; could we confider ourfelves as under the protection and government of God? Would it not be natural and unavoidable for us, to pay homage to thofe who had the difpofal of our lot, and, by all the means which we judged fuitable to that end, to engage their favour, and avert their difpleafure? It was this belief of the power of demons, to difpenfe both good and evil to mankind, that was the foundation of that worfhip which was paid them in the Pagan world. And had they given proof of their power; it would have been unreafonable to deny them worfhip *. To fear or hope without any grounds, is very abfurd: but to fear or hope where there is juft reafon for either, where there is real power either to protect or punifh us, is an evident dictate of the underftanding. The paffions of hope and fear do indeed neceffarily arife in the human mind, upon the contemplation of a power, that may be employed either for our benefit or prejudice; and will ever be accompanied with a fuitable concern to

E   render

* See below, ch. 2. fect. 5. p. 77.

render that power propitious to us *. Concerning the Jews themselves, even after their return from their captivity at Babylon, when they are generally supposed to be entirely cured of their fondness for idolatry, we are told, that on the day of expiation they offered a goat to *Sammael* or *Satan*, that he might not accuse them of their crimes before God, because they believed him to have the power of doing it †.

With regard to Christians, it is in words, chiefly, that many of them differ from the ancient Pagans, who deified the supposed principle of evil. If they refuse the devil the name of God, they go very far in allowing him the attributes and prerogatives of God-head. They conceive of him as a kind of omnipresent

---

* It seems very reasonable to infer from hence, that no miracles were ever performed amongst the Pagans, except by the messengers of the true God, with the express and declared intention of manifesting and distinguishing him from the false: for without this precaution, the Pagans would naturally have referred these works (had any such been wrought amongst them) to their own gods, considered them as new displays of their divinity, and been engaged to worship them with new zeal and ardour. This is evident from the conduct of the idolatrous Lycaonians, who, before they were better instructed by St. Paul, concluded from the miracle he performed upon the cripple, that the gods were come down in the likeness of men, and proceeded without delay to perform the rites of adoration. Acts xiv. 8—18.

† See Buxtorf's Chald. Talmud. & Rab. Lexicon, on the word *Sammael*, p. 1495, and Bochart's Hierozoic. l. 2. c. 54. p. 652.

niprefent and omnifcient fpirit *; and afcribe to him
fuch a dominion over the human race as can belong
to none but the fovereign of the univerfe. To the
devil they afcribe frofts, and tempefts, and infectious
air, blights upon the fruits of the earth, the difeafes
of cattle, the difafters and diftempers of mens bodies,
phrenfy and the alienation of their minds, and the
power of inflicting even cruel deaths †. This error
has begotten amongft Chriftians, though not an idolatrous worfhip, yet endlefs and cruel fuperftitions ‡,
particularly witchcraft, which alone has occafioned a
vaft effufion of human blood; as the records of every
country can witnefs. No lefs than nine hundred
witches have in fome very fmall provinces been put
to death in the fpace of a few years ‖. Neverthelefs,
the grand principle upon which this deteftable art is
built, viz. " the natural power of the devil to de-
" ftroy mens bodies and lives, to bring upon them
" innumerable other calamities, and to work mira-
E 2   " cles,

* Tertullian. Apol. c. 22.

† Tertullian. Apol. c. 22. & de anim. c. 57. and Dr. Mac-
night's Truth of the Gofpel Hiftory, p. 172, 173. Dr. Whitby
on Luke xii. 16. Heb. ii. 14. Jofephus de B. I. l. 7. c. 25.
and Tobit vi. 7. ch. viii. 2. ch. iii. 8.

‡ We hence fee, with how little reafon it is affirmed, that
inafmuch as we are liable to evils, it can make no difference to
whom they are afcribed. Befides, did the evils we fuffer proceed from the power and pleafure of evil fpirits; why are they
not greater and more numerous?

‖ Mead's Medica Sacra, præfat. p. 11, 12.

" cles *," is ftill maintained by the greateft names in
the republic of learning.   On this foundation, laid
for him by philofophy, the wizzard eafily raifes his
own fuperftructure.   While the philofopher afferts
the power of wicked fpirits to produce the moft extraordinary effects, out of the common courfe of nature;
the wizzard prefumes, and not unreafonably, that
they have the *ufe* of this power : for a power which they
cannot ufe, is, in effect, no power at all.   And he
advances only one ftep farther, when he pretends to
a familiar intercourfe with them, or to be fkilled in
the manner of fetting them to work.   Now this difference between them is very trifling; fince, if the
devil can interpofe in the manner fuppofed by both,
it matters not whether he does it with, or without
the inftrumentality of human beings.   Moft melancholy is it to reflect, how much the general principle we
are here oppofing, viz. the power of Satan to work
miracles, and the various fuperftitions grounded upon
it; have contributed in all ages, and in all nations,
to the difquiet and corruption of the human race,
and to the extinction of rational piety.   This confideration alone, were there no other, fhould check
the zeal of Chriftians to maintain an opinion, fo deftructive to our virtue and happinefs; and which the
wifeft heathens, from principles of benevolence and
piety, earneftly wifhed and laboured to extirpate †.

In

---

* Dr. Clarke's Serm. V. 2. p. 700, folio.

† Superftitio fufa per gentes, oppreffit omnium fere animos,
atque hominum imbecillitatem occupavit.—Multum enim &
nobifmet

In a word, if we entertain juft and honourable fen-timents of the conftitution of the univerfe, and its all-wife and benevolent author; can we believe that he has fubjeᵭed us to the pleafure and difpofal of fu-perior beings, many of whom are fuppofed to be as capricious and malevolent as they are powerful? Has God put our very life, and the whole happinefs of it, into fuch hands? This fome maintain he has done; and this he muft have done, if he has granted them the power of working miracles at pleafure: an opinion, which cannot fail to rivet Heathens in their idolatry, and Chriftians in the moft deteftable fuperftitions.

S E C T.   V.

If miracles were performed in favour of falfe doᵭrines ; mankind would be expofed to frequent and unavoidable delufion.

MIRACLES may be confidered either apart by themfelves, or in their relation* to the mif-fion and doᵭrines of a prophet. It is in the former view, that they have been confidered in the preceding feᵭions of this chapter : we fhall now examine them in the latter; which will furnifh us with new evidence of their being works peculiar to God. What I fhall

E 3   attempt

nobifmet ipfis, & noftris profuturi videbamur, fi eam funditus fuftuliffemus. *Cicero de divinat.* l. 2. c. 72.

* What circumftances are neceffary to point out this rela-tion, is particularly fhewn below, ch. 5. at the beginning.

attempt in this fection, is to fhew, that were evil fpirits at liberty to work miracles to impofe upon mankind, the error might be abfolutely invincible. In
proof of this affertion, I appeal to the *natural fenfe* of
mankind concerning miracles, and to thofe impreffions which they always make upon the mind, when
free from the bias of prejudice.

It is certainly more natural, to refer miracles to
God, than to any other invifible being : for reafon
informs us clearly and certainly, that God can, but
does not equally inform us that any other being can,
perform thefe works *. And inafmuch as the courfe
of nature is a divine conftitution, it muft be unnatural to fuppofe, that any being, befides God, is at liberty to controul it †. Accordingly it appears in fact,
that mankind confider miracles as the works of God,
and as divine teftimonials to a prophet, whenever
they are performed and appealed to as fuch. This is
evident, not only from the immediate regard ‡ which
has been fhewn to genuine miracles, whenever they
have been wrought; but alfo from the frequent pretenfions to them, in all ages, and in all nations of the
world. Had they not been generally confidered as
divine works, and authentic proofs of a divine miffion ; they would not have been forged in fupport of
every falfe religion that pretended to come from God.

Nay,

---

* Ch. 2. fect. 2.

† Ch. 2. fect. 3.

‡ 1 Kings xvii. 24. ch. xviii. 39. John iii. 2. Mat. xv.
30, 31. ch. ix. 8. Luke xiii. 13, 17. Acts iii. 10. ch. iv. 31.
ch. xiv. 11.

Nay, fo ftrong an impreffion of their own divinity do genuine miracles leave upon the human mind, that their force is felt even by thofe, whofe natural fenti- ments concerning them are moft perverted by the er- rors of fuperftition, and the refinements of learning. It is ftrongly felt by the whole Chriftian world, not- withftanding their fpeculative opinions are calculated to defeat it * ; and not lefs by infidels and atheifts, who never think themfelves fafe in rejecting religion, till they have perfuaded themfelves, that every hiftory of miracles is falfe. Spinoza himfelf, as Mr. Bayle † affures us, faid to his friends, " That if he could be " convinced of the refurrection of Lazarus, he would " break his whole fyftem into pieces, and readily em- " brace the common faith of Chriftians." The very Pharifees, when moft blinded and hardened by their malice againft Chrift, confeffed the force of this evi- dence in his favour, when they faid, " This man " does many miracles. If we let him thus alone, " all men will believe on him ‡." And indeed the whole world would have believed on him on account of his miracles, had they not been prejudiced againft his doctrine. I add, that Chriftians muft allow, that miracles, when performed in atteftation of a profeffed miffion from God, conftitute an evidence adapted to the frame of the human mind, and the genuine fenti- ments of nature; for both our Saviour and his apof-

E 4   tles

---

* Preface.

† General Dictionary, article Spinoza, note R.

‡ John xi. 47, 48.

tles contented themſelves with the mere exhibition of this evidence, and then left it to produce its proper effect.

Now, if miracles, by their own natural influence, are calcuıated to procure immediate credit to the doctrine they attest; if they conſtitute an evidence a-dapted to the common ſenſe and feelings of mankind; if they make an impreſſion which ſcarce any reſiſtance can totally prevent or efface: it is an eaſy and obvious inference from hence, that if they were performed in favour of falſe doctrines, the generality of mankind would be neceſſarily expoſed to frequent deluſion. And thoſe would be the leaſt able to reſiſt the impreſſion of miracles, who had the ſtrongeſt ſenſe of God upon their minds, the moſt honourable apprehenſions of his natural and moral government, and were the moſt fearful of incurring his diſpleaſure, by rejecting any revelation of his will.

Here it will be objected, " That if miracles were " wrought to confirm falſehood, the nature of the " *doctrine* might ſerve to guard us againſt being de-" ceived, and direct us to aſcribe the works to ſome " evil agent, who was *permitted* to perform them for " the *trial* of mankind." In anſwer to this objection, it might perhaps be ſufficient to obſerve, that what ſome call God's *permitting*, would be in reality *em-powering* and *commiſſioning* evil ſpirits to work miracles. For God's removal of the reſtraint or diſabi-lity which thoſe ſpirits are under at all other times, amounts to his giving them both a power and a com-miſſion to work miracles on this particular occaſion*.

And

* See above, ch. 2. ſect. 2. 54.

And this God cannot do in confirmation of falfe-hood.

But much ftrefs being laid on this objection, we will offer fome farther obfervations upon it. The moft arbitrary and unnatural fuppofitions, when they have been long made, are thought at laft to have fome foundation to fupport them, and require the fame notice to be taken of them as if they had. It is not true in fact *, that any miracles have ever been performed in fupport of error, on purpofe to try our faith. At leaft, no fufficient evidence appears of the truth of any fuch miracles. Nor do the ends of the divine government feem to require, that mankind fhould be expofed to this particular trial. The temptations which occur in the ordinary courfe of providence, are abundantly fufficient to exercife our virtue; and it is quite needlefs that miracles fhould be wrought, merely to put it to a farther proof. Now, if reafon cannot fhew, that mankind *ought to be*, and experience convinces us that they never *have been*, expofed to the delufion of falfe doctrines inforced by miracles; the notion that they may be fo, muft be confidered as a mere fiction. Befides, how unlike would fuch a trial be to thofe ordained by God? The latter arife from paffions planted in our nature for the moft valuable purpofes, and from the moft ufeful and neceffary relations of life. But our adverfaries fuppofe, miracles may be atchiev-ed with no other view, than as *mere* matter of trial to mankind: which is repugnant to all our knowledge

of

* See ch. 2. fect. 2.

of the divine difpenfations. Not to obferve, that errors inforced by miracles, would, very frequently at
leaft, conftitute a trial rather of the underftanding,
than of the heart; and in this refpect likewife, it
would differ from thofe to which God has fubjected
mankind.

To convince us more fully, that no miracles can
ever accompany a falfe doctrine, merely for the trial
of mankind; I would obferve, that they are not capable of anfwering this end, upon the principles of
thofe by whom it is affigned. Were a falfe doctrine
to be attefted by miracles; it muft be afferted, either
that the falfhood of it was difcerned, or that it was
not. If the falfhood of the doctrine was difcerned,
and it was at the fame time known, that the miracles
attefting it might and muft be performed by fome
evil agent: in this cafe, where would be the trial?
The miracles, it would be allowed, were no evidence
of the truth or divinity of the doctrine; and contained no recommendation of it, or motive to embrace
it; nay, they could only ferve to furnifh an invincible prejudice againft it, on account of the known
malevolence of their author. If, on the other hand,
the falfehood of the doctrine was not and could not
be difcerned; the miracles attending it being confidered only as proofs of the interpofition of fome fuperior being, the mind muft be thrown into a ftate
of perplexity and fufpence about the author of the
works, and remain void of all inducement either to
embrace or reject the doctrine. And confequently
here alfo there would be no trial at all. We are never more in danger of charging God foolifhly, than

. when

when we judge of him, not by what he has done, but by what we prefume it becomes him to do. It might convince us, how little a way bare fpeculation can carry us in all refearches into the nature and government of God, to find the ftrongeft minds, when trufting to fpeculation alone, afcribing to him unworthy meafures, and inventing defigns and ends for them, which they are not adapted to anfwer. The very fcheme which affigns the trial of mankind, as the end of God's permitting miracles to be performed in confirmation of error, does itfelf fhew, it could not be promoted by them. Now, whoever calls upon us to believe, that miracles may be wrought without any neceffity, and even without any ufe, demands our affent to what contradicts all our ideas of divine wifdom, and the whole courfe of the divine difpenfations, as well as the feveral reafons before urged to fhew, that no variations from the eftablifhed laws of nature can take place, except when they are indifpenfably neceffary to promote the moft important purpofes of God's adminiftration.

Though miracles wrought in fupport of error, according to the idea fome have formed of thefe works, would not conftitute any trial of mankind ; yet, if we confider them in their true light, they carry fo much weight and authority with them, as moft powerfully and effectually to recommend to the belief of mankind the doctrine which they atteft. And, confequently, were they to accompany error, they could not fail, in very many inftances, of procuring it credit ; as we endeavoured to fhew at the beginning of the fection. In order to confirm what was there advanced, it is
only

only neceffary to add, that, in this cafe, the confideration of the *doctrine* which the miracles attefted, could
not univerfally fecure men from deception. Man is
a creature liable to error, and his judgment (eafily
impofed upon by fpecious appearances) often pronounces that to be reafonable which is not fo. And
even when a doctrine appears doubtful, or ftrongly
fufpicious, mankind are more ready to call in queftion
their own reafonings concerning it, than to difpute
the authority of the miracles which are thought to recommend it. Innumerable cafes there are, in which
human reafon, in its moft improved ftate, is unable
to form any judgment concerning the probability or
improbability of a divine interpofition to confirm particular doctrines. Do not the moft learned, and even
the wifeft of mankind, differ widely concerning the
reafonablenefs of certain opinions? Nay, what contrary cenfures do they pafs upon them? Is there a
fect of Chriftians which does not reprefent the diftinguifhing tenets of all the other fects as unworthy
of God, however credible they appear to thofe who
hold them? How then can the bulk of mankind, the
moft ignorant and illiterate, and thofe in particular
who have been educated in all the darknefs of idolatry; how can they in every cafe judge with certainty,
whether a doctrine be worthy a divine interpofition,
or detect the falfehood of it, when it brings the tefti-
monial of miracles?

Let us put a cafe the moft favourable of any to
thofe whom we here oppofe. They affirm, " That
" if the moft numerous and illuftrious miracles were
" performed in fupport of idolatry, we ought to dif-
                                        " regard

" regard them; that the doctrine being falfe, the
" works could not be divine." Let us then fuppofe,
that fuch miracles were actually wrought for the purpofe here affigned, the confirmation of *idolatry*, in the
fenfe they imagine it to have been practifed by many
in the Pagan world, that is, in confirmation of the
worfhip of certain powerful beings, to whom the government of particular parts of nature was delegated
by the fupreme Divinity. From what was obferved
above *, it appears, that had miracles.been performed
among the Heathens, thefe works muft, by their own
natural influence, have inflamed their devotion towards the reputed authors of them. And in farther
juftification of their idolatry, they might be ready to
plead, " That the honour paid to inferior deities was
" warranted by the miracles which they performed;
" becaufe fuch changes in the order of nature could
" not take place, but by the appointment of the great
" Lord of nature; and becaufe they were in them-
" felves difplays of that authority and dominion over
" mankind with which he he had invefted them:
" and confequently that difowning their authority,
" and refufing them their due homage, was acting
" contrary to the will of the fupreme Being, and to
" the truth of things; refufing to ackowledge thofe
" inferior deities to be, what they really were, our
" divinely appointed governors and guardians." If
a Heathen offered this plea, the validity of which, or
of one very fimilar to it, feems to be admitted in
Scripture;

* Ch. 2. fect. 4. p. 65.

Scripture*; it would be difficult to convince him of
the weaknefs of it, efpecially as it gave a fanction to
all his ftrongeft prejudices and inclinations †. Now
if in a cafe thought to be fo plain, and certainly of
the firft importance, mankind are liable to delufion;
in how many thoufand inftances befides would they
not be open to it, if miracles were·performed to give
a fanction to impofture?

And even fuppofing the doctrine attefted by miracles, to be immoral, or favourable to our corrupt paffions; this confideration would indeed awaken the
caution and prejudice of a few good men againft it,
but would only fo much the more ftrongly recommend it to the affection of the greateft part of mankind. When I confider upon what accounts the
Heathen world did not like to retain the true God in
their knowledge, what vices they afcribed to their
chief divinities, what flagrant immoralities they practifed as rites of religion, even without any fuch fanction as that of miracles: when I farther reflect, how
often the moral precepts of the Gofpel have been cenfured as impracticable, and their ftrict purity urged as
an objection againft their divinity; and that even
Chriftians themfelves, of all denominations, are continually corrupting the fanctity of their religion, or
relaxing its rigour, and ftriving, under different pretences, to bring it nearer to the level of human frail-
ty·

* If. xli. 21—23. cited below, ch. 3. fect. 2.
† What is here offered to fhew, that miracles would have
rivetted *Pagans* in their idolatry; is apparently true with refpect to *Papifts*, were fuch works to be performed by'them.

ty: I cannot help being of opinion, that a doctrine mild and gentle to mens favourite paffions and pur- fuits, if it was fupported by miracles, would be a temptation too ftrong for human nature to refift, and fuch as God therefore will never fuffer it to be expofed to.

A very learned writer, who has done fingular fer- vice to the caufe of religion, has afferted, " Suppof- " ing that the miracles pretended in favour of Pa- " ganifm were all real miracles, yet as they lead men " to a corrupt religion and idolatrous worfhip, no " reverence, no regard is to be paid to them.*" The worfhip which men pay to God, will ever be fuitable to the ideas they form concerning his nature. The moft immoral rites of Pagan devotion were conform- able to the character of the objects of that devotion. And while men entertain corrupt notions of their gods, they are not likely to difcern the abfurdity of a corrupt religion. And therefore miracles performed in fupport of it, would ftrengthen, and (in their opi- nion, at leaft) juftify their attachment to it. In a word, whoever confiders the true nature of miracles, the power which they neceffarily imply, and the for- cible impreffions they make on the human heart, to- gether with the real character of mankind, will hard- ly deny, that, if they were wrought to give evidence to falfehood, they would unavoidably, in numberlefs inftances, procure it credit; efpecially if he farther.

takes

---

* Dr. Newton's Differtations on the Prophecies, V. 2. p. 275. Dr. Clarke likewife had advanced the fame doctrine, V. 2. p. 699, 700, 702. fol. edit.

takes into the account, the underftanding and fagacity afcribed to created fpirits. We are indeed expofed
to the danger of delufion by the artifices of men.
Neverthelefs, againft human craft, human caution is
a fufficient fecurity: but men are not a match for fuperior beings.

Now if God's allowing to evil fpirits the liberty of
working miracles in confirmation of falfe doctrines,
would neceffarily fubject mankind to great delufion;
will it not follow from hence, that he cannot have
granted them any fuch liberty? This confequence
will be allowed by thofe, who think honourably of
the divine government. Who, without being compelled by fuch evidence as cannot be refifted, would
reprefent the Deity as placing his rational creatures,
even thofe who with upright hearts were endeavouring to learn his will, under a difpenfation, which,
without any fault of theirs, would promote their deception, in matters which concerned their moral conduct, and their eternal happinefs? Such a difpenfation as this feems to be utterly inconfiftent with God's
wifdom and goodnefs, with his effential rectitude, and
love of righteoufnefs and truth, and with all the nobleft perfections of his nature. If God *does not*, and
indeed, (for the reafons affigned above *,) *cannot*, fuffer the order of the *natural* world to be difturbed at
the will of created agents at any other time; can it
be thought, that he will permit and employ them to
make this miraculous difturbance, merely to promote
a farther and much greater evil, the delufion, depra-
vity

* Ch. 1. fect. 2. p. 18. & fect. 3. p. 58.

vity and mifery of the *moral* world ? Scarce is it poffible for us, to difhonour the deity more, tha: by fo
groundlefs and injurious an imputation. If falfrhood
and vice are objects of God's difapprobation, he muft
have referved in his own hands the power of working miracles. Now, it is not more impoffible, that
this prerogative of God fhould be ufurped by violence ; than that it fhould be voluntarily refigned and
proftituted to unworthy purpofes.

S E C T. VI.

*If miracles may be performed without a divine interpofition, and
in fupport of falfehood ; they cannot be authentic credentials of a
divine miffion, and criterions of truth.*

IT is a thing too obvious to require any laboured
argument, that if miracles, in themfelves, are e-
vidences only of the interpofition of fome fuperior
beings, not of God more than any other ; they can
never be, in themfelves, a certain criterion of a perfon's being fent of God. " You could not know I
" came from, and was fent by fuch a prince, by
" my bringing his feal along with me, if other
" people had the fame feal, and would lend it to o-
" thers to ufe as they faw fit †." If you cannot point
out, with clearnefs and certainty, the fpecific difference between thofe miracles which are peculiar to

F   God,

† Fleetwood's Effay on Miracles, p. 6, 7.

God, and thofe which the devil can either perform
or imitate, you will be in perpetual danger of mif-
taking the one for the other *.   Accordingly we find
Chriftians themfelves, from the earlieft ages down to
the prefent, difparaging the evidence of mere miracles, as doubtful and uncertain ; cautioning the world
againft receiving doctrines as true and divine, upon
the bare atteftation of thefe works, and cenfuring
a faith founded upon them as manifeftly *rafh and
groundlefs* †.   Can it then be matter of furprize to us,
that unbelievers fhould treat miracles with very little
reverence, and except to the evidence arifing from
them ?   It has long provoked their fcorn and indignation, to have that offered them as a valid proof of
the truth, which equally attefts falfehood ; to fee the

very

---

* Dr. Prideaux in his letter to the Deifts, p. 2c6, and many others have undertaken to fhew, what fort of miracles the
devil may perform or imitate.   The tafk however feems to
have been too hard for them ; which it might well be, if it be
true, as Dr. Clarke and others tell us, that there is no knowing how far the power of created fpirits, good and evil, may
extend.   Why then do thefe writers undertake to determine
the limits of their power ? See Dr. Clarke, V. 2. p. 696, &c.

† Temerariam Plane.   Tertullian in Marc. 3. 2. Origen, in
his anfwer to Celfus, l. 3. p. 124, fpeaks of prophecies and fupernatural cures, as things of an indifferent nature.   And Jerome, or whoever is the author of the Breviary upon the Pfal-
ter, apud Hieron. T. 2. p. 334, 335, makes no difficulty of
allowing to Porphyry, that the magicians of Egypt, Apolloni-
us, and an infinite number of other perfons, wrought miracles.
Non eft autem grande facere figna, feems to have been the
principle common both to Porphyry and Jerome.

very fame works ufed to recommend fome to their
regard as divine meffengers, and to difgrace others
as magicians *. For, I think, there is hardly a fingle
miracle, either in the Old or New Teftament, which
Chriftians ‡ have not thought they could parallel with
fome fimilar miracle amongft the Pagans. There are
two cafes, however, in which miracles are confidered
as evidences of a divine miffion, by fome who plead,
that fuch works may, on other occafions, be performed without the order of God.

I. It is urged, " that in cafe of a conteft between
" two oppofite parties working miracles for victory ;
" the party which works the *moft* and *greateft* mira-
" cles, may reafonably be fuppofed to be affifted by
" God ; and therefore that his doctrine fhould be re-
" ceived as divine." To this we anfwer, 1/, That
if fupernatural operations were brought to fupport
oppofite miffions, it would be difficult to determine
which of them required the greater degrees of power.
Scarce, perhaps, would any two perfons pronounce
the fame judgment concerning them. *The driving of*

F 2 *the*

* It was this which afforded Celfus fuch matter of infult and
triumph, Πᾶς ἂν ὃ σχέτλιον, ἀπὸ τῶν αὐτῶν ἔργων τὸν μεν Θεὸν, τὸς δὲ γό-
ιτας ἡγῆθαι. Celfus apud Origin. contra Celf. l. 2. p. 93. This
it is that feems to have created the ftrongeft prejudice in Mr.
Rouffeau againft miracles : " Can it be imagined," fays he,
" that God ufes the fame means to inftruct men, as he knows
" the devil will ufe to deceive them ?" Lettres ecrites de la
Montagne, p. 104.

‡ This tafk was undertaken by the learned Huetius, in his
Quæftiones Alnetanæ.

the traders out of the temple, is called by St. Jerome *,
*the moft wonderful of all the miracles which Jefus per-
formed:* and yet a very learned modern † fcarce allows it to be any miracle at all.   To change the *form
of a creature*, is pronounced by Dr. Lightfoot‡ the
greateft miracle; and he applies the obfervation to
that wrought at Cana: but Dr. Lardner ‖ calls it,
" one of the *leaft* miracles any where afcribed to
" Chrift."   How can miracles of a *different kind* be
brought into a comparifon with each other?   Were
this difficulty overcome, there ftill remains a greater.
For, 2*dly*; It would be impoffible to fhew, on the
principles we are here examining, that thofe miracles
which carried marks of a *fuperior* power were really
divine.   The moft learned Dr. Clarke feems indeed
to have thought §, that where *fuperior* power appeared, " there it was *neceffarily* to be believed, that the
" commiffion was truly from God;" and the ingenious and acute Bifhop Sherlock affirms ¶, " that mi-
" racles are an immediate and direct proof of what
" they are brought to affert, the fupremacy of God:
" For, when the fingle queftion is, who is the
" Mightieft, muft it not be decided in his favour
" who vifibly exerts the greateft acts of power?"
                                                    But

* In Matt. tom. 9. p. 31. ed. Baf. 1516.
† The miracles of Jefus vindicated, by Dr. Pearce, p. 26.
‡ V. i. p. 504.
‖ Vindication, p. 26.
§ Serm. Vol. 2. p. 700.
¶ Difcourfes, V. i. p. 285.

But if created spirits of very different ranks and orders, are at liberty to work miracles without any
commiffion from God; who can determine the limits of their refpective capacities, and take upon him
to fay, how far the power of the higheft created fpirit may extend ? Dr. Clarke tells us *, " that (un-
" lefs we knew the limit of *communicable* and *incommu-*
" *nicable* power, we can hardly affirm with any cer-
" tainty, that *any* particular effect, *how great or mi-*
" *raculous foever* it may feem to us, is beyond the
" power of all created beings in the univerfe to have
" produced." I admit, that in cafe of fuch a conteft
as is fuppofed above, the party which performs the
moft and greateft miracles is *fuperior* to the oppofite.
But I am not able to difcern, how this *fuperiority* of
the one to the other neceffarily proves an *infinity* of
power, or an abfolute fupremacy over all other beings. On the principles of Dr. Clarke, the miracles
on both fides, feparately confidered, *might* be performed by beings inferior to God, and are proofs only of the interpofition of fome invifible agents fuperior to man. How then can the circumftance of their
being performed in a conteft for victory, demonftrate
that they could have no other author than God ? *3dly;*
On the contrary, this circumftance would incline us to
believe, that *both* parties were affifted only by created
intelligences, fuperior to one another in power: for
it feems much more likely, that there fhould be a contention for power and fupremacy between different

F 3   created

* V. 2. p. 697.

created agents, than between any creature and his
omnipotent Creator. With whom would the almighty Maker and Sovereign of the univerfe deign
to enter into a conteft?. And fuperior fpirits, (as
Dr. Clarke * himfelf allows) " could not poffibly be
" fo abfurdly ignorant, as to imagine that finite could
" prevail by *force* againft infinite, or not know that
" the Almighty could, if he pleafed, annihilate them
" fwift as thought." From hence it feems to me to
follow, that if oppofite miffions were fupported by
miracles, the fupreme Being could have no concern
in the difpute. *4thly;* According to the rule of
judging concerning the divinity of miracles, here laid
down ; thefe works will, at different times, both prove
and difprove the divine commiffion of their performer. While the conteft is continued between two
oppofite parties working miracles for victory; he who
to-day, by working more and greater miracles than
his rival, is received as a divine meffenger, muft be
rejected as an impoftor to-morrow, if his rival fhould
then exceed him in the number and greatnefs of his
miracles. At the next trial, however, he may exceed his rival, recover the advantage he loft, and
from being an impoftor, become again a divine meffenger. How long the conteft may laft, none can
tell ; but every one may fee, that there can be no
force in that proof, which alternately eftablifhes and
deftroys oppofite claims. In fuch a fuppofed conteft,
each of the miracles, in itfelf confidered; is of no
value :

* Sermons, V. 1. p. 60. folio ed. & p. 587.

value: and add as many of thefe ciphers together as
you pleafe, they will be but cyphers ftill.

II. Thofe Chriftians * who are of opinion that miracles may be wrought by inferior beings, do neverthelefs afcribe fuch to God, as are performed for an
end not unworthy of him. " Though the works,"
fay they, " do neceffarily prove nothing more than
" the interpofition of fome fuperior being; yet the
" nature of the *doctrine* will enable us to determine
" who that being is: and if the doctrine has a ten-
" dency to promote piety and virtue, or be only in-
" different in itfelf, and not abfolutely inconfiftent
" with thefe ends; then the miracles, and confe-
" quently the doctrine, muft be divine: for fhould God
" in fuch cafes as thefe, permit evil fpirits to work mi-
" racles and impofe upon men, the error would be ab-
" folutely invincible; and that would in all refpects be
" the very fame thing, as if God worked the miracles
" to deceive men himfelf." This reafoning feems
liable to feveral objections. Why fhould the mere *in-
difference* of the doctrine engage us to afcribe the miracles to God, rather than to other fuperior fpirits
fuppofed capable of performing them? Is it not more
honourable to the Deity to fuppofe, that he will not
atteft a doctrine merely indifferent in itfelf? It is
what his wifdom will not permit. With regard to
doctrines of a *moral or ufeful tendency;* it is not in all
cafes eafy for the bulk of mankind, or even for the
wife and learned, to form a certain judgment con-

F 4   cerning

* Dr. Clarke, Vol. 2. p. 700. Dr. Chandler, and others.

cerning them. What to men appeared to have a
tendency to promote virtue and happiness; superior
beings, who discerned its remotest effects, might
know to be a curse rather than a blessing, and give
it countenance from a motive of malevolence. On
the other hand, a doctrine really subservient to the
cause of piety and virtue, men might judge to be
prejudicial to it. And were the sanctity of the doctrine ever so evident, it would not (on the principles
of those with whom we are here arguing) certainly
follow from hence, that the miracles recommending
it were wrought by God; inasmuch as other beings,
from motives unknown to us, might interest themselves in favour of such a doctrine. Concerning
none but the divine Being can it be demonstrated,
that he is absolutely incapable of deceiving or being
deceived. Nor is there any reason to plead, " that
" if miracles were performed by evil spirits in sup-
" port of a doctrine good or innocent, mankind
" would be *necessarily* deluded into a belief of its di-
" vine original:" unless it be allowed that miracles
bear upon themselves evident and certain characters
of divinity. But those who make this plea, suppose
it to be a thing known and certain, that no miracles
whatever do necessarily argue a divine interposition.
Were I to see miracles performed in favour of all
forts of doctrines, I would not ascribe any of them to
God: I should be unable to persuade myself, that infinite wisdom employed any works as the distinguishing test of his own extraordinary interposition, which
may be performed by inferior beings; or that the
Deity would use that as a seal of truth, which the

                                                    devil

devil ufes to gain credit to impofture. And therefore if miracles may be performed by created agents
of different and oppofite characters, and in fupport
of falfehood as well as truth; I am not able to perceive, how any doctrine can be proved by miracles *,
or at leaft any fuch doctrine as wants the atteftation
of thefe works.

It is neceffary to obferve farther, that the making
the doctrine the teft of the divinity of the miracles,
is, to make the doctrine the rule of judging concerning the miracle, not the miracle the rule of judging
concerning the doctrine. The proper and immediate defign of miracles is, to eftablifh fome truth
unknown before, and fuch as is not demonftrable by
reafon, or capable of other evidence befides that of
miracles; to prove, for example, the miffion of the
prophet by whom they were performed, and the divine

* In confirmation of what is urged above to fhew, that, on
the principle maintained in the objection we are now examining, no doctrine whatever can be proved to come from God by
miracles; it may be obferved, that if the doctrine be fuch, as
natural reafon can clearly and certainly difcover to be *true;*
the miracles are unneceffary and fuperfluous, and for that reafon cannot be divine. And if the doctrine be fuch as reafon
can clearly prove to be *falfe;* it will be ftill more impoffible
to afcribe the miracles to God. If the doctrine be *doubtful,*
and natural reafon be unable to determine whether it be true or
falfe; it muft be equally doubtful who the author of the miracles is. But it is fufficient to have fhewn, that, if miracles are
not peculiar to God, no doctrine that wants the atteftation of
thefe works, can be proved by them.

vine original of his meſſage or doctrine, and to engage men to·receive and comply with it, however
contrary it may be to their prejudices and paſſions.
But according to ſome learned men, the doctrine
muſt firſt be examined without paſſion or prejudice,
and then employed to prove the divinity of the miracles: But is not this repugnant to the proper uſe
and intention of miracles? It is making the whole
force of the proof, to depend upon the doctrine to
be proved. It is of importance to add, that miracles
are intended more eſpecially for the conviction of the
ignorant and unlearned, who are eaſily impoſed upon
by the ſophiſtry of ſcience, and the ſpecious diſguiſes
of error, as well as utterly diſqualified to determine
by abſtract reaſonings concerning the abſolute neceſſity, or the fitneſs and propriety, of ſpecial divine interpoſitions. It is neceſſary therefore that miracles,
when they are offered as evidences of a divine commiſſion, ſhould contain in their own nature, a clear
demonſtrative proof of their divine original: for
otherwiſe their ſpecial deſign could not be anſwered.
It is quite unnatural to ſuppoſe, that the doctrine
muſt firſt eſtabliſh the divinity of the miracles, before
the miracles can atteſt the divinity of the doctrine;
and it is abſurd to expect that a new revelation and
offenſive truths, (which are not received without re-
luctance, even where there is a prior conviction of
the divinity of the miracles atteſting them,) ſhould
themſelves effectually engage men to aſcribe thoſe
works to God, which might be performed by num-
berleſs other inviſible agents.

Now, can it be imagined, that God will·ever allow
superior

fuperior beings to work miracles in fupport of falfehood; if hereby he would deftrey the proof from
thefe works of his own immediate interpofition, and
put it out of his own power to employ them as certain credentials of a divine miflion? Miracles (under
which term I comprehend thofe of *knowledge* as well
as *power*) being the *only* * mean, whereby God can
affure the world of the truth of a new revelation, he
muft have referved the ufe of it to himfelf alone,
without ever parting with it to ferve the purpofes of
his rivals and oppofers.

With regard to the rule, of making miracles
then a proof of the divine original of the doctrine,
when the works difplay a *fuperiority* of power, and
when the doctrine is either fubfervient to, or not inconfiftent with, piety and virtue; it may be farther obferved, that were this rule true in general, it could
not be applied to the cafe either of Judaifm or Chriftianity; if it fhould appear, that the great founders
of both thofe religions have eftablifhed rules directly
oppofite to this, and reprefented miracles as *abfolute*,
not as *conditional* proofs of a doctrine's coming from
God.   And this is the point which comes next under confideration.

But before we proceed farther, it may not be improper to recapitulate what has been already offered
from reafon, to fhew that miracles can never be performed without a divine interpofition. Reafon, it
has been obferved, makes known to us but one almighty

* See below, ch. 5.

mighty being, who is at liberty to act every where, and in what manner he pleafes, and whofe omnipotence is the only adequate caufe, we are capable of difcovering in the whole compafs of exiftence, of thofe effects which are called miraculous. To him therefore it is moft natural to afcribe them. The beft arguments which reafon can employ to prove the exiftence of fuperior created intelligences, do much more ftrongly prove, that they can act only within that particular fphere appointed them by their Creator. It has likewife been fhewn, that the obfervation and experience of all ages are a full demonftration that they are not at liberty to perform miracles in this lower world; no fuch works having ever been performed in it, but fuch as may be fitly afcribed to God. The laws of nature being the eftablifhed rules of the divine government, and effential to the order and happinefs of the world; it feems very unreafonable to fuppofe, that God fhould delegate to any of his creatures a power of fuperfeding or controuling thefe laws. Miracles are famples of dominion over them, and argue the immediate interpofition and authority of that great Being by whom they were at firft ordained. Deifts more efpecially, who deny the exiftence both of angels and devils, muft allow, that if any miracles are performed, they can have none but God for their author, and that the fettled courfe of things is unalterable but by his immediate will. Were inferior beings at liberty to difturb the wife order of nature, we fhould lofe our beft evidence of God's exiftence and providence; and the very foundation of all the homage he claims would be overturned,

turned. The opinion we are here oppofing has in all ages been fatal to true piety, and given birth to endlefs fuperftitions and idolatries. And did fuperior beings really poffefs the miraculous powers afcribed to them; the exercife of thofe powers by good and evil agents, would either expofe mankind to necef-fary and invincible error, or entirely deftroy the credit and ufe of miracles under the idea of criterions of truth, and authentic credentials of a divine miffion.

C H A P.

CHAP. III.

ARGUMENTS FROM REVELATION, TO PROVE THAT MIRACLES ARE, IN THEMSELVES, CERTAIN EVIDENCES OF A DIVINE INTERPOSITION.

IT is neceſſary on this occaſion, to appeal to the ſacred writings; not merely for the conviction of thoſe who acknowledge their divine authority, though they miſtake the meaning of many paſſages relative to our preſent inquiry; but alſo to convince thoſe, who, denying their authority, are ready to avail themſelves of the miſinterpretations of the former, in ſubverting the foundation on which their authority reſts. I will endeavour to ſhew, that the Scriptures both of the Old and New Teſtament (ſtrictly correſponding with right reaſon) always repreſent miracles as the peculiar works of God; and never attribute them to any other beings, unleſs when acting by his immediate commiſſion. The ſubject muſt be conſidered in its full extent; and comprehends under it the following topics, which demand a cloſe and candid examination.

SECT.

'

S E C T. I.

The view which the Scripture gives us of good angels, of the devil and his angels, as alfo of the fouls of departed men; inconfiflent with their liberty of working miracles.

I. WITH regard to *good angels ;* the Scripture never reprefents them as capable of working miracles at their own pleafure, or as invefted with any dominion over mankind. Very fre-' quent mention indeed is made of angels, either as the inftruments or fymbols of an extraordinary providence. When Jacob * in a dream faw a ladder, reaching from earth to heaven, on which the angels of God feemed to afcend and defcend, and on the top of which the divine glory itfelf appeared ; this vifion, perhaps, was defigned only as a fymbol or figurative reprefentation of God's fpecial care of Jacob, and readinefs to interpofe at all times for his protection. It is in allufion to this vifion, that our Saviour exprefles himfelf, when he foretold to Nathaniel that furprizing train of miracles which attended his miniftry† ; " From this time ‡ you fhall fee hea-
" ven

* Gen. xxviii. 12.

† John i. 51. That Chrift here foretels his miracles, and not the vifible afcent and defcent of angels upon him during his miniftry, is evident from hence, that the prophecy was not accomplifhed in this latter fenfe of it.

‡ Aπ' αρτι.

" ven open, and the angels of God afcending and
" defcending upon the Son of man." Now, inafmuch as the miracles of Chrift are elfewhere afcribed,
not to angels, but to God *; the former cannot be
regarded as the proper authors of thefe works; and
our Saviour might mean only to affirm, that his miracles would be fenfible difplays of the divine power
in his favour, or open proofs of an immediate intercourfe between heaven and earth. We do not however deny, that Chrift might employ angels in executing his orders, and particularly in working miracles: for they are all made fubject to him. Neverthelefs, it does not appear from the Scriptures, that
they can perform miracles of themfelves, and without
an immediate divine commiffion. Ou the contrary,
according to the Scripture account of them, if they
bring any meffages to men, they firft receive them
from God; if they controul the courfe of nature, it
is by authority from the Lord of nature; and if they
interpofe at all in the affairs of our fyftem, it is not
as they fee fit themfelves, but according to the command of God, as the minifters of his will, which
they execute as punctually as thofe paffive inftruments
of his providence, the luminaries of heaven, and the
elements of nature †. The word, *angel* or *meffenger*,
denotes only one employed in the execution of fome
commiffion. Hence it is applied, not merely to intelligent

---

* See below, fect. 6.

† Pf. xviii. 9, 10. Pf. lxviii. 17. Pf. ciii. 20, 21. If. vi.
1, &c. Dan. vii. 9. Matt. xviii. 10. Heb. i. 14. ch. ii. 5.
Rev. v. 13. ch. vii. 11. ch. xix. 10.

telligent beings acting by the order of God, but even to the inanimate parts of the creation, which he employs as the inftruments of his government. The Pfalmift, when celebrating the empire of God over the *material* world, fays, " He maketh the winds " his angels or meffengers, and lightnings his mi- " nifters *. For fire and hail, fnow and vapour, and " ftormy winds, fulfil God's word †." But all that

G   is

---

* This is the true rendering of Pf. civ. 4. (Compare Exod. ix. 23, 24. Pf. lxxviii. 48, 49.) Nor is it certain, that thefe words are applied Heb. i. 7. to intelligent beings; as the apof- tle feems to have had no other view in citing them, than to obferve, that the very name of *angels* (however applied) im- ported *miniftry* and *fubjection;* whereas that of *Son* implied *au- thority* and *dominion.* Very probably the Scripture may repre- fent the moft active parts of nature as God's angels, in oppo- fition to the Heathens, who conceived of them as deities. See below, ch. iii. fect. 2.

† Pf. cxlviii. 8. According to this general import of the word *angel*, many learned writers underftand it in the follow- ing and other paffages of Scripture. " The angel of the Lord fmiting Herod," they think is explained in the text itfelf of an *extraordinary diftemper* inflicted by God, Acts xii. 23. God threatened Sennacherib, " that he would fend a blaft upon him," a peftilential blaft, or burning wind, which deftroyed his army; and this being done under the direction of God, and in execution of his defigns, the blaft or wind is called the *angel*, the meffenger and fervant of God, 2 Kings xii. 6, 7. ch. xix. 35. " God's fending an angel to Jerufalem to deftroy it," feems only another form of expreffion for " his fending a pefti- lence upon Ifrael," 1 Chron. xxi. 14, 15. 2 Sam. xxiv. 15, 16. We read Exod. ix. 23, 24. that the Lord " fent upon the E- gyptians thunder and hail and fire :" and the Pfalmift fpeaking

is of importance here to obferve, is, that the Scripture teaches us, that angels, of whatever dignity, are
only *miniftring fpirits*, the fervants of Jehovah, " do-
" ing his commandments, and hearkening to the
" voice of his word," without having themfelves any
power over mankind, or over thofe laws by which
the fyftem to which we belong is governed.

II. We are next to enquire, whether the Scripture
afcribes the power of performing miracles to *the devil
and his angels*. It is generally fuppofed, that thefe
wicked fpirits were originally inhabitants of the celeftial regions, and equal in rank and dignity with
thofe who preferved their innocence. Now, fuppofing this to be the cafe; yet, if even good angels, who
continue in a ftate of favour with God, have no power
of working miracles at their own pleafure, or any dominion over mankind, (as we endeavoured to fhew
under the preceding article;) what reafon can there
be for afcribing fuch dominion and power to evil angels, who are fallen under the divine difpleafure?
Would the Deity, unchangeable as he is in rectitude
and juftice, reward their difobedience, by enlarging
                                            their

of thefe judgments, fays, " God fent evil angels amongft them."
Pf. lxxviii. 48, 49. See Mr. Lowman's three Tracts, p. 60—74.
On the other hand, it may be alledged, that the facred writers
feem to have thought, that God adminiftered *a particular pro-*
vidence by the inftrumentality of his angels; and confequently
in defcribing the effects of a fpecial divine interpofition, would
very naturally make mention of the agency of thofe miniftring
fpirits, much in the fame manner as is done in the paffages here
cited.

their fphere of action, and advancing them to new dominion over his own creation, fuch as is denied to the higheft archangel? Is the latter only *a miniftring fpirit*, while the former reign as fovereigns over nature, as fellow-fovereigns with the eternal God? The apoftles * Peter and Jude fpeak a very different language, when they tell us, that inafmuch as the angels.
" did not keep their principality †, but deferted their
" own habitation, God did not fpare them, but caft
" them down to Tartarus ‡, and (there) referves them
" in everlafting (or perpetual) chains, under dark-
" nefs, to the judgment of the great day." If Peter and Jude are here fpeaking of fuperior fpirits; it is evident, that even prior to their fall, they did not enjoy the liberty of a boundlefs range, but had a certain limited fphere of action affigned them, or their *proper habitation :* which we have fhewn to be highly probable from reafon ‖. And in their prefent ftate, they are fubjected to new reftraints, like prifoners confined for their crimes, in a doleful dungeon, where they remain in fafe cuftody, till they are brought forth to an ignominious execution. The place of their confinement is called *Tartarus ;* by which fome underftand

a deep

---

* 2 Pet. ii. 4. Jude 6.

† Τὴν ἱαυτων ἀρχὴν, Jude 6.

‡ Ταρἰαρώσας.

‖ Ch. 2. § 1.

a deep gulf under the earth *, and others the *dark air* †
near the earth: but whatever place it refers to,
they can have no *dominion* there; it is not their *kingdom*, but their *prifon*, their *conftant* and *perpetual* prifon.   How inconfiftent is this reprefentation of their
cafe, with their fharing with God the empire of the
world, and controuling the laws of nature and providence ! Nor does the Scripture on any occafion contradict this reprefentation: it never afcribes to the
devil the ability of revealing fecrets, foretelling future
events, or working miracles; never guards mankind
againft being deceived by the outward effects either
of his miraculous power or infpiration; neceffary as
fuch a caution would have been, had he been able to
infpire prophecies and work miracles; and earneftly
as it warns us againft a lefs danger, the pretences of
men to divine miracles and infpiration, when they
were not fent and affifted by God.

It is, indeed, urged by fome ‡, that the Scripture
reprefents evil fpirits as " prefiding over diftinct re-
" gions, by the direction of Satan their prince." In
proof of this affertion, we are referred to that paffage
in

* This feems to be the ftrict import of the word.   Homer.
Il. 8. l. 13, 14.   Hefiod. Theogon. l. 119, 718.   Plato in
Phædone, p. 399. ed. Ficini.   Virg. Æn. 6. l. 577.

† Confult the commentators on 2 Pet. ii. 4.   Ephef. ii. 2.
ch. vi. 12.

‡ Dr. Doddridge's **Fam.** Expof. V. i. p. 427. 2d ed. note f.
on Luke viii. 31.

in the book of Daniel*, where mention is made of Gabriel's being oppofed by the princes of the kingdom of Perfia, and of his fighting the prince of Perfia. It is not the defign of this vifion, to affert the prefidency even of good angels, (who at moft only execute the divine orders;) but to reprefent *the peculiar providence* which God exercifed over the Jewifh nation, and his care to fruftrate the councils of their enemies. As to evil fpirits, there is here no reference to them. For by the princes of the kingdom of Perfia, the prophet intends the nobles of that kingdom, and efpecially Cambyfes, the fon of Cyrus, who, in his father's abfence, ftopt the execution of his decrees, and forbad the building of the temple†. It is the more reafonable to underftand this paffage, of fome oppofition againft the Jews in the court of Perfia, by the prince and fome of the nobility; inafmuch as the prince of Grecia mentioned in the very fame paffage, cannot fo well be referred to an angel or evil fpirit, as to Alexander the Great, who overturned the empire of Perfia : he and his fucceffors being the main fubject of the following prophecy.

Some learned writers afcribe to the devil a power " of changing the conftitution of the air ‡." This element " is fo wonderfully contrived as at one and " the fame time to fupport clouds for rain, to afford " winds for health and traffick, to be proper for the

G 3 " breath

---

* Ch. x. 13, 20.

† See the Affembly's Annotations in loc.

‡ Dr. Macknight's Truth of the Gofpel Hiftory, p. 173.

" breath of animals by its fpring, for caufing founds
" by its motion, for tranfmitting light by its tranf-
" parency *." And therefore if the devil can change
the conftitution of this element, on which the material, the vegetable, and the animal creation abfolutely
depend; this world is in a ftate of perfect fubjection
to him; and inftead of being a prifoner in Tartarus,
he is the fovereign of nature. It has been a prevailing opinion amongft Chriftians, that the devil raifes
ftorms, and lays them; in direct contradiction to the
facred Scriptures, which reprefent the winds and
waves as fubject to the controul of God alone †, and
every change of their natural ftate as the certain evidence of his peculiar interpofition, particularly the
miraculous ftorm of thunder and hail in Egypt ‡, the
dividing the Red Sea by the rod of Mofes ‖, and
Chrift's calming the winds and waves upon the lake
of Gennefaret §. God interpofes to controul the elements very rarely, and only on great and extraordinary occafions: can we then believe that the devil,
and forcerers by his affiftance, controul them at pleafure every day? So ftrange a doctrine requires fome
clearer

---

* Dr. Clarke's Sermons, vol. i. p. 5.

† See Pf. lxv. 7. Pf. cxxxv. 7. Pf. cxlvii. 18. Prov.
xxx. 4. If. xxvii. 8. Jerem. x. 13. Amos iv. 13. Job
xxxvii. 10, 11.

‡ Exod. ix. 27—29. Compare If. xi. 15.

‖ Exod. xiv. 15.

§ Mark iv. 41. Matt. xiv. 33.

clearer proof, than the mention made by St. Paul, of
" the prince of the power of the air *." It is evident in general, that the apoftle is defcribing, not
the *natural*, but *moral* ftate of the world. Who
the perfon here referred to is, there may be fome difficulty to determine. If St. Paul refers to " the
prince of the Heathen deities," who were thought to
have their ftation in the higher regions of the air †;
he could not allow their having any real dominion
over the aerial regions, and muft be underftood as
reproaching the grofs ftupidity of idolaters, in being
as ftrongly actuated by their regard to thefe idols, as
if they had been powerful divinities. The very fcope
and defign of this paffage, as well as the principles
which the apoftle avows on other occafions, are fufficient to convince us, that he could only intend to
defcribe the Heathen deities by their ufual appellations, without allowing their claims. Suppofe the
apoftle, to make the Ephefians afhamed of their
former debaucheries, had reproached them with having been the votaries of the god Bacchus, or the goddefs Venus : who would have inferred from this language, that he believed Venus or Bacchus to be
powerful divinities ? Our Saviour himfelf ufes language fimilar to this, when he fpeaks of mens *ferving Mammon*, the god of riches. If (as is more ge-

G 4 nerally

---

* Ephef. ii. 2.

† See Whitby on Ephef. ii. 2. with whom compare Fabricius on Sextus Empiricus, note F. p. 571, and Dr. Harwood's
New Introduction, p. 303.

nerally and probably fuppofed) St. Paul refers to *the devil*, or any fpirit notorious for his difaffection to God, and for having feduced others from their allegiance; he defigned to upbraid the world with following fuch a leader and example, who was confidered by the Jews as the prince or chief of all thofe wicked fpirits, who were believed to have their refidence in the air *. The apoftle is here reminding the Ephefians of their character and ftate before their converfion to the Chriftian faith: " In time paft ye " walked according† to the courfe of this world," (in conformity to the manners and idolatries of the Heathen world,) " according † to" (or after the example of) " the prince of the power of the air," even the prince " of the fpirit ‡" (or difpofition and temper)

---

* The Jews had adopted the notion of the Heathens, that the air was inhabited by *evil fpirits*. See Whitby on Ephef. ii. 2. And to this notion the apoftle feems to refer, when he fpeaks of *the prince of the power of the air*, or the prince of the aerial power; defcribing him in this manner, becaufe it was his ufual appellation, and becaufe he really was the ringleader and chief of thofe wicked fpirits, who were commonly confidered as inhabitants of the air.

† Κατα.

‡ Inftead of, *the fpirit*, the original (τον πνευματος) ought to be rendered, *of the fpirit;* which Dr. Doddridge well explains by *difpofition* and *temper*. And that the word, *fpirit*, does often bear this fenfe, is evident from Pf. li. 10. Luke ix. 55. Rom. viii. 15. 2 Tim. i. 7. and other places. It muft bear this fenfe here; for if by *the fpirit that now worketh in the children of difobedience*, you underftand the devil, who is *the prince of that fpirit*, after whofe example the Ephefians had walked?

per) " that now worketh in the children of difobedience," or in thofe who have not been perfuaded to
embrace the Gofpel. The apoftle is not here excufing
idolatry, from the confideration of mens being urged
to commit it by a fupernatural power, but aggra-
vating its guilt and fottifhnefs, from the confideration
of its conformity to the moft odious character, to the
example of " the prince of the power of the air,"
even " the prince," captain and leader of " that temper *" or fpirit of difatfection to God, which ftill ac-
tuates and governs the unconverted Heathens.

III. We proceed to confider the view which the
S:ripture gives us of *the fouls of departed men.*

Many eminent writers maintain, that men fink
at death into a ftate of total infenfibility till the general refurrection. But we will not avail ourfelves
of this opinion; being perfuaded, that the fouls of
men, though formed with a great dependence upon
the body, with regard to the exercife of all their faculties, are neverthelefs feparable from it, and do
(by the appointment of God, on which it muft depend) exift in a ftate of confcious reflection, when
actually

---

* The fame manner of fpeaking is ufed, Micah i. 13. where
Lachifh is called in the Septuagint, αρχηγος αμαρτιας, the *prince*
or *ringleader of fin;* for this city fet Judah an *example* of idolatry. And in Maccab. ix. 61. mention is made των αρχηγων της
κακιας, *of the leaders of that mifchief,* or the *chief* in it. The
fame manner of fpeaking was familiar with the Latins. Veftri
pulcherrimi facti ille furiofus me principem dicit fuiffe. Cicer.
ep. Princeps atque architectus fceleris. Id. Princeps fceleris
atque concitator belli. Hirt. ap. Cæf. B. G. 8. 38.

actually feparated from it.   In this ftate however the foul can have no intercourfe with the prefent world. It is the body alone which links us to the world, and the organs of it are the neceffary and only means both of our receiving any notices and impreffions from outward objects, and of our exercifing any dominion over them.   And confequently when this animal fyftem, with all its wonderful powers of fenfation and activity, is diffolved by death, the foul can have no communication with the material creation. To renew this communication, it muft again be united to an organized body.   This feems to me moft agreeable to reafon *, and is unqueftionably the fenfe of divine revelation.   Can lefs than this be implied in thofe paffages of Scripture, which reprefent death, and the ftate to which it reduces us, *by fleep* †, in which the organs of the body are bound up; and even by *a negation of* (corporeal) *life and action* ‡ ? The facred writers conftantly affirm, that the dead " know not any thing ‖," which concerns the prefent world; that they are ftrangers to the affairs of their neareft relatives §, " (Abraham being ignorant

" of

---

* See above, ch. ii. fect. 1. p. 64.

† Deut. xxxi. 16. Job iii. 13. Pf. lxxvi. 5. Dan. xii. 2.

‡ Job iii. 11, 16. Pf. xxx. 9. Pf. lxxxviii. 10, 12. Ecclef. ix. 5, 6.

‖ Ecclef. ix. 6.

§ His fons come to honour, and he knoweth it not; and they are brought low, but he perceiveth it not of them, Job xiv. 21.

" of his own defcendants, and Ifrael acknowledging
" them not *," neither acquainted with their fufferings, nor capable of affording any relief:) and in
a word, that there is " no work, nor device, nor
" knowledge, nor wifdom in the grave †." In this
ftate, the moft eminent *faints* remain till the general
refurrection : for David is not yet " afcended into
" the heavens ‡." Much lefs are the fouls of *wicked* men advanced to dignity and power. St. Peter
calls thofe who were formerly difobedient in the days
of Noah, *fpirits in prifon* ‖ ; and our Saviour expreff-
ly teaches, that the fouls of the dead are in a ftate,
where they can have, of themfelves, no poffible intercourfe § with the living; and that they are never
releafed from it by God ; no not for fo important a
purpofe, as that of perfuading their vicious relatives
to reclaim their lives ; and confequently not for any
lower end.

Notwithftanding thefe feveral paffages of Scripture,
and the general idea which it gives us of death, as a
punifhment for fin, from which we are delivered by

a

* Ifaiah lxiii. 16.
† Ecclef. vi. 10.
‡ Acts ii. 4.
‖ 1 Pet. iii. 19.

§ " Between us and you there is a great gulf fixed : fo that
" they which would pafs from hence to you, cannot; neither
" can they pafs to us, that would come from thence." Luke
xvi. 26, 31.

a proper refurrection *; are well calculated to fubvert the foundation of Pagan fuperftition and idolatry; yet, from too ftrong a relifh of both, the *Fathers* of the Chriftian church (as they are ftiled by their true *fons*, who inherit their principles and difpofitions) adopted the wild fictions of the Heathen priefts and philofophers concerning the ftate of the dead †; and like them maintained, that the fouls of the

---

* The word αναστασις is δευτερα στασις, *reftoration*. Suidas in voc. Death deftroys our peculiar and diftinguifhing nature, as beings compounded of matter and fpirit; yet it does not deftroy the fubftance either of the material or fpiritual part of our compofition. The refurrection of the dead confifts in their *reftoration* to that kind of life which they formerly enjoyed, and which they loft by death, or in *a return* to their former ftate. In the age of the Gofpel, all who believed a refurrection, or any future ftate of retribution, believed the permanency of the human foul after death; and all who rejected the latter, denied the former. This was the cafe particularly with refpect to the Pharifees and Sadducees amongft the Jews. See Acts xxiii. 8, and the hiftory of Jofephus. So that our Saviour by afferting the refurrection, would be underftood rather to affert, than deny, an intermediate ftate.

† Even in the age of the apoftles, fome profeffing Chriftians denied the refurrection of the dead, 1 Cor. xv. 12. or faid, it was *paffed already*, 2 Tim. ii. 18. Having been taught by the Heathen philofophers, to look upon the body as the prifon of the foul, and upon death as the means of its liberty and enlargement; they pronounced the refurrection of the dead to be equally undefirable and impoffible, and interpreted what Chrift and his apoftles declared concerning it, of a renovation to a life of holinefs from a ftate of fin, defcribed as a ftate of death. See Whitby on 1 Cor. xv. 35, and compare Peters on

Job,

the deceafed have fome fenfe and knowledge of what is doing here*; that they are clothed with *fubtle bodies*, in which they frequently appear to mankind †; and that perfons of eminent virtue become after death a kind of inferior deities, whofe images and fepulchres ought to be honoured and adored.

In order to juftify the worfhip of deified or beatified fouls, they forged innumerable miracles, pretending them to be wrought by apparitions of the faints in dreams, by their interceffion, by the touch of their fepulchres, their bones or other reliques. Sir Ifaac Newton

---

Job, p. 403. And becaufe fome of the antient philofophers had taught, that the fouls of illuftrious perfonages afcended, immediately after death, into the celeftial regions; many Chriftians maintained, that the *martyrs* (and they only) enjoyed the fame privilege.

* Plato, ep. 2. fays, εστι τις αισθησις τοις τεθνεωσι των ενθαδε.

† The Jews alfo had imbibed this Pagan principle: for the difciples were *terrified* at the firft appearance of Chrift after his refurrection, and " fuppofed that they had feen a fpirit," Luke xxiv. 37. It is obfervable, that our Saviour, in his reply, neither countenances nor controverts the opinion, that ghofts can render themfelves vifible to human fight, and that in their priftine form; but contents himfelf with arguing on their own principles, in order to convince them of the truth of his refurrection; *q. d.* " If you will feel and handle my body, you will " foon perceive from the folidity of it, that I am not a mere " ghoft, which you conceive of as prefenting itfelf to the eye, " and yet eluding the grafp of the hand; but a real man, rai-" fed from the dead in the very fame body, compounded of " flefh and bones, in which I fuffered death."

Newton * has fhewn this concerning the Fathers in
the eaft; and the fame is equally true concerning
thofe in the weft. To guard all honeft minds againft
fo dangerous an impofture, it pleafed God to fortel
it, and to brand the authors and fupporters of it
with the character they fo well deferve, that of " a-
" poftates from genuine Chriftianity," while they retained the outward profeffion of it, and " profligate
" venders of lies. Now the Spirit fpeaketh expreff-
" ly, that in the latter times fome fhall depart † from
" the faith, giving heed to feducing fpirits, and doc-
" trines concerning demons ‡," (the fouls of men
deified after death,) " through the hypocrify (or,
                                                 " feigning)

* Obfervations on Daniel, ch. xiv.

‡ This *apoftacy* or *revolt* from the Chriftian faith, refers to
the corruption of it by the introduction of an *idolatrous worfhip;* as is fhewn by the eminently learned Mr. Jofeph Mede,
Works, p. 625. ed. 4.

‡ διδασκαλιαις δαιμονιων, *doctrines concerning demons.* Compare Heb. vi. 2. Acts xiii. 12. Jerem. x. 8. in the lxx. and
Mede, p. 626. St. Paul here fpecifies the idolatrous worfhip
which would prevail amongft Chriftians, which is that of demons, deified human fpirits. See Rev. ix. 20. and below,
ch. iii. fect. 2. By demons, it is impoffible here to underftand
devils, (in the common acceptation of that word;) becaufe the
Chriftian church, notwithftanding its dreadful degeneracy in
many other inftances, never defiled itfelf with the worfhip of
devils. In Epiphanius (adver. Hær. lxxviii. p. 1055. tom. 1.
ed. Petav.) there is a claufe added to the forecited paffage
from St. Paul, which at leaft ferves to explain it, and which
feems to have been a part of the original text, " for they fhall
" be worfhippers of the dead, as in Ifrael alfo they were wor-
                                                    " fhipped,"

" feigning) of lyars *," (who will fupport their own erroneous doctrine concerning the divinity and wor-fhip of dead men, by falfe miracles and other legendary tales, and whom therefore Chriftians ought to deteft as perfons) " having their confcience feared " with a hot iron †." Thus the facred Scriptures both give us fuch a reprefentation of the flate of the dead as is inconfiftent with their poffeffing a miraculous power, and refolve the whole hiftory of their intercourfe with mankind into the falfhood of its compilers; notwithftanding, under various pretences, (fuch as " forbidding to marry," and " com-" manding to abftain from meat ‡,") they have af-fumed a claim to extraordinary fanctity.

SECT. II.

The Scripture reprefentation of the nature and claims of the Heathen gods, confidered.

THE gods of the Heathens taken notice of in Scripture, are of two different kinds; the world,

" fhipped," that is, when the Ifraelites fell into the Heathen idolatry. See Mills and Beza in loc. and Mann's critical notes on fome paffages of Scripture, p. 92.

* Εν υποκρισει ψευδολογων.

† 1 Tim. iv. 1, 2.

‡ 1 Tim. iv. 3.

world, together with all its conftituent parts and principles ; and demons.

1. The Heathens deified the world, together with all its conftituent parts and powers. Conceiving the world to be pervaded and animated * by a vital and intelligent fubftance, they regarded it as a divinity †, which contained, framed and governed all things. The world poffeffing animal life and intelligence, they concluded the fame concerning the feveral portions of it, efpecially its moft illuftrious parts and active principles, the elements, the heavens and all their hoft, the winds alfo, and whatever other beings partook

* Principio cælum, ac terras, campofque liquentes,
  Lucent-mque globum lunæ, Titaniaque aftra
  Spiritus intus alit, totamque infufa per artus
  Mens agitat molem, et magno fe corpore mifcet.

                              Virgil. Æn. l. 6. l. 724.
  Vide etiam Virg. Georg. l. 4. v. 221. & Plutarch. de Placitis Philofoph. l. 2. c. 3. p. 886.

  † Nec magis approbabit nunc lucere, quam, quoniam Stoicus eft, hunc mundum effe fapientem, habere mentem, quæ & fe & ipfum fabricata fit, & omnia moderetur, moveat, regat, Cicero's Acad. Q. l. 2. c. 37. Nihil mundo perfectius,—fapiens eft, & propterea deus, Id. de Nat. Deor. l. 2. c. 14. Omnium rerum parens eft mundus, c. 34. The Platonifts indeed fometimes fpoke of the world as only a fecondary and begotten god, (as we learn from Origen. contr. Celf. l. 5. p. 235. and Plato's Tim. p. 1049. E. F. 1090. A.) but the doctrine of the Stoics, which reprefented the world as the chief god, (Diogen. Laert. l. 7. fegm. 137, 146. Plutarch de Placit. Philofoph. l. 1. c. 7. and Senec. ep. 94.) was more conformable to common creed of the Pagans.

partook of a fimilar fubftance; and confidered them
all as fo many diftinct deities. The fentient nature
and divinity of the fun, moon and ftars more efpecially, was ftrenuoufly afferted by the philofophers *,
as well as believed by the common people; and was
indeed the very foundation of the Pagan idolatry.
This point was allowed by all, except atheifts †, or
thofe who were reputed fuch. Anaxagoras, though
he maintained the exiftence of an infinite mind, and
its efficiency in the formation of the univerfe, was
neverthelefs accufed of atheifm and impiety, for
teaching that the heavenly bodies were inanimate and
unintelligent beings, and the fun itfelf a mafs of inflamed matter. Thus it came to pafs, that the Pagan
nations loft fight of the argument, from the admirable contrivance of the natural world, in favour of the
exiftence of the true God, the original caufe of all
things. Balbus, the Stoic, in Cicero's fecond book
concerning the nature of the gods, difcourfes ad-
mirably on the order and harmony of the univerfe,
and the ufe and beauty of the parts that compofe
it: but what is the inference he draws from thefe
premifes? " that the world was a god, and the

H   " habitation

* Particularly by Pythagoras and his followers, (as we learn
from Diogen. Laert. 1. 8. p. 509.) and by the Stoics. Thus
Balbus expreffes himfelf, (in Cicer. de Nat. Deor. 1. 2. 15.)
Atque hac mundi divinitate perfpecta, tribuenda eft fideribus
eadem divinitas. See above, note p. 112; and below, note
p. 114.

† Stob. Ecl. Phyf. c. 25. Plotin. Enn. 4. 1. 3. c. 7. and
Plutarch. adv. Colotem. p. 1123. A.

" habitation of the gods *," and that it was governed by " the providence of the gods †." Thefe were
the firſt deities of all the idolatrous nations; and
were eſteemed eternal, fovereign and fupreme ‡.

They

---

* Eſſe mundum deum, & deorum domum.

† Deorum providentia.

‡ Ariſtotle mentions it as a doctrine delivered down from
their very earlieſt anceſtors, and he himſelf applauds it as a divine ſaying, *that theſe firſt ſubſtances are gods,* Θεους ειναι τας πρω-
τας ουσιας, Metaphyſ. l. 14. c. 8. in fin. Plato condemns the
doctrine of Anaxagoras, becauſe it was inconſiſtent with the
divinity of the ſun and moon, which have προσκυνησεις ελληνων τε
και βαρβαρων παντων, " the adorations of all the Greeks and Barbarians." He makes Socrates diſclaim this doctrine of Anaxagoras as abſurd, and puts the following words into his mouth,
" What! do not I believe as other men do, that the ſun and
" moon are gods?" ουδε ηλιον, ουδε σεληνην αρα νομιζω ειναι Θεους, ωσ-
περ οι αλλοι ανθρωποι; Plat. Apol. Socrat. p. 362. F. G. ed. Ficini. And he directs a more excellent worſhip to be paid to
the heaven, than to the other gods, becauſe all men confeſſed
it to be the cauſe of all good things, Epin. p. 1006. A. Plutarch cenſures the Epicureans for aſſerting, that the ſun and
moon are void of intelligence, whom all men worſhipped, Adv.
Colotem. p. 1123. Sanchoniathon (apud Euſeb. Præp. Ev. l.
1. c. 9.) repreſents the moſt ancient nations, particularly the
Phenicians and Egyptians as acknowledging only the natural
gods, the ſun, moon, planets and elements. And Plato declares
it as his opinion, that the firſt Grecians likewiſe held theſe only to be gods, as many of the Barbarians in his time did. In
Cratyl. p. 273. F. See alſo Herodot. l. 1. c. 131, 138. l. 3.
c. 16. Diodor. Sic. l. 1. p. 10, 11. ed. Rhodomani. Strab.
Geogr. l. 15. p. 732. Polyb. Hiſt. l. 7. p. 699, 700. ed. Gronov. Euſeb. Præp. Ev. l. 2. c. 2. p. 59. Even Philo (lib. de
Somniis,) and Origen (in his books περι αρχων,) maintain, that
" the ſtars are ſo many ſouls incorruptible and immortal."

They are diſtinguiſhed by the title of *natural gods* *.

2. The Heathens likewiſe believed, that there were certain ſpirits who held *a middle rank* † between the gods and men on earth, and carried on all intercourſe between them; conveying the addreſſes of men to the gods, and the divine benefits to men ‡. Theſe ſpirits were called *demons* ‖, *diſtributors* or *diſpenſers* of good and evil to mankind. Their name is ex-preſſive of their office, and of that power and au-thority which they derived from the celeſtial gods §.

H 2   It

---

* Φυσικοὶ θεοί. Philo Byblius apud Euſeb. Præp. Ev. l. 1. c. 9. p. 33. ed. Paris.

† Πᾶν τὸ δαιμόνιον μεταξύ ἐςι θεοῦ τε καὶ θνητοῦ. Plato in Sympos. p. 202. tom. 3. ed. Serrani. Plutarch (de defect. Orac.) ſays, " Thoſe ſeem to me to have ſolved very many and great " difficulties or doubts, who place the demons," ἐν μέσω θεῶν κJ ἀνθρώπων.

‡ Plutarch de defect. Orac. p. 415, 416, 417, 421. E. Platon. Sympoſ. p. 202, 203. tom. 3. ed. Serrani. Apuleius de deo Socrat. p. 674, 677. ed. Delph. Jamblichus de myſter. & Auguſt. de civit. Dei, l. 8. c. 18. l. 9, c. 9. 21.

‖ They were called *demons*, παρὰ τὸ δαῆναι τὰ πάντα, ἢ μερίζειν τὰ ἀγαθὰ κJ κακὰ τοῖς ἀνθρώποις, Proclus in Heſiod. See alſo the ſcholiaſt on Homer, Il. 1. v. 222. Others derive δαίμων from δαήμων, ſciens, Plato Cratylus, p. 397. and Lactantius, II. 14. Demons were thought to be intruſted with the *inſpection* and *government* of mankind.

§ Plutarch (de defect. Orac.) informs us, that each demon was called by the name of that celeſtial god, παρ' ἒ δυνάμεως κJ τι-μῆς ἔιληχεν. Apuleius (De deo Socratis, p. 675, ed. Delph) ſays,. Cuncta

It was the opinion of many, that the celeftial divinities did not themfelves interpofe in human affairs,
but committed the entire adminiftration of the government of this lower world to thefe fubaltern deities *.   Hence they became the grand objects of the
religious hopes and fears of the Pagans, of immediate
dependence and divine worfhip.   " If idols are no-
" thing," fays Celfus †, " what harm can there be
" to join in the public feftivals ? If they are demons,
" then it is certain that they are gods, in whom we
" are to confide, and to whom we fhould offer facri-
" fices and prayers to render them propitious."   In
the moft learned nations, they did not fo properly
fhare, as *ingrofs* the public devotion.   To thefe alone
facrifices were offered, while the celeftial gods were
worfhipped only with a pure mind, or with hymns
and praifes ||.

It has been often faid, that the demons of the Heathens

Cuncta cœleftium voluntate, numine, & authoritate, fed dæmonum obfequio, & opera, & minifterio fieri arbitrandum eft.
Apuleius here refines the vulgar fyftem, when he reprefents
demons merely as a minifterial order of beings.

* Neque enim pro majeftate deum cæleftium fuerit, hæc cu-
rare. Apuleius de deo Socratis, p. 677. ed. Delph.   Plato (in
Sympof. p. 202. tom. 3. ed. Serm.) fpeaks to the fame effect,
" No god has any immediate intercourfe with man : all com-
" merce betwen the gods and men is carried on by the media-
" tion of demons."   Does not Plato's Θεὸς ἀνθρώπῳ ὁ μίγνυται
explain Dan. ii. 11 ?

† Apud Origen. c. Celf. l. 8. p. 393.

|| Mede's works, p. 636.

thens were fpirits of an higher origin than the human race. Thofe who hold this opinion, lay the chief ftrefs on the following arguments ; the force of which we fhall take the liberty to examine. 1ft, " The fu- " preme deity of the Pagans is called *the greateft de-* " *mon.*" Suppofing this to be the cafe, it is perhaps one proof, amongft many others, that their fupreme deity fuftained a human character, and had once been a mortal man. Notwithftanding the magnificent titles by which the heathens defcribe their fupreme deity; yet they do at the fame time inform us, that he had a father and a mother, a grandfather and a grandmother, and was of the fame kindred with the other gods of whom he was chief. And though he was fuperior to any of them fingly, he was no match for two or three of them in conjunction; as appears from the dread he was in of being feized and bound by Neptune, Juno and Minerva; from whofe violence he was not faved without the affiftance of Briareus with his hundred arms. This is related by Homer * of that very Jupiter, whom he ftyles " the father and fovereign of gods and men, " who thunders on high, and fhakes all heaven with " his nod." Such likewife is the reprefentation made of Jupiter by the other Heathen writers † : they afcribe

H 3   to

* Il. 1. v. 398. See Lucian. Deor. dialog! inter oper. v. 1. p. 228. ed. Varior.

† Hefiod, in particular, fpeaks of Jupiter in the very higheft terms, in his Theogony, v. 47, 457, 481, 506, 548 : and yet he tells us, that he was the youngeft fon of Rea and Saturn, and dethroned his father, v. 453, 490.

to him the prerogatives, titles and epithets of their fupreme natural divinity, and at the fame time cloath
him with the weakneffes, vices *, and all the properties of a human being. It is plain therefore that he
fuftained two chara&ers, that of a natural, and that of
a hero god. It feems difficult, if not impoffible, to
reconcile the different reprefentations made of him,
on any other fuppofition. It is allowed by all, that a
mixture of phyfiology and herology runs through the
Pagan fyftem of divinity †. It. is likewife evident,
that as amongft the natural, fo alfo amongft the hero
gods, there was a diftinction of rank and dignity,
and one was confidered as prince of the reft. It farther appears, that deified human fpirits were (according to the Pagan fyftem of theology) affociated with
and reprefented the natural gods, and that both were
called

---

* Chærea (in Terence, Eunuch. Act. iii. fc..5.) hardens
himfelf into the commiffion of a rape, by the example of Jupiter, the god, who fhakes with his thunder the lofty battlements
of heaven; qui templa cœli fumma fonitu concutit.

† That the firft fubftances are gods, and that the deity contains univerfal nature, Ariftotle tells us, was delivered *in the
form of a fable*, ἐν μύθυ σχήμαʈι, Metaphyf. l. 14. c. 8. in fin.
Thefe fables were the means of corrupting their theology, and
occafioned the Heathens to transfer their worfhip to new objects. Specimens of the manner, in which they accommodat-
ed the fabulous traditions concerning their hero gods to the
deified objects of nature, may be feen, in Cicero de Nat. deor.
l. 2. c 24, 25.

called by the fame names *. The fun, or æther, or air, or whatever other part of nature was efteemed the fupreme deity of the Pagans, was called in Egypt, Ofiris; in Chaldea and Phenicia, Bel or Baal; and in many other countries, Jupiter. Now it is univerfally known, that Jupiter, Bel and Ofiris had once been mortal men, who were fuppofed to be advanced after death to a deified ftate. For the fame reafons, therefore, for which the chief Heathen numen was called Ofiris, or Bel, or Jupiter, he might be called a demon; fuppofing the word to denote a deified human fpirit. It was under this laft character that he was principally regarded by the common people. 2dly, It is further urged, " that demons are defcrib- " ed as beings placed *between* the gods and men." This defcription refpects, not their *nature*, but their *office* †, (which was that of *mediators* and agents be-

H 4   tween

---

* Diodorus Siculus (l. 1. p. 12. ed. Rhodomani,) fays, that fome of the earthly gods had the fame names with the celeftial, ὁμωνύμως ὑπαρχῶν τοῖς ἐρανίοις. See Plutarch cited above, p. 175. note 1. From Philo Biblius (apud Eufeb. Præp. Ev. l. 1. c. 9. p. 33. ed. Paris.) we learn, that the ancient nations " gave the names of their kings to the elements of the world," τοῖς κοσμικοῖς ϛοιχείοις, which were their natural deities, whom alone they acknowledged to be ftrictly and properly gods. Lord Herbert obferves, (De Relig. Gentil. c. 11.) Initio heroas in aftris plerumque, aftra in heroibus colentes, adeo ut cognomines ita effent, neque fatis judicari poffet, num aniles de iis contextæ fabulæ ad aftra myftice, an ad homines mythice pertinerent.

† See above, p. 115.

tween men on earth, and the celeſtial gods;) and conſequently agrees with ſuch human ſpirits (and it is not to be denied, that there were ſome ſuch) as were thought to be advanced to the office of demons. It may be proper to take notice farther, that when Jamblichus *, the Pythagorean philoſopher, makes it the reward of good men at death, to be converted *into angels and angelical ſouls†;* he has the ſame meaning, as if he had called them *demons.* The learned allow, that Jamblichus, Hierocles, Simplicius and others, uſe the word *demons* and *angels* indiſcriminately. Hierocles ſays expreſsly ‡, that the middle kind of beings were called indifferently *angels,* or *demons,* or *heroes.* Now it is univerſally admitted, that the latter were human ſpirits : and conſequently the former were ſo likewiſe. Philo ſays ‖ " Souls, demons and " angels are only different names, but imply one and " the ſame ſubſtance." And in another place § he affirms, " that Moſes called thoſe angels, whom the " other philoſophers ſtyled demons." 3dly, It is pleaded, " that demons are expreſsly diſtinguiſhed " from *heroes,* who were the departed ſouls of men."

             Demons

---

* Apud Stob. Eclog. Phyſic. l. 1. p. 144.

† Εἰς ἀ[γίλυς ἢ κὴ ἀ[γελικὰς ψυχὰς.

‡ In Car. Pythag.

‖ De Gigantibus, p. 286.

§ De Somn. p. 586. ἓς ἄλλοι φιλόσοφοι δαίμονας, ἀ[γέλυς Μωσᾶς εἰωθεν ὀνομάζειν.

Demons were advanced to a *rank* and *flation* * fuperi-
or to that of heroes; and this difference occafioned
the diftinction. Plutarch † teaches, " that, accord-
" ing to a divine nature and juftice, the fouls of vir-
" tuous men are advanced to the rank of demons ;
" and that from demons, if they are properly purifi-
" ed, they are exalted into gods, not by any politi-
" cal inftitution, but according to right reafon." The
fame author fays ‡, " That Ifis and Ofiris were, for
" their virtue, changed from good demons into gods,
" as were Hercules and Bacchus afterwards, receiv-
" ing the united honours of both gods and de-
" mons ‖."

I do not affirm, that the Heathens had no demons
of

* On this difference of rank and ftation, fee Hierocles in fe-
cundum Aur. Carm. p. 41.

† Plutarch. Vit. Romul. p. 36. A. ed. Paris. and in his book
de defect. orac. he fpeaks of human fouls as commencing firft
heroes, then demons, and afterward advanced to a more fublime degree.

‡ De If. & Ofir. p. 361.

‖ Καὶ Θεῶν κỳ δαιμόνων. Thefe fentiments of Plutarch are confirmed by other writers. Diodorus Siculus (p. 3. ed. Rhodomani.) after fpeaking of Hercules, adds, τῶν ỷ ἄλλων ἀΓαθῶν ἀνδρῶν
οἱ μὲν ἡρωïκῶν, οἱ δὲ ἰσοθέων τιμῶν ἔτυχον. It alfo appears from the
cafe of the Greek Hercules, as related by Paufanias, (Corin-
thiac. l. 2. c. 10. p. 133. ed. Kuhnii.) that heroes rofe by degrees to the rank of gods, and came to be worfhipped as fuch.
(For the worfhip paid to the gods, was different from that paid
to the heroes.)

of a different kind from thofe who were of human extract *. The foregoing reflections were merely defigned to fhew, that the higher order of demons is not fo frequently fpoken of, as is generally fuppofed; and that the common hypothefis is built upon weak grounds. I fhall now affign thofe reafons which induce me to think, that by demons (fuch, I mean, as were " the more immediate objects of the eftablifhed worfhip" amongft the ancient nations, particularly the Egyptians, Greeks and Romans,) we are to underftand beings of an earthly origin, or fuch departed human fouls as were believed to become demons. Hefiod †, and many other poets ‡, who have recorded the ancient biftory or traditions, on which the public faith and worfhip were founded, affert, that the men of the golden age, who were fuppofed to be very good, became demons after death, and difpenfers of good things to mankind. This account of demons is fully confirmed by the other writings of the ancient Heathens. Many paffages have been produced from thofe writings by feveral learned moderns ‖, in which demons muft have the fame meaning as in Hefiod.
                                                            And

---

* Some of the lateft philofophers, in particular, (fuch as Apuleius, de deo Socrat, p. 690.) fancied that there was a higher kind of demons, who had never inhabited human bodies. Ammonius in Plutarch entertained the fame fentiment. De defect. orac. p. 431. tom. 2. ed. Paris. 1624.

† Hefiod. Oper. & dier. l. 1. 120.

‡ Plato's Cratylus, p. 398. tom. 1. ed. Serrani.

‖ Mr. Jof. Mede, and Dr. Sykes.

And there are many more, which I do not remember
to have met with in any former writers on this fubject. Some of thefe paffages have been already cited ;
and a much greater number we fhall have occafion to
cite in the fequel. I will here only take notice of two
from Celfus, becaufe they ferve to fhew, how long
the word preferved its original import, and was ufed
to defcribe a deified man. Thus Celfus * infults
Chriftians under their fufferings : " Your demon, or
" as you fay, the Son of God, gives you no help."
In another place †, after fpeaking of the followers of
Marcion, he adds, " Others form to themfelves ano-
" ther mafter and demon." Perhaps it would be as
ufelefs, as it would be endlefs, to collect all the paffages from the writings of the Heathens, in which
mention is made of demons, in the fenfe here afferted.
For ftill fome would allege, that the word occurred
frequently in a different meaning. Our main defign
(which is, to explain and juftify the Scripture-repre-
fentation of the Heathen deities,) will be anfwered ;
if it can be fhewn, that the more immediate objects
of divine worfhip in the moft polifhed Heathen nations were deified mortals. This, at the fame time,
may ferve to fhew, in what fenfe it is moft natural to
underftand the word, demons, when it is ufed to defcribe thofe gods.

That the more immediate objects of popular adoration amongft the Heathens were deified human beings,

---

* Apud Origen. c. Celf. l. 8. § 39. p. 803.
† P. 272.

ings, is a fact attefted by all antiquity, whether Pagan,
Jewifh or Chriftian.   Let the *Heathens* themfelves
fpeak, and let us credit the united teftimony of their
hiftorians, their poets, and their philofophers, to a
fact which they could not but admit, though it re-
dounded fo much to their difhonour.   We fhall begin with the doctrine of the *hiftorians ;* becaufe it is
clear and explicit, and may ferve to guide us through
the labyrinths of the Pagan theology.   Herodotus *,
when fpeaking of the Perfians, fays, " They have
" neither ftatues, nor temples, nor altars.—What I
" take to be the reafon, is, that they don't believe,
" like the Greeks, that the gods are of the race of
" men †."   Now, inafmuch as the Greeks derived
their religion from the Phenicians and Egyptians, and
fpread it amongft the Romans, there can be no doubt,
but that the gods of all thefe people were of human
race.   Philo Byblius ‡, the tranflator of Sanchoniathon's hiftory of the gods, exprefsly affures us, " That
" the Phenicians and Egyptians, from whom other
" people derived this cuftom, reckoned thofe amongft
" the greateft gods, who had been benefactors to the
" human race : and that to them they erected pillars
" and ftatues, and dedicated facred feftivals."   Diodorus Siculus ‖ treats largely concerning the Gentile
theology ;

* Lib. 1. c. 131.

† Οὐκ ἀνθρωποφυίας ἐνόμισαν τὸς θεὸς, καθάπερ οἱ Ἕλληνες, εἴναι.

‡ Apud. Eufeb. Præp. Ev. l. 1. c. 9. p. 32.

‖ Lib. 1. & 5.

theology; and he fpeaks of it as the opinion of antiquity, " that there were two claffes of gods; the one
" eternal and immortal," (the natural gods fpoken
of above;) " the other fuch as were born upon the
" earth, and arrived at the titles and honours of di-
" vinity, on account of the bleffings they beftowed
" upon mankind *." He confiders Saturn, Jupiter,
Apollo and the reft, as the primary gods of Paganifm; and yet fpeaks of them as illuftrious men.

The *poets* deliver the fame fentiments concerning
the gods, as the hiftorians do. In their theogony †
or generation of the gods, (which was the fame thing
with their cofmogony or generation of the world)
and in their fabulous theology, we have an account
both of their natural and hero gods; though by mixing together their herology and phyfiology, they have
introduced much confufion into their fyftem of divinity. With regard to the principal objects of popular worfhip, they have given us an account of their
birth and parentage, of their marriage and offspring,
and have entered into a detail of their actions ‡.
Whatever fublime titles the poets beftow upon them,
they hold them out to our view chiefly under a human character. Nor is there any juft reafon to affirm,
that the poets invented what they fay concerning their
gods. For their works are either faithful records of
ancient

* Lib. 1. p. 12. ed. Rhodomani.

† See Hefiod's Theogony, and Homer's Il. 14. v. 201.

‡ See what was faid above concerning Jupiter, p. 117.

ancient traditions, or accurate reprefentations of life
and manners. Epic and dramatic writings do not
allow any deviation from truth and juftnefs of character.

It is when reading the *philofophers*, that it becomes
us moft to be upon our guard, if we would not be led
into miftakes concerning the Pagan deities. When
they began to reafon upon the nature of the gods, innumerable objections arofe in their minds againft the
vulgar fyftem of theology; which fome of them derided, and others endeavoured to refine and improve.
Shocked at the abfurdity of the worfhip paid to dead
perfons, they might be willing to perfuade themfelves
and others, that their demons were fpiritual fubftances of a more noble origin than the human race.
They undertook to determine, with what fort of beings all the different regions of the univerfe were peo-
pled; and fome of them filled the æther with fuch
demons as had never been men. But we have no
concern here with *the fpeculations* of the philofophers,
who on this, as on other points, contradicted one
another, and themfelves likewife. It is fufficient to
our prefent purpofe to obferve, that they were not
able to deny, that the public worfhip was directed to
men who had been raifed to the rank of gods and demons. Socrates *, indeed, judged it difficult to declare the origin of demons; which at firft fight feems
fcarce confiftent with a perfuafion, that they were of
human extract. Neverthelefs, he thought they were
                                                natives

* Plato's Timæus, p. 481. ed. Bafil.

natives of this lower world, proceeding from the commerce of celeftial with mortal beings. Perhaps this ftrange commerce was what created the difficulty in the breaft of Socrates : for he rejected many of the common fables concerning the gods. Nor does it certainly appear, that even the celeftial beings concerned in thefe amours, were not originally mortals, though afterwards advanced to a deified ftate. Plato commends Hefiod and the other poets, who affirmed, that whenever any good man dies, *he becomes a demon* *. He elfewhere fpeaks to the fame purpofe †. The latter Platonifts, though they endeavoured to foften the abfurdity of the eftablifhed fyftem of theology, could not but admit a clafs of gods and demons, that had been human fouls. Varro, the moft learned of all the Romans, afferted, as St. Auguftin informs us ‡, that one would be at a lofs to find, in the writings of the ancients, gods who had not been men. Cicero ǁ contends, " that the whole

" heaven

---

* Γίνεται δαίμων. Plat. Cratyl. p. 398. tom. 1. ed. Serrani. See alfo Maxim. Tyr. Diff. 27. p. 283. ed. Davis.

† " All thofe who die valiantly in war are of Hefiod's golden " generation, and become demons; and we ought for ever to " worfhip and adore their fepulchres, as the fepulchres of de- " mons." He affirms the fame concerning all who were judged excellently good in life, in whatever manner they die. Plato de Republ. l. 5. p. 468. tom. 2. ed. Serrani.

‡ De civit. Dei, l. 8.

ǁ Quid ? totum prope cœlum, ne plures perfequar, nonne humano genere completum eft ?—Ipfi illi, majorum gentium dii

" heaven was almoſt entirely filled with the human
" race, that even the greater deities * were originally
" natives of this lower world, that their ſepulchres
" were ſhewn in Greece, and the traditions concern-
" ing them preſerved in the myſteries." In like
manner Pliny †, Labeo ‡, Servius ‖ and others, ſpeak
openly of the origin of the gods. And Plutarch himſelf vindicates the deification of human ſouls, by the
principles of reaſon and philoſophy ¶. Not only did
Atheiſts and Epicureans aſſert, that the Heathen gods
had been men ; this was a point allowed by the zealous ſupporters of the eſtabliſhed religion, even in an
age

dii qui habentur, hinc a nobis profecti in cœlum reperientur.
Quære, quorum demonſtrantur ſepulchra in Grecia: reminiſ-
cere, quoniam es initiatus, quæ traduntur myſteriis: tum de-
nique, quam hoc latè pateat, intelliges. Tuſc. Quæſt. l. 1.
c. 12, 13. It is affirmed in Cicero's dialogue de Nat. deor.
l. 1. that every age honoured the inventors of the uſe of food,
ut deos omnium clariſſimos. See alſo l. 1. c. 42. l. 3. c. 15,
23. and compare Lactant. l. 1. c. 15. p. 85. l. 2. c. 2. p. 146.
Euſeb. Dem. Ev. l. 8. p. 364.

* The greater deities were
Juno, Veſta, Minerva, Ceres, Diana, Venus, Mars, Mercurius,
Jovis, Neptunus, Vulcanus, Apollo.

† Plin. Nat. Hiſt. l. 2. c. 7.

‡ Servius (upon the 3d Æneid) ſays, Labeo in libris qui
appellantur, De diis quibus origo animalis eſt, ait eſſe quædam
ſacra, quibus animæ humanæ vertuntur in deos.

‖ Serv. ad Æn. 8. l. 319.

¶ See the paſſage from Plutarch cited above, p. 182.

age when the improvements in fcience expofed it to contempt.

Thefe teftimonies of the Heathens are fully con-firmed by *facts*, which cannot be difputed: particu-larly by the very nature of the worfhip paid to the Heathen deities. If no argument can be drawn from the facrifices * which were offered them; yet their images, columns, fhrines, reliques, altars (or grave-ftones) and temples (which were their fepulchres), are fufficient proofs, that the objects of public worfhip were fuch dead men and women as fuperftition deified †.

I   Even

---

* Deified human ghofts might more naturally be fuppofed to be nourifhed by the fumes of incenfe, and the fteams of flaughtered beafts afcending from their altars, than the fun, moon and ftars. See Origen. c. Celf. l. 7. c. 334, 335. Con-cerning the idea of facrifices, as the nourifhment of the gods, confult Ariftoph. Avef. v. 183, 1515. Eufeb. Præp. Ev. l. v. p. 181. Lucian. Prometh. tom. 1. p. 183. ed. Græv. De Sa-crificiis, ib. p. 366. Porphyr. de Abftin. l. 2. c. 42. p. 86. ed. Cantabr. We are told by Eufebius (Præp. Ev. l. 2. c. 9.) that in the earlieft ages, when the ftars only were adored, they were not honoured by animal facrifices : which feem therefore to have been principally directed to the hero gods. See above, p. 176. Neverthelefs, it muft be acknowleged, that fuch Pa-gans and Chriftians as believed the Heathen gods to be a dif-ferent order of demons from human fouls, reprefented thofe demons as nourifhed by libations and facrifices.

† See Sir If. Newton's Chronology, p. 159, 160. and efpe-cially Mr. Jof. Mede's works, p. 632, 634. That the ftately tombs of the Heathen gods became public temples, is alfo fhewn by Eufebius, Præp. Ev. l. 2. c. 6.

Even *funeral rites* * were performed in their honour. Euhemerus therefore in his facred hiftory,
befides recording the pedigree and actions of the
Heathen gods, pointed out the very places where
they were buried. His hiftory was tranflated into
Latin by Ennius, and is mentioned by Diodorus Siculus without any marks of difapprobation. Thofe
who cenfured †, were not able to confute, the fubftance

---

* Mede's works, p. 628, 630. Lowth on If. viii. 19. Cicero de Nat. Deor. l. 1. c. 15. Lucan thus addreffes Egypt,
—Tu plangens hominem teftaris Ofirin. l. 8. v. 833.

† It has been faid by learned men, upon the authority of a
paffage in Cicero, (de Nat. deor. l. 1. c. 42.) that the opinion
of Euhemerus was generally regarded by the Heathens as
atheifm, or at leaft as great impiety. Were this true, the
moft that it would prove, is, that the Heathen gods were not
regarded as dead men by their worfhippers, though they were
really fuch. But what fome reprefent as the general fentiment
of the Heathens, is nothing more than the objection of Cotta,
under the character of an *Academic*, which he could not fuf-
tain, without propofing the difficulties and objections, with
which his fubject was embaraffed. See Cicero de Nat. deor.
l. 3. c. 39. and l. 1. c. 5. Cotta fays, Ab Euhemero autem
& mortes, & fepulturæ demonftrantur deorum; and then afks
the following queftion : Utrum igitur hic confirmaffe videtur
religionem, an penitus totam fuftuliffe ? This objection is not
defigned to difprove the fact, that the Heathens worfhipped
dead perfons ; but to expofe the abfurdity of that worfhip.
Cotta admitted the fact, and knew that the worfhip itfelf
pointed out the objects of it: Quo quid abfurdius, quam—
homines jam morte deletos reponere in deos, quorum omnis
cultus effet futurus in luctu ? Cicero de Nat. deor. l. 1. c. 15.
Plutarch alfo cenfures the doctrine of Euhemerus as productive
                                                              of

ftance of his fyftem. If the mere abfurdity of an opinion would prove that it was never entertained; what
a blank would this reafoning make in the hiftory of
religion amongft the Pagans?

We go on to examine the opinion of the *Jews*
concerning the Heathen gods. With refpect to the
writers of the Old Teftament; though they knew,
that the Pagans believed in fidereal and elementary
deities, yet they very properly defcribe their gods as

I 2   *dead*

of atheifm, De If. & Ofir. p. 359, F. p. 360. Neverthelefs,
from this treatife it appeais, that the Egyptian priefts acknowledged, that Ofiris and the other gods of Egypt had been
men. Nay, Plutarch himfelf confeffes, (p. 359. E.) that thofe
who hold this opinion, ἔχουσιν ἀπὸ τῶν ἱσορουμένων βοηθείας, *have
the fupport of hiftory* : to which he oppofes fpeculation, p. 360.
This confirms what was obferved concerning the philofophers,
p. 189. I admit, however, that the doctrine of Euhemerus
might even in the opinion of the vulgar Heathens, be very liable to the cenfure of impiety; and certainly was liable to this
cenfure, if he maintained, (as poffibly he did, or might be
thought to maintain) that the Heathen gods were *mere* men,
not advanced to a deified ftate; or that the Heathens had no
other gods but thefe. In this view he might well pafs for an
atheift. The deification of men prefuppofed the exiftence of
the natural gods, with whom they were affociated, and from
whom they derived their power and authority. And therefore
if he rejected the natural gods, he would be thought not to believe in any gods at all. With this he feems to be charged by
Theophil. Antiochen. ad Autolyc. l. 3. p. 210. ed Oxon.
Concerning Euhemerus, fee Eufeb. Præp. Ev. l. 2. c. 2. p. 59,
where there is an extract from the 6th book of Diodorus Siculus, now loft. See alfo Lactantius, Div. Inftit. l. 1. c. 2.
p. 62. et de ira Dei, c. 2. p. 62. ed. Lugd. Bat. 1660.

dead * perfons; becaufe it was to fuch that the public worfhip was more immediately directed. Here it
fhould be obferved, that when they defcribe the Heathen gods as *dead* perfons; they confider them as
what they *really were*, not what they were *conceived
to be* by their worfhippers; as fome have afferted:
for their worfhippers regarded them as men advanced
to divine power and dominion. In contradiftinction
from thefe, the ancient prophets called Jehovah the
only *living* † God. Thofe Jews who tranflated the
Old Teftament into the Greek language, (I mean the
authors of that verfion which is called the Septuagint)
ftyle the Heathen gods, *demons* ‡. And it has been
generally

---

* This is implied in that declaration, which Mofes required
each Ifraelite to make, at offering the firft fruits of every year,
Deut. xxvi. 14. " I have not given ought thereof for (or to)
the dead," to any Heathen deity : which fuppofes, that each
of thofe deities was nothing more than a dead perfon. Such
was Ifis, to whom Spencer and Le Clerc think there is here a
peculiar reference. Thofe who partook of the facrifices offered to the Pagan gods, are faid " to eat the facrifices of the
dead," Pf. cvi. 28. compared with Numb. xxv. 1, 2, 3. It
was becaufe the Heathen deities were dead men, that Ifaiah
reproaches thofe who had recourfe to their pretended oracles,
as " feeking for the living to the dead." If. viii. 19.

† Deut. v. 26. Jofh. iii. 10. 1 Sam. xvii. 26. 2 Kings
xix. 4. Jerem. x. 10. Dan. vi. 26. and many other places.

‡ " They facrificed unto demons," δαιμονίοις, Deut. xxxii.
17. " All the gods of the Heathen are demons," δαιμόνια,
Pf. xcv. 6. " They facrificed their fons and their daughters
unto demons," δαιμονίοις, Pf. cvi. 37.

generally fuppofed, that by demons they meant certain *created* fpirits of a celeftial origin, who, though
fallen from God and virtue, poffefs a very extenfive
power over this lower world. This however is a
point that ought not to be taken for granted. The
authors of the Septuagint were not unacquainted with
the Greek learning. They could not therefore be
ignorant, that the Heathens did not acknowledge any
created fpirits; or at leaft, that according to their
eftablifhed fyftem of theology, the world and every
thing in it, was either eternal or begotten, not created. As little reafon is there to fuppofe them ignorant, in what fenfe the word, demons, was ufed by
the Heathens, both in their writings, and in their
common difcourfe. No word in the Greek language
could be more familiar to them, efpecially as applied
to the objects of popular adoration, or fuch human
fpirits as were fuppofed to become demons, whether
confidered as good or evil. Now, why fhould it be
prefumed, that thefe writers ufe this word in a fenfe
different from all the Greeks, when fpeaking upon
the fame fubject? Befides, did not the authors of
the Septuagint verfion know, (what all the world
knew) that the Heathen gods had once been men?
Could they be ignorant, that in the books which they
tranflated, and which they acknowledged to be infpired, thefe gods were reprefented in this their true
light? Or, fhall it be taken for granted, that in
open contradiction to the infpired writers, and in
defiance of their own inward convictions, they were
capable of affirming, that *all* the Heathen gods were
of a different origin from mankind? Such a degree

I 3   or

of extravagance and wickednefs as this implies, ought not to be charged upon any writers, without the ftrongeft proofs. For thefe reafons, it appears to me moft probable, that they ufed the word to exprefs fuch human fpirits as became demons. And I am confirmed in this opinion, by attending to the particular occafions on which they ufe it *. As to the other Jews who wrote in the Greek language, they were no ftrangers to this meaning of demons. We have already had occafion to explain the fentiments of Philo †. With refpect to Jofephus, he fays exprefsly, " Demons are the fpirits of wicked men ‡." This fhews, that in the writings of the Helleniftic Jews, particularly thofe who lived near the commencement of the Chriftian æra, the word is to be underftood of fuch departed human fpirits as became demons.

Is it not natural then to fuppofe, that it bears the
fame

---

* It will be fhewn below, that the paffages in the Hebrew text which correfpond to thofe cited above (p. 132, n. ‡.) from the Septuagint, manifeftly refer to the hero gods of the Heathens; I add here, that when the authors of this verfion fay, If. lxv. 11. that the Jews " prepared a table to a demon," τῷ δαιμονίῳ; it feems to me more natural to underftand them, as reproaching the Jews with facrificing to fome Heathen demon, than to any fallen angel. See Lowth in loc. and compare Dr. Sykes's Further Enquiry; p. 35.

† See above, page 120.

‡ Τὰ γὰρ καλύμενα δαιμόνια, ταῦτα δὲ πονηρῶν ἐςιν ἀνθρώπων πνεύματα, De Bel. Jud. l. 7. c. 6. § 3.

fame meaning in *the New Teftament?* There the Heathen deities are called demons: " Thofe things " which the Gentiles facrifice, they facrifice to de- " vils, or demons *.." St. Paul, whofe language this is, was a perfon of extenfive learning, and well ac- quainted with the theology of the Gentiles, which re- prefented human fpirits as becoming demons after death. He knew, that thefe demons were the very perfons to whom the Gentiles offered their facrifices. At the fame time he was converfant in thofe writings . of the infpired prophets, which taught, that the Hea- then gods were men and women deceafed. He him- felf (in imitation of thofe prophets) diftinguifhes Je- hovah from them by the title of the *living* ‡ God: Now, if he knew them to belong to the human fpe- cies; would he deny that they had been men, and affirm that they were angels? To fuppofe that he would, is to charge him, not with error, but with wilful falfehood : a charge that cannot be fupported, but by putting a fenfe upon his language, which, to fay the leaft, was not the moft ufual and common one. Befides, this apoftle was not only himfelf well ac- quainted with the theology of the Gentiles, but was

I 4   writing

---

* Δαιμονίοις. The apoftle adds, " I would not that ye fhould " have fellowfhip with devils, δαιμονίων, demons. Ye cannot " drink the cup of the Lord, and the cup of devils, δαιμονίων, " demons : ye can not be partakers of the table of the Lord, " and of the table of devils, δαιμονίων, demons," 1 Cor. x. 27, 21.

‡ Acts xiv. 15. 2 Cor. vi. 16. 1 Theff. i. 9.

writing to Gentiles, who knew that, according to
their theology, human fpirits became demons after
death; and who would naturally underſtand him as
referring to Jupiter, Venus, and other men and women, whom they had once worſhipped under this
very chara&ter. Would not St. Paul then uſe the
word, *demon*, in the ſame ſenſe in which he knew it
would be underſtood, by thoſe Gentiles to whom he
was writing? If you ſay he borrowed it from the
Jews who ſpoke the Greek language, particularly the
authors of the Septuagint; you ſuggeſt a new proof
of the point we would eſtabliſh: for it muſt be admitted, that he would employ it, as we have ſeen they
did, to deſcribe ſuch human ſpirits as were called demons. There are paſſages in St. Paul's writings, and
in other places of the New Teſtament, where it cannot bear a different meaning *.

In

---

* When St. Paul preached to the Athenians Jeſus Chriſt as
riſen from the dead; he ſeemed to ſome of his hearers, *a ſetter
forth of ſtrange gods,* δαιμονίων, *demons,* (A&ts xvii. 18, 22.)
which, as our tranſlators themſelves were ſenſible, cannot ſigni-
fy *devils,* (in the ordinary acceptation of that word) but muſt
denote *deified men*; the Athenians imagining that St. Paul was
recommending a new deity, who had once been a man. Nor
can it be ſuppoſed, that St. Paul himſelf, in his addreſs to the
Athenians, would uſe the word in a ſenſe different from what
they did, when he calls them δεισιδαιμονεςέρας, (v. 22.) " perſons
much addi&ted to the worſhip of demons," or gods of human
original; for to ſuch gods all the devotion of the Athenians
and other Greeks was dire&ted. The worſhip of cannonized
ſaints amongſt idolatrous Chriſtians, is called " the do&trine
" concerning demons," i Tim. iv. i. explained above, ch. 3.
ſe&t.

In the late controverfy upon this fubject, both parties feem to have committed feveral great miftakes. I fhall take notice of a very effential one, relative to our prefent argument. On the one fide, it was afferted, that demon never fignifies an evil being, till after the times of Chrift: whereas the word is indifferent in itfelf, and is ufed in a bad as well as a good fenfe by very ancient writers *. On the other fide, it was affirmed, that

fect. 1. p. 109. And the fame corruptors of Chriftianity are reproached, for not repenting of the works of their hands, that " they fhould not worfhip demons." Rev. ix. 20: which muft refer to *faint worfhip* and *image worfhip*: for who can charge Chriftians with the worfhip of wicked fpirits, as fuch?

* If the firft demons were all good, as Dr. Sykes afferts; it is becaufe the firft men, (whofe fouls they were) the men of the golden age, were all good. For we fhall fhew, that the Heathens thought, that the departed fpirits of good and bad men became refpectively good and bad demons. There is therefore ground to prefume, that as foon as mankind degenerated, their departed fpirits would be reprefented as wicked and mifchievous, that is, as bad demons. The common or conftant ufe of demon in the earlieft ages in a good fenfe, unlefs when κακος, or fome fimilar epithet is joined with it; is owing to its being applied at firft to the deified fouls of good men. Plutarch tells us, in his life of Dion, near the beginning, p. 958. ed. Paris. 1624. " that it was the opinion of the " ancients, that evil and mifchievous demons, out of envy and " hatred to good men, oppofe whatever they do." In his treatife concerning Ifis and Ofiris, p. 360. he fpeaks of demons who had a mixture of virtue and vice in their character, and reprefents Xenocrates and Empedocles as believing there were fuch demons. From thofe writings of the ancients which are come down to us, we accordingly find, that they ufed the word

that demons in general, and the bad in particular, were fpirits of a celeftial origin, and that it was of the latter, (or of apoftate angels) that the word was to be underftood, both in the Septuagint, and in the paffages of St. Paul cited above. We may allow, (what however has not hitherto been eftablifhed by clear and certain * evidence) that in the places under

our

word demon in a bad fenfe, and applied it not only to the principle of evil, but to other malignant fpirits. Pythagoras held demons who fent difeafes to men and cattle; Diogen. Laert. Vit. Pythag. p. 514. ed. Amft. And though fome of the Heathens might regard evils as the inflictions of juftice; and it is poffible that κακ⊙· δαιμων may fignify fometimes (and particularly in Homer, as Dr. Sykes contends) an *adverfe* demon; neverthelefs, the hurtful demons were generally confidered as violent and cruel in their nature, and were accordingly to be appeafed by cruel rites. Befides, they were thought to inftigate men to wickednefs. Zaleucus in his preface to his laws, apud Stobæum, ferm. 42. fuppofes, that an evil demon might be prefent with a man, τρέπων πρὸς ἀδικίαν, *to influence him to injuftice.* Empedocles (according to Plutarch, de If. & Ofir. p. 361, and in lib. περὶ τȣ μὴ δανείζεϑαι.) fpoke of demons who were punifhed for their crimes. And Ocellus Lucanus, in a paffage to be cited immediately, makes exprefs mention of wicked demons. Thefe inftances are fufficient to fhew in general, what alone they are here produced to fhew, that the moft ancient writers, believed in bad as well as good demons. Accordingly δαιμονες freqently occurs in them, as a term of reproach, as well as praife.

* It feems to me difficult to determine with abfolute certainty, whether demon is ufed in a good or in a bad fenfe in the lxx. It might, *poffibly*, be chofen on account of its ambiguity: for the authors of that verfion were not difpofed to

give

our prefent confideration, the word is to be taken in a bad fenfe, and is applied to wicked fpirits. Neverthelefs, it cannot be inferred from hence, that thefe wicked fpirits were originally of a higher order than mankind. For as the fouls of many good men were thought to become good demons after death; fo it was a prevailing opinion, that the departed fouls of many

give offence to the Pagans, amongft whom they lived; nor were they free themfelves from every tincture of Paganifm. Were we certain, in what fenfe it was to be underftood in the lxx, we fhould be equally certain of the meaning of it in the writings of St. Paul; inafmuch as this apoftle and indeed all the writers of the New Teftament adopted the ftyle and diction of the lxx. That in both, demon is to be taken in a bad fenfe, feems to me fomewhat *probable*, for the following reafons. Some of the Heathens themfelves inferred from the actions afcribed to their gods, and the rites by which they were appeafed, that they were not gods, but evil demons. See Plutarch de If. & Ofir. p. 361, B. p. 362, E. & de defect. Orac. p. 417, C. D. compare Porphyr. de Abft. l. 2. fect. 36, 37, 42. The Jews who wrote in the Greek language, ufe demon in a bad fenfe, particularly Jofephus cited above and the tranflator of Tobit, ch. iii. 8. ch. vi. 17. Grotius thought " that " the Hellenifts ufed δαίμων in an ill fenfe, as the Hebrews " did *Baal*; though both originally indifferent in their figni- " fication;" Note on Math. iv. 23. Laftly, the New Teftament does certainly, on fome occafions, by demons mean evil fpirits, Matth. ix. 34. James ii. 19: and therefore the word may have the fame meaning, when it is applied to the Heathen gods. On the other hand Philo tells us, that the people fpoke as commonly of good as of evil demons, ὥσπερ δὲ ἀγαθὸς δαίμονας κỳ κακὸς λέγυσιν οἱ πολλοί. De Gigantibus, p. 286. ed. Paris. Philo however more frequently fpeaks the language and fentiments of the Platonic philofophers, than of the Jews.

many bad men became bad demons. Thales, Pythagoras, Plato, and the Stoics, as we learn from Plutarch *, reprefented " heroes as fouls feparated from
" their bodies, and as being good or bad according
" to their refpective characters." The Platonifts
commonly held the very fame language with refpect
to *demons* †. From fo early a writer as Ocellus Lucanus we learn, that " fuch as are begotten with in-
" jury and intemperance, are wicked, and will be
" evil demons ‡. And there is no notion which prevailed more generally over the Heathen world, from
the earlieft ages, than that concerning the power of
ghofts to haunt and torment mankind, particularly
the ghofts of thofe who died a violent death‖: which

may

---

* De Placit. Phil. l. 1. c. 8.

† Plerique tamen ex Platonis magifterio, dæmones putant
animas corporeo munere liberatas : laudabilium quoque viro-
rum æthereos dæmones, improborum vero nocentes, Chalchid.
in Platon. Tim. c. 135. p. 30. p. 330.   Compare Origen contra Celf. l. 7. 334.   Dr. Hammond on Matth. viii. 28. refers
to Hieronymus Magius (Mifcell. l. 4. c. 12.) in proof of its
having been the opinion of the ancients, that human fouls were
turned into devils.   But as I have never feen the works of
that author, (which, I am infoimed, are in the Bodleian libra-
ry at Oxford) I cannot tell what authority he cites.

‡ Εἰ ἢ καὶ γεννήσωσιν οἱ τοιοῦτοι μεθ' ὕβριως, καὶ ἀκρασίας, μοχθηροὶ
οἱ γενόμενοι, καὶ κακοδαίμονες ἔσονται.   Ocellus Lucan. p. 532. ed.
Galei.

‖ In Horace's Epodes, l. 5. ep. 5. v. 91. the boy whom
the forcerefs intended to murther, thus menaces her,

Quir,

may eafily incline us to believe, that the doctrine of the philofophers concerning evil men's becoming evil demons after death, was the creed of the vulgar. From the Heathens, the fame or fimilar opinions paff- ed to the Jews, whofe doctors taught*, " that the " fouls of the damned are for fome time changed in- " to devils, in order to be employed in tormenting " mankind." Jofephus (as we have already feen †) affirms, *that demons were the fouls of wicked men.* E- ven Afmodeus (who is often defcribed as the prince of evil fpirits, and reckoned the very fame as Sam- mael and Belzebub) is reprefented by the Jews, as having for his mother Nahemah, the fifter of Tubal- Cain ‡. Some of them taught, that demons were the offspring of Sammael (the prince of demons) and Eve, before Adam knew her: others faid, Adam was their father, and Lilith their mother ‖: and fome

Quin, ubi perire juffus exfpiravero,
   Nocturnus occurram furor ;
Petamque vultus umbra curvis unguibus;
   Quæ vis Deorum eft Manium.
Compare Dido's threatening to Æneas, Virg. En. iv. 384; and what Tertullian fays concerning the aori and the biæothanati, whom the magicians invoked, De Anima, c. 57. p. 305.

* See Calmet's Dictionary, under the article *Demon*; and Theophylact as cited by Grotius on Mat. viii. 28.

† Page 201.

‡ Elias Levita in Lexico fuo.

‖ See Calmet's Dictionary, under the article, *Demon*, Van- dale de Origin. ac progreffu idolat. p. 111, 112, 115, 116·
                                                            Buxtorf's

some might affign them a ftill different origin. It was a common opinion, that demons were the degenerate fons of God defcribed by Mofes*, and their iffue by the daughters of men, the latter efpecially. To thefe they added the fouls of other wicked men. Thefe were the demons with which they were beft acquainted ; of whom therefore they moft frequently fpeak. Had Dr. Sykes and his opponents attended to thefe fentiments of antiquity ; the former would not have found his account in denying, nor the latter in afferting, that demons, in the paffages in queftion, (from the Septuagint and the writings of St. Paul,) were wicked fpirits : for when the Jews ufed the word in a bad fenfe, they underftood by it the fpirits of fuch wicked men as were thought to be changed into demons. So that whether the tranflators of the Old, and the writers of the New Teftament, took the word in a good or a bad fenfe ; the arguments urged above, to fhew that human fpirits were intended, hold good.

The *Chriftian Fathers*, inftead of contradicting the fentiments here advanced, (as is generally fuppofed) feem to me in fome meafure to confirm them. There
is

Buxtorf's Lexic. Chald. almud. Bafnage's hiftory of the Jews, Book IV. ch. 11.

* Gen. vi. 2. Some of the Jews miftook thefe fons of God for angels ; as was obferved above, p. 42, n. *. Many thought that the angels were firft corrupted by the love of women ; as appears from the Apocryphal book of Enoch. See Calmet and Bafnage.

is no one point, that they more unanimoufly or ftrenuoufly maintain, than that all the Heathen deities had
been men and women *.

Here it will be objected, that the Fathers affert,
" that the Heathen gods were demons †; and that
" by demons they meant fallen angels." In order
to our forming juft conceptions of this fubject, it will
be neceffary to attend to the proper point, which the
Fathers undertook to maintain againft the Heathens:
which was this, " that thofe beings whom the Hea-
" thens regarded as gods, were demons ‡." It was
an

---

* Tertullian in his Apology, c. 10, 11. affirms, that Saturn and Jupiter, and the whole fwarm of Heathen deities were
men, and that they were reprenfented as fuch by the Pagans
themfelves, whofe confciences would condemn them, if they
did not allow all thofe whom they worihipped as gods, once to
have been men, omnes iftos deos veftros homines fuiffe. See
alfo c. 28, 29. According to Lactantius, 1. 3. c. 15. their
having no knowledge of any kings before Uranus and Saturn,
is the reafon why thefe were regarded as the moft ancient divinities. St. Auftin. (de civit. Dei, 1. 6.) fays, Euhemerus,
omnes tales deos, non fabulofa garrulitate, fed hiftorica diligen-
tia, homines fuiffe, mortalefque confcripfit. Vide Minuc. Fel.
c. 22. Lactant. l. 1. c. 15. p. 85, 86. l. 2. c. 2. p. 146. Eufeb.
de Vit. Conftant. l. 2. c. 16. l. 3. c. 26. Dem. Evang. l. 8. p.
364. Arnob. paffim. According to Minucius Felix (p. 121.
122. ed. Davis.) Cyprian (de idol. vanit. p. 12.) and Auftin
(de civ. Dei, l. 8. c. 5, 27.) Leo, the Egyptian chief prieft,
difcovered to Alexander the Great, that moft of the Heathen
gods had been men.

† Δαιμόνια ἐιςι οἱ θεοὶ τῶν ἐθνων. Juft. Mart. c. Trypho. p. 310.

‡ Thus Tertullian addreffes the Heathens, Ipfi putatis eos
effe deos, quos nos demones fcimus. Ad Scap. init. c. 2. Juftin
Martyr

an article of the common creed amongſt the Pagans,
that the ſouls of deified men were taken up into heaven, advanced to a ſtate of divine dominion there,
and ranked with the immortal gods *. Herein, their
deiſication did properly conſiſt. Theſe gods were
commonly regarded as good † beings, whoſe merit ‡

to

Martyr alſo, in his Apology, reproaches the Pagans with miſ-
taking evil demons for gods. See Tertullian's Apol. c. 22.
and de Anima, c. 57.

* Good demons inhabited the higher regions of the air.
When they commenced gods, they were exalted to heaven.
Diodorus Siculus (l. 1. p. 12. ed. Rhodomani) ranks the gods
taken from earth with thoſe in heaven, ἄλλας ἐκ τέτων [τῶν ἐν ἐρανῷ θιῶν] ἐπιγείας, κ. τ. λ. Arces attigit igneas, Horace, Carm.
l. 3. od. 3. v. 10. ſays of Hercules. The Egyptian prieſts (according to Plutarch de Iſ. & Oſir. p. 359.) taught, that the
ſouls of their earthly gods, ἐν ἐρανῷ λάμπειν ἄερα. They became
immortal, according to the golden verſes aſcribed to Pythagoras,

Ἐσσεαι ἀθάνατⓆ· θιὸς ἄμβροτος, ἐκ ἔτι θνητός.

The change from a demon into a god, is from *a mutable, paſſi-*
ble, mortal nature, into a nature *immutable, impaſſible, and im-*
mortal, Plutarch de defeเ. Orac. p. 416. See alſo the paſſage from Plutarch cited above, p. 182. and Cicer. de Nat.
Deor. l. 2. c. 24.

† Menander ſays, " We muſt not think any demon to be
evil, hurtful to a good life, but every god to be good." And
Euripides makes Iphigenia (in Taur. v. 391.) ſay, Οὐδένα γὰς
οἶμαι δαιμόνων ἐῖναι κακόν. Vid. Herc. fur. 1341.

‡ Quos in cælum merita vocaverint, colunto; was part of
the Roman law. And from Cicero de Nat. Deor. we learn,
that the cuſtom was, Ut beneficiis excellentes viros in cælum
fama & voluntate tollerent.

to mankind gave them a title to the honours of divinity. Now it is evident, that the Heathens might
affert, and Chriftians deny, their deification; and at
the fame time both of them allow, that they had once
been men. When Chriftians affirmed, that the Heathen gods were demons, I acknowledge, that they
ufed the word in a bad fenfe *, as they generally do
on other occafions, and thought the Scriptures did †.
But it will not neceffarily follow, from their ufing
the word in a bad fenfe, that they applied it to fallen
angels: for they might refer it to fuch human fpirits
as, in thofe ages, were thought to become evil and
mifchievous demons.

It muft, however, be allowed, that they did believe, as the Heathens alfo did, in demons of a celeftial origin ‡, who had never been united to human
bodies; and that feveral of them maintained, that
thefe demons were the gods of the Heathens. And
inafmuch as the authority of thefe writers has been
K often

* Origen, c. Celf. l. 8. p. 377, See alfo p. 234.

† Id. l. 5. p. 234. Eufeb. Præp. Ev. l. 4. c. 5. St. Aug. de
civ. Dei, l. 9. c. 19.

‡ Lactantius, II. 15, fays, " Trifmegiftus calls demons, evil
" angels: fo well was he acquainted with this, that they had
" been celeftial beings, but were depraved, and fo were be-
" come terreftrial." And in ch. 14, he affirms, " that there
" are two forts of demons, the one celeftial, the other terreft-
" rial: that the latter are the authors of the ill things that
" are done, whofe prince is the devil, whom Trifmegiftus calls
" the demonarch" (prince of demons.)

often oppofed to (what we judge to be) the proper
meaning of demons in the New Teftament; it will
be worth our while to inquire, what regard is due to
it in the cafe before us.   The Heathens did not worfhip any fuch beings as we call fallen angels : it was
falfe therefore to affirm, that they did.   The Fathers
themfelves taught, that the Heathen gods had all been
men : they contradicted themfelves therefore when
they afferted, that they were a different order of beings.   Nor is this the only inconfiftency with which
they are chargeable, in relation to the prefent fubject.
They very frequently boafted, that Chriftians could
compel the Heathen gods to confefs themfelves to be
demons ; and that none of them dared to lie to a
Chriftian *.   Neverthelefs thefe gods, inafmuch as
they were human fpirits, did lie to Chriftians, when
they declared that they were celeftial demons.   The
Fathers themfelves conftantly maintain†, that Saturn,
Jupiter, Serapis, Æfculapius, and all the Heathen gods
had been mortal men.   Now if the Heathen gods had
all been men, with what truth could they deny this,
and call themfelves fallen angels?   Tertullian tells

us,

---

* Edatur hic aliquis fub tribunalibus veftris, quem dæmone
agi conftet.   Juffus a quolibet Chriftiano loqui fpiritus ille,
tam fe dæmonem confitebitur de vero, quam alibi deum de fal-
fo.   Dæmones—Chriftiano mentiri non audentes. Tertullian.
Apol. c. 23. p. 22. Vide etiam Minuc. Fel. c. 27. Cyprian. ad
Donat. p. 3. De Idol. Vanit. p. 10. Ad Demetrian. p. 133.
Lactant. II. 15.

† Tertullian. Apol. c. 23. Minucius Felix, c. 27. compared with the paffages cited above, p. 143, note *.

us, that the Heathen gods and demons were only different names of the fame beings* ; and yet on other occafions, he reprefents the demons as *perfonating* † the Heathen gods : which manifeftly fuppofes that they were different beings. Lactantius ‡ affirms, that the very names by which the Heathen gods were worfhipped. were the names of demons ; though the whole world knows, that they were the real names of men and women. Laftly, fuch of the primitive Chriftians as affert, that the gods of the Heathens were fallen angels, not only contradict certain and evident matter of fact, and their own avowed opinion of the Heathen gods ; but they alfo contradict thofe facred writings, which reprefent them as nothing more than mortal men.

K 2   From

---

* Sed hactenus verba, jam hinc demonftratio rei ipfius, qua oftendemus unam effe utriufque nominis qualitatem. Apol. c. 23.

† He fpeaks of a demon, fub perfonis defunctorum delitefcentis. De Anima, c. 57.

‡ " They not only confefs themfelves to be demons, but " alfo declare their own names by which they are worfhipped " in the temples. Lactant. II. 15. Juftin Martyr fays, that " impure fpirits under various apparitions went in unto the " daughters of men, and defiled boys ; and that each of them " was invoked by fuch a name as he had given to himfelf." Apol. I. p. 10. ed. Tirlb. He imagined Jupiter, Apollo, &c. were the proper names of the demons : but Tertullian feems to have thought, the demons only procured themfelves to be worfhipped under thofe names, which belonged to deceafed men and women.

From the Scriptures, it is plain, the Fathers did not borrow their fentiments concerning the Heathen gods. The facred writers do, perhaps, brand as evil demons, thofe whom the Heathens regarded as *worthies*, and worfhipped as gods: but they never reprefent fallen angels as the gods of Paganifm, nor as perfonating thofe gods, nor as paffing under the fame names. Why then has the language of the Fathers on this fubject, been adopted by all fucceeding ages, with the reverence due only to that of immediate infpiration? Though I do not remember to have feen it taken notice of by others; yet it feems highly probable, that this language was borrowed from the Pagan philofophers. Several of the latter afferted, as the former did, that thofe beings whom the Heathen world worfhipped as gods, were evil demons. Both of them, in fupport of this affertion, urged the fame arguments; fuch as the actions afcribed to the Heathen gods, the rites appointed to placate them, and their oppofition to the caufe of true piety. Both taught that evil demons were fpirits of a celeftial origin; and that they were infpirers and authors of prophecies and miracles *. Nor can we wonder, that the

---

* Plutarch (in his treatife de If. & Ofir. p. 360. ed. Paris. 1624.) mentions it as the opinion of the moft ancient theologifts, and declares his own approbation of it, that what is related of Ofiris and Ifis, and other hero deities, is not to be confidered as an account either of gods, or of men; but of certain *great demons*, who tranfcend mankind in power, but, like them, have a mixture of vice in their character. And in his book de Oraculorum defectu, (p. 417.) he argues from the obfce-nity

the Fathers fhould be too ready to adopt the fentiments and language of the philofophers. They had
been educated in the fchools of Pagan philofophy :
and who can make fufficient allowance for the prejudices of education ? Certain it is in fact, that upon

K 3   their

nity, cruelty and folly of the worfhip paid to the gods, that it
was inftituted to avert the wrath of *wicked demons.* Compare
Plutarch de If. & Ofir. p. 361. Porphyry (de Abftin. fect.
36, 37. p. 80, 81.) fays, that a man who is ftudious of piety,
does not offer animal facrifices to the gods, δαίμοσι δὲ, *but to demons.* He defcribes wicked demons, very much in the manner
the Fathers do, as endeavouring to draw the regards of mankind to themfelves, as being ambitious of paffing for gods, and
as calumniating *the beft deity,* τὸν ἄριϛον Θεόν. Sect. 39, 40, 42.
p. 83, 84, 85, 86. He affirms, as the Fathers do, that evil
demons are nourifhed by libations and the fteams of the facrifices, fect. 42. p. 86, and that they perfonate the gods, fect.
40. p. 84. Philo, who was more properly a Platonift than a
Jew, had faid long before, that " evil fpirits ufurp the names
of angels." De Gigantibus, p. 286. C. ed. Paris. Porphyry
(fect. 41. p. 85.) afcribes the whole efficacy of magic to the
power of evil demons ; as the Fathers likewife did. There is
no ground to affert, that Porphyry borrowed his notions from
the Chriftians, to whom he bore an implacable hatred. He
fpeaks agreeably to the principles of the Pythagorean and Platonic philofophy ; nor does he advance any new doctrine. Jamblichus delivers the like fentiments concerning evil demons
(de Myfteriis, Segm. 3. c. 32. et paffim.) with Porphyry ; profeffing at the fame time to have borrowed them from the Chaldeans ; to whom (I apprehend) they of right belong. J. Ger.
Voffius, in his book de fectis philofophorum, fays, Mea autem
hæc fententia ; non poffe aliunde melius, quam ex hoc opere,
quid et Platonici de divinis rebus fenferint, cognofci. Ægyp-
tiorum et Chaldæorum opinionem exprimit. Voffius is here
fpeaking of Jamblichus de Myfteriis.

—

their embracing Chriftianity, though they adopted
fome new opinions, they dropt very few of their old
ones; and in too many inftances, inftead of rectify-
ing their preconceived opinions by the Scriptures,
tortured the Scriptures (as all men are apt to do) to
fupport their preconceived opinions. In the cafe
under our prefent confideration; they were not perhaps governed entirely by prejudices of their own;
they are fufpected at leaft of acting in fome meafure
from a principle of conformity to the prejudices of
others; (as will be fhewn in the fequel.) However
this may be; they ought not to have countenanced
an opinion, that was repugnant to revelation, as well
as to the common fenfe of mankind, and fupported
merely by the authority of the moft fuperftitious of
all the Pagan philofophers.

Notwithftanding the attachment of the Fathers to
the Pagan fyftem of demonology; fome of them
maintain, and Juftin Martyr in particular, that demons were " the fouls of dead men *." When this
learned writer is proving, that the foul does not die
with the body, he argues from the cafe " of thofe
" who are feized and tormented by the fouls of the
" deceafed, whom all call demoniacs and madmen †."
Athenagoras, who flourifhed in the fecond century,
as Juftin alfo did, reckons " the fouls of the giants
                                                amongft

---

* Ψυχαὶ ἀποθανόντων.

† Οἱ ψυχαῖς ἀποθανόντων λαμβανόμενοι, κỳ ῥιπτόμενοι ἄνθρωποι, ὖς
δαιμονολήπτὒς και μαινομένὒς καλὖσι πάντες.   Apol. 1. al. 2. p. 65.
Paris. 1620. p. 54. ed. Bened. p. 27. ed. Thirlb.

amongft the demons *." Tatian, indeed, who believed that the human foul dies, could not allow,
that any human fouls became demons †: but his reafoning againft this notion, is a proof that it was entertained by others. Tertullian likewife conceived
the ftate of the foul after the death of the body, to
be fuch as ill confifted with the idea of demons, who
wandered about in the region of the air near the
earth. Accordingly we find, that he fpeaks principally of fuch demons as were never united to human
bodies. Neverthelefs, even from Tertullian it appears, that there was a current belief in his time of
demons that had once been men; and that he himfelf
did not wholly reject them. He tells us in his Apology,
that " from a corrupted ftock of angels, there fprung
" a ftill more degenerate race of demons ‡." It is
univerfally allowed, that Tertullian here refers to *the
fons of God* in the hiftory of Mofes ‖, who mixed
with the daughters of men, and who were believed
to be angels by Tertullian, and by almoft all the Fa-

K 4

thers

---

* —— κ̀ αἱ τῶν γιγάντων ψυχαὶ, οἱ περὶ τὸν κόσμον εἰσὶ πλανώ-
μενοι δαίμονες. Athenag. Apol. p. 28. B.

† Tatian (Orat. contr. Græcos, p. 154.) fays, " Demons
are not the fouls of men:" and (p. 146.) he affirms, " that they
were ejected from the heavenly converfation."

‡ Sed quomodo de angelis quibufdam, fua fponte corruptis,
corruptior gens dæmonum evaferit, &c. Tertullian. Apol.
c. 22. p. 21.

‖ Gen. vi. 2.

thers of the four firſt centuries *, upon the authority
of Philo, Joſephus, and the ancient editions of the
ſeptuagint, which had ſubſtituted *the angels of God*,
inſtead of *the ſons of God.* So that according to Tertullian, and I believe I may ſay, according to the general ſenſe of thoſe ages, the worſt kind of demons
are in part, at leaſt, of human original. In another
place, however, Tertullian expreſſes himſelf in the
following manner †: " We diſcover (if I be not miſ-
" taken) the fallacy of an evil ſpirit, lurking under
" the maſks of dead men, by facts; when, during
" his being exorciſed, he ſometimes affirms himſelf
" to have been a man, one of our progenitors, ſome-
" times a gladiator, or one who fought with wild
" beaſts ‡, as elſewhere he would ſay he was a god ;
" being concerned for nothing more than this, that
" he

---

* See Whitby's Strictur. Patrum, in Gen. c. vi. 4. p. 5.
Some think the Fathers were drawn into this error, by the authority of the apocryphal book of Enoch.

† Hanc quoque fallaciam ſpiritus nequam ſub perſonis defunctorum delitreſcentis, niſi fallor, etiam rebus probamus, quum
in exorciſmis interdum aliquem ſe ex parentibus hominem ſuis
affirmat, interdum gladiatorem, vel beſtiarium, ſicut et alibi
deum ; nihil magis curans, quam hoc ipſum excludere quod præ-
dicamus, ne facile credamus animas univerſas ad inferos redigi,
ut et judicii et reſurrectionis fidem turbet. Et tamen ille dæ-
mon poſtquam circumſtantes circumvenire tentavit, inſtantia di-
vinæ gratiæ victus, id quod in vero eſt, invitus confitebitur.
Tertullian de Anima, c. 57. p. 305, 306. ed. Paris.

‡ This confirms what is obſerved above, p. 141. and below,
p. 155. concerning ſuch as ſuffered a violent death.

" he may contradict what we preach, and prevent
" us from believing that all fouls go to the fhades
" below * ; and this in order to difturb our faith of
" a judgment and a refurrection. Yet will this de-
" mon, after he has tried to delude the company,
" be fo far over-ruled by the prefence of divine grace,
" as unwillingly to confefs himfelf to be what he
" really is." Tertullian here contradicts what he
himfelf elfewhere advances concerning thofe demons,
who were the iffue of the daughters of men ; as well
as what he afferts with refpect to the power of Chriftians, to compel demons to declare what they truly
were, and to prevent them from telling lyes in their
prefence. For here a demon, though in the end he
owns his real character, is guilty of lying, even under the exorcifm of Chriftians, by afferting he had
been a man. It is more material to obferve farther,
1ft, That it muft have been at that time a very common opinion, that demons were the fouls of dead
men: for otherwife this evil fpirit would not have
been reprefented as affirming, that he had been *a man.*
2dly, The reafon affigned by Tertullian for rejecting
this opinion, was his believing that all fouls remained
in the fhades below till the day of judgment : which
is mentioned amongft the errors and paradoxes † of
this learned writer ; and therefore could have no
weight

* Or, *to hades*, the region underneath the earth : which according to many of the Heathens, as well as Tertullian, was
the region of the dead.

† See Tertullian, p. 306. note b, ed. Paris.

weight with thofe Chriftians, who taught, that human fouls either afcended the etherial regions, or
wandered about the earth, according to their refpective characters.

The fentiments concerning the ftate of feparate
fouls, which were entertained by Chriftians in general, and by Origen in particular, the moft learned
of all the Fathers, were very different from thofe of
Tertullian.   Near the beginning of his feventh book
againft Celfus, Origen undertakes to fhew, that the
ancient oracles were not infpired *by any gods*, as the
Heathens commonly thought, but on the contrary
by *evil demons* *.   In proof of this point, he obferves †, (amongft other things,) " that all men,
" whether Jews or Chriftians, Greeks or Barba-
" rians, believe that the *human* foul furvives the dif-
" folution of the body : that it is agreeable to rea-
" fon to think, that the *pure* foul afcends the pure re-
" gions of ether, leaving the grofs body, and its pol-
" lutions behind ; but that the *wicked* foul is borne
" downwards by its fins, flying about the earth, or
" living near fepulchres."   He then afks the following queftion ‡ : " What fort of fpirits fhould we
" judge thofe to be, which are tied down whole ages,
" as one may fay, to particular buildings or places,
" either by certain charms, or by their own wicked-
" nefs ?" that is, Are they fuch purified human fpirits as reafon tells us afcend the fublimer regions,
and

and the Heathens efteem as gods; or are they thofe polluted human fpirits who are detained near this lower earth, and are evil demons? This queftion does not appear to concern any but human fpirits; no mention having been made of any other. Origen refolves this queftion in the following manner:— " Reafon tells us, that they ought to be regarded as " wicked fpirits, who ufe prophecy (a thing of an " indifferent nature in itfelf) to deceive mankind, " and to draw them from the pure worfhip of God *." There has been occafion to obferve, that the ancients were of opinion, not only that *wicked* human fpirits became demons, but alfo that " thofe who fuffered a violent death became fuch." Now from St. Chryfoftom we learn, that even this was the belief of the meaner people in his time †. And had it not, at that time, been generally thought, that demons were the fouls of the deceafed; would demoniacs have faid, as from the fame author we learn they did, that " they were poffeffed by the foul of fuch or fuch a monk ‡ ?"

The forecited paffages from the Fathers appear to me to contain a fufficient proof, that whatever they teach

---

* Ibid.

† Πολλοὶ τῶν ἀφελεστέρων νομίζυσι τὰς ψυχὰς τῶν βιαίω θανάτω τελευτῶντων δαίμονας γίνεσθαι. .De Laz. Serm. 2. tom. 1. p. 727. E.

‡ Τί ἔν, ὅτι οἱ δαίμονες λέγυσι, τῦ μοναχῦ τῦ δεῖνος ἡ ψυχή εἰμί, φησι, Chryfoft. de Lazaro, tom. 1. p. 728. Αὐτοί, φησιν, οἱ δαιμονῶντες βοασιν, ὅτι ψυχὴ τῦ δεῖνος ἐγώ. In Matt. hom. 28. al. 29. tom. 7. p. 336. C.

teach concerning the miraculous powers and operations of celeſtial demons, was borrowed froṁ the Pagans: that many of them did aſſert, that ſome human ſouls after the diſſolution of their bodies became
demons: and that for ſeveral ages after the coming
of Chriſt, demons did very commonly denote ſuch
human ſouls; agreeably to the meaning affixed to
them by the ancient Heathens and Jews, and by the
apoſtles of Chriſt. The writings of the Fathers,
therefore, inſtead of deſtroying, do in ſome meaſure
confirm the explication we have given of the demons
mentioned in Scripture, as the objeᴄts of Pagan devotion. At the ſame time, they bear expreſs teſtimony to this great truth, (the eſtabliſhment of which has
been our main view, in what has been hitherto advanced in this ſeᴄtion,) that all the Heathen gods,
except the deified parts and powers of nature, belonged to the human race. The forming a true idea
of the Heathen gods, being a matter of no ſmall importance to a juſt defence of the Scripture; we hope
to be excuſed, for having taken up ſo much time in
diſcuſſing it.

If the foregoing account of the Pagan gods be
juſt; there will be no difficulty, in vindicating the
cenſures paſſed upon them in the ſacred writings.
With regard to the parts and powers of nature, which
the Heathen world deified; they are repreſented in
Scripture as the creatures of God's power, and the
paſſive inſtruments of his decrees *. Even " the ſun,
                                                " and

* See above, p. 97.

" and the moon, and the ftars, and all the hoft of
" heaven," however revered by the Pagans as the
chief deities; " the Ifraelites are forbidden to wor-
" fhip and ferve; becaufe Jehovah, their God, pla-
" ced them in the firmament of heaven;" not for the
ufe of any one particular nation, but " for the com-
" mon benefit of the whole human race *." It
is extraordinary that Mofes, at a time when the
world was univerfally regarded as animated and divine, and the elements and the heavenly bodies were
thought to poffefs an internal power to exert themfelves in all their admirable effects; it is very extraordinary, that Mofes, at this time, fhould difcover,
publifh, and (by fuitable miracles) confirm the oppofite doctrine. His doctrine is perfectly agreeable to
the modern philofophy, which reprefents the whole
natural world as a merely material, inert, inactive
thing, without any wifdom or power of its own, and
refifting any change of ftate, whether of reft or motion; and which muft therefore be continually upheld and directed by the wifdom and power of God,
to whom the whole train of natural caufes and effects is to be afcribed. The doctrine alone of Mofes,
fo remote from the fentiments and philofophy of his
age, and fo agreeable to truth, creates a ftrong prefumption of his having received it by immediate revelation.

As to the other gods of Paganifm, whether they
were fuch human fouls as became demons, or (as
fome

* Deut. iv. 19. compared with Gen. i. 17.

fome apprehend) created fpirits of a fuperior order;
we have already * feen, that the Scriprure gives us
fuch a view of them, as is inconfiftent either with
their infpiring prophecies or working miracles. And
it will be fhewn in the fequel, that all fupernatural
effects are referred to God alone by the facred writers. Is it poffible for them to contradict themfelves,
as they muft do, if they afcribe fuch effects to the
Heathen gods? But fo far are they from doing this,
that they conftantly reprefent thofe gods as utterly
impotent and infignificant; either as having no real
exiftence, or no more power than if they did not
exift. They call them *vanities* †, things of no kind
of value or efficacy. Nor is this cenfure confined to
a part only of the Heathen gods; it is extended to
all, without a fingle exception. " They are ALL
vanity ‡." " ALL the gods of the nations are idols,
or nothings ‖:" not powerful evil fpirits, but mere
nullities. In this manner, the ancient prophets of
God fpoke of the Pagan deities; and the apoftles of
Chrift ufed the fame language: " We know that an
                                                " idol

---

* Ch. 3. fect. 1.

† Deut. xxxii. 21. 1 King. xvi. 13, 26. Jerem. viii. 19.
ch. xiv. 22. ch. xviii. 15. In 1 Sam. xii. 21. they are called
" vain things which cannot profit." They are called " lying
vanities," Pf. xxxi. 6.

‡ xii. 29. Jerem. x. 8.

‖ ch. Elilim, *nothings*, or things of no value. Pf. xcvi. 5.
(xviii. 4.) See alfo Levit. xix. 4. 1 Chron. xvi.
Ezek. xxx. 13. and compare 1 Kings xviii. 27. If. xlv. 5.

" idol is nothing in the world *." This is not to be underftood of the mere images of the gods : for the Heathens did not regard thofe images, in themfelves confidered, as real gods. They believed them to be the reprefentatives and the receptacles † of their gods, and in this view they fpoke of them as gods, and the objects of divine worfhip; and it is in reference to the divine powers fuppofed to refide in, them, that the Scriptures affirm, that they are nothing. On all occafions, the facred writers deride thefe pretended refidences of the Heathen deities, as mere earthly materials, polifhed by the hand of the artificer, and the deities themfelves as equally void of underftanding, or rather as being nothing diftinct from thofe fenfelefs materials, and exifting only in the imagination of their deluded worfhippers. " The ftock is a doc-" trine of vanities ‡." " Their idols are filver and " gold, or wood and ftone, the work of mens hands, " which neither feé, nor hear, nor eat, nor fmell ‖." Agreeably hereto the Scripture reprefents the votaries of thefe divinities as perfons utterly loft to reafon, and

* 1 Cor. viii. 4. ch. x. 19.

† Various ceremonies were ufed, to induce the gods to take up their refidence in the temples and ftatues erected to receive them. See Arnob. l. 6. p. 203, 207. Sozom. H. E. l. 7. p. 724. Origen, c. Celf. l. 7. p. 378.

‡ Jerem. x. 8.

‖ Deut. iv. 28. Pf. xcvii. 7. Pf. cxv. 4. Pf. cxxxv. 15. If. xl. 18. ch. xlii. 17. ch. xliv. 9. Jerem. ii. 27. ch. x. 3. Dan. v. 4, 23. Habak. ii. 18. Acts xviii. 29. 1 Cor. viii. 4. ch. x. 19. ch. xii. 2. 1 Theff. i. 9.

and without a fhadow of excufe. " They are altogether brutifh and foolifh," and difcover no more
underftanding than the idols they make *.

Oracles, prophecies, prodigies were afcribed by the
Heathens to their demons: and on their favour the'
good or evil ftate of mens lives was thought to depend. This perfuafion was the ground of their worfhip. And the proper point in difpute between idolaters and the prophets of the true God, was, whether that perfuafion was fupported by *facts*. We find
the meffengers of God challenging idolaters, to juftify their worfhip of idols; and the idol gods themfelves, to give proof of their divinity, by a difplay of
knowledge, or by fome exertion of power, fuch as
was either hurtful or beneficial to mankind; and ev-
en admitting, that by fuch a difplay of their power
or knowledge, the Heathen deities would have eftablifhed their claim to divinity, and their title to the
homage of mankind. " Produce your caufe, faith
" the Lord, bring forth your ftrong reafons.—Let
" them fhew the former things what they be, that
" we may confider them, and know the latter end
" of them:" produce your ancient oracles, that we
may judge whether they were fulfilled by correfpon-
dent events; *or*, now " declare to us things for to
" come. Shew us things for to come hereafter, that
" we may know that ye are gods; yea, do good, or
" do evil, that we may be difmayed," that it may
                                           appear

---

* Jerem. x. 8. Pf. cxv. 8. Pf. cxxxv. 18. Habak. ii.
18, 19.

appear ye have, what your votaries aſſert, a title to the reverence and worſhip of mankind. " Behold, ye are nothing, and your work of nought * ;" and therefore there can be no ſhadow of reaſon for paying you homage. How very different is this language of the ancient prophets, from that of our learned moderns, who tell us, that idolatry cannot poſſibly be juſtified by any miracles, however numerous or ſplendid ; and that whatever power over mankind the Heathen gods might poſſeſs, they could have no right to worſhip? The prophets would have allowed their title to worſhip, had they admitted their power †. Their utter impotence is the only reaſon of the Scripture's remonſtrating againſt paying them homage. I add, that theſe remonſtrances of Scripture, which are frequently repeated ‡, are confirmed by facts, by many ſtriking teſtimonies of the utter inability of the Heathen deities, to interpoſe either for the conviction of gainſayers, or for the benefit of their worſhippers, or in vindication of their own honour. They could not interpret Nebuchadnezzar's dream ||, nor the hand-writing upon the wall of Bel-

L ſhazzar's

---

* Iſ. xli. 21, 24.

† The reaſoning urged above, p. 76, 77, 78, may ſerve to juſtify the deciſion of this caſe by the prophets.

‡ Jerem. x. 3, 5, 15. Iſ. xliii. 8. ch. xliv. 7. ch. xlv. 16, 20. ch. xlvi. 5. ch. xlviii. 3. 1 Cor. viii. 4. ch. x. 19. ch. xii. 2. 1 Theſſ. i. 9.

|| Dan. iv. 7.

shazzar's palace*; nor were they able to anfwer by fire, in the public trial between their own prophets, and the prophet of Jehovah†; though on thefe feveral occafions, but efpecially the laft, all their credit was at ftake. Nor did they oppofe (how much foever it might be their intereft to do it) any miracles of their own, to thofe either of Mofes or the Meffiah; as we hope to fhew in the fequel.

In oppofition to all this evidence, it has been afferted, that the fyftem of Pagan idolatry was fupported by prophecies and miracles, delivered and performed, not by the fictitious deities of the Heathens, but by *devils*, or wicked demons of a higher order than mankind, who perfonated the gods, lurked within their confecrated images and ftatues, infpired the vates, animated the fibres of the entrails of victims, governed

---

* Dan. v. 7.

† 1 Kings xviii. If fpirits (as learned men have affirmed) can do *invifibly*, all that men can do *vifibly;* why, in the conteft related in this chapter, did not evil fpirits bring fire in a fecret manner from fome neighbouring place to the altar, to confume what was laid upon it? There feems to be no *peculiar* difficulty in fuch a miracle.

Should any object to what is here urged concerning the impotence of the Heathen gods, that in 2 Chron. xxviii. 23, the facred hiftorian is reprefented as faying, that " the gods of Damafcus fmote Ahaz:" I anfwer in the words of Mr. Halett (V. 2. p. 79.) " All this difficulty is avoided, if we follow the " old Hebrew copies, from which the Greek tranflation was " made, which reads thus, And king Ahaz faid, I will feek to " the gods of Damafcus who fmote me."

governed the flight of birds, guided the lots, framed the oracles, and exerted themfelves to the utmoft in promoting idolatry, in order to involve men in the guilt of it, to draw all adoration to themfelves, to fe-cure proper food and nourifhment from the rich fteams and blood of the victims, which were offered to them, and hereby to ftrengthen themfelves for the enjoyment of their luftful pleafures with boys and women. It has been farther afferted, that thefe wicked fpirits were, properly fpeaking, the gods of the Heathens ; rather than thofe imaginary beings, whom they feem-ed to themfelves to worfhip. In fupport of thefe af-fertions, appeal is made to the writings of the Fathers, and the authority of Scripture.

For the honour of human nature, who would not wifh that fuch extravagant opinions as thefe had ne-ver been broached by any writers ? Neverthelefs, it muft be owned, they are clearly contained in the writings of the Fathers †. Thefe opinions however are there only afferted, not proved ; and perhaps were never really believed, by the very perfons who main-tained them, and upon whofe authority alone they have been received in fucceeding ages. For the Fa-thers, though they fometimes taught, or allowed, that

L 2 Pagan

---

† Juftin Mart. Apol. p. 113. ed. Thirlb. Tertullian de ani-ma, c. 57. Minucius Felix, c. 27. Cyprian de Idolor. Van. p. 206. Arnob. c. Gent. l. 1. 26. Lactant. de Orig. Error. l. 2. c. 16. De vera Sapient. l. 8. c. 16. ed. Spark, p. 399. Eu-feb. Præp. Ev. l. 5. c. 4. St. Auguft. de Civ. Dei, l. 8. c. 16. See alfo Middleton's Free Inquiry, p. 66, 70, 77. and Mede's works, p. 680, 681.

Pagan idolatry was supported by oracles and miracles;
do neverthelefs on other occafions confefs or clearly
intimate, that Paganifm had no other fupport, than
human craft and impofture *. They pretended, indeed, that any Chriſtian was able to compel the Heathen gods to confefs themfelves to be devils, as well
as to eject † them from the bodies of men ; but every one now knows, that there was no miracle ‡ in the
cafe. To me it feems to be a matter of no great importance, what fentiments the Fathers entertained on
the fubject under our confideration; and therefore
we will proceed to examine thofe of the facred writers. Several general reafons have been already ‖ fuggefted, to fhew how unlikely it is, that the Scriptures
fhould affert or allow, that idolatry was fupported by
the miraculous interpofition of any wicked fpirits;
whether they did or did not counterfeit the fouls of

men

* Origen, c. Celf. p. 333. Eufeb. Præp. l. 4. c. 1, 2, 3.
Clemens Alexandrinus, Strom. l. 3. See Fontenelle's Hift.
of Oracles, ch. 9. p. 76. and Clerici Hift. Ecclef. prolegom.
p. 54. With regard to the refidence of invifible beings in the
confecrated images of the Heathens; it is frequently treated
by the ancient apologifts with the fcorn it fo well deferved.
See Arnob. l. 6. p. 200. Lactant. l. 2. p. 147. Perhaps one
reafon why on fome occafions the Fathers allow, that Paganifm was fupported by miracles, was their finding the Pagans
more difpofed to refer them to evil agents, than to difbelieve
their reality.

† See Dr. Whitby's general preface to the epiſtles, p. xxvi.

‡ See Dr. Middleton's Free Inquiry, p. 80, &c.

‖ See above, p. 157.

men deccafed. To what has been already offered, I would add the few following obfervations on the cafe before us.

1ft, The Scripture has never given the leaft intimation, that the gods of the Heathens were of two different kinds, the one fuch as they *feemed to themfelves* to worfhip, the other the *real* objects of their devotion. Much lefs has the Scripture afferted or intimated, that, though the former were utterly impotent, the latter were powerful wicked_ fpirits, who were always promoting idolatry by prophecies, prodigies, and miracles. Now, is it credible, that the prophets of God, who were in the higheft degree anxious for the welfare of the Ifraelites, fhould never give them any notice of their hourly danger from fuch powerful demons? and that they fhould tell the people, they had nothing to fear or hope from the gods they were fo prone to worfhip; without dropping a fingle hint that thofe gods had a thoufand abettors, who were allowed to work miracles, in order to involve them in the guilt of idolatry? This will appear ftill more incredible, if we confider, 2dly, That had the claims of the Heathen deities been fupported by other invifible agents, affuming their names, and acting their parts: this would have been the very fame thing, *to the apprehenfions of mankind*, as if thofe deities had themfelves interpofed in fupport of their own divinity. For had miracles been performed in the name of the Heathen gods: the fpectators muft have referred them to thofe gods; rather than to any other beings, of whom they were entirely ignorant. And if, to the fpectators, the Heathen gods *neceffarily appeared*

L 3   to

to poffefs a miraculous power; would not this have produced, and very juftly too, the fame effect as if they had *really* poffeffed it? If the exercife therefore of this power, for the benefit or to the prejudice of mankind, by the idol gods, would have juftified the worfhip of them, (as the prophets of God allow it would;) the exercife of the fame power by others, under the circumftances here fuppofed, would have done fo too. 3dly, The prophets of God could not with truth or fincerity affirm, that apoftate angels were, properly fpeaking, the gods of the Heathens; becaufe they reprefent their gods as *dead men*. Nor do they fpeak of them in this manner, in order to accommodate themfelves to the common opinion of the Heathens concerning them, as fome have imagined *; for the Heathens regarded them as *deified fouls of their worthies*. They call them dead men; becaufe they were really and truly fuch; and not evil fpirits mafking themfelves under their names. 4thly, They could not without the groffeft violation of truth, reprefent the ftatues and images of the Heathen deities as mere fenfelefs materials, if they were inhabited by *any* fpiritual beings whatfoever. 5thly, Moft fallacious and dangerous would it have been in the prophets, to inculcate it perpetually upon the Ifraelites as a moft certain and evident truth, that all the Heathen gods were imaginary beings, who had no *exiftence*, or no degree of *power* over mankind; without informing them at the fame time, (what it concerned them

---

* See above, p. 132.

them much to know, if it was true,) that the real objects of the Heathen worfhip, were poffeffed even of
miraculous powers, which they were continually exerting to the deception of the human race. This
would have been egregious trifling on a moft folemn
occafion, and grofs prevarication: it would have
been not only leaving the people in ignorance of their
danger, but deceiving them into a falfe and fatal opinion of their fafety. Include in the number of the
Heathen gods whatever fpirits you pleafe, apoftate
angels of every rank and order, as well as human
fouls; that declaration of God muft hold true,
" They are all vanity, their works are nothing *."
If you chufe to fay, that the prophets of God conceived the Heathen deities to be devils, in the fenfe
in which the word is ufed at prefent; you make them
deny, that devils have any power at all: for in reference to all the Heathen deities, they thus admonifh
the Ifraelites, " Be not afraid of them, for they
" cannot do evil, neither alfo is it in them to do
" good †."

It is true, indeed, that both according to the ancient and modern verfions of the Bible, the Heathen
gods are reprefented as devils in that facred volume.
But thefe verfions do great injuftice to the original;
if by devils you mean a diftinct order of beings from
human fouls. Let us examine the feveral paffages,
where the Heathen gods are defcribed as devils, in
the Englifh tranflation.

L 4   Mofes,

---

* Ifaiah xli. 29.   † Jerem. x. 5.

Mofes, in his *prophetic* hymn concerning the apoftacy of the Ifraelites, takes notice of it as a proof and
aggravation of their idolatrous difpofition, " that
they facrificed - unto devils," *(fchedim,)* whom he
calls " new gods that came newly up, whom they
" knew not, and their fathers feared not *." The
Pfalmift in like manner thus reproaches them:
" Yea, they facrificed their fons and their daughters
" unto devils †," *(fchedim).* If all the Pagan gods
were devils, why are the *fchedim* diftinguifhed from
their other gods? Why are they called *new* to the
Ifraelites, who had of old worfhipped the Pagan deities ‡? Why is the worfhip of thefe *fchedim* mentioned as matter of *peculiar* reproach? And if thefe
fchedim were devils, who have a real and extenfive
power over mankind; why are they called *vanities*
and *idols* ‖? The word, *fchedim,* is derived from a
verb § which fignifies *to lay wafte, to deftroy,* and
ought to have been rendered, *the deftroyers.* It expreffes the fuppofed cruel nature and character of
thefe falfe gods, who were thought to delight in,
and who were accordingly worfhipped by, *the de-*
ftruction of the human fpecies, and who required, as
appears from the context, even " the blood of their
fons

---

* Deut. xxxii. 17.
† Pf. cvi. 37.
‡ Gen. xxxv. 2, 4.   Jofh. xxiv. 2.
‖ Deut. xxxii. 21.   Pf. cvi. 36.
§ שדד

fons and daughters *." Who the gods were, that were worfhipped by human facrifices, all hiftory informs us; and fo has the Pfalmift in the moft exprefs terms †, " They ate the facrifices of the dead." They were the great warriors, who in their mortal ftate delighted in the flaughter of the human race. The revolt of the Ifraelites from the worfhip of God their *Saviour*, to that of thefe *wafters* and *dcftroyers* of mankind, argued the higheft degree of folly and wickednefs. This worfhip was *new* to the Ifraelites, what they had never practifed either in Egypt, or before they went into that country; but what they afterwards learnt of the Canaanites. Accordingly the fchedim are exprefsly called by the Pfalmift, " the idols of Canaan ‡." What one circumftance is there that can lead us to fuppofe, that either Mofes or the Pfalmift, in the forecited paffages, are fpeaking of *devils*, in the common acceptation of that word?

The fame defect either of candour or judgment, our tranflators have fhewn in the explication of another word, which they render *devils*. " They fhall " no more offer their facrifices unto devils," *fcirim*, or, *fehirim* ‖. This prohibition of Mofes to the Ifraelites after they had left Egypt, implies that they had, during their ftay there, defiled themfelves with that

---

* Pfalm cvi. 38.

† V. 28. See the learned Mr. Merrick's annotations on the Pfalms, p. 218.

‡ Pfalm cvi. 38.

‖ Levit. xvii. 7.

that particular species of idolatry here condemned. And from other passages of Scripture, it sufficiently appears, that the Israelites were no strangers to the worship of the Egyptian deities *. It is allowed, that the word, *seirim*, signifies *hairy beings*, or *goats* †. And the learned Bochart ‡ has fully shewn, that the *sacred* animals of Egypt were *hairy;* and that the *goat* in particular was worshipped, (on the same account as *Priapus* was amongst the *Greeks;*) and that Pan was represented under the image of this animal. It is plain, therefore, that as the *schedim* were the idols of Canaan, so the *seirim* were the idols of Egypt. This will more clearly appear from another place in which this latter word occurs : " He (Jero- " boam) ordained him priests for the high places, " and for the devils, *(seirim,* the goats,) and for the " calves he had made ‖." Did Jeroboam make devils,

* Josh. xxiv. 14. Ezek. xx. 7. ch. xxiii. 2, 3. Acts viii. 39.

†·In Levit. iv. and ch. xvi. and other places, it signifies a goat. In many places it signifies *hair* or *hairy*. Lev. xiii. 10, 25, 26, 30, 32. Gen. xxv. 25. Psalm lxviii. 21. The word also occurs, If. xiii. 21. where the prophet is foretelling the utter destruction and desolation of Babylon : " The satyrs," the seirim, " the goats or hairy creatures shall dance there ;" i. e. it shall be inhabited by beasts, and not men. And in If. xxxiv. 14. this word is rendered *satyrs*, where the prophet is describing the desolation of Idumea, representing it as the haunt of goats and other wild beasts.

‡ Hieroz. l. 2. c. 53.

‖ 2 Chron. xi. 15.

vils, or the ftatues and images of devils ? The word, *feirim, (goats,)* no more fignifies devils, than the original word tranflated *calves*, or any other word throughout the Bible. Some very learned † men indeed plead, that devils were reprefented by goats, becaufe they appeared to mankind in the form of thefe animals. But, till they produce fome better authority, than the reports of witches, and the fables of the Heathens concerning fauns and fatyrs, in proof of the devil's appearing in the fhape of goats; this plea cannot be admitted. What the hiftorian affirms, is plainly this; that Jeroboam lately returned from Egypt, eftablifhed the worfhip of the deities of that country, which was eminently that of goats and calves; or at leaft fet up the images of thefe animals as fymbols of the Divinity. There could be no reference to devils, as this word is now underftood; becaufe the Ifraelites are never charged by their prophets, with fo deteftable a fpecies of idolatry, as the worfhip of devils. The inftitution of fuch worfhip would not have fuited with the policy of Jeroboam, who was defirous of attaching the Ifraelites to himfelf. Nor did the Egyptians, whofe example Jeroboam copied, ever reprefent devils under the figures of goats and calves.

With regard to the paffages in the New Teftament, in which the Heathen gods are ftyled *devils*, or (according to the original) *demons* ‡ ; it has already been

fhewn,

---

† See Patrick in particular.

‡ 1 Cor. x. 20, 21, cited above, p. 135.

shewn *, that thereby we are to underſtand ſuch human ſpirits as were ſuppoſed to be converted into demons. It is ſcarce neceſſary to obſerve, that when St. Paul in theſe paſſages calls the objects of Pagan worſhip, demons, and in other places, *gods* and *lords* †; it is merely for the ſake of deſcribing them by their uſual appellations, or to expreſs what the Heathens believed them to be; without having any intention of allowing them any real power or divinity: for he elſewhere upbraids them as vanities ‡, and mere nullities ‖. This likewiſe is the view which all the ſacred writers give us of the gods of Paganiſm: a view abſolutely inconſiſtent with their poſſeſſing a power of working miracles.

S E C T.

---

* Page 135, 136.

† " There be gods many, and lords many," i. e. ſuch as are ſo called, 1 Cor. viii. 5. The lords here ſpoken of, anſwer to *Baalim* in the Old Teſtament, and to *demons* in the New; the ſuppoſed diſpenſers of good and evil according to the Pagans. But Chriſtians acknowlege only one God, and one Lord.

‡ Acts xiv. 15.

‖ 1 Cor. viii. 4, 5, 6.

SECT. III.

*The character and pretenfions of the magicians, diviners and for-
cerers of antiquity, examined; with the Scripture account concerning them. And the various pleas alledged by Chriftians in
fupport of the credit, and efficacy of the ancient magic, refuted.*

IT will be my bufinefs in this fection to fhew, that
the *magicians, diviners* and *forcerers* of antiquity,
who pretended, by the affiftance of the Heathen deities, to foretel future events or to work miracles, are
branded in Scripture as mere impoftors, incapable of
fupporting their pretenfions by any works or predictions beyond human power or fkill. It is natural to
fuppofe this, from what has been advanced in the
foregoing fection; but it will admit of a much fuller
confirmation. In order to our clearly difcerning the
juftice, with which the Scriptures cenfure and ex-
plode all the Pagan pretences to prophecy and miracles; it will not be improper to inveftigate the falfe
principles upon which they were founded, the knowlege of which will be of fervice to us on feveral occafions, in the fequel of the argument.

The magi were originally the priefts of the gods *,
and

---

* Plato's Alcibiades, 1. Lucian ἐν Μακροβίοις. Porphyry, in
his book, de Abftinent. 1. 4. § 16, fays, Παρὰ γε μὲν τοῖς Πέρσαις,
οἱ περὶ τὸ θεῖον σοφοὶ, καὶ τύτε θεράποντες, Μάγοι μὲν προσαγορεύονται.
See alfo Plato apud Apul. Apol. p. 290, and Dio Chryfofto-
mus, Orat. 36. F. 499.

and the profeſſors of ſcience, particularly phyſic and aſtrology *. They undertook to interpret dreams, to foretel future events, and to accompliſh many wonderful things, by their ſuperior knowledge of the ſecret powers of nature, of the virtues of plánts and minerals, and of the motions and influences of the ſtars. Diodorus Siculus informs us, that " the prieſts " of Egypt foretold future events by aſtrology, and " the inſpection of ſacrifices †." And from the ſame author we learn ‡, " that the Egyptians obſerved " with great exactneſs, the motions, revolutions and " ſtations of the planets, and their reſpective power " and operation in the generation of ánimals, and " the production of good and evil; that they fore-" tel very frequently future events ‖; and that by long " obſervation they foreknow many things, which are " commonly thought to be beyond the reach of hu-" man knowlege." Cicero § gives us the ſame account

account

---

* Plin. Nat. Hiſt. l. 30. c. 1.

† Διὰ τῆς ἀϛρολογίας καὶ τῆς ἱεροσκοπίας, p. 66. D. ed. Rhodomani.

‡ Τάς τε τῶν πλανήτων ἀϛίρων κινήσεις κỳ περιόδȣς κỳ ϛηριϛμὸς, ἔτι δὲ τὰς ἱκάϛȣ δυνάμεις πρὸς τὰς τῶν ζώων γειίσεις, τίνων ἐσὶν ἀγαθῶν ἢ κακῶν ἀπεργαϛικαὶ, φιλοτιμότατα παρατετηρήκασι, κ. τ. λ. p. 73.

‖ Particularly, ſcarcity and plenty, epidemical diſeaſes, earthquakes, and comets, (which have been generally thought to portend ſome extraordinary events) as well as the accidents of private life.

§ Principio Aſſyrii, trajectiones motuſque ſtellarum obſervaverunt; quibus notatis, quid cuique ſignificaretur, memoriæ prodiderunt.

count of thefe men, both amongft the Egyptians,
and other ancient nations. To the former of whom,
as the original difcoverers, Herodotus afcribes, " the
" afcertaining the month and day which belonged to
" each particular deity; and the foretelling the fu-
" ture difpofitions and fortunes of men, by obferving
" the day on which each perfon was born *." He
alfo acquaint us†, " that when a prodigy happens,
" they keep an account of the events which fucceed
" it; and conclude that when a like prodigy appears,
" the fame events will happen after it." In Cicero's
firft book of divination, in which the feveral kinds
of it are explained and defended ; it is refolved into
many caufes very different from that of an immediate revelation from fome fpiritual being. He divides
divination into *artificial* and *natural.* Under divination by *art* and obfervation, he comprehends that
drawn from the infpection of the entrails of victims,
the interpretation of prodigies and thunders, the ufe
of

prodiderunt. Chaldæi—diuturna obfervatione fiderum, fcien-
tiam putantur effeciffe, ut prædici poffet, quid cuique eventu-
rum, & quo quifque fato natus effet. Eandem artem etiam
Ægyptii, &c. Cicero de Divinat. l. 1. c. 1. According to
Diodorus Siculus, p. 73, the Chaldeans were a colony of E-
gyptians, who had been inftructed in aftrology by the priefts
of Egypt.

* Euterpe. c. 82.

† Γενομίνου γὰρ τέρατ@-, φυλάσσσσι γραφόμενοι τῶ ποραῖνον· καὶ ἦν
κοτι ὕσερον παραπλήσιον τῦτω γίνηται, κατὰ τῶὖτο νομίζυσι ἀποσησίσθαι.
Herodot. ubi fupra.

of aufpices, the practices of lots and aftrological predictions, and all the varieties of prefages and figns.
In a word, as in almoft every object they looked for
fignifications of the divine purpofes, and the prefages
or indications of future events; fo in the right underftanding of thefe *external* figns, confifted divination by art. By *natural* divination (which was *internal*) Cicero means, the forefight of future events by
the mind under a particular emotion and agitation;
as in *dreaming*, or when actuated by *vaticinations* or
prophefyings by fury; and fuch *oracles* as proceeded
from a *divine inftinct and afflatus* *. It was thought,
that divination by fury (or when the mind was in an
extacy) might be excited by certain vapours or exhalations of the earth; and that a draught of water from
a particular fpring would render perfons oracular and
prophetical †. It was alfo afferted, that prodigies and

figns

* Cicero de divinat. l. 1. c. 2, 6, 18, 49, 55.

† Of the *waters* which infpired the poets and prophets,
mention is made by Statius Silv. I. II. 6. Et de Pieriis voca-
lem fontibus undam; by Anacreon, xiii, Λαλον πιοντες ὑδωρ; by
Tacitus, Haufta fontis arcani aqua,—edit refponfa; (Annals, l.
2. c. 54.) and by Pliny, l. 2. c. 103. l. 5. c. 29. *Oracular exhalations* are fpoken of in Cicero, de Div. l. 1. c. 50, Credo
etiam anhelitus quofdam fuiffe terrarum, quibus inflatæ mentes
oracula funderent. The ftrange agitations into which the goats
of Coretas, and afterwards Coretas himfelf fell, upon their ap-
proaching the top of a cavern on the hill of Parnaffus, and receiving the influence of the fubterranean blaft; gave occafion
to the building the temple, and eftablifhing the famous oracle
at Delphi. It was fuppofed, that " that virtue of the earth,
" which agitates the mind of the prieftefs of Apollo with a di-
" vine

" vine afflatus, may in length of time vanifh." Poteft vis illa
terræ, quæ mentem Pythiæ divino afflatu concitabat, evanuiffe
vetuftate, ut quofdam exaruiffe amnes, aut in alium curfum
contortos & deflexos videmus. *c.* 19. Strabo likewife fpeaking concerning the Delphic Oracle, fays, there iffued out of a
cavity πνῦμα ἐνθυσιαςικὸν, *an enthufiaftic gale*, or *wind*, rendering
perfons prophetical. But this matter is treated at large in
Plutarch de defectu Oraculorum, where he allows indeed that
demons might be appointed by the gods to prefide over divination and oracles, (p. 418. D. & p. 436. F.) and to be the
guardians of the temperature of thofe exhalations, to which
they are afcribed; but at the fame time it is afferted, that the
foul is naturally endued with the faculty of divining, and that
certain exhalations of the earth were the means of exciting
that prophetic power or virtue. This *prophetical blaft* or *fpirit
of divination* (for it is called μαντικὸν ῥεῦμα κ̀ πνεῦμα, p. 432.)
was thought to owe its virtue to the fun or Apollo, (for they
were both efteemed to be the fame god, p. 433. D. p. 434. F.)
When the infpiration was too ftrong, the prophetefs was faid
to be poffeffed with a *dumb and evil fpirit*, p. 438. B. vide p.
431—438. From Ammianus Marcellinus we learn, that divination was afcribed to the " fpirit of all the elements, and
" to the fubftantial powers, which were appeafed by different
" rites, and over which the goddefs Themis was faid to pre-
" fide." Elementorum omnium fpiritus, utpote perennium
corporum præfentiendi (*al.* præfentienti) motu femper & ubi-
que vigens, ex his quæ per difciplinas varias affectamus, parti-
cipat nobifcum munera divinandi: & fubftantiales poteftates
ritu diverfo placatæ, velut ex perpetuis fontium venis vaticina
mortalitati fuppeditant verba, quibus numen præeffe dicitur
Themidis: quam ex eo, quod fixa fatali lege decreta præfcire
facit in pofterum, que τιθεμένη fermo Græcus appellat, ita cog-
nominatam, in cubili folioque Jovis vigoris vivifici theologi ve-
teres collocarunt. Auguria & aufpicia non volucrum arbitrio
futura nefcientium colliguntur: (nec enim hoc vel infipiens
quifquam dicet) fed volatus avium dirigit Deus, ut roftrum fo-
nans, aut prætervolans pinna turbido meatu vel leni futura præ-

M   monftret.

figns might be procured by difcipline *. So that divination was a fcience, in which they thought them-felves fure of fuccefs, if they proceeded according to certain eftablifhed rules.

We are not, however, from hence to infer, as fome have done, that the ancient magicians or priefts were mere naturalifts and aftrologers. There have indeed been Atheifts and Chriftians, who have been much addicted to divination and aftrology †; but thefe arts amongft the Pagan nations were founded in their fyf-tem of theology. Great things, it was thought, might be produced in nature; but not for that reafon with-out the gods: for they had deified all the parts and powers of nature ‡, and more efpecially the heavenly bodies:

monftret.—Extis item pecudum attenti fatidicis, in fpecies converti fuetis innumeras, accidentia fciunt.—Aperiunt tunc quoque ventura, cum æftuant hominum corda, fed loquuntur divina. Sol enim (ut aiunt Phyfici) mens mundi, noftras men-tes ex fefe velut fcintillas diffunditans, cum eas incenderit ve-hementius, futuri confcias reddit. Unde Sibyllæ crebro fe di-cunt ardere, torrente vi magna flammarum. Ammianus Mar-cellinus, l. 1. c. 1. p. 204, 205. ed. Gronov.

* Cumque magna vis videretur effe—in monftris procuran-dis in harufpicum difciplina, Cicero de div. l. 1. c. 2. See Liv. l. 22. c. 44, cited below, ch. 3. fect. 4. article 1.

† Le Clerc de L'Incredulité, ch. 1. p. 32. and Mr. Bayle fur une comete.

‡ See the beginning of the preceding fection. Lord Bol-ingbroke reprefents infpiration, according to the Pagan idea of it, merely as a *natural* phenomenon, and as grounded on a *phyfical* principle, the intoxicating wind or vapour explained above:

bodies; afcribing to the latter not only life and intelligence, but a *fore-perceiving motion**, and a fovereign influence on every thing here below. This notion lay at the foundation of divination by art. With regard to natural divination, as by fury, for inftance, excited by certain exhalations; this was founded on a fuppofition of the divinity of the earth, out of which thofe exhalations are generated, and of the fun, (called the mind of the world) to which they owe their virtue †. The human foul itfelf (which was thought to be " a particle of the divine air or fpirit, to be taken out from God ‡," and to have exifted from eternity,) was believed to have a prefaging faculty, which exerted itfelf under feveral favourable circum-

M 2

ftances.

above : whereas from the paffage in Cicero's firft book of Divination, c. 19, cited above, p. 176. note p. it appears, that that very vapour was confidered as a *divine* afflatus. See his philofophical works, V.. 1. Effay 1. It muft be acknowleged, however, that Lord Bolingbroke was in this inftance mifled by men more learned than himfelf, who have confidered that as *natural* magic, (according to the modern acceptation of it) in which *demons* were not thought to be concerned; without reflecting, that what we now call *inanimate nature*, was regarded by the ancient Heathens as *animated* and *divine.*

* Perennium corporum præfentiendi (*al.* præfentienti) motu, &c. Ammianus Marcellinus, cited above, p. 177.

† Plutarch de defeᵭu orac. p. 436, E. See alfo above, p. 176. note †, and note * below, p. 181.

‡ Ex ipfo Deo decerptus, ex univerfa mente delibatus. Cicero's Tufc. Quæft. v. & de Seneᵭut.

ftances *. As from the imagined exiftence of thefe
gods, they concluded there muft be divination; fo
from the apprehended reality of divination, they confirmed themfelves in the belief of the exiftence of the
gods †. Hence Maimonides reproaches every magician as an idolater‡; and Pliny afcribes all the fplen-
dor of magic to religion ‖. The Heathens had other
gods, befides the objects of nature, viz. demons, or
deified human fpirits; and from their fubordinate
miniftry and mediation, and that of wicked fpirits;
divination, prophecy, and magic, were thought to
proceed §. The affiftance or influence of the gods
was obtained by a great variety of rites and facrifices,
adapted to their refpective natures ¶; by the ufe of
charms and fuperftitious words **, by ceremonies and
fupplications.

* Cicero de Divinat. l. 1. c. 5, 31, 49, 51, 59.

† Si divinatio fit, dii fint; & fi dii fint, fit divinatio. Cicero
de Nat. Deor.

‡ Mor. Nevoch. p. 445. Omnis magus citra dubium eft
Idololatra.

‖ Nat. Hift. l. 30. c. 12.

§ Herodot. l. 2. c. 83. Plato in fympof. in Epinomide, in
Phædro; Porphyr. apud Eufeb. præp. Ev. l. 4, 5, 6, & de
Abftinentia, l. 2. Jamblich. de Myft. Apul. Apol. Id. de deo
Socrat. Plutarch de defect. Orac. cited above p. 176. n. †. &
Pythagoras apud Diogen. Laert. in vita Pythag. n. 32. p. 514.

¶ Ritu diverfo placatæ. Ammianus Marcellinus, l. 21. init.

** The famous *Ephefian Letters*, which were certain barbar-
ous words ufed as charms, may be feen in Hefychius, or in Dr.
Sykes'

fupplications. Sometimes we find the power of in-
chanting afcribed to noxious herbs and drugs *, but
not exclufively of the affiftance of the gods, who were
invoked to give them efficacy †. The magicians pretended in the proper ufe of their art, (for it was
taught as fuch) to a power of *compelling* ‡ the gods to
execute their defires and commands.

Upon the principles here explained, all the pretences amongft the Pagans to divination and forcery (and
every other ‖ fpecies of magic) were founded ; whe-

M 3   ther

Syke's Inquiry, p. 61. See his Further Inquiry, p. 66. Ovid
fays,

  Carmina fanguinea deducunt cornua lunæ
  Et revocant niveos folis euntis equos.

 * Thus the witch in Virgil, Ecl. 8. fays,
  Has herbas, atque hæc Ponto mihi lecta venena
  Ipfe dedit Mœris; nafcuntur plurima Ponto.
  His ego fœpe lupum fieri, & fe condere fylvis
  Mœrin, fæpe animas imis excire fepulchris,
  Atque fatas alio vidi traducere meffes.

 † Theocritus Id. 2. They likewife thought, Quamvis plan-
tam fuam habere ftellam, quemadmodum & omnibus animali-
bus & metallis certa fydera adfcribunt. Maimon. Mor. Nevoc. l. 3. c. 37.

 ‡ They acted cæca coactorum numinum violentia. Enchan-
treffes boafted that they had power over the gods. Lucan. l. 6.
v. 606, 742. Ovid. Metamor. l. 7. 192.

 ‖ I have taken no notice of that fpecies of magic, called *theurgy* (θεϋργία,) becaufe it principally confifted in a fanatical
pretence to communion with demons, and a vifion of their ef-
fence. So far as it was thought, to inveft thofe who practifed
                 it,

ther thofe pretences were carried on by the prieft, under the protection, and for the fervice of the ftate *; or for the purpofes of private gain, by the loweft orders of magicians †, conjurers and witches, generally (though feldom effectually) profcribed or prohibited by law ‡. Whatever difference there might be between them, the Scripture brands them all as fhamelefs impoftors; and reproaches them with an utter inability of difcovering or accomplifhing any thing fupernatural. The prophet Ifaiah having fore-told the deftruction of Babylon, fo famous all over

the

it, with the power of the gods; it differed in one refpect from that fort of magic called forcery (γοητεία;) *theurgy* invoking only the *benevolent* divinities; *forcery* the *mifchievous ones*, whofe operations were fuitable to their nature.

* That the public minifters of religion practifed forcery as well as divination, is certain from their curfing the enemies of the ftate, and devoting them to deftruction.

† They were rather more extravagant, as well as more mif-chievous, than the eftablifhed priefts; inafmuch as they pre-tended to know other people's fortunes, to difcover what was loft, to bewitch, to procure love, to walk upon the water, to fly through the air, to raife or lay ftorms, to turn themfelves or others into any fhapes, to remove corn from one field into another, to draw down the moon, to raife ghofts, to ftop the courfe of rivers, and to kill or cure both men and cattle, &c. See Ovid's Metamor. l. 7. v. 199.

‡ Concerning conjurers and fortune-tellers, who were called *mathematici*, Tacitus fays, they are a *fallacious* fort of men, quod in civitate noftra & vetabitur femper, & retinebitur. Hift. l. 1. c. 22.

the world for divination and aftrology; thus proceeds to infult that proud city * : " Stand now with
" thine inchantments, and with the multitude of thy
" forceries, wherein thou haft laboured from thy
" youth ; if fo be thou fhalt be able to profit, if fo
" be thou mayeft prevail. Thou art wearied in the
" multitude of thy councils : let now the aftrologers,
" the ftar-gazers, the monthly prognofticators, ftand
" up, and fave thee from thofe things which fhall
" come upon thee," from that deftruction, which, he
tells them, with their various methods of divination
and forcery, they would be unable either to forefee
or prevent. The fame prophet thus warns the Ifraelites againft having recourfe to the Heathen diviners
for inftruction ; " Should not a people feek unto
their god ?" Whom then fhould you confult but the
God of Ifrael ? " For the living to the dead † ?" that
is, Is it not abfurd to confult the dead concerning
the ftate of the living, of which the former are ignorant ? Or the meaning may be, Inftead of the living
God, will you have recourfe to the dead? The Heathen gods were dead men : and the oracles were placed in their temples, which were their fepulchres.
Moreover, the Heathen diviners pretended to call
up the fouls of the departed, which were fuppofed to
poffefs a prophetic virtue ; nay, by an infpection of
the entrails of boys who had fuffered a violent death,

M 4   they

* Ifaiah xlvii. 11—13.

† Ifaiah viii. 18, 19.

they hoped to dive into futurity*. The language of Iſaiah implies, that it was unpardonable ſtupidity, in any or all theſe ways, to expeɛt any inſtruɛtion or information from the dead. When Jeremiah thus warns the Jews, " Learn not the way of the Hea-" then, and be not afraid of the ſigns of heaven," whoſe appearances were thought to portend particular calamities ; he pronounces " the cuſtoms of the Heathens vain," on account of the utter ignorance and impotence of their gods †, who could not be ſuppoſed to convey to others, that knowledge and power which they did not poſſeſs themſelves. And thus Jeremiah deſcribes the prophets who were not ſent of God, " They prophefy unto you a falſe viſion " and divination, and a thing of nought, and the " deceit of their heart ‡." On other occaſions, he addreſſes the people of God in the following ſtrain : " Hearken not ye to your prophets, nor to your di-" viners, nor to your dreamers, nor to your enchan-" ters, nor to your ſorcerers. For they prophefy a " lie unto you ‖." The ſacred writers do at all times brand thoſe, who exerciſed the arts of divination and ſorcery, *as liars* §; and the arts themſelves *as lying vanities,*

---

* To theſe methods of divination Juſtin Martyr refers, A-pol. 1. p. 27. ed. Thirlb. Νικυομαντεῖαι μὲν γὰρ, ᾗ αἱ ἀδιαφθόρων παίδων ἐποπτεύσεις, ᾗ ψυχῶν ἀνθρωπίνων κλήσεις.

† Jerem. x. 2, 3—8, 14. Compare Iſ. xli. 23, 24.

‡ Jer. xiv. 14.

‖ Ch. xxvii. 9, 10.

§ Iſaiah xliv. 25. Jerem. l. 36.

vanities *, the moft abfurd and groundlefs delufions imaginable. What ftronger language could they have ufed, fuppofing them to have believed (as they certainly did believe) all the magic of the ancients to have had no other fupport, than human artifice and falfehood?

Notwithftanding this clear decifion of the point by the divine oracles, many Chriftians have contended for the fupernatural power and efficacy of Pagan divination and forcery. This point was maintained by the Fathers in particular, who afcribed the efficacy of magic to evil demons; as fome of the Heathen philofophers alfo did†. It was a very prevailing opinion in the primitive church ‡, that magicians and necromancers, both amongft the Gentiles and heretical Chriftians, had each their particular demons, perpetually attending on their perfons, and obfequious to their commands, by whofe help they could call up the fouls of the dead, foretel future events, and perform miracles. " In the cafe of idolatry, " they imagined demons to affume the names, and
" to

---

* Pfalm xxxi. 6. Jonah ii. 8.

† Eufebius's Præp. Ev. l. 5. c. 4, has this infcription, Περὶ τᾶ πονηρῶν δαιμόνων ἔναι, τὰ παρὰ τοῖς ἔθνεσι μαντεῖα τε καὶ χρηστήρια. And St. Auftin (de civ. Dei, l. 8. c. 16.) fays, Inter cætera etiam dicit [Apuleius] ad eos [dæmones] pertinere divinationes augurum, arufpicum, vatum, atque fomniorum. Vid. Minuc. Fel. p. 30. ed. Lugd. Bat. and fee above, p. 180. note §. Porphyry de Abftin. l. 2. § 41. p. 85, fays, διὰ μέντοι τῶν ἐναέρων ἡ ἡ πᾶσα γοητεία ἐκτελεῖται.

‡ See Dr. Middleton's Free Inquiry, p. 66.

" to act the parts of the Heathen gods; and in ma-
" gic to affume the forms of departed fouls, and to
" appear under the names of thofe, who were called
" up from the dead; and as fuch, to anfwer all quef-
" tions, which fhould be demanded of them *." As
what was urged above † againft the former fuppofition, concludes with equal force againft the latter; I
need not fhew, how inconfiftent this is with the Scripture account of the magicians, as utterly unable to
fupport their pretenfions, by any works or predictions
beyond human power and fkill. It will be neceflary however to examine what is alledged, in fupport
of the contrary doctrine.

1. It is alleged, " that the *names* by which the
" feveral forts of diviners are defcribed in Scripture,
" imply a communication with fpiritual beings."
Thofe who urge this argument, do not always diftinguifh between the Scriptures in their original languages, and in the tranflation now in ufe, which
(like moft other tranflations, whether ancient or modern) was made by perfons deeply tinctured with
the vulgar fuperftition, and often on that account
does great injuftice to the original. That phrafe ‡, *a*
familiar

---

* Id. p. 70.   † Page 240.

‡ This phrafe (which occurs Lev. xix. 31. chap. xx. 6, 7.
Deut. xviii. 11.   1 Sam. xxviii. 3, 7, 8, 9.   2 Kings xxi. 6.
ch. xxiii. 24.   1 Chron. x. 13.   2 Chr. xxxiii. 6.   If. xxix.
4. ch. viii. 19.) has nothing in the original to anfwer to it but
ob (or *oboth* in the plural number) which fignifies *a bottle,* (which
amongft the ancients fomewhat refembled our bladders,) Job
xxxix. 19; and hence came to denote a perfon whofe belly is
diftended

familiar fpirit, or *familiar fpirits*, which occurs fo often, is thought to be an inftance of this kind. But
even fuppofing the original word to be rightly tranflated; it cannot be inferred from hence, that the facred writers believed, that any perfons were really
affifted and infpired by a familiar fpirit. They could
not allow, and meant only to chara&erize, their pretenfions. The Scripture, as it defcribes the Heathen
deities by their ufual appellations, (gods, lords, demons,)

diftended as a bottle, and is applied particularly to thofe perfons who delivered oracles as from their bellies, fwelled, as it
was believed, by fome divine afflatus. Accordingly, it is generally tranflated by the LXX. ἐγγαςρίμυθος; a word which fignifies thofe who fpeak with their mouths fhut, fo as to feem to
fpeak out of their bellies. But though the word, according to
its ftri&eft etymology, might denote only *a bottle-bellied perfon;* yet as it is the word ufed to defcribe thofe, who pretended that their bellies were inflated by a divine energy, by the
perfons who believed the reality of thofe prentences; our
tranflators are not, perhaps, whblly to be condemned, for the
manner in which they render it. (See below, ch. 4. fe&. 2.)
    But it is not fo eafy to excufe them, for the manner in which
they have acquitted themfelves on another occafion. I refer
to their reprefenting Simon, the magician, as *bewitching* the
Samaritans; and hereby giving a fenfe to the word, ἐξιςᾶν,
A&s viii. 9, different from what they themfelves have put upon ἐξίςατο, in the 13th verfe : which they juftly render, *he won-
dered.* Simon had been exercifing the magical arts in Samaria,
and thereby *raifing the aftonifhment* of the inhabitants. But
the fight of genuine miracles difcovered at once the vanity of
the moft artful imitations of them, and *aftonifhed* and convinced Simon himfelf, who had fo long *raifed the aftonifhment* of
others. Vid. Schmidium ad A&. viii. 13.

mons,) which are expreffive, not of what they really
were in themfelves, but of what their votaries believed them to be * ; fo it calls all thofe perfons, who
pretended to any intercourfe with the gods, by their
common names, (prophets, magicians, necromancers, ·
diviners, forcerers, monthly prognofticators, &c.)
though thefe names were at firft affumed by the pre-
tenders themfelves, to enable them more fuccefsfully
to carry on their impoftures ; or conferred on them
by the fuperftition of the people.   Whatever pretenfions or claims thefe names may imply, it is fufficient
that the Scriptures deny them any anfwerable powers
or performances.   And therefore, when St. Luke
fpeaks of the damfel at Philippi as " poffeffed with a
fpirit of divination, or of Apollo †," he meant only
to defcribe her pretenfions, and the common belief
concerning her.   Dr. Sykes was of opinion, that this
woman had merely acquired a trick of fpeaking in-
wardly, as from her belly ; by the difcovery of which
fhe was difabled from playing it any longer : while
others

---

* See above, p. 172.   In like manner Jeremiah calls particular celeftial appearances, " the figns of heaven," becaufe the
Heathens regarded them as fuch, ch. x. 2.   And who fcruples
to fay, fuch a perfon tells fortunes, when nothing more is
meant, than that he pretends to do it ?

† Acts xvi. 16, 18.   Πνεῦμα πύθωνος, *a fpirit of Python* or *A-
pollo*: this is manifeftly the language of the Pagans, which St.
Luke adopted, becaufe it ferved to defcribe the cafe of the
damfel.   He cannot be fuppofed to allow, that Apollo (whether the word here denotes a hero god, or the fun) imparted
to her the power of prophefying.

others plead that fhe was really infpired. Both parties equally forget, that *a fpirit of Python* or *Apollo*,
denoted in the language of antiquity, not only the
infpiration of Apollo, but alfo that raving and madnefs, which were the effect of that fuppofed infpiration and poffeffion *. And therefore the miracle performed upon the damfel, or the cafting out of her
the fpirit of Apollo, confifted in curing her madnefs,
and reftoring her to her right mind; in confequence
of which the people would confider her no longer as
infpired or poffeffed.

2. The *laws of Mofes* † againft divination and witchcraft are thought to prove the *efficacy* of thefe arts;
though thofe laws do really prove nothing more than
their execrable *wickednefs* and *impiety*. By the credit of thefe arts, the people were drawn away from
the true God to falfe ones. The arts themfelves
were founded upon the principles of idolatry ‡; and
the

---

* No prophetefs was thought to be infpired, but when fhe
was mad and raving. Ἡ τι γὰρ δὴ ἐν Δελφοῖς προφῆτις, αἵ τ᾽ ἐν Δοδώ-
νη ἱέρειαι, μαινεῖσαι, κ. τ. λ. Platon. Phædr. p. 1220, C. D. E.
ἐδεὶς γὰρ ἔννυς ἐφαπτέται μαντικῆς ἐνθέα κ, ἀληθᾶς. Id. Tim. p. 1074.
D. It appears from Meric Cafaubon, (cited by Dr. Macknight,
Harmony, v. 1. p. 179, 2d ed.) that to the natural difeafes of
melancholy, madnefs, epilepfy, &c. enthufiaftic divinatory fits
are (thought to be) incidental: and that when the difeafe is
cured, the enthufiafms go away.

† Exod. xxii. 18. Lev. xix. 26, 31. ch. xx. 27. Deut.
xviii. 10, 11. Would it not be in vain to make laws againft
thofe, whofe miraculous power could prevent their execution?

‡ This was proved above concerning divination, p. 178.
Witchcraft alfo, and all magical rites, had a reference to the
heavenly

the rites and placatory facrifices which attended them,
were in their very nature acts of idolatry, that is, of
high treafon againft the Jewifh ftate, over which Jehovah prefided as fupreme Governor. It was neceffary therefore that every magician fhould be put to
death, becaufe every magician, was an idolater. I
add, that many of the rites of magic were flagrant
immoralities. For thofe who anciently practifed witchcraft, mingled dangerous drugs with their compofi-
tions, and, on account of the real mifchief they hereby did, are often ranked with *poifoners* *. Amongft
other deteftable methods of divination, one was the
murther of infants and others, who were facrificed on
purpofe, that by raking into their entrails, they might
gain an infight into futurity ; as appears from the
teftimony of Herodotus, Cicero, Lucan, Juvenal, Tacitus, Philoftratus, Porphyry †, and many other learned

heavenly bodies. Nullum autem magicum opus fine fiderum
refpectu & confideratione poteft perfici. Maimon.. `or.
Nevoc. pt. 3. c. 37. He farther obferves, that the belief of
their power to hurt or help, neceffarily led mankind to worfhip
them. Accordingly both witchcraft and divination are joined
with idolatry, 1 Sam. xv. 22, 23. If. ii. 6—8. ch. xlvii. 12,
13. Jerem. xxvii. 9, 10. Ezek. xxi. 21, 22. Nahum iii. 4.
Micah v. 12.

* The Hebrew word, mecafhephim, which we tranflate *forcerers*, the LXX render by φαρμακὺς.

† Jacobus Geufius, in his book entitled, Victimæ humanæ,
Pars I. c. 19—21, cites thefe and other Heathen writers, to
fhew how very frequently human facrifices were employed by
thofe, who practifed divination and magic. The *Cimbri* ripped
open

ed Pagans; as well as from the intimations of the facred writers *. Sorcerers and forcereffes were fuppofed to perform all their amazing works by the affiftance of the fouls of young boys, who had been
violently put to death for that purpofe, and then
called up from the dead, by ineffable adjurations †.
Now might it not be very fit, feverely to punifh thefe
external acts of forcery ‡, without entering into the
queftion

open the bowels, and from them formed a judgment of future
events. Strabo, l. 7. p. 451. (compare Porphyry de Abft. l. 2.
§ 51.) The *Celtæ* divined by the agonies and convulfions of
the men, who were offered for a facrifice, and from the effufion of their blood, Diodor. Sic. l. 5. p. 308.

* Deut. xviii. 10, 11. 2 Kings xvii. 17. chap. xxi. 6. 2
Chron. xxxiii. 6. Ezek. xx. 26, 31.

† In Horace's epodes, l. 5. epod. 5. v. 12, 13, the perfon
murdered by the forcerefs, Canidia, is puer, impube corpus.
The author of that very ancient, though fpurious work, the
" Recognitions of St. Clemens," reprefents Simon Magus as
faying, Pueri incorrupti, & violenter necati, animam adjura-
mentis ineffabilibus evocatam adfiftere mihi feci; & per ipfam
fit omne quod jubeo. Ed. Cotelerii, p. 523. See Eufeb. Hift.
Ecclef. l. 7. c. 10. Chryfoftom and others, cited by Cotele-
rius in his note on this paffage of Clemens. This kind of divination was called βριφομαντεια. On fuch rites of magic, fee
Broukhufius on Tibullus, 1. 11. 45. and Fabricius, Bibl. Antiq. p. 417, 419.

‡ This is not a groundlefs diftinction; for the laws of Mofes are levelled wholly againft the *external acts* of forcery, as
appears from all the laws referred to above, p. 189. note †, and
particularly from Deut. xviii. 10, 11, 14, " There fhall not be
" found amongft you any one that maketh his fon or his daugh-
" ter

queftion, whether they were or were not of any *effi-cacy* to procure fupernatural affiftance?

3. Pretenfions to divination (it is farther pleaded) could not have fupported " their credit in all the " Heathen nations, and through all ages ;" if fome inftances of true divination had not happened, how-ever rare we may fuppofe them to have been.   This laft argument (which was confidered in a former chapter *) proceeds on a fuppofition notorioufly falfe : for diviners of all forts, obfervers of times, inchant-ers, witches, wizzards, ventriloquifts, and necroman-cers, did not fupport their credit in the manner here alledged,

" ter to pafs through the fire, or that ufeth divination, or an " obferver of the times, or an enchanter, or a witch, &c." Amongft thofe who believed the fupernatural power of force-ry, laws were framed againft its fuppofed *effects*.   The Roman law forbad bewitching the fruits of the earth, and drawing their neighbours corn in their own fields by charms.   Apud nos in duodecim tabulis cavetur, ne quis alienos fruêtus excan-taffit.   Seneca, Nat. Quæft. l. 4. c. 7.   Seneca adds, " our " ignorant anceftors imagined, that fhowers could be procur-" ed or driven away by charms ; but we need not go to any " fchool of philofophy to teach us otherwife."   As the Ro-mans became more enlightened, the ftyle of their law was al-tered.   The Lex Cornelia, ufually cited as a law againft for-cery, forbids *poifoning*, & mala facrificia, Liv. Decad. 1. l. 8. which may ferve both to explain and vindicate the laws of Mofes for the punifhments denounced againft the fame crimes, and to fhew how unreafonably this divine legiflator has been reproached, on account of thefe laws, with a fpirit of perfe-cution.

* Chap. 2. feĉt. 2.

alleged, and never were in any reputation with Pagans of a liberal mind and education. And from Chriftians, whofe zeal for the credit of ancient magic thus tranfports them beyond the bounds of truth, we appeal to Heathens of underftanding and virtue, in vindication of the cenfure paffed upon every fpecies of magic by the prophets of God. Cicero, the greateft mafter of reafon and learning amongft the Romans, and in all refpects a very able judge of this fubject, condemns the oracles of the Heathen gods as either *falfe*, or *obfcure*, or *ambiguous*, (fo as to require other oracles to explain them) or as true only by *chance* or *accident* *. We find both Sophocles and Euripides, upon the public theatre at Athens, (a city greatly addicted to fuperftition and idolatry,) paffing a fimilar cenfure upon the Pagan foothfayers and diviners †, or reprefenting them as men actuated only by the love

N   of

---

* Partim falfis, ut ego opinor ; partim cafu veris, ut fit in omni oratione fæpiffime ; partim flexiloquis & obfcuris, ut interpres egeat interprete, et fors ipfa ad fortes referenda fit ; partim ambiguis. De Divinat. l. 2. c. 56. In the 25th chapter, he argues againft divination by *art*, in the whole extent of it, from the *obfcurity* of the figns. It appears likewife from Cicero in the fame book, (as alfo from Strabo, l. 15.) that aftrology was rejected by aftronomers, and the beft philofophers.

† —— Τίς ἢ μάντις ἐς᾽ ἀνὴρ ;
Ὃς ὀλίγ᾽ ἀληθῆ, πολλὰ ἢ ψευδῆ λέγει
Τυχών· ὅταν ἢ μὴ τύχη, διοίχεται.
In Aulide, v. 956.

of money *. Pindar in his Olympic odes †, which
were all compofed to be fung on the moft public occafions, and probably at the folemn facrifices offered
to the gods, affirms, " that they have beftowed upon
" mortals no fure prefage of things to come." And
in ftill earlier times, Hefiod ‡ had maintained the fame
opinion. What various rites of fuperftition were practifed by fuch Heathens as were loft to all reflection,
whereby they gueffed what fhould happen to them;
we learn from Theophraftus in his characters of fuperftition, and from Plutarch in his book on the fame
fubject ‖: but we find them derided by Terence in
his Phormio §. Nor were there any men of underftanding, who gave countenance to any of the modes
of divination, unlefs from a principle of compliance
with vulgar prejudices, or for reafons of ftate ¶.
Amongft the Heathens no impofture was cenfured as
unlawful,

* Τὸ μαντικὸν γὰρ πᾶν φιλάργυρον γένΘ-. Sophocles Antigone,
1607· Vide etiam Oed. Tyr. 395. et Euripid. Iphig. in Aul.
520.

† Ode xii. l. 10.

‡ Μάντις δ' ἐδεὶς ἐσιν ἐπιχθονίων ἀνθρώπων
'Οσις ἂν εἰδείη Ζηνὸς νόον αἰγιόχοιο.
Hefiod. Fragment.

‖ See alfo Maimonides de Idolatria, c. 11. § 4, 5, 6.

§ Act. 4. fc. 4.

¶ Exiftimo jus augurum, etfi divinationis opinione principio conftitutum fit, tamen poftea reipublicæ caufa confervatum
ac retentum. Cicero de Divinat. l. 2. c. 35. fee alfo c. 33.
From

unlawful, which was judged to be ufeful *. With regard to forcery; the pretended effects of it, as they are defcribed by the Heathen poets †, are too extravagant to be confuted, and their beft writers treat the art itfelf with derifion. In proof of this, I appeal to Horace ‡, Cicero ||, Seneca §, Dion Caffius ¶, Quintus Curtius **, Tacitus ††, and Pliny ‡‡, befides others already taken notice of; and indeed to all the Heathens, whofe underftandings were not totally depraved by fuperftition. The miracles faid to be wrought amongft the Pagans, were not believed by the hifto-

N 2   rians

From the fame political motives, the wifeft Heathens countenanced the popular idolatry. See Auguft. de Civitat. Dei, l. 4. c. 3, 22, 27, 31.

* Plutarch. l. de Socrat. Genio, p. 579, 580.

† Ovid. Met. l. 7. fab. 2. l. 199, &c. Virgil. Eclog. 8. Æn. 4. Lucan. l. de bello civili, 6. Manil. l. 1. Tibullus, l. 1. Eleg. 2. See above, p. 182. note †.

‡ Epift. l. 2. ep. 2. l. 208.

|| De Nat. Deor. l. 1. Cum poetarum autem errore conjungere licet portenta magorum, Ægyptiorumque in eodem genere dementiam. And in his fecond book of divination, where he delivers his own fentiments, he fays in reference to magical operations, Num igitur me cogis etiam fabulis credere? &c.

§ Nat. Quæft. l. 4. c. 67.

¶ L. 52. p. 490.

** L. 7. c. 4.

†† L. 1. c. 22.

‡‡ Nat. Hift. l. 30. c. 1, 2, 3. l. 26. c. 4.

rians * who relate them ; and the philofophers treated them as fables †. If magic was able to fupport fome reputation in ages of grofs ignorance, through the fuperior knowlege and fraudulent contrivances of thofe who exercifed it ; yet when learning revived and became general, it never failed to fink into contempt. It did fo in the fame age, in which the Gofpel gained a general eftablifhment by the credit of undeniable miracles. In vain did the Roman emporor, Nero, by difcovering the moft extravagant fondnefs for magic, and fending for the moft eminent profeffors of it from every quarter of the world, endeavour to fupport its finking reputation. Pliny informs us, that all that Nero gained by his attempts, was an entire conviction of the folly of magic. And he obferves himfelf, that if at any time magicians perform extraordinary things, it is owing to the efficacy of their drugs, not of their magic art ‡. Now, inafmuch as

---

* Quæ ante conditam, condendamve urbem, poeticis magis decora fabulis, quam incorruptis rerum geftarum monumentis traduntur, ea nec affirmare nec refellere in animo eft. Datur hæc venia antiquitati, ut mifcendi humana divinis, primordia urbium auguftiora faciat. Liv. Proem. After reciting feveral prodigies, Livy adds, Et alia ludibria oculorum, auriumque, credita pro veris. L. 22. c. 44. See Liv. l. 24. c. 10. l. 22. c. 3. et Quintus Curtius, l. 9. c. 1.

† In reference to Heathen miracles, Cicero fays, l. 2. de Divinat. Nihil debet effe in philofophia commentitiis fabellis loci. Concerning Cato, he tells us in the fame book, Mirari fe aiebet, quod non rideret arufpex, arufpicem cum vidiffet.

‡ In his Veneficas artes pollere, non magicas, Nat. Hift. l. 30. c. 2.

as magic did conftantly lofe its credit, juft in the degree in which men exercifed their underftandings, it certainly was not fupported by any fupernatural power.

S E C T. IV.

Concerning the falfe prophets as fpoken of in Scripture, in which the following paffages are explained, Deut. xiii. 1—5. Matt. xxiv. 24. 2 Theff. ii. 9. Rev. xiii. 13, 14; *together with feveral others relative to the falfe teachers in the apoftolic age.*

THAT the pretences to infpiration and miracles, made by falfe prophets, in fupport of error and idolatry, fhould be branded in Scripture as the fole effects of human craft and impofture; is what might be naturally expected from thofe writings, which do not allow the power of infpiring predictions, or of working miracles, to any Pagan deity, or to any evil fpirit. For from what other quarter was it ever imagined, that a falfe prophet could receive any fupernatural fupport? It will be neceffary, however, to examine the feveral paffages of Scripture, which fpeak to this point; inafmuch as they have had a fenfe affigned them, abfolutely inconfiftent with the principles already eftablifhed.

I.

I fhall begin with confidering that celebrated warning of Mofes to the Ifraelites: " If there arife among

N 3   " you

" you a prophet, or a dreamer of dreams, and giveth
" thee a fign or a wonder, and the fign or the won-
" der come to pafs, whereof he fpake unto thee, fay-
" ing, Let us go after other gods, (which thou haft
" not known,) and let us ferve them ; thou fhalt not
" hearken unto his words :—for the Lord your God
" proveth you, to know whether you love the Lord
" your God with all your heart.—And that prophet,
" and that dreamer of dreams, fhall be put to death,
" becaufe he hath fpoken to turn you away from the
" Lord your God, which brought thee out of the
" land of Egypt, and redeemed you out of the houfe
" of bondage *."

It has been contended that Mofes, in this paffage,
is laying down this general rule, viz. " that the true
" *divinity* of miracles is to be determined by the *doc-*
" *trines*, which they are applied to confirm." It is
farther afferted, that the Jews are here required, to
make *his law,* in particular, the ftandard by which
to judge of miracles ; to difallow the force and evidence of thofe which oppofe that law, and even to
put to death the prophet who performed them, becaufe he taught the worfhip of a ftrange god †. The
learned Dr. Benfon ‡ and Dr. Lardner ‖, as well as

many

* Deut. xiii. 1—5.

† Hence Rouffeau concluded, that the Pagans had an equal
light to put the apoftles to death, for preaching up to them
the worfhip of a ftrange god, though they proved their miffion by miracles.

‡ Life of Chrift, p. 202.

‖ Jewifh and Heathen Teftimonies, V. 1. p. 255, 256.

Though

many others, were of opinion, that Mofes here puts a cafe, which never would happen; but if it did happen, and a miracle was performed to induce the Ifraelites to worfhip other gods, it was to be difregarded. Here it is natural to enquire, whether any prophet did ever arife amongft the Ifraelites, who performed real miracles to draw them into idolatry. If no fuch prophet did arife, (and there is not the leaft reafon to believe there did;) how needlefs was it to caution the Ifraelites againft him? Nay, Mofes knew that it was impoffible any fuch prophet fhould arife; becaufe he appropriates all miracles to God *, and denies that the Heathen deities could fupport their claims by any fupernatural works. He always reprefents them as fenfelefs idols, and could not therefore allow them any power or dominion over mankind. On all occafions he appeals to miracles, as abfolute proofs of the divinity of Jehovah, and of his own miffion *: and can he, without grofs felf-contradiction, here reprefent thefe works as common both to the true God and to rival deities; to a divine meffenger and a falfe prophet? And indeed why

N 4 fhould

Though this judicious, candid and excellent writer afferts, that Mofes here refers to miracles; yet, contrary to his ufual method, he produces no proof of his affertion. Nay, he allows it to be a rule of Scripture, that if any man propofes, and performs a miracle in proof of his miffion, it would be decifive in his favour: and yet in the cafe, ftated above, he fuppofes that a miracle determines nothing.

* This will be fhewn below, ch. 3. fect. 5. and ch. 4. fect. 1.

should not a real miracle equally gain credit to both or neither ? be of as great weight *againſt* Moſes as *for* him ? Moſes neither does, nor could allow, that an idolatrous prophet would perform works truly miraculous : and the very order to put ſuch a prophet to death, ſhews that there was no danger of his being protected from puniſhment by a miraculous power.

The Jewiſh lawgiver here refers, not to true miracles, but to thoſe *divinations* amongſt the Pagans, by which the credit of idolatry was ſupported. Amongſt other methods of divination, one was by the interpretation of *portents, oſtents, prodigies, monſters* *, rare and extraordinary appearances and occurrences, which were falſely deemed ſupernatural, and thought to preſignify † future events. Theſe are *the ſigns and wonders* ‡ here ſpoken of by Moſes, and which it was the

---

* The ſeveral ſpecies of divination are enumerated in Cicero de Nat. Deor. l. 2. c. 65. Multa cernunt haruſpices; multa augures provident; multa oraculis declarantur; multa vaticinationibus; multa ſomniis; multa portentis.

† See the paſſage from Herodotus, cited above, p. 175, and note ‡, below.

‡ Heb. *Oth*, a *ſign*, and *mopheth*, a *wonder*, like the correſpondent Greek words σημεῖον and τέρας, though often applied to miraculous works, yet very commonly bear a different application. *Oth* denotes any *mark* or *token*, Gen. xvii. 11. Exod. xii. 13. Ezek. xx. 12, 20; and ſo likewiſe does the word σημεῖον, Matt. xxvi. 48. Luke ii. 12. Rom. iv. 11. 2 Theſſ. iii. 17. Nor can *mopheth* denote a miracle, Pſ. lxxi. 7. Iſ. xx. 3. Ezek. xii. 6. ch. xxiv. 24; or τέρας in the ſame paſſages of the LXX. *Oth* and *mopheth* are both applied to

ſuch

the bufinefs of the Pagan prophet (or interpreter of
the will of the gods) and diviner by dreams to ex-
pound *. And that Mofes does not here refer to any
miraculous works performed *upon the fpot*, but to a
prodigy or fign of fome future event, is farther evident

fuch things as point out, and prefignify future events, 1 Kings
xiii. 3. If. viii. 18. ch. xx. 3. Ezek. xii. 6, 11. ch. xxiv. 24,
27; and fo are both σημεῖον and τέρας, Luke xxi. 11, 25. Acts
ii. 19. In Ælian's Var. Hift. l. 12. c. 57. we are told, that
when Alexander led his forces againft Thebes, οἱ μὲν Θεοὶ σημεῖα αὐτοῖς ᴶ τέρατα ἀπέςελλον, προσημαίνοντες τὰς περὶ αὐτῶν ὅσον οὐ-
δήπω τύχας, " the gods fent *figns* und *wonders* amongft them,
" prefignifying their impending fate." Polybius alfo (lib. 3.
c. 10. p. 365. l. 9. cited by Raphelius on Mat. xxiv. 24.) ufes
both thefe words together in the fame fenfe as Ælian. See alfo
the citation from Herodotus, fect. 3. p. 175. note †, where τέρας
fignifies a prodigy. The following paffage from Livy, (l. 22.
c. 44.) may ferve farther to explain the nature and ufe of prodigies. Confules duabus urbanis legionibus fcriptis, fupple-
mentoque in alias lecto, priufquam ab urbe moverent, prodigia
procurarunt, quæ nuntiata erant. Murus ac portæ tactæ, &
Ariciæ etiam Jovis ædes de cælo tacta fuerat. Et alia ludibria oculorum, auriumque, credita pro veris. The prophetic
fign and portent was fometimes preternatural, Homer. Il. 2. l.
308—324, but often nothing more than fome very rare and
uncommon accidents and occurrences, Terent. Phormio Act.
4. fc. 4. l. 24, 25, 26. Hence the Roman orator fays, (De
Div. l. 2.) Si quod raro fit, id portentum putandum eft, fapientem effe portentum eft, fæpius enim mulum peperiffe arbi-
tror, quam fapientem fuiffe.

* In Homer (Il. 1. v. 62.) *a prophet*, and *an expounder of
dreams* are reckoned amongft the perfons, capable of explaining the meaning of Apollo in fending the plague amongſt the
Greeks. Compare Jerem. xxvii. 9.

dent from his fpeaking of the fign given, as a thing
that *might come to pafs*, or afterwards happen.   To
give a fign or a wonder, therefore, muft mean, the
propofing and appealing to any particular prodigy or
portent, as a token or proof of a divine interpofition,
as a declaration of the decrees óf the gods, and an
indication of futurity.   It is indeed fuppofed, that
the prodigy might poffibly be followed by the very
event it was faid to prefage; neverthelefs Mofes did
not, and could not admit, that this completion of the
prediction was a proof of any fupernatural infpiration.
For the Heathen gods, according to his reprefentation of them, were as unable to foretel, as they were
to accomplifh, any thing.   Predictions no lefs than
miracles, are propofed in Scripture as figns of a prophet's miffion.   When a prophet fpoke in the name
of the *true God*, and the event foretold did not come
to pafs; the Ifraelites were to conclude, that the
prophet fpoke entirely from himfelf*; it being impoffible that Jehovah fhould either be deceived himfelf, or deceive his creatures.   On the other hand,
if his prediction (of fuch future events as human reafon could not forefee) received its accomplifhment,
they were to regard him as a prophet †.   But a perfon who fpoke in the name of a *falfe* or *idol god*, was
to be rejected, notwithftanding the accomplifhment
of his (conjectural) prediction; becaufe the deity by
whom he profeffed to be infpired, was a mere nullity,

and

* Deut. xviii. 18—22.

† Jerem. xxviii. 9.   If. xli. 23. ch. vii. 14.

and therefore could not infpire him with any fupernatural knowlege. The very fuppofition, that the
Pagan prognofticator might, in a particular inftance,
divine aright; implies, that this was not likely to be
a common cafe, but that this predictive fign would
more generally fail of its accomplifhment; and confequently was nothing more than human conjecture *.

To difcern the full meaning and propriety of this
prophetic admonition, we muft recollect both *the
temper*, and *the circumftances* of the Ifraelites. They
were continually expofed to the artifices of the numerous Heathen priefts and diviners †; who in virtue of their fuperior fkill in the laws of nature, were
able to make very probable gueffes concerning fome
events, which were thought to be beyond the reach
of human forefight; and who, no doubt, by habit
acquired a conjectural fagacity more than common;
and who, at leaft, by the very frequency of their conjectures, could fcarcely be *always* ‡ in the wrong.
Whenever their predictions came to pafs, they urged
the accomplifhment of their fign (fent, as they affirmed, by the gods) as a divine interpofition. To
facts

---

* Againft the divinity of figns and oftents, we find the Heathens objecting their obfcurity, Quæ fi figna Deorum putanda
funt, cur tam obfcura fuerunt? Cicero de Div. l. 2. c. 25. See
above, p. 193.

† 1 Kings xviii. 19. Jerem. xxvii. 9, 10.

‡ For as Cicero obferves, (de Divinat. l. 2. c. 4.) Quis eft
enim qui totum diem jaculans, non aliquando collimet?

facts of this nature we know the Pagans were wont to appeal. But this was not the worst of the case. Those who are strongly addicted to superstition, easily give credit to every thing that seems to favour it; they remember and regard a single oracle that proves true, while they overlook the more numerous instances in which the oracles have failed. With regard to the Israelites, their whole history shews, that they had too little esteem and relish of the chaste and pure worship of the true God, and were inflamed with the love of idolatry, on account of its licentious rites, and the indulgence it allowed to their lusts. This made them an easy prey to the delusion of false prophets, and is the ground of the frequent warnings against them in Scripture. Moses here puts the case as strongly as possible, when he tells them: " Suppose that a Pa-
" gan prophet or diviner should propose some pro-
" digy or extraordinary appearance, as a proof of
" the interposition of a false god, and an indication
" of futurity; and that the event should correspond
" to the prophecy; do not on this account hastily
" conclude, that there is any thing supernatural or
" miraculous in the case; neither expect that the true
" God should interpose * in an extraordinary manner
" at every turn, to prevent such occurrences as these;
" which he will permit for the trial and discovery of
" your temper. If doubtful appearances and lucky
                              " conjectures

---

* For such purposes God might on some great occasions interpose, " He frustrateth the tokens of the liars, and maketh diviners mad." Isaiah xliv. 25. See Psalm xxxi. 10.

" conjectures ferve you as reafons to defert his wor-
" fhip; this will be a full proof
" oufly difal
" ply he dev
" minion o   all
" the g   ) and
" laid you a   obli-
" gations to his worfhip, and fervi   mofe ftu-
" pendous a d underiable mirac'   ch accom-
" plifhed your deliverance from the bondage of
" Egypt."

From this view of the paffage, it appears, that Mofes does not make the fuppofition, of a prophet's
working real miracles in the name of the Pagan deities; nor require the Ifraelites to difregard fuch works,
on account of the abfurdity of the doctrine they are
defigned to atteft. Nor the moft diftant intimation
is given, that we are in any cafe to make a prophet's
doctrine, the ftandard whereby to judge of the divinity of his miracles. He is here guarding the Ifraelites againft the pretended divination and prodigies
of the Pagans. And the reafon he affigns, why they
fhould not fuffer themfelves to be feduced by prodigies and ftrange events, or by the accidental completion of a conjectural prediction, into the worfhip of
falfe gods, is, that the claims of Jehovah had been
already eftablifhed, and confequently theirs confuted,
by miracles; the validity of his claims neceffarily in-
ferring the falfehood of theirs. It is to miracles
alone,

† See below, ch. 3. fect. 5.

alone, that Mofes here appeals; by this fingle proof
he decides the queftion concerning the fole right of
Jehovah, to the worfhip of the Ifraelites. And his
reafoning is defigned to prove, that the fign or wonder of the prophet, who announced any other god,
than the God of Ifrael, could not be really fupernatural. In thofe early ages, when eclipfes, meteors,
earthquakes, inundations, and all the uncommon phenomena of nature, were reprefented by Pagan impoftors or enthufiafts, as the productions of their fictitious deities; how could Mofes more effectually
guard the Ifraelites againft thefe frauds and delufions,
than by reminding them, how fully Jehovah had afferted and vindicated his fole dominion over · the
whole natural world; and thus fhewing them, that
the events in queftion were the effects of that order
and difpofition, which God had eftablifhed at the beginning?

II.

We are in the next place to examine that warning of the Chriftian lawgiver to his difciples, " There
" fhall arife falfe Chrifts and falfe prophets, and fhall
" fhew great figns and wonders, infomuch that (if it
" were poffible) they fhall deceive the very elect *."

Here our Lord has (very erroneoufly, as I apprehend) been fuppofed to make his gofpel, (juft as
Mofes in the foregoing paffages was fuppofed to make
his law,) the criterion whereby to judge of the divinity

* Mat. xxiv. 24. Mark xiii. 22.

nity of miracles; and to direct men to confider the like works as marks of impofture when wrought by others, which he had appealed to, when wrought by himfelf, as indubitable figns of a divine miffion. But if miracles proved *him* to be the Meffiah; muft they not equally eftablifh the claim of any *other* perfon to that character? Were it poffible, they fhould be wrought in confirmation of oppofite claims; they would mutually deftroy each other. The wonders here fpoken of, are emphatically ftyled *great ;* and the end propofed by them, was the deliverance of God's people; which, to a Jew at leaft, could not appear to be an end unworthy of a divine interpofition. And therefore, fuppofing the miracles to have been really performed by falfe Chrifts and falfe prophets; the Jews muft either have admitted their claims inforced by great miracles, or have rejected thofe of every other. At leaft, might it not have been expected, that our Lord, to prevent the deception of his followers, would have laid down fome fure and perfpicuous rule, to enable them to judge, in what cafes *great* miracles are proofs of a *divine* agency, and when they are evidences only of a *diabolical* one? When a prophet has eftablifhed his own miffion by miracles; is his barely *foretelling* thofe of his rivals and oppofers, a fufficient criterion whereby to judge of their author? Would it not rather be a confeffion, that miracles are no certain figns of a divine miffion?

But our Lord is not here warning his difciples againft admitting the *divinity* of unqueftionable miracles, but againft haftily crediting the *truth* of thofe

pretences

pretences to miracles, which would be made by the persons of whom he is speaking. This appears, as well from the natural import of this prophecy in its original language; as from the history and character of the impostors, to whom it refers. Christ does not say, " False prophets shall *shew* * (that is, really *exhibit* and *perform*) great signs;" but (as the original word should have been rendered) " they will GIVE †," that is, appeal to, promise or undertake to produce, such signs; using the very language of the Jewish legislator explained above, who represents a prophet as *giving* ‡ (that is, proposing or appealing to)

* Had this been our Lord's meaning, he would have expressed it, as Josephus does in the passages cited below, (p. 210. note †. and p. 211. note †.) by the word δείξειν.

† This is the most natural sense of δωσουσι. Dr. Lardner, in a letter which is now before me, after taking notice, that although Whitby, Le Clerc, and other commentators allow, great things were done by the impostors, referred to by Christ in this prediction, yet that no miracles are ascribed to them by Josephus; adds, " I shall be obliged to Mr. Farmer, if he " will let me know his solution of this difficulty." In compliance with this request, I communicated to him my explication of the word δωσουσι, which I had never met with in any writer, and which intirely solves the particular difficulty proposed by Dr. Lardner, as well as removes the general objection against the authority of miracles, which unbelievers have hitherto raised from this passage. The doctor in his reply expresses himself in the following terms : " Your answer is very " agreeable, and will be of use to me." Accordingly he inserted it in his *Testimonies*, V. 1. p. 67.

‡ Deut. xiii. 1. in the Septuagint.

to) a fign or wonder, whether it did or did not come to pafs. The phrafe itfelf does not determine, whether the fign given, be it the promife of a miracle, or the prediction of an event, would be confirmed or confuted, when it was expected to be accomplifhed. It might be engaged for, and yet never be exhibited. And every circumftance of the prophecy contained in this context, ferves to prove, that the perfons here foretold would only undertake to fhew great figns, without performing what they undertook. But I fhall argue chiefly from the hiftory of thofe perfons, in whofe appearance and pretenfions this prophecy received its completion, and which muft be allowed to be the beft key to the interpretation of this prophetic warning.

Our Saviour here refers to thofe impoftors, who fprung up in Judea in the interval between the delivery of this prophecy, and the deftruction of Jerufalem. As early as the 45th or 46th year of the Chriftian æra, one Theudas, who called himfelf a prophet, perfuaded great numbers to follow him to Jordan, by telling them that he would, by his own command, divide the river : but this confident boaft ended in his own deftruction, as well as that of many of his followers *. About nine or ten years afterwards, Judea fwarmed with thefe deceivers, who led the people into the wildernefs, and *undertook to exhibit divine wonders* †. One who came out of Egypt promifed to caufe the walls of Jerufalem to fall down ; but the deluded multitudes who followed him were

O   difperfed

* Jofephus Antiq. l. 20. c. 5. § 1.

difperfed or deftroyed by the Romans, " fuffering"
(to ufe the language of Jofephus) " the juft punifh-
" ment of their folly §." The nearer the Jews were
to deftruction, fo much the more did thefe impoftors
multiply, and fo much the more eafy credit did they
find with thofe, who were willing to have their miferies foothed by hope. Even during the conflagra-
tion of the temple, a falfe prophet encouraged the
people with miraculous figns of deliverance * : nor
did the total deftruction of the city cure this madnefs;
as appears by the conduct of an impoftor at Cyrene †,
who " promifed to fhew them figns and appari-
" tions."

There is the moft perfect correfpondence between
the impoftors defcribed by Jofephus, and thofe foretold by Chrift, in the following particulars. 1. According to Jofephus, their appearance both preceded
and accompanied the deftruction of Jerufalem ; and
by Chrift alfo they were diftinctly foretold both as
the diftant ‡ figns and fore-runners, and as the nearer ‖ and more immediate attendants, of that great
and awful cataftrophe. 2. Our Saviour defcribes
them as feverally affuming the double character of a
prophet and of the Meffiah : and according to the
Jewifh hiftorian, they both pretended to infpiration
                                                        and

§ Jofeph. Ant. c. 8. § 6. & de B. J. l. 2. c. 13. § 4, 5.

* Jofeph. de B. J. l. 6. c. 5. § 2.

† Id. ib. l. 7. c. 11. § 1. σημεῖα ἡ φάσματα δείξειν ὑπισχνέμενος.

‡ Mat. xxiv. 5.   Mark xiii. 6.   Luke xxi. 8.

‖ Mat. xxiv. 24.   Mark xiii. 22.

and prophecy ¶, and undertook the peculiar office of the Meffiah *, the deliverance of God's people from their enemies. 3. " They fhall give" (or undertake to exhibit) " great figns and wonders," fays the prophecy: and the hiftory relates the fact in perfectly correfponding language, " They *promifed* to fhew or " exhibit evident wonders and figns †." 4. Does our Saviour fay, that by their confident promifes of miracles, they would *deceive many* ‡ of the unbelieving Jews, and *the very elect,* or *Chriftians themfelves* ‖, *were that poffible;* that is, could this be well fuppofed of perfons, who certainly knew that the Meffiah was already come? Jofephus informs us that thefe impoftors drew away vaft multitudes after § them; and that *under pretence of divine infpiration,* they raifed the enthufiafm of the people to a degree of *madnefs* **. 5. The very places of their appearance are the fame in the prophecy, as in the hiftory; " the

O 2 " defart

¶ As they ftyled themfelves prophets, fo they profeffed to act προσχήματι θεασμῷ, " under pretence of a divine afflatus." Jofeph, de B. J. l. 2. c. 13. § 4.

* Luke xxiv. 21. et Grot. in loc.

† Δείξειν γὰρ ἔφασαν ἐναργῆ τέρατα κỳ σημεῖα. Jofeph. Ant. l. 20. c. 8. § 6. This language of Jofephus ferves both to explain and verify our Saviour's prediction, fo as to remove all reafonable doubt concerning either its meaning or truth.

‡ Matth. xxiv. 5.

‖ V. 24. compared with Rom. xvi. 13. Coll. iii. 12. 1 Theff. i. 4.

§ On one occafion he mentions fix thoufand; B. J. l. 6. c. 5. § 2. on another thirty thoufand; l. 2. c. 13. § 5.

** Δαιμονᾶν ἀνέπειθον. Id. ib. § 4.

" defart or wilderne fs,and the fecret chambers or
" places of fecurity in the city*." 6. If our Saviour calls them *deceivers*, and fuppofes *all* their pretences (and confequently their pretences to miracles, as
well as to the Meffiahfhip) to be founded in *falfehood :*
Jofephus calls them by the fame name †, and reprefents them as utterly difappointing all the promifes
they had made to their followers, and every expectation
they had raifed. Now, if no miracles were actually
performed by thefe impoftors; it is great weaknefs
in Chriftians to affirm, that any were foretold by
Chrift; as it is virtually branding him as a falfe prophet. But in the fenfe of the prediction affigned
above, it received the moft perfect accomplifhment
in the conduct and appearance of the Jewifh impoftors, who only pretended to miracles. And confidering how backward the Jewifh Chriftians themfelves were, to give up all hope of deliverance from
their fubjection to the Romans; it was an inftance
of the wifdom and goodnefs of our Saviour, to fore-
warn them againft trufting to the fallacious promifes
of perfons, who affirmed confidently that they were
divinely raifed up to accomplifh fuch a deliverance;
and by confiding in whom, the infatuated Jews were
deceived and deftroyed beyond all recovery or redemption.

III.

---

* Mat. xxiv. 26. Jofeph. Ant. l. 20. c. 8. § 6. et B. J.
l. 2. c. 13. § 4. et l. 6. c. 5. § 2.

† Πλάνοι γὰρ ἄνθρωποι ἰ ἀπατιῶνες. B. J. l. 2. c. 13. § 4. Seq
alfo Antiq. l. 20. c. 8. § 6.

III.

All the falfe teachers in the apoftolic age, whether they rejected or corrupted Chriftianity, are reprefented as deftitute of fupernatural gifts.

With regard even to the true apoftles of Chrift, and others who really performed miracles; thefe works could not be applied by them to any other purpofe, than the confirmation of the miffion and doctrines of Chrift; inafmuch as they were always performed by his immediate power, in profeffed atteftation of his authority, and not without the actual exercife of faith in his name, at the time of their performance. How then could real miracles be performed, in oppofition to the claims or genuine doctrines of Chrift, by falfe apoftles? When St. Paul fays, " We can do nothing againft the truth * ;" does not this language imply, that no miracles could be wrought in atteftation of falfehood? He, threatens his oppofers at Corinth, with coming to them in a fhort time, that † " he might know, not the fpeech " (the eloquence) of them that were puffed up, but " the (miraculous) power ;" with the want of which, it is evident, he here upbraids them. He adds, " For " the kingdom of God is not in word, but in " power ;" it is erected and fupported by the immediate exertions of omnipotence : language that plainly intimates, that his oppofers were not imme-

O 3   diately

---

* 2 Cor. xiii. 8.

† 1 Cor. iv. 19, 20. ch. v. 4.

I

diately commiffioned to publifh the gofpel by God, becaufe he did not fupport their claim by miracles. The power of miracles he elfewhere calls " the fign of an apoftle * ;" and on a ftill different occafion, he thus defcribes and diftinguifhes himfelf, " He that " worketh miracles amongft you †." could miracles then be common both to him and his opponents ? He warns the Corinthians againft giving him occafion to exercife his miraculous power in their punifhment: " What will ye ? fhall I come unto you with a rod ?" This is not the language of a perfon expecting miracles to be oppofed by miracles. Nay, he reprefents the leaders of the oppofite party as fupporting themfelves wholly by artifice and fraud: " ‡ Such are falfe " apoftles, deceitful workers (or labourers in the " gofpel ‖) transforming themfelves into the apoftles " of Chrift. And no marvel, for Satan himfelf is " transformed into an angel of light." It may be doubted, whether St. Paul is here fpeaking of any transformation of Satan, in the literal fenfe of the word : for the falfe apoftles did not in this fenfe change themfelves into the apoftles of Chrift, or af- fume their *external fhape and form.* But the falfe apoftles here referred to, *pretended* to preach *gratis ;* which is what St. Paul really did at Corinth : and this groundlefs pretence was the fole foundation of their

* 2 Cor. xii. 12.
† Gal. iii. 2, 5.
‡ 2 Cor. xi. 13, 14.
‖ Locke upon the place.

their claim to the apoftolical character. To prevent the Corinthians from being deceived by fuch or any other fpecious appearances or difguifes, he reminds them, that the very worft characters might eafily affume the outward femblance of virtue; that there was not any *temptation* *, even of the moft *infernal kind*, which did not ftrive to conceal its deformity, and affume an alluring and *celeftial* form. It is poffible, however, that St. Paul may here refer to an opinion, common amongft the Heathens, that evil fpirits could render themfelves vifible at pleafure, and affume the appearance of gods and demons †. Nor is it neceffary to fuppofe, that the apoftle is here delivering his own opinion; he may be barely illuftrating his argument, by a commonly received fentiment concerning evil fpirits ‡.

O 4

Both

* Dr. Doddridge upon the place.

† Porphyry (de Abftinent. 1. 2. § 39, 40.) fpeaking of fpiritual beings, and evil demons in particular, fays, " All thefe " are naturally invifible to men ; but they make themfelves " vifible at pleafure, change their forms, and perfonate the " gods." Apuleius (in Apol. Socrat.) fays, At enim Pythagoricos mirari oppido folitos, fi quis fe negaret unquam vidiffe drœmonem. See Jamblichus, fect. 2. c. 3. and Porphyry cited below, ch. 4. fect. 2. article 2.

‡ Thus our Saviour draws a comparifon between the Jews, and " the fpirits who walk through dry places ;" and the Pfalmift fpeaks of the " deaf adder that ftops her ear to the voice of the charmers," (perfons who ufed forbidden arts, Deut. xviii. 11.) with regard to which the authors of the Univerfal Hiftory obferve, " There is no more occafion to underftand it literal-
" ly,

Both Paul and Peter reprefent the falfe teachers as feducing their followers, not by miracles, but by *fair fpeeches*, and by a condefcenfion to mens criminal paffions *. Jude defcribes them as " not having the fpirit †;" and John brands all their pretenfions as impofture, " Thou haft tried them which fay they " are apoftles, and are not; and haft found them " liars ‡." He lays it down as un univerfal maxim, " Every fpirit" (or pretender to a fpiritual and divine afflatus) " that confeffeth not that Jefus Chrift " is come in the flefh, is not of God ‖." And Paul in like manner declares, " that no man fpeaking by " the fpirit of God, calleth Jefus accurfed ¶." Neverthelefs, becaufe fuch oppofers of Chriftianity as thefe apoftles fpeak of, could not be infpired by *God;* it has hence been inferred, that they were enabled to work miracles by the *devil.* But the former does by no means infer the latter. To underftand thefe paffages we muft recollect, that John moft certainly,

---

" ly, than if he had compared an evil tongue to the voice of a " fyren, the claws of an harpy, the eyes of a bafilifk, or any " other fabulous creature." V. 3. p. 491. 8vo ed. The words of the Pfalmift, however, are differently interpreted by others. See the learned Mr. Merrick's annotations on Pfalm lviii. 4, 5.

* Rom. xvi. 18. 1 Cor. iv. 9. Col. ii. 4, 8. 2 Pet. ii. 18.

† V. 19.

‡ Rev. ii. 2.

‖ 1 John iv. 3.

¶ 1 Cor. xii. 3.

tainly, and Paul * poffibly, refers to the Jewifh antichrifts †, fome of whom affumed to themfelves the
character of the Meffiah, and all of whom oppofed
the claims of Jefus; and did it under the pretence of
a *divine* afflatus and infpiration. Now, fince thofe
who denied Jefus to be the Meffiah, pretended to be
prophets of the true God, (herein differing from the
idolatrous prophet mentioned by Mofes ‡); the apoftles direct their fellow Chriftians to conclude, that
fuch pretences muft be falfe; for this felf-evident
reafon, that God cannot contradict himfelf. Since
Chriftians allowed, that God had borne teftimony to
Jefus, it was impoffible he fhould ever bear teftimony
againft him. As to any intercourfe with *evil* fpirits,
or affiftance from them, thefe prophets did not pretend to it; nor do the apoftles charge them with it;
but

* It is immaterial to our prefent purpofe, whether St. Paul
refers to the Jewifh antichrifts, or to the unbelieving Jews in
general, who had long taught, that the Spirit of God could
reft on none but on thofe of their own nation, and ftill pretended to fome of his gifts. The apoftle therefore with great propriety here reminds Chriftians of two felf-evident truths:—
" that no man fpeaking by the Spirit of God, calleth Jefus"
(one fo highly approved of God!) " accurfed;" and " that no
" man can fay that Jefus is the Lord," (or affert and maintain
Chrift's divine authority,) " but by the Holy Ghoft." Does
not this language imply, that all genuine miracles proceed
from the fpirit of God?

† See what was obferved above in the explication of Mat.
xxiv. 24. and compare Whitby on 1 John iv. 1, 2.

‡ Deut. xiii. 1.

but refolve their pretenfions into human delufion and forgery, as we have already feen.

IV.

St. Paul's prophecy * concerning the man of fin, " whofe coming is after the working of Satan †, with " all power, and figns, and lying wonders‡;" though frequently urged to fhew, that the papal hierarchy was to be fupported by real miracles, proves the very contrary. Whoever confiders the nature of the papal empire, (that moft flagitious and daring ufur‑ pation on the government of God, and all the valuable rights of mankind!) will readily admit, that if ever the devil had a hearty zeal for any caufe, it muft be for this; and that he would have exerted his utmoft power for its fupport. Neverthelefs the apoftle, inftead of allowing that popery would have the advantage of *true* miracles, affirms that the coming of the man of fin was to be " with all power, and figns, " and wonders of a lie ‖;" that is, " with lying, or " fictitious

---

* 2 Theff. ii. 9, 10.

† That this phrafe, *the working of Satan* or an adverfary, does not imply a *miraculous* agency, appears from the ufe of it, Ephef. ii. 2.

‡ Whoever compares this paffage with Heb. ii. 4. will find the fame terms applied both to the miracles of popery and Chriftianity; and confequently will be forced to maintain, that they are both *equal*, unlefs the latter alone were genuine, and the former counterfeit.

‖ This is the true rendering of the original words, ἐν πάσῃ δυνάμει

" fictitious power, and figns, and wonders." The apoftle docs not fay, that the wonders are wrought with an intention to deceive; but that the wonders themfelves are a lie, the fole effect of falfehood and impofture. The church of Rome lays claim to a miraculous power, glories in it as a mark of the true church * ; and from hence infers the validity of her pretenfions. Many learned proteftants have allowed in part the truth of this claim, and admitted that fome real miracles have been performed in the Roman church. But the infpired apoftle brands them all as deceitful tricks, and fabulous legends. Such, many of the beft attefted are allowed to be, by the members of the Roman communion †; and fuch

with

δυνάμει κỳ σημείοις κỳ τέρασι ψεύδες. The word, *lie*, refers equally to all the preceding terms, and ought not to have been limited to the laft. That " the power, and figns, and wonders of a lie," denote " lying" or " fictitious power, figns and wonders," by a ufual hebraifm; appears from Deut. xxxii. 20. 2 Sam. xii. 15. Pf. v. 6. Luke xvi. 6. Ephef. ii. 2. ch. iv. 24. Col. i. 3 ; and from the context alfo, where the like form of fpeech is ufed. " The man of fin" denotes a notorioufly finful man: and the deceivablenefs of unrighteoufnefs fignifies unrighteous deceptions. Nay, in the very place in queftion, the prefent tranflation renders " wonders of a lie," " lying wonders."

* Undecima nota eft gloria miraculorum. Bellarmin. de notis ecclefiæ, l. 4. c. 14.

† They confefs many even of thofe miracles, which were attefted by witneffes upon oath, to be mere impoftures. Maraccius, fpeaking of certain bones, which were miftaken for thofe of fome eminent faints, fays, Vix credi poteft, quot ftatim miracula

with equal reafon we may fafely pronounce them all.
It is not therefore the power of miracles, (as fome
maintain *) but *the making falfe pretences to it*, that
St. Paul here (and elfewhere †) affigns as one of the
characteriftics

racula de iis in vulgus emanaverint, quæ etiam adjuratis tefti-
bus confirmabantur. Et tamen nullum hic erat, nec effe po-
terat, verum miraculum. Prodr. pars 2. Melchior Canus com-
plains, that the lives of the philofophers, and the hiftories of
the Cefars, are written by Laertius and Suetonius with greater
regard to truth, than the lives of the faints by the Catholics.
And fpeaking of *the golden legend*, he fays, it contains for the
moft part, rather monfters of miracles, than true miracles. O-
ther learned papifts have made the like complaints, as may be,
feen in Geddes's Tracts, V. iii. tract 2. p. 49. Even the miracles afcribed to the miffionaries of the Roman church in In-
dia, where they are moft wanted, are denied by their graveft
writers, Hofpinian de Origin. Jefuitar. p. 330. Middleton's
prefat. Dif. to his Letter from Rome, p. 97. and Acofta de
procuranda Indorum falute, cited by the Criterion, p. 77, I
add, that whenever any one of the orders of the Roman church
endeavours to fupport its peculiar tenets by fupernatural works;
the other orders feldom fail to detect the cheat, or to treat it
with all imaginable contempt. Will any one undertake, to
produce one popifh miracle, which is either more credible in
its nature, or more ftrongly attefted; than thofe which learned papifts themfelves have condemned as impudent falfehoods?

* " Admitting (fays a very learned writer) that any of the
" Romifh miracles were undeniable matters of fact;—yet I
" know not what the Bifhop of Rome would gain by it, but a
" better title to be thought antichrift." Bifhop Newton's
Differtations on the Prophecies, V. 2. p. 279, and Vol. 3. p.
273.

† See 1 Tim. iv. 1, 2. explained above, ch. 3. fect. 1. p.
111.

characteriftics of the man of fin ; and by which he is remarkably diftinguifhed from Mohammed and other impoftors, to whom this prophecy has been improperly applied.

· V.

The papacy feems to be farther charaterifed in the Revelation of St. John *, " He doeth great won-
" ders (or figns †) fo that he maketh fire come down
" from heaven on the earth, in the fight of men ;
" and he deceiveth them that dwell on the earth, by
" means of thofe miracles (or figns) which he has
" power to do in the fight of the beaft."

Whatever be the true fenfe of this obfcure paffage, it ought not to have any meaning affigned it, repugnant to the numerous more plain declarations of the divine word. If the predition of St. Paul which we laft examined, brands all the miracles of popery as *forgeries* ; this of St. John cannot allow them to be *realities.* Befides, there is this material difference in the two cafes : the prophecy of St. Paul is delivered in much plainer terms, not under the cover of fymbolical reprefentations ; but the revelations made to St. John, were in the way of *vifion*, in which there was frequent ufe of *emblems* and *fymbols*, with which we find the whole Apocalypfe abounds. And therefore

* Ch. xiii. 13, 14.

† Σημεῖα. The fame word is ufed in the original in both verfes, though rendered by our tranflators *wonders* in the 13th, and *miracles* in the 14th verfe.

fore it is more natural to give a figurative, than a literal conftruction to this language of St. John.
" The making fire to come down from heaven,"
may poffibly refer to the *anathemas* and *excommunications* of the Roman church, ftyled the *thunders* of the
Vatican, which are fhocking imprecations for fire
from heaven, and were thought to expofe men to its
hotteft vengeance ; (as a fymbol of which they ufed
in pronouncing their excommunications, to fwing
down a lighted torch from above *) and which have
actually fet whole kingdoms in a flame, being inforced by princes and perfons in authority, who in the
prophetic language are reprefented by *the heavens*.
On either, or both thefe accounts, but more efpecially the former, the fire may be faid to come down
from thence.   The *great figns* he is here faid to perform, include thefe and other amazing artifices ufed
by the pope, to perfuade an ignorant and credulous
laity, that the vengeance of heaven will be armed a-
gainft all his oppofers. The fuccefs of thefe frauds,
and the credit they would gain with the members of
the Roman communion, may be intimated in their
being fpoken of as done, " in the fight of men," and
in " the fight of the beaft."   However this may be,
I can fee no ground to conclude, that amongft the
figns here referred to, we are to include true miracles †;
                                                                both

---

* Sir If. Newton, in his Obfervations on the Apocalypfe, p.
319.

† The word, σημεῖα, denotes figns and tokens, even though
they are not miraculous ; as we fhewed above on Deut. xiii.

both becaufe the word is applied to other e-
vents; and the fign here particularly fpecified, " the
" making fire to come down from heaven," if underftood figuratively, agreeably to the ftyle of St.
John's prophecy, was not miraculous. Moreover true
miracles are never reprefented as means of *delufion*,
but of conviction.

We have now diftinctly examined the feveral paffages of Scripture, which are generally thought, to
allow the claims of falfe prophets to infpiration and
miracles; and, I hope, it appears, either that thofe
paffages do not refer to any fuch claims, or exprefsly
deny their validity. Whether thefe prophets fpoke
in the name of the true God, or in the name of falfe
gods, the Scriptures reprefent them as totally deftitute of fupernatural knowledge and power, and exprefsly refolve all their pretences to them, into human
artifice and falfehood *. This has been already
fhewn,

1; and it is in the Apocalypfe applied to furprifing events, ch.
xii. 1, 2. ch. xv. 1. There may be a reference in this chapter
to thofe ftrange appearances, (fuch as the bowing of c... .es,
the fhaking and ftirring their hands and feet, motions per... rin-
ed by fecret fprings; and a thoufand other things of the like
kind;) which though mere human artifices, are reprefented as
the effects of the divine power. The fraud practifed by the
Roman clergy with regard to thefe things, was expofed in
fome remarkable inftances at the Reformation. See Burnet's
Hiftory of the Reform. V. 1. p. 232.

* Some of our lateft and moft approved writers upon miracles affirm, that God will not fuffer falfe prophets to work miracles, " fo as to lay men under a neceffity of being deceived,
" or without giving honeft men plain evidence of the impof-
" ture."

shewn, both with respect to their pretended miracles and prophecies. I will here add a few passages, which more immediately refer to the latter. Moses ascribes them to *the arrogance* or *presumption* * of the prophet. Jeremiah calls them, " the vision of his own heart†," not the supernatural suggestions of the devil. And Ezekiel describes the false prophets, as prophesying " out of their own hearts, and following their own " spirit, and as having seen nothing ‡."

Before

" ture." See Mr. Hallet on miracles, and Dr. Benson's Life of Christ, p. 202, 203, 219, 220, 222, 234, 235, 236. The Scriptures seem to me to deny the power of false prophets, to perform miracles under any circumstances whatever. And indeed if " the whole nature of miracles lay in being such " things, as are above the power of men," (as the doctor affirms, p. 236, compare p. 204;) if they may be performed by false prophets, when they do not necessarily subject honest men to delusion; and if performed by such prophets, are to have no regard paid to them, (p. 202;) how are they, in their own nature, signs of *a divine* interposition, and a divine mission? Besides, there could be very little danger of any man's being deceived by the miracles of a false prophet, if he was clearly and certainly persuaded, that these works are no distinguishing test of a divine interposition; (as was shewn above, p. 88.) There would, in this case, be more probability of mens rejecting the miracles of a true prophet; from an apprehension, that infinite wisdom would not employ ambiguous proofs of a divine mission.

* Deut. xviii. 22. " The prophet has spoken it presumptuously;" per superbiam vel tumorem animi sui.

† Ch. xxxiii. 16. In ch. xiv. 14, he says, " They prophesy unto you a false vision,—and the deceit of their heart."

‡ Ezek. xiii. 2, 3. See also Zechar. xiii. 4.

Before we proceed any farther; let us recollect how far we are advanced in examining into the fenfe of Scripture, concerning the author of miracles, whether of power or knowledge. We have attempted to fhew, that the Scripture denies the ability of performing any miracles, to angels, whether good or evil; to the fpirits of departed men; to the Heathen deities; to magicians, who pretended to an intercourfe with them; and laftly, to all falfe prophets, upon whatever principles they grounded their pretenfions. Now thefe are the only agents, who have ever been conceived as capable of working miracles, either in oppofition to God, or without an immediate commiffion from him. And confequently the Scripture, by denying the miraculous power of all thefe, does, in effect, deny, that any fingle miracle has ever been performed without the immediate interpofition of God. Farther evidence of this important point will occur in the following fections.

P S E C T.

S E C T. V.

The Scriptures reprefent the one true God, as the fole creator and
fovereign of the world, which he governs by fixed and inva-
riable laws. To him they appropriate all miracles, and urge
them as demonftrations of his Divinity and fole dominion over
nature, in oppofition to the claims of all other fuperior beings.
The ancient controverfy between the prophets of God and ido-
laters, ftated.

IN direct oppofition to the numerous fictitious deities of the Pagans, whether they were fuppofed
to poffefs an original, or only a delegated power and
authority; the prophets of the true God affirm, that
he alone is God : " He is Jehovah, and there is no
" God befides him : He is Jehovah, and there is
" none elfe *." The Heathens maintained the exiftence of local† deities, whofe power and prefence were
circumfcribed within narrow bounds. Ariftotle very
juftly obferves, " that it was by no means agreeable
" to the fyftem of religion eftablifhed by law, to fup-
" pofe God to be one moft powerful and excellent
" being ; the gods in that fyftem being mutually bet-
" ter one than another, as to many things ‡." Accordingly

---

* Deut. iv. 35. If. xlv. 5, 6, 18, 21, 22. compare ch. xliii.
10—13. ch. xliv. 8. 2 Sam. vii. 22.

† 1 Kings xx. 23.

‡ When arguing againft Zeno, Ariftotle fays, εἴπερ ἅπαντα
ἐπικράτισον

cordingly we find, that as each nation * had its chief
deity; fo feveral of the gods held by the fame people were each of them fupreme in their refpective
provinces, and independent of the reft. One was
fupreme ruler over *the heavens,* another over *the air*
and *winds,* and others ftill different from thefe over
the fea and *earth* and *hell.* But the language of revelation is, " Jehovah he is God in heaven above,
" and upon the earth beneath, there is none elfe †:"
he exifts and operates in all places, without limits,
and without controul ‡. To underftand this language,
it is neceffary to recollect, that the word, God, in
Scripture denotes a governor or king; nor is more
included in the general idea, than authority and dominion. Mofes is called *a god to Pharoah* ‖; becaufe
he was appointed to controul and govern him. Judges and kings are frequently called *gods* with refpect
to their fubjects, over whom they rule ¶. And therefore when the facred writers affert, that there is no

P 2   other

ἐπικράτισον τὸν Θεὸν λαμβάνει, τῦτο δυνατώτατον καὶ βέλτισον λέγων, ὐ
δοκεῖ δὲ τῦτο κατὰ τὸν νόμον, ἀλλὰ πολλὰ κρείτῦς εἶναι ἀλλήλων οἱ Θεοί.
De Xenophane, Zenone, et Gorgia, c. 4. inter por. V. 2. p.
841, 842. ed. Paris.

* Judges xi. 24.

† Deut. iv. 39.

‡ 1 Kings viii. 27. Pf. cxxxix. 1—12. If. xliii. 13.

‖ Exod. vii. 1.

¶ Exod. xxi. 6. ch. xxii. 9, 28. Pf. lxxxii. 1, 6. Compare John x. 34, 35.

other God but Jehovah ; they mean, that there is no superior being befides him, who has any power or dominion over mankind.   Had there been other fuperior beings, who were vefted with power over the human race ; the Scripture, we have feen'*, would have allowed, that they were our gods or rulers.

The Heathens either believed the eternity † of the world, or afcribed its origin, and the generation of animals ‡, to elementary and fidereal deities. According to the eftablifhed fyftem of theology, the world was *begotten,* not created ; at once *the offspring* and *the parent* of gods, and *itfelf* a god ‖.   On the other hand, the facred penmen afcribe its creation to the fole operation (or rather to the almighty fiat ¶) of the one eternal Jehovah : " He made the fea, his hand " formed the dry land **. He formed the light, and " created darknefs ††.   He created the heavens, and " the earth, and all the hoft of them ‡‡ ;" that is, the

whole

---

* Ch. 3. fect. 2. p. 237, 238.

† Diodorus Siculus, p. 6. ed. Rhodomani.

‡ See above, p. 174.

‖ See above, 111—114. What we call the creation or formation of the world, was in the Pagan fyftem its *generation,* or a *cofmogony.* And their cofmogony or generation of the world was *a theogony,* or *generation of gods.*

¶ Pf. xxxiii. 6, 9.   Pf. cxlviii. 5.   Gen. i. 3.

** Pf. xcv. 5.

†† If. xlv. 7.

‡‡ Gen. i. 1. ch. ii. 1. Pf. xxxiii. 6.

whole world, all the parts which compofe, and all the creatures that inhabit it, whatever divine attributes and operations might be foolifhly afcribed to any of them by the Heathens. God afferts his fole prerogative in fuch language as this: " I am Jeho-
" vah who maketh all things, who ftretcheth forth
" the heavens alone, who fpreadeth abroad the earth
" by myfelf *." This truth is often inculcated, with the exprefs defign of guarding the Ifraelites from wor-fhipping the objects of nature †.

To thefe falfe gods, and to demons the Heathens afcribed the government of the world, the direction of all human affairs, the calamities and profperity of perfons and nations. But the Scriptures celebrate Jehovah as the univerfal fovereign, who exercifes an abfolute dominion over all without any rival, without any co-adjutor or partner of his throne ; " I am Je-
" hovah, and befides me there is no Saviour.—There
" is none can deliver out of my hand : I will work,
" and who fhall let it ‡ ? I make peace, and create
" evil ‖." It was, indeed, the main defign of the Jewifh difpenfation, to convince the Ifraelites and the whole world, that as Jehovah created the world at firft, fo he referved the government of it in his own hands ; and that there was no fuperior invifible being whatever, befides Jehovah, on whofe favour, the

P 3   good

* If. xliv. 24.

† Deut. iv. 19. Jerem. xiv. 22.

‡ If. xliii. 11, 13.   ‖ Ch. xlv. 7.

good or evil ftate of their lives did in any degree depend.   This is the doctrine every where inculcated,
in direct oppofition to thofe who taught, that there
were invifible beings, who were the authors both of
bleffings and calamities to mankind.   The order of
the natural world is reprefented, as fixed " by his
" decree, which fhall not pafs away;" and governed by his laws " which fhall not be broken," by laws
" which he has eftablifhed for ever and ever *;" and
confequently which cannot be controuled by any authority, except that by which they were at firft ordained.   If you fay, that the allowing a liberty to
fuperior created intelligences to interpofe in human
affairs, is one of thofe very laws which God has ordained : I anfwer, that if they can do this of themfelves, and without an immediate commiffion from
God; then what the Scriptures affirm is not true;
there are other fuperior invifible beings befides God,
who can difpenfe both good and evil to mankind;
and the order of events in the natural world is *not*
fixed at all, but is dependent upon the pleafure of
thofe fuperior beings †.

With regard to miracles, or deviations from the
ordinary courfe of nature; the Scriptures refer them
to God as their author.   Nor do they afcribe them to
him *eminently*, as fome ‡ pretend ; but abfolutely *ap-*
propriate

---

* Pf. cxlviii. 6.   Pf. lxxxix. 37.   Pf. cxix. 90, 91.   Jerem.
xxxi. 35, 36. ch. xxxiii. 25.

† See above, ch. 2. fect. 3.

‡ Dr. Sykes on miracles, and others.

propriate them to him *alone.* Witnefs the fong of Mofes, " Who is like unto thee, O Jehovah, amongft " the gods? who is like unto thee,—doing won- " ders * ?" What words can more ftrongly deny to all other beings the power of working miracles, and challenge it as the fole prerogative of the true God, than the following paffages? " Bleffed be Jehovah " God, the God of Ifrael, who only doeth wondrous " things †. Thou art great, and doeft wondrous " things, thou art God alone ‡." Such language of- ten occurs, " Thou art the God that doeft wonders ‖. " To him who alone doeth great wonders §." When- ever the facred writers occafionally mention any par- ticular miracles, whether of power or knowledge; they affirm concerning every one of them feparately, what they do concerning all of them in general. Thus they affirm it to be the fole and exclufive pre- rogative of God, to raife the dead ¶, to open the eyes

P 4 of

---

* Exod. xv. 11. That by *wonders*, in this and the follow- ing paffages, we are to underftand miracles, appears from the connection in which the word is ufed. The miracles more e- fpecially referred to are thofe wrought in favour of the Ifrael- ites; concerning which Mofes declares, that all the annals of time could afford no inflance of a like nature, Deut. iv. 32— 36.

† Pf. lxxii. 18,

‡ Pf. lxxxvi. 10.

‖ Pf. lxxvii. 14.

§ Pf. cxxxvi. 4.

¶ Deut. xxxii. 39. 1 Sam. ii. 6. 2 Cor. i. 9.

of the blind *, to tread upon the waves of the sea †, to still the noise of its waves ‡, to reveal secret and distant transactions ‖, to foretel future events §, and to search the heart of man. These declarations of Scripture, though they are particularly levelled against the false pretences to prophecies and miracles amongst the Pagans, are no more to be reconciled with the notion of the devil's possessing a supernatural power, than with the opinion of any Heathen gods possessing that power. If any being whatever can perform miracles, besides God, it is not true that God alone can perform them.

As the Scriptures represent miracles as works peculiar to God; so they urge them as proofs of his sole Divinity, or of his claim to the distinguishing character of Jehovah. To give us a clearer idea of this very important point, we must look back to the first account of miracles. When Moses, on his being appointed God's ambassador to the people of Israel, and the court of Egypt, desired to be instructed by what title he should describe him; God was pleased to assume a name, which of all others was the most expressive of his nature, I AM, or JEHOVAH¶.

Both

---

* Pf. cxlvi. 8.

† Job ix. 8.

‡ Pf. lxv. 9.   Pf. cvii. 29.

‖ Dan. ii. 28, 29, 47.

§ If. xlii. 9. ch. xlv. 21. ch. xlvi. 9, 10.

¶ Exod. iii. 13, 14, 15. In the 13th verse what is commonly

Both thefe names are in fenfe the fame; and exprefs
" his eternal, underived and immutable exiftence
" and excellence *." They likewife affert this as his
fole prerogative; and therefore neceffarily imply
(what fome think they directly exprefs) " his giving
" being to all other things †," or his being the fovereign

ly tranflated, I AM THAT I AM, is rendered by Mr. Pur-
ver, I AM HE WHO AM. Accordingly God ordered Mofes to tell the Ifraelites, I AM has fent me unto you. Though
the word *ehjeh* be in the future, yet according to the genius of
the Hebrew tongue, it is applicable to the prefent tenfe.

* Eft autem hoc nomen, Ehjeh afcher Ehjeh, derivatum a
verbo hajah, quod fignificat effentiam vel exiftentiam. Maimon. Mor. Nevoc. p. 1. c. 63.

† Ainfworth and others are of opinion, that Jehovah is a
participle of hajah in *piel;* and that it does not only fignify *to
be,* but *to caufe to be.* Univerfal Hift. V. 3. p. 360, 361.
In the foregoing part of that note, p. 358, the learned authors
condemn our verfion for. rendering Jehovah by LORD, and
the LXX. for rendering it κύριος; though bifhop Beveridge
(V. 1. p. 111.) alledges, that κύριος comes from κύρω *to be,* as
Jehovah from hujah. The laft mentioned writer obferves, p.
112, that the word, Jehovah, is never ufed with any other ge-
nitive cafe after it, but *fabaoth,* though this occurs fo frequently. The title of Jehovah or LORD of hofts (or fabaoth) does
not denote *the God of battle;* as thofe affert it does, who would
degrade the God of Ifrael to a level with the Heathen god of
war, whofe peculiar province it was, to prefide over battles.
This very magnificent title is given to God, on account of his
being the creator and fovereign of all other beings; the monarch, not of fome particular people and province, but of the
whole univerfe. He created " the heavens, and the earth,
and all the hoft of them," Gen. ii. 1. " He is the former of
all

reign creator and abfolute lord of the univerfe. This was defigned to prevent both the Ifraelites and Egyptians, from degrading him to the level of the *tutelary* deities of the Pagans, (whofe influence was thought to be confined to a particular country and people;) and by afferting his proper diftinguifhing charaƈter, to deny the claims of all their gods to any fhare in the creation and government of the world. In direƈt oppofition to thefe falfe gods, mere fiƈtions of the human imagination, the God of Ifrael ftyles himfelf

all things,—the LORD of hofts is his name," Jerem. li. 19. ch. x. 16. " Thus faith Jehovah, who giveth the fun for a light by day,—the LORD of hofts is his name," Jerem. xxxi. 35. See ch. xxxii. 18, 19. If. xlii. 5. ch. xliv. 24. ch. xlv. 5. Dan. iv. 35. The Englifh reader fhould be reminded, that whenever LORD, in capital letters, occurs in our tranflation, Jehovah is ufed in the original, which I have generally retained in the paffages cited in the fequel.

After I had drawn up the preceding part of this note, I found, that the celebrated Le Clerc was of the fame fentiment with Ainfworth, with refpeƈt to the meaning and derivation of Jehovah; though the former declares, he had never met with it in any author. I will tranfcribe a part of his note on Exod. vi. 3. Dubium non eft quin vox ab הָיָה fuit derivetur, quo faƈtum ut fufpicarer Deum vocabulum יְהֹוָה fibi fumfiffe, non quod fua natura fit, adeoque æternitate gaudeat, fed quod efficiat ut res fint, quafi effet futurum Hiphil aut Pihel faciet ut fit. We may, however, allow, that the word, Jehovah, was only defigned to exprefs God's eternal and immutable exiftence, and to affert this as his fole prerogative; inafmuch as it neceffarily follows from hence, that all other beings owe their exiftence to his fovereign pleafure. And the miracles defigned to prove the former, ferve to afcertain the latter.

felf Jehovah *, " him who is †, and from whom all
" other beings are derived." This conftruction of
the word is confirmed by the fequel: God faid to
Mofes, " I am Jehovah: and I appeared unto Abra-
" ham, unto Ifaac, and unto Jacob, by the name (or
" under the character) of God ALMIGHTY; but by
" my name (or character of) JEHOVAH was I not
" known unto them ‡." God had called himfelf by
the name, Jehovah, to the Patriarchs ‖; and they had
invoked him by it: in what fenfe then was it unknown to them? Critics have fuppofed, that it refers
to God's giving being or life to his *promifes*, by their
actual accomplifhment §. But this feems a very groundlefs limitation of the word. Underftand it in its juft
latitude, and God will appear to fpeak to the following effect: " I took your fathers under my powerful
" protection,

* " I am Jehovah, that is my name, and my glory will I
" not give to another, neither my praife to graven images."
Ifaiah xlii. 8.

† As on other occafions he is ftyled the *living* God, in oppofition to *dead* men, whom the Heathens worfhipped as gods.

‡ Exod. vi. 3.

‖ Gen. xv. 7, 8. chap. xxvi. 24. ch. xxii. 14. ch. xxviii.
13.

§ Both Ainfworth and Le Clerc fuppofe, that the word, Jehovah, expreffes God's caufing his promifes to receive their
accomplifhment: but many of the paffages cited by the latter,
and particularly If. xlii. 5. ch. xlv. 5—7. Jerem. xxxi. 35,
fhew, that it muft be taken in a ftill more extenfive fenfe, and
that it expreffes his character as univerfal creator.

" protection, and granted them marks of my pecu-
" liar favour; hereby acting rather under the cha-
" racter of *their God,* than as *the one eternal Deity,*
" *and only sovereign of the universe.* And though
" your pious anceftors always entertained juft ideas
" of me as Jehovah; yet I did not make this my
" true character *known* * and *evident,* in the confpi-
" cuous manner I am now going to do. To your
" fathers I revealed myfelf chiefly by *private dreams*
" *and visions:* but now I shall fully vindicate and
" proclaim my eternal Divinity, and my boundlefs
" dominion, by the moft *public and stupendous mira-*
" *cles.*" It was neceffary to explain, what is included in the term, Jehovah; inafmuch as the miracles
of Mofes were defigned to prove, that this term was
appropriate to the God of Ifrael.

To the Ifraelites God commanded Mofes to fay,
" I AM hath fent me unto you; Jehovah, the God
" of your fathers appeared unto me †." Mofes was
farther inftructed to tell the Ifraelites, " Ye shall
" know, that I am Jehovah your God, which bring-
" eth you out from the burdens of the Egyptians ‡."
The miraculous means of their deliverance were defigned, as Mofes fays in exprefs terms, for the conviction

---

* *To know* often fignifies *to make known*: " I determined not
to know any thing amongft you, fave Jefus Chrift," that *is,*
this was what I determined to " make known amongft you,"
1 Cor. ii. 2. See alfo ch. viii. 3, and Locke upon it.

† Exod. iii. 14, 15.

‡ Exod. vi. 7.

viction of the Ifraelites, or " that they might know,
" that Jehovah he is God, and that there is none
" elfe befides him *." When Mofes went to Pharaoh, and told him that Jehovah, the God of Ifrael,
demanded the relcafe of his people; and the king of
Egypt afked, " Who is Jehovah," and faid, " I
know not Jehovah :" God declares to Mofes, " The
" Egyptians fhall know that I am Jehovah, when I
" ftretch forth mine hand upon Egypt, and bring
" out the children of Ifrael from amongft them †."
Nay, each particular miracle is frequently alledged as
a full demonftration of this grand point. God (by
his prophet) faid to Pharaoh, IN THIS (that is, by
turning the waters of the river into blood) " thou
fhalt know that I am Jehovah ‡." The miraculous
                                        plagues

---

* Deut. iv. 35. compare Exod. x. 1, 2. ch. xi. 7. 2 Sam.
vii. 22—24.

† Ch. v. 1, 2. ch. vii. 5. ch. ix. 14. ch. xiv. 4, 18, 25.

‡ Exod. vii. 17. In like manner Mofes promifed Pharaoh,
to remove the fecond plague, that of frogs, " that he might
" know there was none like unto Jehovah," (ch. viii. 10.) or
none befides him who could perform true miracles, (compare
ch. xv. 11.)—The fwarms of flies were fent upon Egypt, while
Gofhen was preferved from them, " to the end thou mayeft
know," (as God faid to Pharaoh) " that I am Jehovah, in
the midft of the earth," (ch. viii. 22.) or, " the fovereign of
" the whole earth, not of one particular diftrict only." The
metaphor, as Paulus Fagius obferves upon the place, is taken
a regibus, qui fedes fuas fere habent in mediis provinciis, ut
ex æquo illis profpicere poffint.—To the fame effect, it is faid,
the hail fhould be removed, that Pharaoh might know, " that
the earth is Jehovah's." ch. ix. 29.

plagues of Egypt were not defigned, merely or principally to accomplifh the deliverance of the Ifraelites
from the bondage of Egypt ; which might have been
effected with fewer (or without any vifible) deviations from the ordinary courfe of nature. The principal end which God had in view, was infinitely more
important, and the very fame with that which he
propofed by taking the Ifraelites to be his peculiar
people, viz. the manifeftation of himfelf to the world.
For it was not from any partial regards to them, that
they were at firft feparated from the reft of mankind, but to accomplifh the defigns of God's general providence, and (amongft other important
purpofes) to recover and preferve the knowlege of
the true God, and to propagate it amongft the Heathen nations, (and thereby to prepare the world for
the coming of Chrift.) The nations were already
funk into the groffeft idolatry, fuch as gave a fanction
to the fouleft crimes. Egypt was the parent and
nurfe of this idolatry. From hence it was propagat-
ed through many other nations. By their refidence
in this country, the Ifraelites themfelves *were defiled
with its idols**. . Jehovah, therefore, in his infinite
wifdom and goodnefs, was pleafed to accomplifh their
redemption, in a manner the moft proper to convince
them, and the Egyptians, and the other nations, of
the evil and folly of idolatry, and to make himfelf
known and adored as the only living God†.   Pharaoh

* Ezek. xx. 7. ch. xxiii. 2, 3. Jofh. xxiv. 14.
† See Exod. ix. 14, 16. ch. xi. 7. ch. xiv. 4, 18. and compare If. xix. 21. Pf. xxii. 27, 28.

raoh was preferved, after he deferved to have been cut off for. his oppreffion and impiety, that by the new wonders his obftinacy would occafion, " God's " name might be declared through all the earth *."

The

---

* Exod. ix. 16. Though the paffages cited above, are ful-ly fufficient to prove, that the refcue of the Ifraelites from their cruel bondage, was not (what too many have reprefented it) the whole defign of God in the punifhment of the Egyp-tians; and there can be no neceffity therefore of producing a-ny farther proofs of this point: yet I cannot forbear obferving, that what has been advanced upon it, feems to be confirmed by what God fays to Mofes, Exod. xii. 12. " I will fmite all "the firft born of the land of Egypt, both man and beaft: and " againft all the gods of Egypt I will execute judgment; I " am ·Jehovah." Some indeed think, that by gods we are here to underftand the *princes* and *rulers* of Egypt: but they weie very few in number, in comparifon with the multitudes who fuffered the lofs of their firft born. Others are of opinion, that God threatens the *idols* of Egypt here, (as he does elfe-where, If. xix. 1. Jerem. xliii. 13.) and that they fuffered fome fuch judgment as befel ·Dagon, 1 Sam. v. 3, 4. This however is not fupported by the hiftory. Why fhould we not underftand God as fpeaking concerning *the deities* of Egypt? Let it be confidered, that the miraculous judgments hitherto inflicted upon Pharaoh and the Egyptians, were the wifeft means that could be employed to convince them of the claims of Jehovah, and of the utter impotence of their own gods. For the Nile, the elements, and other objects of nature which they worfhipped, were themfelves employed by Jehovah as the inftruments of their punifhment. The death of the firft born, both of man and beaft, was a farther condemnation of their falfe religion. For in ancient times the priefthood was the pri-vilege of primogeniture; in Egypt, their gods were taken from amongft the firft born of their flocks and herds; and thefe _ni-mal gods were worfhipped with a reference to their elementa-

ry

The effect they produced was anfwerable to this intention: for both the Ifraelites, and many of the E-
gyptians " feared Jehovah, and believed Jehovah *."

The miracles of fucceeding prophets had the fame
moft benevolent intention, with thofe of Mofes. The
paffage of the Ifraelites over Jordan, as well as that
through the Red Sea, and their difpoffeffion of the
Canaanites, had this ultimate view, " that all the
" people of the earth might know the hand of Jeho-
" vah, that it is mighty †." When God interpofed
for the deliverance of his people; it was that both
they and all the kingdoms of the earth " might know
" that he was Jehovah ‡." Accordingly good men
prayed to God to " maintain the caufe of Ifrael at all
" times, that all the people of the earth might know
                                              " that

ɀy and fidereal deities. The fatal cataftrophe therefore which
befel the firft born of Egypt, from which the Ifraelites were
preferved, was the execution of judgment againft all the gods,
as well as againft the people of that country. Thus was the
great controverfy concerning the claims of Jehovah, as fole
monarch of the univerfe, and his right to demand the releafe
of his people, finally determined. Thofe on whom fuch means
of conviction could produce no lafting effect, were certainly
ripe for utter excifion.

  * Exod. ix. 20, 21. ch. xii. 38. ch. xiv. 31. The like effect was produced by other miracles, Jofh. ii. 10, 11. 1 Sam.
xii. 18. 2 Chron. xx. 29.

  † Jofh. iv. 23, 24. Exod. xxxiv. 10:

  ‡ 2 Kings xix. 15—19, 35. compare 1 Kings xx. 13, 28.
See alfo Pf. lxxxiii. 18.

" that Jehovah is God, and that there is none elfe *."
And indeed the Ifraelites would have been deftroyed,
on account of their great propenfity to idolatry, had
not God intended by their miraculous protection or
chaftifement, as they were obedient or difobedient,
to affert and vindicate his own Divinity in the eyes
of all the nations. The conclufion to be drawn from
every fingle act of miraculous power, by thofe who
attended to its true nature and defign, is the fame as
Naaman expreffed, when his leprofy was miraculoufly cured: " Behold! now I know there is no God
" in all the earth, but in Ifrael†." The king of Ifrael in particular confidered the cure of a leprofy as
a proof of divine power, " Am I God, to kill and to
" make alive, that this man doth fend unto me, to

Q   " recover

---

* 1 Kings viii. 59, 60. Notwithftanding the numerous paffages from the Old Teftament cited above, together with a
multitude of others, affert the God of Ifrael to be " Jehovah,
" the univerfal governor of the world, and the one only living
" and true God;" and notwithftanding the Heathen gods are
a thoufand times reproached in Scripture as mere nullities:
yet the celebrated Voltaire has, in different works, endeavoured to perfuade the world, that the Jews and their prophets acknowledged the *local tutelary* deities of other countries; and
at the fame time infinuated; that they worfhipped their own
God under no higher character than thofe. His great difin-
genuity in quoting the Scriptures, is well expofed by the learned Mr. Findlay, in his " Vindication of the Sacred Books," p.
98. Would writers of fuch eminence as Mr. Voltaire, reft the
caufe of infidelity on the groffeft mifreprefentations, were they
confcious of being able to fupport it by fair reafoning?

† 2 Kings v. 15.

" recover a man of his leprofy * ?" And though the gods of Egypt and Canaan were worfhipped by the moft immoral rites, with which the worfhip of Jehovah could not be charged ; yet the prophets of God never urge this circumftance either in confutation of their claims to divinity, or in proof of his ; but refer the decifion of both thofe claims to miracles alone. Whatever difference there may be between fome miracles and others with refpect to grandeur, the Old Teftament conftantly reprefents all miracles, whether of knowledge or of power, as proofs that the God of Ifrael was Jehovah †. The New Teftament alfo holds the fame language, when it ftyles miracles the works of God ‡, and fpeaks of them as defigned, to recover idolaters to his faith ‖ and worfhip.

How very different a view of miracles is this, from that given us by thofe learned moderns who affert, that they argue only the interpofition of fome power more than human ; that the loweft orders of fuperior intelligences may perform great miracles ; and

higher

* V. 7.

† If. xli. 21—26. ch. xlii. 8, 9. ch. xliii. 9—13. ch. xliv. 8. ch. xlv. 18, 21, 22. ch. xlvi. 9, 10. ch. xlviii. 3. Jer. x. 5—16. Dan. ii. 11. 27, 28, 29. 47. In thefe paffages, revealing fecrets, foretelling future events, delivering and faving, and the doing either good or evil in a fupernatural manner ; are not only afferted as the fole prerogatives of the true God ; but urged as the decifive proofs of deity.

‡ See below, fect. 6.

‖ 1 Pet. i. 21. 1 Theff. i. 9.

higher orders of beings, greater miracles ftill; that no miracle recorded in Scripture can be pronounced beyond the power of all created beings in the univerfe to produce; and that in no cafe whatever, can the immediate interpofition of God be diftinguifhed certainly by the works themfelves *? When the adverfaries of revelation ufe fuch language, with a view to deftroy its evidence, they fpeak in character. But what raifes our wonder is, its being held by fome of its ableft votaries and advocates, notwithftanding that revelation ftrongly afferts the fole dominion of Jehovah over nature, and every deviation from the laws of nature, (that is, every miracle) to be in itfelf a demonftration of his being its creator and lord. Which of thefe two opinions is moft confonant to reafon, is a point difcuffed in the fecond chapter. We only obferve here, that they cannot both be true. Can thofe works be the fole prerogatives of Jehovah, and a proof of his fole and unrivalled fovereignty; which *others* befides him, and even when acting in oppofition to him, have a power of performing as well as he? And can we fuccefsfully maintain the argument from miracles in favour of revelation, if we do not adhere to the ufe which revelation itfelf makes of miracles?

The moft able of our modern writers feem not to have attended to the true ftate of the antient controverfy between the prophets of God and idolaters. Even the very learned and fagacious bifhop Sherlock,

Q 2   fpeaking

---

* Dr. Clarke at Boyle's Lectures, and others.

speaking of the miracles wrought for the conviction of Pharaoh, says, " Here the question plainly was " between God under the character of the God of " the Hebrews, and the god of the Egyptians, which " of them was supreme *." He afterwards adds *, " When the question is, Who is the mightiest, must " it not be decided in his favour who visibly exerts " the greatest acts of power † ?" All the Heathen nations

---

* Difcourfes, V. 1. p. 281, 285. At p. 279, he had affirmed, " God thought proper to exert himfelf in fuch acts of " power as fhould demonftrate his *fuperiority* above all gods of " the Heathen." And fo little did his Lordfhip attend to the hiftory, that he affirms, after the generality of divines, that the character of diftinction which God affumed, when he commiffioned Mofes to work miracles, was that of the God of the Hebrews, p. 279, 280; notwithftanding its being fo evident, that the diftinguifhing character which God then affumed was that of *Jehovah*; and that the grand defign of Mofes's miracles was to prove, that the God of the Hebrews had a right to this title. The miracles of Mofes were indeed in part defigned to accomplifh the deliverance of the Ifraelites; and in this view they demonftrated Jehovah to be " the God of the Hebrews :" a character under which God now appeared, though it was not now firft affumed; for he had ftood before in the fame relation to their anceftors. But had he appeared under no other or higher character than this ; he would have been confounded with the feveral local deities of the Heathens. Whenever he was thus degraded as only the tutelary god of Ifrael; (as he was by Rabfhakeh, 2 Kings xviii. 33, 34 ;) he vindicated his own proper character as Jehovah God, and fole monarch of the univerfe. 2 Kings xix. 14—35.

† That in the cafe of a conteft, he who performs the *moft* and *greateft* miracles, gives evidence only of *fuperior* power, not

nations had at that time their feveral local deities, whofe refpective claims did not interfere with one another; each deity having a particular province and people of his own. Hence it came to pafs, that the god peculiar to each nation, never had his divinity called in queftion within his own diftrict by the other nations. So that had Jehovah appeared under no higher character, than that of the God of the Hebrews; the Heathens might and would have readily admitted it, without departing from their own principles. But the God of Ifrael affuming the title of Jehovah, and declaring this to be his diftinguifhing name and memorial, by which he would always be remembered and celebrated * ; his claims were abfolutely fubverfive of thofe of all other gods. It was the fundamental article of the Jewifh religion, that their God was Jehovah, and God alone; and that all the Heathen deities had no power or influence over the affairs of mankind, within any limits whatfoever. And therefore the queftion never could be, Who is the *mightieft*, Jehovah or the rival gods of Paganifm. Any figns of power given by the latter, would have overthrown the doctrine of Jehovah's prophets, and infringed his prerogative as the fole author and fovereign of nature. If he was Jehovah,

Q 3   there

not of *abfolute fupremacy*; was fhewn above, ch. 2. fect. 6. p. 83. And how unfatisfactory the bifhop's folution is, when applied to the works of the magicians in Egypt, will be fhewn below, ch. 4. fect. 1.

* Exod. iii. 15.

there could be no other fovereign of nature : and if there was any other fovereign of nature, he was not Jehovah, or the only living and true God.   Accordingly we find in fact, that in the conteft between the Ifraelites and Egyptians, and in every fucceeding conteft, the queftion was, Is the God of Ifrael Jehovah, in the full and proper fenfe of that expreffion? In this there was another queftion involved, Are any of the reputed gods of the Heathens truly Gods? or do they poffefs any of that power and dominion afcribed to them by their worfhippers? And how was this queftion to be decided, but by miracles? A power and dominion over nature cannot be more effectually eftablifhed, than by changing or fufpending the courfe of its operations.   Accordingly Pharaoh demanded of Mofes a fign *, as a proof of his miffion from Jehovah.   And in the grand conteft between Elijah and the prophets of Baal; as the queftion was, Who is God, Jehovah or Baal; fo both fides agreed to have it determined by a fingle miracle. Elijah had no conception, that Jehovah and Baal could both of them be gods, one of them greater than the other. On the contrary, he fuppofes one of them only could be God, or have any dominion over nature, or power of working a miracle, and confequently a title to worfhip; when he fays, " If Jehovah be God, fol-" low him: but if Baal, follow him †." The propofal he afterwards made of deciding the controver-

                                                                            fy

---

* Exod. vii. 9.

† 1 Kings xviii. 21.

ly by a fingle miracle, (not by the greater in number or degree,) " The God that anfwereth by fire, let him be God," whether Baal or Jehovah *; is a demonftration that Elijah had no expectation that both Baal and Jehovah could interpofe in this miraculous manner ; becaufe this would rather have proved both of them to be gods, than that Jehovah alone was God ; which was the point to be decided. And had Baal anfwered by fire, this point had been determined against Elijah, and he muft have acknowledged that Baal was god ; anfwering by fire, being, in his opinion, a valid proof of a divine interpofition ; the very touchftone by which he himfelf had defired the claims both of Jehovah and Baal might be tried, in order effectually to diftinguifh which were genuine, and which were counterfeit. Elijah allowed the priefts of Baal to make the experiment firft, and to try to engage him to anfwer them by fire ; firmly affured of his utter impotence, and defirous of expofing him in the prefence of his deluded worfhippers. All application to Baal being ineffectual, Elijah prayed for fire from heaven, not to manifeft the *fuperiority* of the God of Ifrael, but his fole Divinity, " that " it might be known that Jehovah was God in If- " rael, and Jehovah God†." When the fire of Jehovah fell and confumed the facrifice, the people acknowledged, " Jehovah, he is God ; Jehovah, he is God‡." This conclufion was juft, upon the princi-

Q 4   ple

* V. 24.

† 1 Kings xviii. 36, 37.   ‡ V. 39.

ple maintained above ‖, that the laws of nature being
ordained by God, their operation and effects cannot
be controuled by any superior beings besides him. If
this principle be false, could a single miracle confute
the claims of the Heathen deities, and demonstrate
Jehovah to be the only sovereign of nature? But it
is, I hope, needless to shew, that revelation confirms
the dictates of reason on this subject. Here we have
no other view, than to illustrate the state of the ancient controversy between the prophets of God and
idolaters; and by that means to confirm what has
been already urged to shew, that the Scriptures represent all miracles as the prerogatives of the one e-
ternal Divinity, and as proofs of his being Jehovah,
and God alone. They do this in a manner, that
plainly shews their having no apprehension, that any
superior beings whatever, besides God, had a power
of producing these effects.

‖ Ch. 2. sect. 3.

S E C T.

SECT. VI.

The Scriptures uniformly reprefent all miracles as being, in them-
felves, an abfolute demonftration of the divinity of the miffion and
doctrine of the prophets, at whofe inftance they are performed ;
and never direct us to regard their doctrines as a teft of the mi-
racles being the effect of a divine interpofition.

WHEN God commiffioned Mofes to deliver the
Ifraelites out of Egypt; he at the fame
enabled him to perform figns and wonders, to procure him credit both with the Ifraelites *, and the E-
gyptians †. Miracles were the only teftimonials urged with either, in proof of his miffion from Jehovah.
And it was alfo upon this evidence alone, that the
laws of Mofes were afterwards received by the Ifraelites as divine injunctions ‡, and his authority fupported amongft them; though they were too much difpofed to difobey the one, and murmur againft the
other ‖. They did not however try his miracles by
his

---

* Exod. iv. 1—5, 8, 9. See alfo Numb. xvi. 28—30.
Deut. iv. 39.

† Exod. vii. 8.

‡ Exod. xix. 3—8. ch. xxiv. 3.

‖ When the Ifraelites charged Mofes with ambition and u-
furpation, he appeals to a miracle in proof of his divine commiffion, Numb. xvi. 13, 28, 29, " Hereby ye fhall know that
" the Lord has fent me.—If the Lord make a new thing, and
the

his laws; nor difpute the divine original of the former, merely becaufe many of the latter were expen-
five and painful, and had no intrinfic excellence to
recommend them.   Nor did Mofes, when he proved
by miracles his commiffion to require of Pharaoh the ·
releafe of the Ifraelites, appeal to the equity of his demand, in confirmation of the divinity of his works;
though he might have fhewn, that the bondage of the
Ifraelites was the higheft reproach to the gratitude of
the Egyptians, whofe country had been faved by Jofeph, and a violation of all the laws of hofpitality,
and of all the promifes of protection and kindnefs
made to the Ifraelites, when they firft came into E-
gypt.   But Mofes refted the proof of his authority
upon the fole evidence of his works, as plainly difcovering the hand of God. The fucceeding prophets*
under the Old Teftament, proceeded upon the fame
principle; and appealed to miracles alone, as an unqueftionable demonftration of their miffion from God.
Elijah in particular thus prays to God to anfwer him
by fire, " Let it be known this day, that thou art
" God in Ifrael, and that I am thy fervant, and that
                                                            " I

" the earth open her mouth," &c.   It was by a miracle likewife that Samuel convinced the Ifraelites of their fault in afking a king, 1 Sam. xii. 16—19.

   * Jofh. iii. 7. ch. iv. 14. 1 Sam. x. 1—7. ch. xii. 16—18. 1
Kings xiii. 3. ch. xvii. 24. 2 Kings v. 15. In like manner with
regard to prophecies, by their accomplifhment it fhall be known
that a prophet has been amongft them, Ezek. xxxiii. 33. Jer.
xxviii. 9. 1 Sam. iii. 19, 20. compare Deut. xviii. 22.

" I have done all thefe things at thy word *." The very fame ufe is made of the miracles of the New Teftament. But this being a point which has been controverted both by the adverfaries and advocates of the Chriftrian revelation; (the former fometimes denying, that the miracles of the Gofpel were defigned to atteft Chrift's divine miffion; and the latter often afferting, that they are urged only as conditional atteftations of it;) I will examine diftinctly the paffages which fpeak of the author and end of the Gofpel miracles; efpecially as I do not remember to have feen them collected together, much lefs placed in (what appears to me to be) their true light. The miracles of Chrift, and his apoftles fhall be confidered feparately.

I.

With regard to our Saviour; juft before he entered upon his public miniftry, he was qualified for the difcharge of it, by receiving " the Spirit of God without meafure †," or for univerfal and perpetual ufe, and not as the former prophets had received it, for a limited time and occafion. Accordingly he refers both his doctrine and his works to God as their author. " He fpake as the Father taught him, and gave him commandment ‡." His miracles he ftyles
" the

* 1 Kings xviii. 36.

† John iii. 34.

‡ John viii. 28. ch. xii. 49, 50. In farther proof of his referring his doctrine to God, the following paffages might be appealed

" the works of God," and " the works of his Father * ;" which would have been an improper mode
of expreffion, if any one elfe could have done the
fame works. Chrift exprefsly afcribes them to " the
finger or Spirit of God †;" and affirms on one occafion, " The Son can do nothing of himfelf ‡ ;"
and on another, " The words that I fpeak unto you,
" I fpeak not of myfelf. But the Father that dwell-
" eth in me, he doth the works ‖," whereby thofe
words are confirmed: He reprefents them as a vifible
and very confpicuous difplay of the " glory § and
power † of God." His difciples, in like manner,

appealed to, ch. viii. 26, 38, 40. ch. vii. 16, 17. ch. xiv. 10, 24.
Agreeably hereto we are told, " that the Spirit of the Lord
" was upon him, anointing him to preach the Gofpel," Luke
iv, 18, and that after his refurrection " he through the Holy
" Ghoft gave commandments unto his apoftles," Acts i. 2.
See Whitby's preface to St. John's Gofpel.

* John ix. 3. ch. x. 37. ch. v. 36.

† Mat. xii. 28.   Luke xi. 20.

‡ John v. 19.

‖ John xiv. 10.

§ Ch. xi. 4.   In the 40th verfe Chrift, when going to raife
Lazarus, thus addreffes Martha, " Said I not unto thee, that
" if thou wouldft believe, thou fhouldft fee the glory of
" God ?"

† " To whom hath THE ARM OF THE LORD been revealed ?"
John xii. 37, 38.   It is with a peculiar reference to the miracles of Chrift, that he frequently affirms, " that feeing him,"
was

fpeak of them as works, " which God did by him * ;"
and declare, " God anointed Jefus of Nazareth with
" the Holy Ghoſt and with power, who went about
" doing good, and healing all that were oppreſſed
" with the devil, for God was with him †."

Agreeably to this reprefentation of their author,
Chriſt appeals to his miracles as a demonſtration (not
a partial and conditional, but a compleat and abfolute demonſtration) of his miſſion from God. He
tells the Jews, " The works which my Father has
" given me to finiſh (or to perform) the fame works
" that I do, bear witnefs of me, that the Father has
" fent me." He adds, " Even the Father himfelf
" which hath fent me, hath born witnefs of me ‡."
Juſt as he was going to perform one particular miracle, he made a public appeal to God, " that men"
(by that fingle miracle) " might believe that the Father had fent him ‖." And St. Peter ſtyles him, " a
" man approved of God, (or confpicuouſly demon-
" ſtrated by God § to be his meſſenger) by miracles,
" and

was " feeing God who fent him." John xii. 44, 45. ch. xiv.
9—12. ch. xv. 24.

* Acts ii. 22.

† Ch. x. 38. St. Luke alfo fays, ch. iv. 1, 14. " Jefus returned in the power of the Spirit into Galilee," which is explained Mat. iv. 23, 24, " He healed all manner of difeafes."

‡ John v. 36, 37. See alfo ch. viii. 18, 28, 29, 42, 54.
ch. x. 35, 36.

‖ Ch. xi. 41, 42.

§ Απο τȣ Θεȣ αποδιδειγμενον. Acts ii. 22.

" and wonders, and figns." This language of Chrift and his apoftles implies, that his miracles were works appropriate to the Father, and therefore, in themfelves, and apart from all confideration of his doctrine, a full demonftration of his divine miffion.

The miracles of Chrift were farther defigned to e-vince his peculiar character as *the Meffiah* or *anointed*. But here it will be neceffary previoufly to confider, what is included in this character : a point which has been overlooked * by our beft writers upon the fubject of miracles ; and the overlooking of which has, I apprehend, been one caufe of their not difcerning the peculiar and direct defign of the New Teftament miracles, or at leaft occafioned their fpeaking of it in too vague and indeterminate a manner. The kings of Ifrael (thofe vice-roys of God, who fat upon God's throne,) were inftalled in their office, by the ceremony of anointing them with oil, and very frequently diftinguifhed by this title +, " the Lord's anointed." When this term is applied to Chrift, it conveys to us the idea of " a king, immediately ap- " pointed by God, and qualified for that office by a " divine

* I take notice of this overfight, not merely for the fake of fhewing the neceffity of here laying before the reader, a fuller account of the ends propofed by the Gofpel miracles, than any that has been given by former writers ; but alfo of fhewing in general, how neceffary it is to examine every thing ourfelves, without trufting to the reprefentation even of learned, judicious, and candid men.

+ This title was not indeed peculiar to the kings of Ifrael ; but it belonged to them eminently.

" divine unction," the unlimited communication, and perpetual refidence of the Holy Ghoft. The two grand branches of Chrift's regal office are " legifla- tion," and " the diftribution of rewards and punifh- ments amongft his fubjects," according to their dif- ferent behaviour. In ancient times kings were alfo *judges* * ; and indeed the adminiftration of juftice is a principal act of government, and infeparable from the office of fovereign princes. An authority to difpenfe pardon, is likewife an effential branch of the royal prerogative, and fuch as it was neceffary the fove- reign of mankind fhould be invefted with, in order to his encouraging his fubjects, who were in a ftate of guilt and revolt from God, to return to their alle- giance †. And the kingdom of Chrift not being of a temporal nature, but fpiritual and heavenly, and the chief bleffings of it being fuch as could not be enjoyed in their proper extent in this world, or even

in

---

* " Be wife now therefore, O ye kings: be inftructed ye judges of the earth." Pf. ii. 10. compare 1 Sam. viii. 5, 7. Our Saviour declares, that a *judicial* power belongs to him as the Meffiah, " The Father has given him authority to execute judgment alfo, becaufe he is the fon of man," John v. 27. He fpeaks of himfelf under the character of *a king*, when he de- fcribes his coming to judge the world, Mat. xxv. 34. And St. Paul calls his appearance as the judge of the living and the dead, *his kingdom*, 2 Tim. iv. 1. See Acts x. 42.

† Acts vi. 31. ch. x. 43. It is obferved in Livy, Dec. 1. l. 2. c. 3, that what renders *the kingly government* dear to the people, is the liberty of pardoning; Regem hominem effe, a quo impetres, ubi jus, ubi injuria opus fit : effe gratiæ locum, effe beneficio; & irafci & ignofcere poffe.

in the future ſtate while mankind continued under the power of death ; it was abſolutely neceſſary, that Chriſt ſhould be authorized by God to raiſe the dead, in order to their being judged, and either rewarded or condemned *. All the other exerciſes of his royal power, are only ſo many preparations for the laſt grand act, of inſtating all the children of God in a bleſſed immortality. The notion we are to form of Jeſus as the Meſſiah, is that of the (promiſed and) divinely conſtituted *prince* and *Saviour* †. In his *le-giſlative* and *judicial* capacity, he is ſpoken of as *a king* : and when he exerciſes his power in diſpenſing divine pardon, in recovering mankind from the do-minion of death, and putting the righteous of every age and nation into the poſſeſſion of eternal life, he is deſcribed as a *Saviour*. But, ſtrictly ſpeaking, this latter office is included in the former. Chriſt's roy-alty would have been but an empty title, without the power of diſtributing rewards and puniſhments, to inforce the obedience of his ſubjects. In a word, the Meſſiahſhip of Jeſus denotes his *regal* commiſſion and power, or his right by divine deſignation to domi-nion and judicature over mankind. And this is what the miracles of Chriſt were deſigned to eſtabliſh.

At the firſt opening of his miniſtry, he proclaimed the joyful tidings of the approach or arrival of the Meſſiah, or of the kingdom of heaven ; aſſerted his own authority to give laws, and to adminiſter govern-

ment

* See John v. 27—20.

† Acts v. 31.

ment in this kingdom of God ; and at the fame time urged his miracles as a full and adequate proof of his regal inveftiture and commiffion. In oppofition to thofe who accufed him of a confederacy with Satan, he affirms, " If I caft out demons by the Spi-" rit of God, then is the kingdom of God come " unto you *:" which implied, that he himfelf was the perfon, under whom that kingdom was to be erected. To thofe who defired him, in cafe he was the Chrift, plainly to declare it, he replied, " I told " you who I am, and ye believed not. The works " that I do in my Father's name, they bear wit-" nefs of me.——Say ye of him, whom the Father " has fanctified" (or fet apart to the office of the Meffiah) " and fent into the world" (under fo high a character), " Thou blafphemeft ; becaufe I faid, " I am the Son of God +? If I do not the works of " my Father, believe me not. But if I do, though " ye believe not me," i. e. my teftimony, " BELIEVE " THE WORKS," which are the teftimony of God : " that" by thefe vifible difplays of his power and au-thority, " ye may know and believe, that the Father " is in me, and I in him ‡." To his difciples he fpeaks the fame language, " Believe me that I am " in the Father, and the Father in me : or elfe be-

R   " lieve

---

* Mat. xii. 28. Luke xi. 20.

+ *The Son of God*, and *the Meffiah* or *the Chrift*, are equi-valent terms. Mat. xvi. 16. John. vi. 69. Mat. xxvi. 63. Luke xxii. 66, 70. John i. 34—41. Compare Prov. iv. 3. Pf. ii. 7, 12. 2 Sam. vii. 14.

‡ John x. 24, 25, 36—38. ch. viii. 28, 29.

" lieve me FOR THE VERY WORKS SAKE * :" which
are the moſt authentic teſtimonials of my union with
the Father, and of his dwelling and operating in me
by a permanent influence; ſo that, properly, it is
God who ſpeaks and acts by me. In anſwer to that
inquiry, by a deputation to Jeſus from the Baptiſt,
" Art thou He that ſhould come ?" he refers them
to his miracles for ſatisfaction ‡. And becauſe his
miracles evinced his dignity and authority as the
Meſſiah, he affirms their intention to be, " that the
" Son of God might be glorified thereby ‖." His
divine commiſſion and prerogative to diſpenſe ſpiritual bleſſings, is particularly pointed out, as a moſt
eſſential branch of his office, and at the ſame time
moſt remote from the conception of the worldly-
minded Jews. When he healed the maladies of
thoſe, who, from a principle of faith, applied to him,
he declared he did it with this view, " that men
" might know, that the Son of man had power on
" earth to forgive ſins §." And to the end, they
might regard him as the diſpenſer of eternal life to
good

---

* Ch. xiv. 10, 11.

‡ " The blind receive their ſight, the lame walk," &c.
Mat. xi. 5. Luke vii. 21.

‖ John xi. 4. By his firſt miracle, " he manifeſted forth his
glory." John ii. 11.

§ Mark ii. 10, 11. Chriſt's reaſoning here ſuppoſes, that
the power of healing diſeaſes was no leſs the prerogative of
God, than that of pardoning ſins; and therefore that neither
could be communicated to any, but by God alone.

good men, after having raifed them from the dead; before he called Lazarus from the grave, he ftiles himfelf " the refurrection and the life," and affured his difciples, " he that believes on me, though he " were dead, yet fhall he live *." The power of re-ftoring the dead to life, he elfewhere fpeaks of as the immediate gift of his Father: and then proceeds to affert his power to call·all mankind from their graves, that they might be adjudged to everlafting life or death †. And inafmuch as all his miracles, by prov-ing him to be the Meffiah, eftablifhed his commiffion from God to raife the dead, (without which he could neither judge his fubjects, nor beftow upon them the promifed recompence); we find him upon all occa-fions, and particularly when he fed five thoufand with a few loaves and fifhes, afferting his character as the difpenfer of eternal life ‡; adding, " for him " has God the Father fealed," his miracles being as authentic credentials of his Meffiahfhip, as the royal feal is of a commiffion from a prince, whofe feal it is: which expreffion ftrongly implies, ·that miracles are a feal which none but God can ufe. If impof-tors are allowed to perform them, they are no au-thentic proof of a divine miffion, any more than the royal feal would be of an order from a prince, who permitted others, and even his enemies, to have a

R 2   duplicate

---

* John xi. 25, 26.

† Ch. v. 20, 21, 25, 29. See ch. vi. 39, 40, 44, 45.

‡ " The Son of man fhall give unto you eternal life." John vi. 27.

duplicate or counterpart of the fame. In a word, all
Chrift's miracles were performed, (and all his prophecies * likewife were delivered,) with exactly the
fame view with which they were committed to writing, " that we might believe, that Jefus is the
" Chrift, the Son of God; and that believing we
" might have life through his name †." The *effect*
they produced was anfwerable to this defign of their
performance. They carried along with them a conviction of their divinity: " No man," faid Nicode-
mus to our Saviour, " can do thefe miracles that
" thou doft, except God be with him ‡." And " the
" multitude," when they faw his works, " marvel-
" led, and glorified God, who had given fuch power
" unto men ||." Accordingly his miracles wrought
a perfuafion in fome, that Jefus was a divine prophet §; and in others, that he was the Meffiah §. If
miracles were not conclufive, and even cogent arguments of a divine miffion, the refiftance of thefe
means of conviction would not have been upbraided
                                                    by

---

* " Now I tell you before it come, that when it is come
" to pafs, ye may believe that I am he." John xiii. 19. See
ch. ii. 22. ch. xiv. 29. ch. xvi. 4, 30. 1 Cor. xiv. 25. Rev.
xix. 10.

† John xx. 31. See ch. xi. 15.

‡ John iii. 2.

|| Mat. ix. 8. See John ix. 33.

§ Mat. xii. 23. John ii. 11, 22, 23. ch. iii. 2. ch. iv. 45,
52, 53. ch. vi. 14. ch. vii. 31. ch. ix. 35—38. ch. x. 44.
ch. xi. 45, 47, 48. ch. xii. 11. Luke xxiv. 19.

by Chrift with fo much feverity, nor made a ground of the moft aggravated condemnation *. On the other hand, Chrift declares, " If I had not done " amongft them the works which none other man " did," (that is, fuch as none but a truly divine meffenger can perform,) " they had not had fin : " but now have they both feen, and hated both me " and my Father †."

R 3   On

---

* Mat. x. 15. ch. xi. 20—24. ch. xii. 31. John xii. 37. ch. xv. 22—25. Heb. ii. 3, 4. ch. vi. 4. God proceeded to execute judgment upon Pharaoh, upon his not yielding to the evidence of the firft miracle ; and Zacharias was ftruck dumb, for not giving credit to a fingle divine appearance : which feems to imply, that every miracle bears upon it the vifible ftamp of divinity. And wherein does the common doctrine concerning miracles being wrought by evil fpirits, differ from " the blafphemy againft the Holy Ghoft," (fo feverely condemned in thofe who imputed Chrift's cure of demoniacs to the affiftance of demons,) except in its not arguing malice againft Chrift ? The Jews referred only one fpecies of Chrift's miracles to the devil : many Chriftians affert, that moft, if not all, his miracles might be wrought by evil fpirits.

† John xv. 24. This paffage has been generally thought to affirm, that the perfonal miracles of Chrift were *greater* than thofe of Mofes, or any of the ancient prophets ; which was fcarce true at that time. Chrift is here diftinguifhing himfelf from all *falfe* prophets, whom the Jews were too much inclined to follow, even without any evidence of their miffion, and from a mere relifh of their corrupt doctrine. The expreffion is fomewhat parallel to John x. 37. " If I do not the " works of my Father, believe me not." Both thefe paffages teach us in the ftrongeft manner, that miracles are works which no impoftor, nor any but God, can perform, and in themfelves authentic proofs of a divine miffion.

On the third day after he had suffered death, under the false imputation of blasphemy and imposture; he was raised from the dead : a miracle which the Scripture ascribes " to the working of God's mighty power *," and considers as the capital and most authentic declaration of Jesus's being " the Son of God †," and the true Messiah ; and to which he had often referred his enemies for conviction ‡. The regal power of the Messiah, including in it a judicial as well as a legiflative authority ; the refurrection of Christ, and his advancement to the full possession of his regal power, is spoken of as a completion of the evidence, and as a commanding argument of his being appointed to judge the world ‖.

II.

With regard to the miracles performed by the apostles of Christ, after his ascension into heaven ; as they are ascribed to the agency of the Spirit of God §, even to " the Spirit of truth which proceedeth (cometh forth) from the Father ¶," and is dispensed through the

---

* Ephef. i. 19.　Col. ii. 12.

† Rom. i. 4.

‡ John ii. 18.　Mat. xii. 38. ch. xvi. 1.

‖ Acts xvii. 31.　In this passage; πίστιν παρασχὼν πᾶσιν, " having offered faith to all men;" faith is put for the *evidence* afforded, or the *persuasive argument* whereby it is wrought.

§ Rom. xv. 19.　1 Cor. xii. 4—11.　Heb. ii. 4.

¶ John xv. 26.

the mediation of Chrift * ; fo they are urged as a full
vindication of the character of Chrift from the afperfions
and calumnies of his enemies, as a proof of the truth
of his refurrection and advancement to celeftial dignity
and power, as a confirmation of his claims to be a divine
meffenger and the Son of God, as a teftimony of God
and of Chrift to thofe whom he commiffioned to affert thefe claims, or to atteft the facts (his refurrection in particular) on which they were founded † ; or
in other words, as an indubitable divine teftimony to
the doctrine they preached, when they taught Jefus
to be the Meffiah, by faith in whom pardon and eternal life were to be obtained. Our Saviour promifed
his followers, " that they fhould do greater works
" than he had done, becaufe he went to the Father,"
(or was to be exalted to power in his prefence and
kingdom,) when; as the effect and evidence of his
exaltation, he was to receive from the Father, and
difpenfe to his followers, the Holy Ghoft ‡. " And
" when he is come, he will" (by the miracles he
will enable you to perform in my name) " reprove"

R 4   (or

---

* Tit. iii. 6. " The Father," fays our Lord, " will fend
" him in my name. I will pray the Father, and he fhall give
" you another Comforter or Advocate. I will fend him unto
" you from the Father." John xiv. 26. ch. xv. 26.

† The apoftles received their commiffion from Chrift ; John
xx. 31. ch. xvii. 18. and were appointed to be the witneffes
of his refurrection ; ch. xv. 27. Acts i. 8. ch. ii. 22, 23. ch.
x. 39, 41. ch. xiii. 31. 1 Cor. xv. 14, 15.

‡ John xiv. 12. ch. xv. 26. Acts ii. 33--36.

(or rather, convince) " the world of fin," of their heinous guilt in rejecting and condemning me to death as an impoftor, " and of" the " righteoufnefs" of my character and the juftice of my claims, " and of" the equity of that " judgment," which will be executed upon my enemies *. " He fhall teftify of " me †. He fhall glorify me ‡. At that day," fays Chrift, " ye fhall know, that I am in my Father, and " you in me, and I in you ‖." He intercedes with his Father, on the behalf both of his apoftles, and of their converts, " that they may be one," (by a common participation of the Spirit,) " as § thou, Father, art " in me, and I in thee; that they alfo may be one " in us: that the world" (by the vifible operations of that Spirit, which I fhall receive from thee, and impart to them,) " may believe that thou haft fent " me." And " the glory" (the power and honour of performing miracles by the Spirit) " which thou " haft given me, I have given them: that they may " be one, even as we are one; that the world may " know that thou haft fent me, and haft loved them, " as thou haft loved me." And juft before his af-
cenfion

---

* John xvi. 8—11.

† Ch. xv. 26.

‡ Ch. xvi. 14.

‖ Ch. xiv. 20. ch. xvii. 21—23. Compare ch. x. 38. ch. xiv. 10, 11, cited above; and confult Dr. Whitby on thefe feveral places, and on Ephef. iv. 4.

§ John. xvii. 21—23. *As*, in this place, denotes *refem-blance*, not *equality: for in Chrift dwells all the fulnefs of the Godhead bodily.*

cenfion he tells his difciples, " Ye fhall receive power
" after that the Holy Ghoft is come upon you ; and
" ye fhall be witneffes unto me *."

Conformable to this declared intention of 'Chrift
in promifing and beftowing the gifts and miracles of
the Holy Ghoft, are the feveral ufes to which they
are applied by the apoftles. When they received the
gift of tongues, St. Peter tells the Jews, " Chrift be-
" ing by the right hand of God exalted, and having
" received of the Father the promife of the Holy
" Ghoft, he has fhed forth this, which ye now fee
" and hear †." And from this effufion of the Spirit,
as well as from the teftimony of prophecy, he argues,
" that God had made Jefus both Lord and Chrift†."
" We," fays the fame apoftle afterwards, " are wit-
" neffes of thefe things," (viz. the refurrection and
exaltation of Jefus,) " and fo alfo is the Holy
" Ghoft ‡." The Scriptures likewife inform us on
other occafions, that " with great power" (by very
illuftrious miracles) " gave the apoftles witnefs of
" the refurrection of the Lord Jefus ||." The *manner*
in which the apoftles performed their miracles, fhews
that they were efpecially defigned as an immediate
teftimony to the refurrection and glory of Chrift.
" In the name of Jefus of Nazareth rife up and
" walk §," faid Peter to the lame man at the gate of
the

* Acts i. 8.
† Ch. ii. 33—36.
‡ Acts v. 31, 32.
|| Ch. iv. 30, 33.
§ Ch. iii. 6. Compare ch. iv. 30.

the temple. And he thus farther explains the intention of the miracle to the aftonifhed multitude : " God
" has raifed up, and glorified his Son Jefus ; and his
" name, (or power,) through faith in his name, has
" made this man ftrong." The apoftles conftantly
declared themfelves to be the appointed witneffes of
his refurrection and exaltation ; and accordingly their
miracles are fpoken of as the atteftation of God to
them, in the execution of their commiffion. " God
" bore them witnefs, both by figns and wonders,
" and with divers miracles and gifts (or diftribu-
" tions) of the Holy Ghoft * : they went forth, and
" preached every where ; the Lord working with
" them, and confirming the word with figns follow-
" ing † : the Lord gave teftimony to the word of his
" grace, and granted figns and wonders to be done
" by their hands ‡." St. Paul, in particular, confidered fupernatural interpofitions in his favour, as manifeftations of " the life ‖" of Chrift, " and as a proof
of

---

* Heb. ii. 4.

† Mark xvi. 20.

‡ Acts xiv. 3. By " the word, the word of God, the Gof-
" pel, the word of the Gofpel, the word of the kingdom,"
(which are often ufed as fynonimous terms,) the Scripture
means the joyful news of the approach or arrival of the Meffiah, and the preaching Jefus to be that very perfon, or the
ruler and redeemer of the people of God. Compare Luke iii.
18, 21. ch. viii. 11. ch. ix. 2, 6. Mat. xi. 5. Acts viii. 4.
ch. x. 36, 37. ch. xi. 1, 19, 20. ch. xii. 24. ch. xiii. 42—49.
ch. xv. 7, 35. ch. xvii. 3, 11, 13. ch. xviii. 4, 11.

‖ 2 Cor. iv. 10, 11.

of Chrift fpeaking in him *," and exprefsly calls his miracles, " the figns of an apoftle †." He likewife tells his converts, " that his Gofpel came not unto " them in word only, but alfo in power, and in the " Holy Ghoft, and in much affurance," (or with the fulleft conviction of its truth); " and that his preach- " ing was in demonftration of the Spirit, and of " power, that their faith might not ftand in the wif- " dom of men, but in the power of God ‡." The *effect* produced by thefe miracles, correfponds to and confirms the account here given of their primary de- clared intention : for they demanded and procured an abfolute credit to the doctrine and teftimony of the performers, " concerning the kingdom of God ‖, " and the name of Jcfus Chrift §." And St. Paul tells us, that the Gentiles were made obedient to the faith, " through mighty figns and wonders, by the " power of the Spirit of God," and prefented as an acceptable offering to God, " being fanctified by the Holy Ghoft ¶," imparted to the firft Chriftian con- verts in many extraordinary gifts.

The

---

* Ch. xiii. 3.

† Ch. xii. 12. Compare 1 Cor. iv. 19, 20. and what is urged above, ch. 3. fect. 4. p. 213, 214.

‡ 1 Theff. i. 5. 1 Cor. ii. 4, 5.

‖ See above, note †, p. 266.

§ Acts viii. 6, 7. See ch. ii. 33, 41—43. ch. ix. 35, 42. ch. xiii. 12. Rom. xv. 18.

¶ Rom. xv. 16, 18, 19. It appears from this paffage, that the winning men over to the faith of Chrift, was the defign
with

The paſſages already cited, chiefly refer to the miracles performed by the apoſtles, for the conviction
of unbelievers: I˚ will now ſet down the paſſages
which expreſs the intention of thoſe ſpiritual gifts
which the apoſtles beſtowed upon believers; that we
may ſee the whole ſubject in one-view. The gifts
conferred upon the Chriſtian converts, beſides being
a new confirmation of the Chriſtian faith, or of the
doctrine and teſtimony of the apoſtles concerning
Chriſt *; were farther deſigned as an evidence of the
divine favour to all who received and obeyed the
Goſpel, though they did not ſubmit to the law of
Moſes; as a ſeal of the pardon of their paſt ſins, and
a pledge of their adoption to eternal life †; as a proof
of their election of God to be his church and people ‡;
and as a means alſo of ſupporting the worſhip of God,
and thereby of promoting the edification and improvement of Chriſtians, as well as the conviction of
unbelievers, who might caſually attend the Chriſtian
aſſemblies ‖. With regard to the miraculous judgments inflicted upon ſuch as wickedly oppoſed, corrupted, or diſobeyed the Goſpel; they were deſigned
more immediately for the puniſhment and reformation

with which the miracles were performed, as well as the effect
which they produced.

* 1 Cor. i. 5, 6, 7. 2 Cor. i. 18—22.

† Acts ii. 38. Rom. v. 1, 5. ch. viii. 14—16. 23. 2 Cor.
i. 22. ch. v. 5. Gal. iv. 6, 7. Epheſ. i. 13, 14. ch. iv. 30.
Compare Luke xx. 36.

‡ 1 Theſſ. i. 4, 5.

‖ 1 Cor. xii. 7. ch. xiv. 3, 22, 25, 31. Epheſ. iv. 8—16.

tion of offenders *, though they ultimately termina-
ted in the confirmation of the Chriftian doctrine.

The clear and explicit view, which the foregoing
paffages of Scripture give us of the precife intention
of the miracles of the New Teftament, may ferve to
rectify the miftakes men have run into upon this fubject. In the numerous paffages here cited, the divinity of thefe miracles, confidered in themfelves, is
always either exprefsly afferted, or manifeftly implied; and they are accordingly urged as a decifive
and abfolute proof of the divinity of the doctrine and
teftimony of their performers, without ever taking
into confideration the nature of the doctrine or of the
teftimony to be confirmed.

To what is here advanced, fome will object, " that
" our Saviour, when the Pharifees afcribed his mi-
" racles to a confederacy with demons, appealed to
" his doctrine in refutation of the calumny:" " If
" Satan caft out Satan, he is divided againft him-
" felf; how then fhall his kingdom ftand? And if
" I by Beelzebub caft out devils; by whom do your
" children caft them out? therefore they fhall be
" your judges †." It is fuppofed that our Saviour
in this paffage affirms, that it was abfurd to afcribe
his miracles to the devil, becaufe *his doctrine* was moft
oppofite to all that an evil fpirit could wifh to be pro-
pagated in the world; and that if Chrift was an ac-
complice

---

* 1 Tim. i. 20. Acts xiii. 11. 2 Cor. x. 6. 1 Cor. v. 5.
2 Cor. xiii. 10.

† Mat. xii. 26, 27.

complice of the devil, then the devil was fubverting his own interefts, ruining his own kingdom. This objection, I apprehend, proceeds upon two miftakes.

1ft, It fuppofes, that the Pharifees afcribed the miracles of Chrift *in general* to a confederacy with demons: a fuppofition altogether groundlefs. It appears from the hiftory *, that this calumny, as it was occafioned by, fo it concerned only, one particular fpecies of his miracles, the cure of demoniacs ; whofe diforders were thought to be caufed by the influence of demons ; from whence it was concluded, that they might be removed by the influence of demons. There is no intimation given us, that the enemies of Chrift ever extended this reproach to any of his other miracles ; faithfully as the evangelifts have recorded every other calumny againft him, and particular as they have been in their relation of this. And indeed it is certain, that the Pharifees neither did nor could afcribe the miracles of Chrift in general to a demoniacal agency. They *could not* do it ; I mean, not without grofs felf-contradiction : becaufe they allowed miracles to be a proof of a divine miffion, upon which alone their religion was founded ; and becaufe many of the miracles of Chrift were the very fame with thofe, which their own prophets had produced as divine credentials. And that they *did not* afcribe them to demons, appears from their behaviour on fome remarkable occafions. When they were unable to

deny

---

* The following are the only inftances of this calumny on record : Mat. ix. 32. ch. xii. 22. Mark iii. 22. Luke xi. 14.

deny the reality of Chrift's miracles, at a lofs to evade
the conviction of them, and fully fenfible of the dangerous confequences to their fuperftition and ufurpa-
tion, from their gaining credit; in a word, when reduced by them to the utmoft perplexity, even then
they did not fo much as attempt to argue, that the
works of Chrift proceeded from any evil fpirits *, but
rather acknowleged God was the author of them.
Thus to the man born blind, on whom Chrift had
beftowed fight, they fay, " Give God the praife :
" we know that this man is a finner †." They were
willing to allow, that God might exercife his power,
and convey his favours by a profligate impoftor, rather than that any but God could open the eyes of a
perfon born blind. In this fenfe they were underftood
by the man on whom they were performed, with
whom they were difputing; as appears from his reply, " God heareth not finners ‡," cannot confirm
by miracles falfe pretences to a divine commiffion.
It has, I think, been univerfally affirmed, that the
Pharifees afcribed Chrift's miracles in general to a
confederacy with Satan; though the contrary be fo
very evident. How dangerous is it to adopt any opinion, until it has been ftrictly and impartially examined?

2dly, The objection we are confidering farther
fuppofes, that our Lord in his reply refers the Pharifees to his doctrine for fatisfaction: whereas there is

not

* John xi. 47, 48. ch. xii. 19. Acts iv. 14, 16.
† John ix. 24.   ‡ V. 31.

not one word faid in relation to that, however oppofite it was to the interefts of the devil. As the objeΣion referred only to one particular kind of miracles; fo does the anfwer, which contains an argument in confutation of the objeΣion drawn from the
miracle itfelf. Our Lord is here addreffing himfelf to
thofe, who did.not acknowlege, and were unwilling
to be convinced of his authority; and therefore argues with them (as he was wont * to do) upon their
own principles, in order to filence thofe whom he
could not inftruΣ†: telling them, " that it was un-
" reafonable to impute his cure of demoniacs to the
" affiftance of the prince of demons; fince, if the
" miracle confifted (as they apprehended, and the
" objeΣion implied,) in the ejeΣion of demons; it
" was in its very nature an aΣ of hoftility againft
" them; and Satan could not be fuppofed to affift in
" overturning his own empire." With the fame
view of expofing the abfurdity of this calumny, upon
their own principles and pretenfions, he adds, " If
" I by Beelzebub caft out demons; by whom do
" your children caft them out? therefore they fhall
" be your judges." By the children of the Pharifees
                                                    we

---

* Mat. xi. 12, 13. ch. xxv. 24, 25. Luke xviii. 1—7.

† To the malicious Pharifees, who had been endeavouring
to infnare him, Chrift propofes this queftion, " If David call
Chrift Lord, how is he his Son?" Mat. xxii. 45. not for the
fake of folving the difficulty, but to leave his enemies fpeech-
lefs. And when they afked him, " Who gave him his authority?" Mat. xxi. 23; he anfwered this queftion with another,
to filence thofe who would not be convinced.

we are to underftand their difciples * and followers,
or the Jews who undertook † to .caft out demons in
the name of the God of Abraham, but who certainly
did not fucceed in their attempts ‡. And our Lord
(without either charging their doctrine with ab-
S   furdity,

* In like manner, by " the fons of the prophets," we are
to underftand the difciples of the prophets.

† Acts xiii. 19. That the Jews practifed exorcifms, farther appears from the teftimonies of Jofephus, Juftin Martyr,
Irenæus, Theophilus, and Origen, cited by Grotius, Hammond and Whitby on Mat. xii. 27.

‡ See Middleton's Free Inquiry, p. 84. To what is urged
by this excellent writer to difcredit the teftimony of the Fathers to the efficacy of the Jewifh exorcifms, I would add, that
Origen, notwithftanding his allowing to the Jews in his time
the power of cafting out devils, declares, " That the Jews,
" fince the coming of Chrift, are entirely deferted, have no
" token of the divine prefence amongft them, have no pro-
" phets, no miracles." Contra Celf. l. 2. p. 62. and l. 7. p.
337. And Juftin Martyr fpeaks of the prophetic gifts as
transferred from the Jews to the Chriftians. Dial. Tryph.
p. 308, 315. Indeed the Jewifh exorcifms as defcribed by
their own hiftorian (Jofeph. Ant. Jud. l. 8. c. 2. § 5.) are too
abfurd to be confuted. Accordingly the Jews who had been
accuftomed to the exorcifms of their countrymen, (in which
they made ufe of magical ceremonies and natural remedies,)
when they faw the diforders imputed to demons perfectly and
inftaneoufly cured by Chrift, were ftruck with the higheft aftonifhment. Luke xi. 14. Mark i. 26, 28. ch. v. 20. Luke
iv. 36, 37. The fight was *new*, and the miracle carried an
immediate conviction of its divinity, " They were amazed at
the mighty power of God," Luke ix. 43. and affirm, " It was
never fo feen in Ifrael," Mat. ix. 33. compare Mark ii. 12.
The feventy difciples triumphed in their cure of demoniacs, as
the

furday, or making any mention of the reasonable-
ness of his own,) reproaches the manifest inconsist-
ency of their conduct, in imputing his cure of demoniacs to Beelzebub, when they ascribed to God
the pretended success of their own exorcisms; and
at the same time taxes them as persons of the most
shameless disposition, in countenancing the grossest
impostures, while they resisted a miracle supported
by the clearest evidence. In the sequel of his address to the Pharisees, instead of referring them
to his doctrine, he urges the miracle itself as a full
and decisive proof of his being the Messiah *; which
it could not be, if it could have been performed by
those who opposed and blasphemed his character and
claims. And when he adds, that the ejection of demons argued a power (not only opposite, but) *superior* - to that of Beelzebub; he still reasons from the
nature of the miracle alone, according to their idea
of it. He closes his address in the same strain: " If
" it be a just maxim, that he is to be regarded as an
" enemy, who only refuses his assistance †; will you
" account me a friend and confederate with Satan,
" who directly oppose and dispossess him?'

As

the most wonderful and distinguishing privilege, Luke x. 17.
and the people regarded this miracle as the characteristic of
the Messiah, crying out at the sight of it, " Is not this the
Son of David?" Mat. xii. 23. Nay, the Pharisees themselves were never so far blinded by malice as to oppose the
Jewish exorcisms to Christ's cure of demoniacs: a plain proof
that the difference between them was too great to admit of
any comparison.

    * Mat. xii. 28.   † V. 29.   ‡ V. 30.

As there is no proof that our Lord ever did, fo it is utterly impoffible that our Lord ever fhould, refer the Jews to his doctrine, in order to convince them of the divinity of his works, or to fatisfy them that thofe works were not performed by the affiftance of the devil. For notwithftanding his miracles, they difputed his divine miffion and authority, on account of the apprehended abfurdity and impiety of his doctrine, and his extraordinary character and pretenfions as the Son of God. This was the cafe of thofe who reproached him with blafphemy, when he afferted his commiffion to forgive fin, though at the fame time he confirmed it by a miracle *; and of thofe who difparaged his multiplication of the loaves and fifhes, becaufe he fpoke to them of his fufferings and death †. Indeed the doctrine of his crofs was a ground of general offence both to Jews and Gentiles; and inftead of giving authority to the miracles of the Gofpel, ftood in need of their affiftance to procure it a reception. The Pharifees, who (as we have already obferved) could not but allow the divinity of his works, did neverthelefs conclude, from his performing them on the *Sabbath-day*, (and thus fubverting thofe fuperftitions, which they reverenced as the moft effential branches of religion,) that he muft needs be a wicked impoftor ‡. And the true reafon, why our Saviour, during the courfe of his perfonal miniftry,

S 2   did

---

* Mark ii. 7.

† John vi. 30, 31, 41, 60, 66.

‡ John ix. 14, 16.

did not more clearly and explicitly reveal fome parts
of his doctrine, was, that the prejudices of the Jews
against them were too stubborn to be overcome by the
cleareft evidence of their divinity *. To have directed them, therefore, to try his miracles by the doctrines they were intended to atteft, would only have
fo much the more confirmed them in their difbelief
of the Gofpel. Even after the refurrection of Christ,
when the Gofpel was propofed to them by the apoftles in its fulleft evidence, and the right of the Gentiles to all the privileges of the Christian church, without fubmitting to the Jewish law, was vindicated by
the miraculous donation of the Holy Ghoft to Cornelius and other uncircumcifed Gentiles; yet circumci-
fion was still infifted upon by many, as a neceffary
term of Christian communion.

It is to little purpofe therefore to plead, as the advocates of Christianity are apt to do, that the nature
of the doctrines which miracles are defigned to confirm, will ferve to point out the authors of the works;
inafmuch

---

* If Christ had made his doctrine a teft of the divinity of
his miracles, it would have been neceffary for him to have revealed his *whole* doctrine, before he required men to receive
him as a divine meffenger on account of his miracles: for how
could they judge whether thofe parts of his doctrine which he
had not revealed, were worthy of God or not? Neverthelefs
long after Christ had required men to receive him becaufe of
his works, he tells his own difciples, " I have yet many things
to fay unto you, but ye cannot bear them now." John xvi. 12.
Even at this day, no man, on the principle we here oppofe,
can regard the miracles of Christ as divine works, unlefs he be
previoufly affured, that he perfectly underftands the whole
Christian revelation.

inafmuch as this can do no fervice to Chriftianity. For the divinely authorized teachers of it did not, and confidering the prejudices of the firft converts, could not, make this ufe of its doctrines. Had there been any ambiguity in the proof from miracles, it would have been rejected by thofe to whom it was at firft propofed. In latter ages learned men have adventured (fuch is the prefumption and weaknefs of human reafon, in many perfons endowed with the largeft meafure of it!) to demonftrate a priori, that it became God to interpofe for the reformation of the world, juft at the time, and in the manner related in the Gofpel: and hence they infer the divinity of its miracles, and very often even their truth. But it is certain, that in the age in which the Gofpel was publifhed, nothing feemed more incredible, than its grand doctrine, that Jefus of Nazareth is the Meffiah. And Jefus and his apoftles won men to the belief of this article, by the evidence of prophecies and miracles, without once appealing to the internal credibility of it, or entering into any metaphyfical reafonings and difquifitions concerning the difpenfations of providence.

Indeed, fetting all prejudice afide, the Meffiahfhip of Jefus of Nazareth is a doctrine, which natural reafon cannot, of itfelf, difcover to be either true or falfe. It is a doctrine which admits of no other proof, than the teftimony of prophecies and miracles; and yet can never itfelf ferve to manifeft their divine original*. A late celebrated writer feems to have been

S 3 fenfible

* See below, ch. 5.

fenfible of this when he faid*, that we are " to dif-
" tinguifh between the doctrines we prove by mira-
" cles, and the doctrines by which we try miracles ;
" and that they are not the fame doctrines." With
what a number of fubtle diftinctions have the learned
perplexed the evidence of the Gofpel, fuch as render
it very unfit for being (what it was, by its gracious
author, defigned to be) the religion of the poor and
illiterate! If miracles are common to all fuperior
beings ; is it evident to an ordinary capacity, that
they necefTarily argue the immediate interpofition of
God, when performed by a perfon who teaches lef-
fons of morality ; though at the fame time he alleges
his miracles, in confirmation of claims and powers
quite diftinct from and fuperior to that of a teacher
of morality, fuch as his being the Meffiah and Son
of God? Befides, if the purity of Chrift's moral
precepts be a necefTary teft of the divinity of his works,
wrought to eftablifh his extraordinary pretenfions and
character ; how comes it to pafs, that neither Chrift
nor his apoftles have given us any information concerning this matter? As they have no where told
us, what thofe doctrines are, by which we are to try
their miracles ; if there be fuch doctrines, are they
not chargeable with the moft criminal omiffion ? an
omiffion, which no human wifdom or fagacity can
fupply. Nay, upon the fole evidence of miracles,
they demanded faith in Chrift as the Meffiah, *before*
they inftructed men in any other doctrines; and
therefore

* Sherlock's Dife. V. 1. p. 303, 304.

therefore certainly without fubmitting them to previous examination: which would have been very unreafonable, if thofe other doctrines are a neceffary teft
of the divinity of their miracles.

The plain matter of fact, as it appears to me, is
this: they never taught men to try their miracles either by the doctrine they were immediately defigned
to confirm, or by any other: but, on the contrary,
taught men to judge of their doctrine by their miracles. The very *purity* of the Chriftian doctrine, as
well as the nature of Chrift's perfonal claims, rendered
this conduct neceffary. The Jews in general, and
the Pagans more efpecially, were plunged into the
deepeft corruption. The latter were not only idolaters, but worfhipped their gods by acts of uncleann-
nefs, fuch as were fuitable to their apprehended natures. Would not the purity of the Gofpel create in
fuch perfons a prejudice againft its miracles *? What
could engage them, to embrace a doctrine that contradicted every fentiment and affection of their hearts,
but fuch works as were in themfelves, and according
to the genuine fentiments of nature, certain and evident proofs of a divine interpofition? Thofe therefore who endeavour to prove, that miracles alone are
not a fufficient criterion of a divine miffion; do not
attend to the nature of the Chriftian difpenfation, nor
to the ftate of the world when it was firft erected.
They likewife impeach the conduct of Chrift and his
apoftles, and labour to deftroy (though without de-

S 4   figning

* See above, ch. 2. fect. 5. p. 78-f-80.

figning it) the very foundation on which Chriftianity
is built.   We have fhewn in general, that if miracles
are ever performed in fupport of falfehood, they can
never afford certain evidence of a divine commiffion.
Leaft of all, then, can they ferve to eftablifh the divine miffion and authority of Chrift; which he requires us to acknowlege upon the account of his miracles, as in themfelves a compleat and fufficient evidence.

I have now laid before the reader various arguments from revelation, to prove that miracles are the
peculiar works of God.   Leaving others to judge of
the force of thofe arguments; I fhall conclude this
chapter with obferving, that what has been advanced
in it concerning the author of miracles, feems to me
to be confirmed by the main doctrines both of the
Jewifh and Chriftian revelations.   As it is the diftinguifhing doctrine of the Old Teftament, that Jehovah is the only true God; fo it is the diftinguifhing doctrine of the New Teftament, that Jefus Chrift
is the only mediator between God and man. "Though
" there be that are called gods, whether in heaven,
" or in earth," whether fuperior *celeftial* deities, or
inferior *terreftrial* demons, who are thought to interpofe in human affairs, and to controul the courfe of
events, in a fupernatural manner: " but to us there
" is but one God, the Father, of whom are all things,"
who is the fovereign of the whole world; " and one
" Lord Jefus Chrift, by whom are all things *," who
                                                          is

---

* 1 Cor. viii. 4, 5, 6.   1 Tim. ii. 5.

is the fole agent between heaven and earth, by whofe miniftry God exercifes his government over mankind. But if there are any other fuperior beings who can of themfelves interpofe in our affairs in a fupernatural manner, and controul the courfe of nature, without an immediate commiffion from God and his Chrift; then it is not true, that " there is none other God but one," or that Chrift is the only Lord of mankind. As to the former point, there has been occafion to confider it already * : with refpect to the latter, St. Paul obferves, that it was abfurd in Chriftians, who profeffed to believe in the one Lord, to have communion with other lords or demons †; his power excluding theirs. He charges the Coloffians " with not holding the head," or with fubverting the authority of Chrift, " by the worfhipping of angels," though they only afcribed to them a delegated power and authority over mankind. Others, perhaps, may be-able to reconcile thefe fentiments of the apoftle with the power of fuperior beings to work miracles; to me they feem to corroborate the other proofs from revelation, that miracles argue a divine interpofition.

* Chap. 3. fect. 5.
† 1 Cor. x. 19, 20, 21.

C H A P.

CHAP. IV.

SHEWING, THAT THE SCRIPTURES HAVE NOT RE-
CORDED ANY INSTANCES OF REAL MIRACLES
PERFORMED BY THE DEVIL; IN ANSWER TO THE
OBJECTIONS DRAWN FROM THE CASE OF THE
MAGICIANS IN EGYPT, FROM THE APPEARANCE
OF SAMUEL AFTER HIS DECEASE TO SAUL, AND
FROM OUR SAVIOUR'S TEMPTATIONS IN THE WIL-
DERNESS.

THE obfervations contained in the forego ig
chapter, are, I hope, fufficient to fhew, that
the Scriptures reprefent miracles as works appropriate
to God, and never attribute them to any other beings, unlefs when acting by his immediate power and
commiffion. Neverthelefs, to all this evidence it is
objected, " that the Scriptures cannot confider mira-
" cles as the works of God alone; inafmuch as they
" relate feveral *inftances*, in which evil fpirits have
" actually performed genuine and inconteftable mi-
" racles, without the order of God, in oppofition
" to his meffengers, and in fupport of error and
" wickednefs. This," it is alleged, " appears with
" the cleareft evidence, from the works of the ma-
" gicians in Egypt; from Samuel's being raifed up
" by the forcerefs at Endor; and from our Saviour's
" temptations in the wildernefs by the evil fpirit."

B

But if thefe narratives eftablifh the actual exercife of a miraculous power by the devil; then the Scriptures grofsly contradict themfelves, when (as I think, we have already fhewn) they deny this power to the devil, and appropriate it to God. But before we charge them with fuch grofs felf-contradiction, we ought to inquire, (if we treat them with the fame candour we do other writings,) whether the facts they record, and the doctrine they teach, are not perfectly confiftent. To this end, let us proceed to examine the feveral cafes which are appealed to, in fupport of the devil's power of working miracles. We will begin with confidering ·

S E C T. I.

The Cafe of the Magicians who oppofed Mofes.

VARIOUS are the accounts, which learned men have given of the works of the magicians in Egypt. Some have fuppofed, that God himfelf empowered the magicians to work true miracles, and gave them an unexpected fuccefs *. But whatever they performed, the hiftory afcribes it, not to God, but to their inchantments. Befides, would it not be injurious to the character of the Deity, to fuppofe that he acted in oppofition to himfelf? Would

he

---

* Dr. Fleetwood on miracles, Difc. 1. and Dr. Shuckford's Connexion, V. 2. p. 422. 2d edit.

he work ſome miracles to confront the authority of
Moſes, at the ſame time that he was working other
miracles to eſtabliſh it? And how, in this caſe,
ſhould Pharaoh know, whether it was his duty to
diſmiſs the Iſraelites, or to detain them? Would
God, by a miraculous interpoſition, require him to
do, and not to do, the very ſame thing?

Others imagine, that the devil aſſiſted the magicians, not in performing true miracles, but in deceiving the ſenſes of the ſpectators, or in preſenting
before them deluſive appearances of true miracles.
But we have already ſhewn * in general, that with ,
regard to the ſpectators, there is no manner of difference between *appearing* and *real* miracles, when
the fictions or illuſions are not diſtinguiſhable from
realities. And if Moſes had affirmed the works of
the magicians to be diabolical deluſions, or mere deceptions of the ſight; why might not Pharaoh have
affirmed the ſame concerning the works of Moſes?
If one ſide had pretended, for inſtance, that the devil
ſecretly ſtole away the rods, and ſubſtituted ſerpents
in their ſtead; the ſame might have been ſaid by the
other ſide: and the trial or competition muſt have
ended in a common diſtruſt of the ſenſes by both
parties, in confuſion, or mutual reproaches of fraud
and impoſition.

The opinion concerning the works of the magicians, which has moſt generally obtained ſince the
time of St. Auſtin, is, that they were not only performed

* Ch. 1. ſect. 3. p. 30, 31.

formed by the power of the devil, but were genuine miracles, and real imitations of thofe of Mofes. This opinion, however, has been rejected by feveral eminent writers, and even by fome very zealous affertors * of the power of fuperior beings to work miracles without the order of God; and who therefore might have acquiefced in the common explicaticn of this hiftory, had they not feen other reafons for departing from it, drawn from the circumftances of the hiftory itfelf. What I fhall attempt to fhew, is, that the magicians did not perform works really fupernatural, nor were affifted by any fuperior invifible being. In order to form a right judgment of this fubject, it may not be improper to confider

I. The character and pretenfions of the magicians. It has been already fhewn from the teftimony of Heathen writers, that the ancient magicians undertook to explain and to accomplifh things which were deemed far beyond the reach of other mens capacities †. Conformably to this view of them given us

by

---

* This is the cafe with regard to Dr. Sykes in particular. His account of the magicians contains fome excellent obfervations; neverthelefs his zeal to maintain the power of fuperior beings, and even of *evil* fpirits, to work genuine miracles, prevented him from taking notice of the ftrongeft objections againft the common explication of the performances of the magicians. At the fame time he has given, what I conceive to be, a very falfe account of their character and pretenfions; and left unexplained many circumftances of the hiftory, which are neceffary to the right underftanding of it.

† Ch. 3. fect. 3.

by Pagan antiquity, we learn from the ſacred writeis, that they were applied to by the kings of Egypt and Babylon to interpret and decypher their dreams *, as well as to diſcredit the miracles of Moſes. In the ex-ercife of their art, they relied much on their ſuperior knowledge of the ſecret powers of nature; yet we are not from hence to infer, with a late learned wri-ter †, that they did not pretend to any commerce with ſpirits or demons: for the extravagant prodigies they undertook to perform, their ceremonies, ſuppli-cations and prayers to the gods for aid and ſuccefs, demonſtrate the contrary §. Magic was indeed an art, and might be learnt, like any other art, from perſons ſkilful in it : but it was founded on the Pagan ſyſtem of theology, confiſted in the practice of the rites of ſuperſtition, and pretended even to a power of compelling the gods to execute their deſires. The appellations by which Moſes deſcribes the magicians, agrees with the account here given of their character and pretenſions. They are called *wiſemen, ſorcerers,* and *magicians* ‡. The original word which we render

* Gen. xli. 8. Dan. ii. 10, 27. ch. iv. 7. See below, note ‡, p. 288.

† Dr. Sykes on miracles, p. 142. Becauſe witchcraft was an art, the doctor concludes that witches did not pretend to receive their power from demons: whereas it was confidered as the art of ſetting demons to work.

§ Ch. 3. ſect. 3.

‡ " Then Pharaoh alſo called the wiſemen and the ſorcer-ers : now the magicians of Egypt, they alſo did," &c. Exod. vii. 11.

der, *magicians*, does properly fignify perfons who undertake *to explain things obfcure and difficult* *. It is here ufed as a general term, and comprehends under it *wifemen* and *forcerers*; as is evident from the manner in which they are mentioned ¶. Their being denominated *wifemen*, denotes their being the profeffors of fcience. With regard to the word we render *forcerers* †, it is derived from a verb ‡, which fignifies to ufe juggling tricks, to delude the fight with falfe appearances, fo as to make a thing feem otherwife than it is ‖; or rather to practife fafcination and charms. The word is always joined in Scripture with thofe which fignify *divination, fortune-telling*, or *revea'ing fecrets*: and it is from the fame root that the words which we render *witches* and *witchcraft* are derived §. Dr. Sykes ** and others have taken much fruitlefs pains

* See Le Clerc on Gen. xli. 8. (where the LXX render it by a word that fignifies *interpreters*,) and compare Dan. v. 11, 12. It is often explained by genethliaci or fapientes nativitatum, and is joined with aftrologers and foothfayers, Dan. i. 20. ch. ii. 10, 27. ch. iv. 7.

¶ See note ‡, p. 286.

† Heb. mecafhephim.   ‡ Cafhap.

‖ Vid. Buxtorf & Pagnin. in voc.

§ See Exod. xxii. 18. Deut. xviii. 10. 2 Chron. xxxiii. 6. 2 Kings ix. 22. Mic. v. 12. Le Clerc renders the word mecafhephim, *diviners*, Exod. vii. 11. And as thefe mecafhephim (forcerers or diviners) made ufe of dangerous drugs, and often employed their art in poifoning, the LXX render the word by φαρμακοί.

** On miracles, p. 166. When this learned writers affirms, that magic does not feem to be fo old as the days of Mofes in Egypt,

pains to prove, that all the names by which the magicians are deſcribed, import only *legerdemain ;* as if.
they had been jugglers by *profeſſion,* as well as *practice.*
There has been occaſion * to obſerve, that the Scripture deſcribes the Heathen gods, and thoſe who pretended to any intercourſe with them, by their uſual
appellations. And the names here given the magicians ſeem to exprefs what they were by profeſſion † ;
they affected the reputation of ſuperior knowlege ‡ ;
and pretended both to explain and effect ſigns, prodigies and wonders, by obſerving the rules of their
art. Theſe are the perſons who were called in by
Pharaoh on the preſent occaſion ; and we have ſeen
already that the Scripture denies them the ability of
diſcovering or effecting any thing ſupernatural ‖.

                                                    II.

Egypt, p. 158 ; he contradicts both the hiſtory before us, and
Gen. xli. 8 : which agree well with the later accounts of this
art; as will appear to any one who compares what occurs here,
with what was advanced above, ch. 3. ſect. 3.

* P. 253, 274.

† This is certainly the caſe, as to the two words *magicians,*
and *wiſemen* ; and therefore moſt probably is ſo with regard to
the third, *ſorcerers.* And indeed the word itſelf does more
properly import the practice of faſcination and charms, than of
legerdemain.

‡ In confirmation of what is obſerved here and above (ch.
3. ſect. 3.) concerning the magicians, I add a paſſage from
Tacitus, Hiſt. l. 4. Ptolomæus omine & miraculo excitus, ſa-
cerdotibus Egyptiorum, quibus *mos* talia intelligere, nocturnos
viſus aperit.

‖ Ch. 3. ſect. 3.

II. We are, in the next place, to inquire, with what defign they were fent for by Pharaoh.

To fuppofe that they were fent for, to engage the gods of Egypt to work miracles, in direct oppofition to the God of Ifrael; and thereby to invalidate Mofes's divine commiffion; is to contradict the fundamental principles of the Pagan theology, in which the king of Egypt had been educated. Though the Heathen poets do fometimes reprefent the gods as quarrelling with one another, and taking different fides; fome favouring a particular perfon, others perfecuting him *: neverthelefs, the claims of the different deities of the Pagans were fuppofed to be confiftent with each other †; and their theology, inftead of encouraging its votaries, to hope that one deity fhould protect them from the vengeance, or act in direct defiance of another, rather taught them to appeafe and gain over to their own fide thofe deities, who were fuppofed to be angry with them, and to protect their enemies ‡. So that had Pharaoh admit-

T ted,

---

* Ovid. Trift. l. 1. eleg. 2. v. 4.

† See above; ch. 3. fect. 5. p. 244.

‡ Cyrus endeavoured to appeafe the gods of the countries which he invaded, Xenoph. Cyropæd. l. 3. The Romans evoked the tutelary gods of the cities they befieged, Macrob. Saturnal. l. 3. c. 9. Plin. Nat. Hift. l. 24. c. 17. § 102. Plutarch. Craffum, p. 553. A. The Tyrians, when befieged by Alexander, bound the ftatues of Apollo and Hercules, to prevent them from deferting to the enemy, Quintus Curt. l. 4. c. 3. And the Lacedemonians, during war, prayed very early in the morning; that being the firft folicitors, they might pre-engage the

ted, that the works of Mofes had been performed by
the God of the Hebrews; he would not have applied
to the Egyptian deities to oppofe his operations and
claims *. Befides, on the principles of Pagans, who
held the doctrine of local and tutelary deities, the
performance of miracles by the gods of one country,
would not have deftroyed the claims arifing from the
like miracles performed by the gods of another country. And therefore if Pharaoh confidered the God
of Ifrael as a local deity, he would not have thought
Mofes's commiffion from him invalidated by miracles
performed by the gods of Egypt. But it is apparent,
from the attempts of the magicians, that they did not
ftrive to engage the gods of Egypt to limit, or controul, or in any manner to oppofe, the God of Ifrael.
For, in this cafe, they would have endeavoured to
traverfe and *counteract* the aim of the adverfe divinity, not to *promote* it; and would have entreated their
gods, not to aggravate and inhance the tremendous
effects of Jehovah's difpleafure by inflicting like judgments, but to diminifh or remove thofe already inflicted: not to turn more water into blood, for example, but to reftore the corrupted waters to their natural ftate: not to multiply frogs, but to remove or

deftroy

the gods in their favour, Xenophon de Laced. Rep. When
Balaam was fent for to curfe the Ifraelites, he had no expectation of fuccefs, without the permiffion of their God, Numb.
xxiii. 27. Thofe who conquered any country, adopted the gods
of the vanquifhed people.

* See Shuckford, V. 2. p. 406.

deſtroy them; eſpecially as it was, at leaſt, equally eaſy to do the latter as the former. Could the deities of Egypt more effectually expoſe themſelves to the reproaches and indignation of their votaries, than by committing acts of hoſtility againſt them, inſtead of protecting or delivering them from the plagues and vengeance of the adverſe Divinity? And were the Egyptians likewiſe ſo infatuated, as to deſire the divine guardians of their country, to join with the God of the Hebrews in bringing down more and heavier judgments, and adding to thoſe direful plagues which he had already inflicted? If Pharaoh and his magicians contrived no better for the relief or protection of their country, we may be certain that Egypt, in their days, was not famed for wiſdom.

The real ſtate of the caſe ſeems to have been, that Moſes having in the name of Jehovah, the God of the univerſe, who had taken the Hebrews under his peculiar protection, demanded of Pharaoh leave for them to go three days journey into the wilderneſs, to perform a ſacrifice; and having at the requeſt of the king of Egypt *ſhewn him a miracle**, by turning his rod into a ſerpent, in order to authenticate the divinity of his miſſion; Pharaoh, notwithſtanding this miracle, refuſed to conſent to the demand of Moſes. It is natural to ſuppoſe, that a ſuſpicion that the Iſraelites were meditating an eſcape from that wretched ſlavery in which they were detained, (which might naturally ſpring up in a mind conſcious of its own in-

T 2   juſtice

* Exod. vii. 9.

juſtice and oppreſſion,) and the fear of loſing ſo very
numerous and valuable a body of ſlaves, together
with all their flocks and herds; would prevent Pharaoh from being forward on this occaſion, either to
receive or follow conviction. We ſhall the leſs doubt
of this, if we call to mind the pride of princes, (which
is not eaſily reconciled to a diminution of their grandeur,) or the peculiar rigour of the Egyptian policy,
and the aſtoniſhing magnificence of their public
works *. Pharaoh was, as he told Moſes, a ſtranger
to Jehovah, in whoſe name he came: a Deity worſhipped only by his Hebrew ſlaves, whom he had permitted to groan under the moſt cruel oppreſſions, and
even amongſt them very little, and but lately known.
And his character as the God of the univerſe, the *only* true God, being ſubverſive of the claims of all the
Egyptian deities, would at firſt appear, to one accuſ-
tomed to worſhip a plurality of gods, (many of whom,
and particularly the lights of heaven, were thought to
exhibit continually the moſt conſpicuous proofs of their
divinity,) as the higheſt abſurdity and blaſphemy. The
Egyptians were early famed for wiſdom and learning,
and more eſpecially for their knowlege of the nature
and worſhip of the gods; their ſentiments on this
                                                    ſubject

---

* The pyramids are a proof of the peculiar turn and genius
of the Egyptians to works of magnificence and grandeur;
which is alſo confirmed by the teſtimony of Diodorus Siculus,
l. 1. p. 27. ed. Rhodomani. The Iſraelites were employed in
their public buildings, as appears from Exodus, ch. i. and v.
and, no doubt, in many other ways ſo large a body of people
muſt contribute to the benefit of the ſtate.

fubject feem to have been received with deference and fubmiffion by all the neighbouring nations. At the fame time they exceeded them all in zeal for fu-perftition and idolatry. It muft therefore be difficult for us to conceive, what great offence it gave to their pride and bigotry, to be told, that there was no other God but Jehovah, and that the Ifraelites, at that time the moft defpicable and wretched part of mankind, were his peculiar people. This was upbraiding *Egypt* with ignorance and impiety, as well as with injuftice and cruelty.

Nor is it at all unlikely, that Pharaoh might fome-what doubt at firft, whether the miracle which had been wrought for his conviction, did certainly fur-pafs the powers of nature, and the fcience of magic, and was a proper proof of the fole Divinity of the God of Ifrael. He had never till then feen an exam-ple of this kind ; nor indeed had fuch wonders, as thofe of Mofes in Egypt, ever been performed before this time: which might occafion fome hefitation and furprize. The laws of nature in general, and thofe in particular concerning the generation of animals, the feafons, circumftances and means of their being pro-duced and brought to life, were not fo well under-ftood, as at prefent. And as they conceived of the whole fyftem of nature as animated and divine *, they entertained an extravagant opinion of its hidden pow-ers. Learning was in a few hands; and therefore it was not fo eafy to diftinguifh what was merely un-

T 3   ufual

---

* See above, ch. 3. fect. 2. at the beginning.

uſual and aſtoniſhing, from what was ſupernatural.
A few ages ago our own countryman, friar Roger
Bacon, in virtue of his improvements in natural knowledge, paſſed for a conjurer, without having any deſign on his part to impoſe upon the people. The antient magicians *ſtudied* to raiſe in others the higheſt
poſſible idea of their profeſſion. And it was the received opinion of antiquity, that divination and prodigies (with the laſt of which Egypt * abounded more
than any other country,) were the effect of the natural influence of the elements and planets, and that
magicians who dived into the arcana or ſecrets of nature, and were maſters of their own profeſſion, could
regularly bring them to paſs, according to the fixed
and certain principles of their ſcience. In this ſcience
Moſes himſelf had been inſtructed. And probably
the firſt thought of Pharaoh was, that Moſes was nothing more than a magician †.

In this view of things, what was more natural than
for Pharaoh to ſend for his magicians, in order to learn
from them, whether the ſign given by Moſes was truly
ſupernatural, or only ſuch as their art was able to accompliſh. The nature of their attempts correſpond
                                                    with

---

* Τίϱαῖά τε πλίω ſφι εὕϱηται ἤ τοῖσι ἄλλοισι ἅπασι ἀνθϱώποισι. Herodot. Euterpe, c. 82.

† Moſes had been brought up in the palace of Pharaoh, and
was " learned in all the wiſdom of the Egyptians," Acts vii.
22; and therefore it was natural to account him a magician.
On the very ſame grounds, Daniel and the three children were
accounted magicians at Babylon, Dan. i. 4, 20. ch. iv. 7—9,
ch. v. 11.

with this view of Pharaoh in calling them to his affiftance. For they did not undertake to *out-do* Mofes,
or to *controul* him by *fuperior* or *oppofite* acts of power,
but barely to *imitate* him, or to do the fame works
with his: which they did with a view to invalidate
the argument which he drew from his miracles, in
fupport of the fole Divinity of Jehovah, and of his
own miffion. And had the magicians fucceeded in
their attempt, and, in the exercife of their art, really
performed the fame extraordinary acts as Mofes did;
it would have followed of courfe, that Mofes, whatever he might pretend, was a magician only * and not
an extraordinary divine meffenger; and that Jehovah
was not the only fovereign of nature †. It is of the
laft importance therefore to attend to the true point
in queftion upon this occafion. The queftion was
not, and could not be, " Are the gods of Egypt fu-
" perior to the God of Ifrael? or, Can any evil fpi-
" rits perform greater miracles than thofe which Mo-
" fes performed by the affiftance of Jehovah?" Every circumftance of the hiftory ferves to fhew, that the
queftion was, " Are the works of Mofes proper
" proofs, that the God of Ifrael is Jehovah, the only
" fovereign of nature, and confequently that Mofes

T 4

acts

* Pliny (in his Nat. Hift. l. 30. c. 2.) mentions Mofes a-
mongft the moft illuftrious magicians: which is the higheft
character under which he could be confidered on the common
hypothefis.

† See ch. 3. fect. 5. p. 227, 245. If the magicians had performed real miracles, the confequences would have been the
fame as if Baal had anfwered by fire. P. 247.

" acts by his commiſſion? or, Are they merely the
" wonders of nature, and the effects of magic * ?"
To reſolve this queſtion, Pharaoh ſent for his magicians; and they by their magical feats undertook to
ſhew, that Moſes's works lay within the compaſs of
their art, and therefore could be no proofs of the
high claims of the God of Iſrael, or of Moſes's divine commiſſion.

III. But it may be aſked, what motives could induce the magicians to make ſuch an attempt, ſince
notwithſtanding Pharaoh might, *they* could not be
ignorant of the extent of their own art? When they
were firſt ſent for to court, they as well as Pharaoh
might conceive of Moſes as nothing more than a magician, like themſelves. And though it be too weak
an authority for ſuch an ancient fact, yet it may de-
ſerve juſt to be mentioned, on account of the probability of the thing itſelf, that according to the *Talmud*, when Moſes began to work his miracles, the
magicians bantered him, ſaying, " Thou bringeſt
ſtraw to Affra†," (or, as we ſhould expreſs it, " Thou
bringeſt

---

* It may be worth obſerving, that both Philo (de vita Mo-
ſis, l. 1. p. 616.) and Joſephus (Antiq. Jud. l. 2. c. 13.) place
the ſubject in the ſame light.

† The learned authors of the Univerſal Hiſtory, though
they adopt the common explication of the wonders of the magicians, have taken notice of this Jewiſh tradition. And they
farther obſerve, that Philo introduces them ſpeaking to Pharaoh and his court, to this purpoſe, " Why are you affrighten-
" ed? We are not ignorant of ſuch things, ſeeing we profeſs
" the ſame ourſelves." Univerſal Hiſtory, v. 3. 8vo. p. 373.
note E.

bringeſt coals to Newcaſtle ;") meaning that he had
judged ill to play his tricks in a country ſtocked with
magicians, who were as well verſed as himſelf in the
powers of nature, and in the knowlege of the ſecret
arts. And it is certain, that they muſt ſoon diſcover,
how reluctant the king was to part with the Iſraelites,
and therefore how acceptable to him it would be,
ſhould they by their ſkill and dexterity be able to
imitate, and thereby to diſcredit the miracles of Moſes. And by a mind prejudiced as his was, they well
knew, that mere cavils, and the moſt barefaced ſophiſtry are often eſteemed a ſufficient confutation of
the moſt concluſive arguments. Beſides, the king,
reſolutely determined not to hearken to Moſes, might
be ſo unreaſonable as to require that of his magicians
which was beyond their power*; by which they
might be tempted to have recourſe to artifice, to
ſcreen themſelves from his vengeance. And their
concern at all times, from motives of pride and ambition †, to raiſe the reputation of their art to an extravagant height, continually prompted them to have recourſe to fallacy to ſupport it. And this extravagance
of their pretenſions gave ſome colour to the reſent-
ment of princes, when their boaſted enterprizes failed

in

---

* See Dan. ii. 1—13. The prophets of Baal likewiſe, 1
Kings xviii. 24. made an experiment, without any well-ground-
ed expectation of ſucceſs, becauſe the people approved of Elijah's propoſal.

† Strabo (Geogr. l. 1.) tells us, " that the prieſts of Egypt,
" the Chaldeans and magi obtained great honour and pre-emi-
" nence, becauſe they excelled in all kinds of knowlege."

in the execution. In the cafe before us, the magicians of Egypt were under every temptation to en-
counter Mofes at all hazards, and if poffible to fupply by collufion their defect of power. And they
might the more eafily hope for fuccefs and applaufe,
or at leaft to avoid difgrace and detection, as they
knew the whole court as well as the king would be
forward to avail themfelves of the appearance not only of equality, but of any refemblance between their
performances and thofe of Mofes. From this reprefentation of the motives and aims of the magi, let us
now proceed to confider thofe of Mofes.

IV. If we examine the principles and conduct of
Mofes, we fhall foon be fenfible, that he could not
allow the magicians performed real miracles. For

1. We have already proved, that the Scriptures
ever reprefent the whole body of magicians as impoftors *, who were incapable of fupporting their
pretenfions by any works or predictions beyond human power and fkill.

2. It has been alfo fhewn †, that all the facred writers, and Mofes in particular, reprefent all the Heathen deities (on the belief of whofe exiftence and influence the ‡ magic art was founded) as unfupported
by any invifible fpirits, and in themfelves utterly impotent and fenfelefs; and certainly therefore incapable of imitating the ftupendous miracles of Mofes.

3. This

---

* Ch. 3. fect. 3. p. 182.

† Ch. 3. fect. 3. p. 156, 157.

‡ Ch. 3. fect. 2. p. 178.

3. This divine prophet farther taught, that the God of Ifrael was Jehovah, who alone created the world by his power, and ruled it continually by his providence *. His religion was built on the unity and fole dominion of God, as its foundation. And the point which Mofes *at this very time* was about to eftablifh, was, the fole Divinity of Jehovah †, in direct oppofition to the principles of idolatry, and confequently with a view of expofing the abfolute nullity of all the Heathen gods; the claims of the former being fubverfive of thofe of the latter. If Mofes therefore allowed, that the Heathen idols (or, which we have fhewn to be the fame thing, any evil fpirits‡ fupporting their caufe) enabled the magicians' " to " turn rods into ferpents, and water into blood, and " to create frogs ‖," and confequently any other fpecies of animals, which require only equal fkill and power; he contradicts the great defign of his miffion; and overturns the whole fabric of his religion. For on the fuppofition here made, the Heathen deities are not mere nullities, and Jehovah is not God alone.

* Ch. 3. fect. 5. p. 228.

† Ch. 3. fect. 5. p. 232, 236.

‡ Ch. 3. fect. 2. p. 162.

‖ I might have added, that the advocates of the common hypothefis (in effect) allow, that thofe invifible beings who fupported the magicians, had a power of *turning duft into lice*, when they afcribe their not doing it, to their being *reftrained* by God.

alone. Whatever beings are able to create ſeveral different ſpecies of animals, and to multiply them at pleaſure, (and hereby to deſtroy the wiſe economy of the animal world,) and to change the inmoſt nature both of inanimate ſubſtances, and of living beings; whether we will allow ſuch beings the *name* of God or not, they certainly poſſeſs in a very high degree thoſe *powers*, which, according to the united teſtimony of reaſon and revelation, are the appropriate and diſtinguiſhing glories of the one true God. If the bringing things into exiſtence, be no teſt of a divine interpoſition, to what more authentic teſt can we appeal? The creation of beings endued with *life*, does more eſpecially ſeem to be a branch of the divine prerogative *; the loweſt degrees of animal life having an excellence and dignity ſuperior to all the glories of inanimate nature †. Such a creating power, and

---

* A creating power is repreſented in Scripture as a divine prerogative, Iſ. xliv. 24. and as the foundation of the worſhip which God claims from mankind, Jerem. v. 22. " His glory he will not give to another." Iſ. xlii. 8. ch. xlviii. 11.

† What biſhop Sherlock affirms concerning the miracles of Moſes, (V. 1. p. 283.) would be true alſo of the works of the magicians, had they been, as he ſuppoſes, real miracles: " They " were ſo near akin to the works of creation, that by a juſt " compariſon they might be known to come from the ſame au- " thor." Or rather, ſince works of creation were performed by oppoſite inviſible powers; it would follow of courſe, that there was a plurality of creators; and therefore of rival Gods. See above, ch. 2. ſect. 4. Were the common account of the magicians true; their works muſt neceſſarily have been conſidered by Pharaoh as a full demonſtration of the exiſtence and power

and fuch a fovereignty over nature, as the Heathen deities are here fuppofed to have difplayed, muſt make it difficult, if not impoſſible, to determine, what parts of the creation, and what events of providence are to be afcribed to God alone. Who can tell how far the power of evil fpirits may extend on other occafions, when uncontrouled by God; if they were capable even of oppofing and contravening, in fuch an aſtoniſhing degree, his operations and defigns, at the very time he was publicly afferting his own peculiar honours *?

4. Mofes appropriates all miracles to God, and urges his own as an abfolute and authentic proof, both of the fole Divinity of Jehovah, and of his own miſſion †: which he could not juſtly do, if his oppofers performed miracles, and even the very fame with his. But here it is alleged, notwithſtanding we ſhould admit that the magicians wrought real miracles, yet that in the iſſue it appeared, Mofes was fupported by the true God; becaufe he performed more

and,

power of his own gods, and as a fuller vindication of their worſhip (at leaſt of a fubordinate worſhip,) than the Pagan prieſthood ever produced.

* It is the more incredible, that God ſhould now fuffer any evil fpirit to work miracles in oppofition to himfelf; as this was the *firſt time* of interpofing in a miraculous manner, for the conviction of the world, and no fuch miracles were performed in any fnbfequent conteſt between him and the idol gods. 1 Kings xviii.

† See the paſſages cited above, ch. 3. feᴄt. 5. p. 236. fect. 6. p. 249. and below, p. 304—307.

and greater miracles than his oppofers. "The mira-
" cles performed by the magicians in Egypt," (fays
an able and eloquent writer *,) " were fo far from
" leffening the authority of the works done by Mo-
" fes, that they added to it: For, the greater the
" powers were which God humbled and fubdued,
" the greater evidence did he give of his own fupe-
" riority." Many other learned writers have likewife
pleaded, that the miracles oppofed by the idolatrous
magicians to thofe of Mofes, the prophet of God,
ferved only to fet off the divine power to the greateft
advantage. But I can not perfuade myfelf, that the
power of God appears to any, much lefs to the beft
advantage; but when it performs works peculiar to
itfelf, fuch as no creatures are able to imitate; and
carries the divine defigns into execution, without any
controul. The *fuperiority* however of the true God
to the Heathen deities, was not the point in queftion.
What Mofes propofed to prove, was, that Jehovah
was God alone, and that there was none befides him,
and confequently that the Heathen gods were mere
nullities. Now, if in their names very great miracles
were performed by the magicians, and ftill greater
by Mofes in the name of Jehovah; though we may
allow that hereby Jehovah proved himfelf fuperior †

to

* Bifhop Sherlock, in his Difcourfes, V. 1. p. 285.

† It was fhewn above, ch. 2. fect. 6. p. 83, that in the
cafe of fuch a conteft as is here fuppofed, between two oppofite
parties working miracles for victory; though he who exerts
greater acts of power than his opponent, may be allowed to
poffefs

to the Heathen gods; yet this fuperiority to them will not prove that he is God alone, and that the Heathen gods were nullities, deftitute of that very power which they vifibly exerted. " The greater " the powers were which God humbled and fubdu- " ed;" with fo much the lefs truth could they be reprefented as impotent and fenfelefs idols. Had Mofes, while he allowed to the gods of Egypt a creating power, (or what feems very nearly to approach it;) attempted nothing more than to prove the fuperiority of the God of Ifrael; this would rather have eftablifhed than over-turned the Pagan fyftem, which was built upon a belief of gods of different orders, who poffeffed various degrees of excellence and power.

But a cafe fo very abfurd, as that of two oppofite parties working miracles for victory, would never have been put, had the defenders of revelation more carefully attended to the ftate of the controverfy * between the prophets of God, and the antient idolaters. And were it true in general, that in cafe of a conteft between two parties performing real miracles, he who does the moft and greateft is fent of God; yet this would be of no fervice to the caufe of Mofes; becaufe he places the truth of his miffion on a different footing. Mofes certainly beft underftood the evidence arifing from his own miracles; and it is impoffible

---

poffefs greater degrees of power; yet it will not follow from hence, that he is affifted by the Divine power.

* Ch. 3. fect. 5. p. 243.

impoffible to make a juft vindication of them, unlefs
we vindicate the ufe to which *he* applies them. Now
Mofes never alleges in his own favour, that on the
whole he performed more and greater miracles, than
his oppofers *. He urges his miracles in an abfolute,
not in a comparative view, as full proofs of his miffion from Jehovah: which he could not juftly have
done, at leaft with regard to thofe miracles which
were performed both by him, and his rivals, had
there been any fuch. This will more fully appear
under the next head, where we fhall fhew, that

5. Mofes not only urges his miracles in general,
but even each individual miracle apart, as a compleat
proof both of the Divinity of Jehovah, and his own
miffion. With regard to his firft miracle, the transformation of his rod into a ferpent, he was directed
by God to perform and propofe it both to the Ifraelites and Egyptians as *a fign* †, furely not as a doubtful and fallacious, but as a certain and demonftrative,
fign of his miffion from Jehovah, the God of the Hebrews; without taking into confideration any fuppofed fuperiority he was afterwards to acquire. Yet
how was the transformation of his rod a demonftration of his being fent by Jehovah, if the magicians
produced

* Nor do any of the prophets of God ever plead the fuperiority of their miracles, either in refpect of number or excellence, to thofe of their oppofers; neceffary as fuch a plea would
have been, in cafe their oppofers had performed real miracles.
Thefe divine meffengers appeal to their works, as being in
themfelves, and feparately confidered, figns of a divine miffion.

† Exod. iv. 1—5. ch. vii. 8, 9.

produced the very fame credentials, to fhew the falfehood of his commiffion? Nay, the magicians, in the
firft conteft, if they performed real miracles, not only imitated, but exceeded Mofes; having the advantage over him in the *number* of their miracles. For
they turned not only one rod into a ferpent, which
was all Mofes had hitherto done; but they turned
their feveral rods into ferpents. Now, why is Mofes
to be credited on account of a fingle miracle, if it be
contradicted and overborne by feveral miracles, fully
equal to it? Befides, with refpect to the Ifraelites,
they had not only been inftructed to receive, but
had actually received, Mofes as a meffenger from Jehovah, the God of their fathers *, upon the evidence
of the miraculous converfion of his rod into a ferpent. What doubts then, nay, what fhame on account of their own credulity, and what indignation
againft Mofes, muft they have felt, when they faw
this evidence overturned and deftroyed, which Mofes
had propofed, and they had admitted, as valid in itfelf, without the aid of any further miracle? Afterwards, it is true, Mofes's ferpent fwallowed up thofe
of the magicians: but this after-victory, however
fplendid, could not retrieve the credit of the former
defeat; it could not eftablifh the validity of the proof,
from the change of his rod, which he had appealed
to in the beginning, as a decifive teftimony in his favour: but which was entirely deftroyed by the magicians changing their rods into ferpents. In like manner

U

* Exod. iv. 1—5.

ner, concerning the firſt miraculous plague ; Moſes
was commanded to ſay to Pharaoh, in the name of
God, " IN THIS thou ſhalt know that I am Jeho-
" vah : behold, I will ſmite with the rod that is in
" mine hand, upon the waters which are in the ri-
" ver, and they ſhall be turned into blood *." Now,
if the magicians afterwards performed the very ſame †
kind

---

* Exod. vii. 17.   See above, p. 237, nota ‡, where other
examples are produced, to ſhew what uſe Moſes makes of each
individual miracle.

† I allow indeed, that, on the common hypotheſis, the miracles of turning water into blood, and bringing up frogs, as performed by the magicians, were not ſo extenſive, as the ſame
miracles when performed by Moſes.   But, on that hypotheſis,
the reaſon might be, that when the magicians undertook theſe
miracles, it was impoſſible to carry them to the ſame extent ;
the waters of Egypt being previouſly converted into blood, and
the country covered with frogs, by Moſes.   And to this cauſe,
rather than to any defeƈt of power in the magicians, the Egyptians would naturally aſcribe the difference between their works
and thoſe of Moſes, if the former had been real miracles.   In
caſe you allow the magicians a miraculous power of turning
water into blood, how will you ſhew, that they did not exert
it, as far as the ſcarcity of water would permit, and therefore
as far as it could have been exerted by Moſes himſelf, had he
been in their ſituation ?   Why then ſhould it be taken for granted, by the advocates of the common hypotheſis, that, when the
magicians had (it is ſuppoſed) turned a certain quantity of water into blood, their power was limited to that particular quantity, and could extend no farther ; inaſmuch as the hiſtory contains an obvious reaſon for their not turning more water into
blood, there being very little water on which the experiment
could be made ?   When Chriſt converted into wine, the water
in ſix veſſels ; did he not hereby give proof of a power, which
couƚd

kind of miracle; it was no more a proof that the
God of the Hebrews was Jehovah, than that one of
the Egyptian idols was Jehovah. With what truth
then could it be affirmed to Pharaoh, " By *this* mira-
" cle, the diftinguifhing character of the true God
" fhall be fully made known and difplayed?" Had

U 2   Mofes

could have produced the fame change in a much larger quantity? The limits of the miracle were determined by the occafion and circumftances of it, and do not create the leaft prefumption of any defect of power. I add, that if this miracle of
Chrift was in itfelf a proof of a divine interpofition; why do
men deny the divinity of the fimilar miracle, which they afcribe
to the magicians? From the mere nature of the work itfelf,
no argument can be drawn to its difadvantage. It was indeed
lefs extenfive, than the correfponding miracle of Mofes; but
we have accounted for this difference. Befides, in miracles of
the fame kind, can the abettors of the common hypothefis determine on their own principles, how far the power of the devil reaches, and where the power of God begins? Were we
to allow them, that whenever one miracle exceeds another in
extent, the moft extenfive miracle muft neceffarily proceed
from a being of the moft extenfive power; this would not prove
its divinity, as was fhewn above, ch. 2. fect. 6. Nor did Mofes
ever reft his miffion, on his miracles being more extenfive, than
the fuppofed miracles of the magicians. Nay, God himfelf fays
to Mofes, Exod. iv. 9. " If they will not believe even thefe
two figns," (the turning the rod of Mofes into a ferpent, and
the ferpent into a rod again, and the making his hand leprous
and found,) " thou fhalt take of the water of the river, and
" pour it upon the dry land, and the water which thou takeft
" out of the river, fhall become blood upon the dry land."
Here the quantity of water could not be confiderable; neverthelefs, the converfion of it into blood is propofed as a certain
fign of Mofes's divine miffion.

Mofes on this occaſion referred the king for conviction to his fubfequent miracles : this new evidence,
however forcible, could not have refcued him from
the juſt reproach of having before offered (and by a
pretended command of God) fuch as was futile and
fallacious, and of ſtill claiming a title to a divine le-
gation, which, on the iffue he had put it, had been
already decided againſt him.   Though we ſhould allow Mofes but the common difcretion of a man, and
deny him the divine guidance of a prophet of God ;
we cannot fuppofe him guilty of fo weak a conduct
as this ; which muſt have funk the Ifraelites into de-
fpondency, afforded the Egyptians juſt occaſion of
triumph, and fully vindicated Pharaoh in treating
Mofes as an impoſtor, who had offered falfe teſts of a
divine agency and miffion. Our learned divines would
never have fuppofed, that Mofes believed the magicians performed real miracles, and the fame with his
own ; had they confidered the ufe which this divine
prophet makes of each diſtinct and particular miracle
which he performed.

6. The abfurdity of fuppofing that Mofes allows
the magicians the credit of real miracles, will appear
in a ſtill ſtronger light, if we recollect *the order of
time*, in which their fuppofed miracles, and thofe of
Mofes, were performed. Dr. Clarke*, after moſt o-
ther writers, feems to have inverted the true order of
time, when he places the miracles of the magicians
firſt : " The magicians worked feveral miracles to
" prove

* Vol. 2. p. 700. fol.

"prove Mofes an impoftor, and not fent of God;
"Mofes, to prove his divine commiffion, worked mi-
"racles more and greater than theirs." But, according to the hiftory, Mofes firft of all turns his rod into
a ferpent; and thereby, according to his own and our
reprefentation, fully eftablifhes his divine miffion. Immediately after, his oppofers deftroy the force of that
evidence to which he had appealed, by producing (according to the common hypothefis) the very fame e-
vidence, and in a more perfect degree, to prove him
an impoftor. In the next place, Jehovah interpofes
to recover the loft credit of his meffenger, and the
ferpent of Mofes fwallows up thofe of the magicians.
But the fpectators might juftly doubt, whether one
ferpent's eating another was a greater miracle, than
the turning feveral rods into fo many ferpents; and
therefore muft remain in fufpence on which fide the
fuperiority lay. However that might be, Jehovah a
third time engages to evince his own Divinity, and
the authority of his ambaffador, by turning the waters of Nile into blood. But now the evil fpirit (according to the commonly received account of this
matter) interpofes in his turn, and by rivalling the
operations of Jehovah, defeats his intention, and ex-
pofes the infufficiency of the means ufed to accomplifh it; and hereby gains a temporary triumph over
the profeffed fovereign of the univerfe. God interpofes again, and with the fame view as before, and
brings frogs upon the land of Egypt. But his inten-
tions are again fruftrated by Satan, who performed
the fame atchievement, to convince the world that

U 3

that

that work had been falfely arrogated by God as his
fole prerogative.   Thus (according to the prevailing
hypothefis) were the claims of Jehovah and Mofes on
the one hand, and of the magicians and the devil on
the other, alternately eftablifhed and deftroyed; the
fuperiority of power appearing on both fides at different times: nay, hitherto more frequently, and indeed more inconteftably belonging to the devil, than
to God; inafmuch as it was not Jehovah who controuled the fuppofed miracles of the devil, (one inftance alone excepted,) but the devil who controuled
the miracles of Jehovah.   The abettors of the common hypothefis are concerned to fhew, that their account of this conteft, if traced into its genuine confequences, is not big with impiety, and the moft dif-
honourable apprehenfions of the bleffed God.   Can
they deliberately perfuade themfelves, that the almighty fovereign of nature would engage in an open
conteft for fupremacy with the devil? and that he
would fuffer him to appear on fome occafions as his
rival, and even as his fuperior, capable of fruftrating
his great defigns, invalidating the proofs he thought
fit to give of his univerfal dominion, and hereby rendering him contemptible in the eyes of the Ifraelites
and Egyptians?   Or, could his claim to be Jehovah,
and the only fovereign of nature, be both true and
falfe?   For thefe reafons, (and feveral others which
will occur in the fequel,) Mofes could not reprefent
the magicians as performing real miracles.

V. Here perhaps it may be objected, that Mofes
defcribes the works of the magicians in the very fame
language

language as he does his own * ; and therefore that there is reafon to conclude, that they were equally miraculous. To which I anfwer,

1. That nothing is more common, than to fpeak of profeffed jugglers as *doing*, what they *pretend* and *appear* to do † ; and that this language never mifleads us, when we reflect what fort of men are fpoken of, namely, mere impofers on the fight. Why might not Mofes then ufe the common popular language, when fpeaking of the magicians, without any danger of mifconftruction; inafmuch as the fubject he was treating, all the circumftances of the narrative, and the opinion which the hiftorian was known to entertain of the inefficacy and impofture of magic, did all concur to prevent miftakes?

2. Mofes does not affirm, that there was a perfect

U 4   conformity

---

* " The magicians of Egypt alfo did in like manner with " their inchantments. For they caft down every man his rod, " and they became ferpents." Exod. vii. 11, 12. After Aaron had turned all the waters of Egypt into blood, it is faid, " The magicians did fo with their inchantments," v. 22. And again it is faid, " The magicians did fo with their inchant- " ments, and brought up frogs upon the land of Egypt," ch. viii. 7.

† When Mofes defcribes what the magicians pretended and feemed to perform by faying, " They caft down every man his " rod, and they became ferpents, and they brought up frogs " upon the land of Egypt;" he only ufes the fame language as Apuleius, (Metam. l. 1.) when defcribing a perfon who merely played juggling tricks, Circulatorem afpexi equeftrem fpatham præacutam mucrone infefto devoraffe : ac mox eundem,—venatoriam lanceam,—in ima vifcera condidiffe.

conformity between his works and thoſe of the magicians. He does not cloſe the reſpective relations of
his own particular miracles with ſaying, The magicians' did " that thing *," or, " According to what
he did, ſo did they †;" (a form of ſpeech uſed on
this occaſion, no leſs than three times in one chapter,
to deſcribe the exact correſpondence between the orders of God, and the behaviour cf his ſervants):
but makes choice of a word of great latitude, ſuch as
does not neceſſarily expreſs any thing more than a
general ſimilitude, ſuch as is conſiſtent with a difference in many important reſpects: They did *ſo*, or
in like manner, as he had done. That a perfect imitation of Moſes could not be deſigned by this word,
is evident from its being applied to caſes, in which ſuch
an imitation was abſolutely impracticable: for when
Aaron had converted all the waters of Egypt into
blood ‡, we are told, " the magicians did ſo," that
is, ſomething *in like ſort.* Nor can it be ſuppoſed,
that they covered the land of Egypt with frogs; as
will be ſhewn below. Nay, the word imports nothing more, than their *attempting* ſome imitation of
Moſes: for it is uſed when they failed in their attempt. " They did SO——to bring forth lice, but
" they could not ‖."

3. So

---

* As in Exod. ix. 5, 6.

† Ch. vii. 6, 10. 20.

‡ Exod. vii. 20—25.

‖ Ch. viii. 18. Le Clerc obſerves, Nec raro Hebræi, ad
conatum notandum, verbis utuntur quæ rem effectam ſignifi-
cant.

3. So far is Mofes from afcribing the tricks of the magicians to the invocation and power of demons, or to any fuperior beings whatever ; that he does moft exprefsly refer all they did or attempted in imitation of himfelf, " to human artifice and impofture." The original words which are tranflated *inchantments* *, are entirely different from that rendered inchantments in other paffages of Scripture, and do not carry in them any fort of reference to forcery, or magic, or the interpofition of any fpiritual agents. They import deception and concealment, and ought to have been rendered, *fecret fleights* or *jugglings ;* and are thus tranflated even by thofe who adopt the common hypothefis

---

cant. Gen. xxxvii. 21. Confult him likewife on Exod. viii. 18. ch. xii. 48. Pf. lxvi. 2.

* The original word ufed Exod. vii. 11. is belahatehem; and that which occurs, ch. vii. 22. and ch. viii. 7, 18. is belatehem. The former is probably derived from lahat, which fignifies ' to burn,' and the fubftantive.' a flame,' or ' fhining fword-blade ;' and is applied to ' the flaming fword' which guarded the tree of life. Gen. iii. 24. Thofe who formerly ufed legerdemain dazzled and deceived the fight of the fpecta-tors by the art of brandifhing their fwords, and fometimes feemed to eat them, and to thruft them into their bodies. And the expreffion feems to intimate, that the magicians appearing to turn their rods into ferpents, was owing to their eluding the eyes of the fpectators by a dextrous management of their fwords. In the fucceeding inftances they made ufe of fome different contrivance : for the latter word belatehem comes from a word fignifying ' to cover' or ' hide,' (which fome think the former word alfo does ;) and therefore fitly expreffes any fecret artifices or methods of deception, whereby falfe appearances are impofed upon the fpectators.

hypotheſis with regard to the magicians *. Theſe *ſecret ſleights* and *jugglings*, are exprefsly referred to the magicians, not to the devil, who is not ſo much as mentioned in the hiſtory. Should we therefore be aſked †, How it came to paſs, in caſe the works of the magicians were performed by ſleight of hand, that Moſes has given no *hint* thereof? We anſwer, he has not contented himſelf with a hint of this kind; but, at the ſame time that he aſcribes his own miracles to Jehovah, has in the moſt *direct terms* reſolved every thing done in imitation of them entirely to the fraudulent contrivances of· his oppoſers, to legerdemain or ſleight of hand, in contradiſtinction from magical incantations. Moſes therefore could not deſign to repreſent their works as real miracles, at the very time he was branding them as impoſtures.

VI. It remains only to ſhew, that the works performed by the magicians, did not exceed the cauſe to which they are aſcribed; or, in other words, the magicians proceeded no farther in imitation of Moſes, than *human artifice* might enable them to go; (while the miracles of Moſes were not liable to the ſame impeachment, and bore upon themſelves the plaineſt ſignatures of that divine power to which they are referred.) If this can be proved, the interpoſition of the devil on this· occaſion, will appear to be an hypotheſis invented without any kind of neceſſity,

as

---

* Biſhop Kidder on Exod. vii. 11.

† As we are by Dr. Macknight, in his Truth of the Goſpel Hiſt. p. 372.

as it certainly is without any authority from the sacred text.

1. With regard to the firſt attempt of the magicians, the turning rods into ſerpents; it cannot be
accounted extraordinary, that they ſhould ſeem to
ſucceed in it, when we conſider that theſe men were
famous for the art of dazzling and deceiving the
ſight; and that ſerpents, being firſt rendered tracta-
ble and harmleſs *, as they eaſily may, have had a
thouſand different tricks played with them, to the
aſtoniſhment of the ſpectators. Huetius † tells us,
that amongſt the Chineſe there are jugglers who undertake to turn rods into ſerpents; though, no
doubt, they only dextrouſly ſubſtitute the latter in
the room of the former. Now, this is the very trick
the magicians played: and it appears by facts, that
the thing in general is very practicable. It is immaterial to account particularly, how the thing was
done;

* Thoſe who deſire to ſee inſtances of this from modern authors, may conſult Dr. Sykes on miracles, p. 166—168. Many
pretended to render ſerpents harmleſs by charms, (Pſ. lviii. 5.
Bochart. Hieroz. Part. poſt. l. 3. c. 6. Shaw's travels, preface, p. 5. travels, p. 429. ſupplement, p. 62.) though more
probably they deſtroyed the teeth through which they ejected
their poiſon. Herodotus mentions certain ſerpents which were
quite harmleſs, ἀνθρώπων ἐδαμᾶ δηλήμονες, Euterpe, c. 74. Antiquity attributed to the Pſylli, a people of Africa, the extraordinary virtue of rendering themſelves invulnerable by ſerpents, as well as of curing thoſe who were bit by them. See Dr.
Haſſelquiſt's voyages and travels, cited in the Monthly Re-
view for February 1766, p. 133.

† Alnetan. Quæſt. l. 2. p. 155.

done ; ſince it is not always eaſy to explain in what
manner a common juggler impoſes upon our ſight.
Should it be ſuggeſted, that Moſes might impoſe upon the ſight of the ſpectators as well as the magicians; I anſwer, that as he aſcribes their performances to legerdemain, and his own to God; ſo there
might, and muſt have been a wide difference in their
manner of acting ; the *covered arts* of the magicians
not being uſed by Moſes, the ſame ſuſpicion could
not reſt on him as did on them. What an ingenious
writer aſſerts is not true, that according to the Exodus, the outward appearance on both ſides was pre-
ciſely the ſame: for the book of Exodus ſpecifies a
moſt important difference between the miracle of
Aaron, and the impoſtures of the magicians. For it
ſays, that " Aaron caſt down his rod, before Pha-
" raoh, and before his ſervants, and it became a ſer-
" pent." But with regard to the magicians it uſes
very different language; for at the ſame time it ſays,
" They caſt down every man his rod, and they be-
" came ſerpents," it expreſsly declares that they did
this by their " inchantments, or covered arts." And
what in the moſt effectual manner prevented any ap-
prehenſion, that the ſerpent of Aaron was (like thoſe
of the magicians) the effect only of a dextrous management, not a miraculous production ; God cauſed
his rod to ſwallow up theirs : in which there was no
room for artifice, and which, for this reaſon, the magicians did not attempt to imitate. This new miracle was not deſigned to eſtabliſh the ſuperiority of
the God of Iſrael to the idols of Egypt; nor was it
                                                  capable

capable of anfwering that end * : but in the view here given of it, had much wifdom, by vindicating the credit of the former miracle †, (which might poffibly be more open to fufpicion, than any of the reft,) as well as by affording new evidence of a divine interpofition in favour of Mofes. God confidered this evidence as fully decifive of the point in queftion between his meffengers and the magicians: for from this

---

* It was obferved above, p. 309. that it is far from being evident, that the cauling one ferpent to fwallow feveral, is a greater miracle than the actual creation of a number equal to thofe fwallowed.

† We learn from hence, how little occafion there was for Mofes, to detect the artifices of the magicians; who did not fo much as pretend to any peculiar divine affiftance, and who funk into contempt of themfelves. 2 Tim. iii. 9. The nature of the works of Mofes, and the open unfufpicious manner of their performance, ferved fufficiently to difgrace the attempts of his rivals.——On the other hand, it is an infuperable difficulty attending the common hypothefis, that Mofes never intimated to Pharaoh, or the Egyptians, that the magicians performed their works by the affiftance of the devil, (as without doubt he would have done, if that had been the cafe;) nor taught them to diftinguifh between diabolical and divine miracles; though on the common hypothefis both appeared in feveral inftances to be the very fame. If the devil performed real miracles in fupport of the magicians; it was the more neceffary that Mofes fhould have given exprefs notice of this, both to the Ifraelites and Egyptians.; as the latter certainly had no fufpicion of this kind, and neither could learn any thing concerning the miraculous power of the devil, but by revelation. Mofes, however, inftead of revealing this fecret, has, (by defcribing his rivals as magicians, and their works as impoftures,) in effect, denied their being affifted by the devil.

this time he proceeded to the *punishment* of Pharaoh
and the Egyptians: which affords a new demonftration, drawn from the juftice of the divine Being, of
the falfehood of the common hypothefis, according
to the reprefentation given of it by thofe, who maintain, that the magicians were not plainly vanquifhed,
till they were reftrained from turning the duft into
lice *. Had this been the cafe, it would have been
right in Pharaoh to fufpend his judgment till that
time; nor would God have punifhed him by the two
intervening plagues, that of turning the waters of the
Nile (to which Egypt owed its fecundity) into blood,
and covering the land with frogs: punifhments fo
fevere, as to imply the moft criminal obftinacy on
the part of Pharaoh.

2. With regard to the next attempt of the magicians

---

* According to Mr. Hallet, (on miracles, p. 26, 34, 35.)
the works of the magicians were *real miracles*, fuch as argued
the interpofition of *oppofite* invifible powers to thofe by which
Mofes was affifted; the three firft miracles of Mofes did not
appear to require more ftrength for their performance, than
thofe of the magicians; and the fpectators were in fufpence
which fide gained the victory, till the magicians were prevented from turning the duft of the land into lice. Archbifhop
Tillotfon alfo, (on 1 John iv. 1. V. 1. p. 179. fol. ed.) after
a thoufand other writers of inferior note, fuppofes the evidence till then to be equal on both fides. But, is it poffible,
that the righteous judge of the world fhould punifh Pharaoh
for not complying with his orders, before he had given him
clear evidence that thofe orders came from him, and while he
could not but doubt whether they did come from him; if the
being left in doubt did not itfelf create a fufpicion, that they
could not come from him?

cians to imitate Mofes, who had already turned all
the running and ftanding waters of Egypt into
blood *, there is no difficulty in accounting for their
fuccefs, in the degree in which they fucceeded. For
it was during the continuance of this judgment, when
no water could be procured, but *by digging round
about the river* †, that the magicians attempted, by
fome proper preparation, to change the colour of the
fmall quantity that was brought them; (probably
endeavouring to perfuade Pharaoh, that they could
as eafily have turned a larger quantity into blood.)
In a cafe of this nature, impofture might, and, as we
learn from hiftory, often did, take place. It is related by Valerius Maximus ‡, that the wine poured
into the cup of Xerxes was three times changed into
blood. But fuch trifling feats as thefe could not at
all difparage the miracle of Mofes; *the vaft extent* of
which raifed it above the fufpicion of fraud, and
ftamped upon every heart, that was not fteeled againft
all conviction, the ftrongeft impreffion of its divinity.
For he turned their ftreams, rivers, ponds, and the
water in all their receptacles, into blood. And the
fifh that was in the river (Nile) died, and the river
ftank ‖.

3. Pharaoh not yielding to this evidence, God
proceeded to farther punifhments, and covered the
whole land of Egypt with frogs. Before thefe frogs
were

---

* Exod. vii. 20—25. . † V. 24.
‡ L. i. c. 6.
‖ Exod. viii. 1—7.

were removed *, the magicians undertook to bring
(into fome place cleared for the purpofe) a frefh fupply : which they might eafily do, when there was
fuch plenty every where at hand.　Here alfo the narrow compafs of the work expofed it to the fufpicion
of being effected by human art ; to which the miracle of Mofes was not liable ; the infinite number of
frogs which filled the whole kingdom of Egypt, (fo
that their ovens, beds, and tables fwarmed with
them,) being a proof of their immediate miraculous
production.　Befides, the magicians were unable to
procure their *removal* †, which was accomplifhed by
Mofes, at the fubmiffive application of Pharaoh, and
at the very time that Pharaoh himfelf chofe ; the
more clearly to convince him, that God was the author of thefe miraculous judgments, and that their
infliction or removal did not depend upon the influence of the elements or ftars, at fet times, or in critical junctures.

4. The hiftory of the laft attempt of the magicians, confirms the account here given of all their
former ones.　Mofes turned all the duft of the land
into lice : and this plague, like the two preceding
ones, being inflicted at the word of Mofes, and extended over the whole kingdom of Egypt, muft neceffarily

---

* Exod. viii. 6, 7, 8.　Nor indeed can it be imagined, that
after this or the former plague had been removed, that Pharaoh would order his magicians to renew either.

† Ch. viii. 8.　Had they been able to *inflict* this plague *miraculoufly*; they might have *removed* it in the fame manner.

ceffarily have been owing, not to human art, but to a divine power. Neverthelefs, the motives upon which the magicians at firft engaged in the conteft with Mofes, the fhame of defifting, and fome flight appearances of fuccefs in their former attempts, prompted them ftill to carry on the impofture, and to try " with their inchantments to bring forth lice : " but they could not *." With all their fkill in magic, and with all their dexterity in deceiving the fpectators, they could not even fucceed fo far as they had done in former inftances, by producing a fpecious counterfeit of this work of Mofes. Had they hitherto performed real miracles, by the affiftance of the devil; how came they to defift now? It cannot be a greater miracle to produce lice, than to turn rods into ferpents, water into blood, and to create frogs. It has indeed been very often faid, that the devil was now laid under *a reftraint :* but hitherto no proof of this affertion has been produced. The Scripture is filent, both as to the devil's being now reftrained from interpofing any farther in favour of the magicians, and as to his having afforded them his affiftance on the former occafions. But if we agree with Mofes, in afcribing to the magicians nothing more than the artifice and dexterity which belonged to their profeffion ; we fhall find that their want of fuccefs in their laft attempt, was owing to the different nature and circumftance of their enterprize. In all the former inftances, the magicians knew beforehand what they were to undertake, and

X   had

* Exod. viii. 18.

had time for preparation. They were not fent for by
Pharaoh, till after Mofes had turned his rod into a ferpent: and previous notice had been publicly given of
the two firft plagues *. But the orders in relation to
the third, were no fooner iffued than executed, without being previoufly imparted to Pharaoh†. So that in
this laft cafe, they had no time for contriving any expedient for imitating or impeaching the act of Mofes.
And had they been allowed time, how was it poffible
for them to make it appear, that they produced thofe
animals by which they themfelves, and all the country, were already covered ‡ and furrounded? Or,
what artifice could efcape detection, in relation to
infects, whofe minutenefs hinders them from being
perceived, till they are brought fo near as to be fubject to the clofeft infpection? Now therefore the
magicians chofe to fay, " This (laft work of Mofes)
is the finger of God ∥."

It has been generally thought, that the magicians
here acknowlege, " that the God of Ifrael was
" ftronger than the gods of Egypt, who had hitherto
" affifted § them, but were now reftrained from do-
                                                    " ing

* Exod. vii. 15, 17. ch. viii. 1—4.

† Ch. viii. 16.

‡ V. 18. There " being lice upon man, and upon beaft,"
feems to be affigned as a reafon of the magicians being unable
to counterfeit this miracle.

∥ V. 19.

§ Had the magicians, in the former trials, been affifted by
the gods of Egypt, (or any evil fpirits who fupported their
                                                    caufe;)

" ing it by his fuperior power." But the text makes
no mention of their allowing the God of Ifrael to be
fuperior to the gods of Egypt; much lefs of their
admitting the former to be Jehovah, and the only
true God. Nor do they refer to any fupernatural
reftraint upon the Egyptian deities, but to the laft
miracle * of Mofes, when they fay, " This is the
finger of God;" or " of a god:" for the original
word † admits this fenfe, and very probably was ufed
in no other by the magicians, who believed in a plurality of gods. Being unable to turn the duft of the
earth into lice, (and even to feem to do it,) they allow that this furpaffed the fcience they profeffed, and
argued the fpecial miraculous interpofition of fome
deity. There is no fort of evidence, that this language of the magicians proceeded from a defire of
doing juftice to the character and claims of the God
of Ifrael; or that it was not merely defigned as the

X 2

beft

caufe;) they might have imputed their mifcarriage in the trial
under confideration, to the omiffion of fome ceremony or incantation, judged neceffary to engage their affiftance. The
difappointments of the Pagan diviners were frequently accounted for in this manner, and their credit hereby faved.
Nor was it difficult for idolaters to account for a difparity of
power between different gods; each god having his peculiar
province, as was fhewn above, p. 329.

* The Targum of Onkelos renders the words, " This
plague comes from God." And the Arabic verfion expreffes
the fame fenfe, " A fign of this nature is of God."

† Heb. Elohim.

beft apology they were able to make for their own failure of fuccefs, and to prevent Pharaoh from reproaching them with the want of fkill in their profeffion. Certain it is, that this declaration of the magicians had no good effect upon Pharaoh, but feems rather to be mentioned as an occafion of his continued hardnefs *. Nay, the hiftory plainly intimates, that the magicians themfelves afterwards confronted Mofes, till in punifhment of their obftinacy, they were fmitten with ulcers ‡. I add, that the fenfe here affigned to their language, is perfectly agreeable to the account before given of the ftate of the controverfy between them and Mofes: for it implies, that the magicians had not fo much as pretended to any miraculous interpofition of the gods in their favour, but relied entirely upon the eftablifhed rules of their art; and confequently that Pharaoh's view in

. fending

---

* V. 19. After relating what the magicians faid to Pharaoh, the hiftorian adds, " And Pharaoh's heart was harden-" ed, and he hearkened not unto them," that is, to Mofes and Aaron, (as clearly appears from the ufe of the fame form of fpeech, Exod. vii. 13, 22.) " as the Lord had faid." Its having been taken for granted, that Pharaoh is here reproved for not hearkening to his magicians, (who never perfuaded their monarch to releafe the Ifraelites,) feems to have prevented critics from underftanding the true meaning of the paffage in queftion, " This is the finger of God."

‡ " The magicians could not ftand before Mofes, becaufe " of the boil: for the boil was upon the magicians." Exod. ix. 11. Does not this imply, that till this time the magicians had, in fome method or other, oppofed or difparaged Mofes?

fending for them, was to enable himfelf to determine, whether the works of Mofes lay within the
compafs of it.

I cannot conclude this fubject without obferving,
that the ftrenuous but unfuccefsful oppofition of the
magicians to Mofes, added ftrength to his caufe ; as it
ferved to manifeft the divinity of his miracles, by clear-
ing him from all fufpicion of magic. This art was
thought equal to the moft wonderful phenomena.
In Egypt it was held in the higheft efteem, and carried to its utmoft perfection. Pharaoh, without
doubt; on the prefent moft important and interefting
occafion, engaged the affiftance of the moft able profeffors of it, who, from a regard to their own reputation and intereft, would try every poffible method
to invalidate the miracles of Mofes. Neverthelefs,
their utmoft efforts were baffled ; and the vanity and
futility of the claims of magic were detected and expofed : agreeably to the cenfure paffed upon them by
St. Paul. For, fpeaking of certain perfons, whofe
oppofition to genuine Chriftianity was the fole effect
of their corrupt minds, without the leaft colour of
reafon ; he compares them to Jannes and Jambres *

X 3   who

* Jannes and Jambres, mentioned by St. Paul, 2 Tim. iii.
8. from the Chaldee paraphrafe on Exod. vii. 11. are fuppofed
to have been the two chiefs of Pharaoh's magicians. Nume-
nius, the Pythagorean philofopher, (apud Eufeb. Præp. Ev.
l. 9. c. 8.) fays, " they are inferior to none in magic fkill ;
" and for that reafon chofen by common confent to oppofe
" Mufæus," for fo the Heathens called Mofes). See Le Clerc
on Exod. vii. 12. and Pliny's Hift. l. 30. c. 1.

who withftood Mofes; and did it, he muft mean,
with as little pretence; or there would be no juftice
in the comparifon. He adds, " Their folly was manifeft unto all men * ;" and thus he taxes the conduct of the magicians with the moft glaring abfurdity. He cannot therefore be fuppofed to admit, that
they imitated and equalled for a time the miracles of
Mofes, and then defifted as foon as they found themfelves unable to continue the conteft to advantage,
(which would have been a point of prudence) ; but
to aſſert, that they wickedly and abfurdly attempted
to place the feats of art on a level with the undeniable operations of a divine power; and fo fhamefully
mifcarrying in their undertaking, they expofed themfelves to the contempt of thofe, who had once held
them in high veneration. We proceed to confider,

SECT. II.

The Cafe of Samuel's Appearance to Saul at Endor.
I Sam. xxviii.

I. AMONGST other deteftable methods of divination practifed by the ancient Pagans,
one was their pretenfion of calling up and confulting
the dead †. The foul of man, when feparated from
the

* 2 Tim. iii. 9.

† This cuftom is referred to If. viii. 19. ch. xxix. 4. ch.
lxv. 3. A full account of it may be found in Lucan. l. 6.
v. 591,

the body, was fuppofed to be cloathed with a material covering *, which retained the fhape and lineaments of the body, and was capable of being feen and heard, though of two fine a contexture to be felt or handled. This *image* † or *fhadow* was what the Heathens conceived they could raife by proper facrifices to the earth, to the dead, and to the infernal deities ‡. *Human victims* || were frequently offered up on thefe occafions. At a time when the pretended art of raifing up ghofts was held in high efteem §

X 4   in

v. 591, &c. Virgil. Æn. l. 6. Homer. Il. l. 23. Odyff. l. 10, 11. Statius's Thebaid, iv. v. 477. In Horace (epod. od. ult.) Canidia boafts, Poffim crematos excitare mortuos; and Medea, in Ovid, (Metam. l. 7. v. 199, &c.) that fhe could command, manes exire fepulchris. See likewife Herodotus, l. 5. c. 29. Heliodor. Æthiop. l. 5. p. 293. Jofeph. Antiq. l. 6. c. 14. § 2. Horace, Satir. l. 1. fat. 8. v. 28, 29. And Tibullus, lib. 1. el. 2. v. 45, 46. where the pretenfions of forcereffes are thus defcribed,

> Hæc cantu finditque folum, manefque fepulchris
> Elicit, et tepido devocat offa rogo.

* Cic. Tufc. Difput. 1. 16.

† The Greeks called it, εἴδωλον; the Latins, fimulachrum, imago, umbra.

‡ Homer. Odyff. Λ. 21, &c. Æfchyl. Perf.

|| Servius on Virgil, Æn. l. 6. l. 107. and Patrick on Deut. xviii. 11.

§ Lucian de Aftrol. 24. Homer makes Ulyffes have recourfe to necromancy without any fcruple; but in later and more enlightened ages, the magic arts becoming contemptible and odious, Virgil reprefents Dido as making an apology for ufing them. Æn. iv. 493.

in the Pagan world, and temples were erected where
the ceremony of conjuration was to be performed * ;
Mofes, with the higheft reafon, branded it as a moft
atrocious crime, and punifhed it with death †. Unhappily however this execrable fuperftition (as indeed almoft all the other fuperftitions of Paganifm) was
too much countenanced by the Chriftian converts, and,
particularly by the ancient Fathers, who univerfally
afcribed to magicians and necromancers the power
of calling up the fouls of the dead ‡. A blind deference to the authority of thefe writers, (whofe faith
was an unnatural mixture of Pagan and Chriftian
principles, not lefs oppofite to one another than light
and darknefs,) has too long enflaved the Chriftian
world, and hindered them from duly attending to the
voice of reafon, or what is taught in the facred writings. To this neglect we muft afcribe their embracing an opinion, fo repugnant to the order of the
natural world, and to the doctrines of revelation re-
fpecting the ftate of the dead. Can it be confiftent
with a juft reverence of God, to believe, that he has
fubjected the fouls of the departed to be remanded
                                                        back

* Herodot. l. 5. c. 92. § 7. Paufanius, Bœot. c. 30. Plutarch. Vit. Cimon. p. 482. We read, 2 Chron. xxxiii. 6. 2 Kings
xxi. 6. that Manaffes " dealt with a familiar fpirit ;" which,
according to the LXX, imports, his eftablifhing the practice
of confulting the dead, and erecting temples for that purpofe.

† Deut. xviii. 10, 11. Levit. xx. 27. See above, ch. 3.
fect 3. p. 189.

‡ Middleton's Free Inquiry, p. 66.

back from their deftined abodes, and compelled to
reveal what he has feen fit fhould be concealed ; and
this at the call of fome of the vileft mortals ? Are
even the moft eminent faints and prophets doomed
to fuch difhonour ? And could Pagan priefts and
diviners acquire fuch an extraordinary power over
them, by the practice of the moft execrable rites,
and offering up the moft inhuman facrifices ? Surely
natural reafon confirms the fuffrage of Scripture,
when it brands the whole magic art, to which evo-
cations of the dead, and all necromantic divinations
appertain, as founded in impofture *.

II. There are fome who admit, that witches cannot difturb the fouls of good men, much lefs of prophets; who neverthelefs are of opinion that thefe
wretched women can caufe " the devil to counterfeit
the fouls of the dead ;" and that in the cafe before
us, " an evil fpirit appeared before Saul in the like-
nefs of Samuel †." This is not advanced upon the
teftimony of reafon or experience, or upon the authority of divine revelation; but in conformity to
the wild fictions of the Platonic philofophers ‡, invented to deceive the credulous, and to confirm their
attachment to the worfhip of falfe gods. Suppofe
the

* See ch. 3. fect. 3. p. 182.

† See Patrick on 1 Sam. xxviii. 12.

‡ Porph. de Abftinentia, l. 2. thus defcribes certain fallacious fpirits, Γένος ἀπαταλῆς φύσεως παντόμορφον κ̀ πολύτροπον, ὑπο-
κρινόμενον κ̀ θεὸς, καὶ δαίμονας, κ̀ ψυχὰς τεθνηκότων. Compare Iam-
blichus de Myfter. fect. 3. c. 31.

the forcerers and diviners amongſt the Heathens had been able, by offering up ſacrifices to their infernal deities, and by other rites of necromancy, to cauſe evil ſpirits to aſſume the ſhape of dead men, and to appear with their full reſemblance before their former acquaintance: would not this deception, eſpecially when accompanied with true prediſtions, have ſupported idolatry as effeſtually, and done as much miſchief in the world, as a power of calling up the dead themſelves *? Beſides, the very apparition of a ſpiritual and incorporeal being, and the gift of prophecy, are real miracles, and as ſuch cannot take place, but by divine appointment; unleſs all the arguments hitherto offered on this point are inconcluſive. Laſtly, the hiſtorian calls the appearance to Saul, Samuel †; which he could not do with truth, if it was no other than the devil, who here appears, not as a tempter, but as a very ſevere reprover of impiety and wickedneſs.

III. Many learned men have maintained, that it was neither Samuel, nor an evil ſpirit, who now appeared to Saul; but that the whole was the work of human impoſture. In ſupport of this opinion, it may be pleaded, that the woman to whom Saul applied to call up Samuel, though ſhe is ſaid to have *a familiar ſpirit* ‡, and pretended to be able to call up the dead,

and

---

* See above, ch. 3. feſt. 2. p. 165.

† 1 Sam. xxviii. 12.

‡ It was obſerved, ch. 3. feſt. 3. p. 186. note ‡, that the Hebrew word *ob*, and the plural *oboth*, is generally rendered

by

and by their help to foretel future events; was merely a ventriloquift, one of thofe who had the art of
fpeaking

by the LXX, ἐγγαστριμύθυς, ventriloquifts: In If. xix. 3, it is
rendered by them, τὰς ἐκ τῆς γῆς φωνῦντας, ' thofe that fpeak out
of the earth.' I allow, that this art requires no evil fpirit; nor
had the woman whom Saul had confulted the affiftance of any.
Neverthelefs, as thefe ventriloquifts pretended to be, and were
thought to be, infpired by thofe who applied to them to call
up the dead; our tranflators had fome ground for rendering
the word *ob*, ' a familiar fpirit.' Somewhat of this import, the
word muft have in the mouth of Saul, when he faid, " Seek
" me a woman, that is miftrefs of ob; Divine to me by ob,"
(1 Sam. xxviii. 7, 8.) and denote either ' a fpirit of divination' in general, or a ' fpirit by which (it was believed) fhe
could call up the dead.' Saul muft fuppofe fhe was agitated
and fwelled by fome fpirit. See Le Clerc on Levit. xix. 31.
It appears from Plutarch, (De Defeʿct. Orac. tom. 2. p. 414.)
Suidas, (tom. 1. ad voc. ἐγγαστριμύθῳ, p. 667.) and Jofephus,
(Antiq. l. 14. p. 354.) that thofe who were antiently called
ventriloquifts, had afterwards the name of *pythoneffes*; which
implies a pretence to divination. *Python* is the word ufed by
the Vulgate verfion, 1 Sam. xxviii. 7, 8. And Mr. Voltaire
(in his Philofophy of Hiftory, ch. 35.) fays, " It is ftrange
" that the word *Python*, which is Greek, fhould be known to
" the Jews in the time of Saul. Many learned men have con-
" cluded from hence, that this hiftory was not written, till the
" Jews traded with the Greeks, after the time of Alexander."
But in the original Hebrew no fuch word as *Python* is ufed,
(as Mr. Voltaire himfelf knew); but a term fo remote in found
from it as *ob*. And for the credit of learning one would hope,
(what I really believe to be the cafe,) that Voltaire is the
only learned man, who ever undertook to determine the date
of a Hebrew book, from the ufe of a word in a Latin tranflation, made many hundred years after it, and not to be found
in the original. See Mr. Findlay's Vindication, p. 389.

ſpeaking with their mouths ſhut, ſo as to ſeem to ſpeak out of their bellies, and who could throw their voices as if they came out of the earth, or from other places: an art which muſt neceſſarily have been very ſerviceable to thoſe who counterfeited the anſwers of the dead. With regard to Saul; how eaſy muſt it have been to impoſe upon a man, whoſe reaſon had been ſo long diſturbed by jealouſy, and who was now ſunk into deſpair, by the invaſion of his enemies, and a ſenſe of his rejection by God? If he had been maſter of himſelf, would he have applied to a witch to raiſe up Samuel, and to extort from him the know-lege of futurity? or have expected God to anſwer him by a dead prophet, when he refuſed anſwering by the living; eſpecially as he knew God had for-bidden the conſulting the dead? Saul came to the Pythoneſs *by night*: a ſeaſon the moſt proper for carrying on a fraud; and for this reaſon always * choſen for magical practices. Thoſe who ſupported any reputation in this profeſſion, as the woman ap-plied to by Saul ſeems to have done, were perſons of great artifice, and of very extenſive intelligence †, ſo as very ſeldom to be ſtrangers to the character and ſituation of thoſe who came to conſult them. We are not therefore to be ſurprized at the ſaga-city and addreſs of the witch at Endor. She ei-ther knew Saul by the advantage of his ſtature, or

picked

---

* See either Patrick on 1 Sam. xxviii. 8. or Le Clerc on v. 13. or Dr. Chandler's Life of David, V. 1. p. 241, 273.

† Le Clerc on 1 Sam. xxviii. 16.

picked out the fecret from his attendants, or inferred it from his giving her a promife not of *fecre-*
cy, (all that a private perfon could give,) but of *im-*
punity *, which Saul alone could make. When fhe
pretended to have brought up Samuel, Saul was not
allowed to fee him †, but received his account of the
apparition from the woman herfelf, whofe great fright
was a mere artifice ‡. The queftion which is put into the mouth of Samuel, " Why haft thou difquiet-
"; ed || me, to bring me up ?" by acknowledging the
efficacy of magic, and the power of this pythonefs to
difturb his reft, and to bring him into this world at
her pleafure, even againft his own confent, and therefore without a commiffion from God ; is highly abfurd in itfelf, and injurious to the character of this
divine prophet. And though he is afterwards made
to read Saul a very grave lecture, and to denounce
his doom ; yet fhe ran no rifque by fo bold an admonition

---

* V. 13. † V. 13, 14.

‡ It may however be objected, that if the woman had a
mind to make Saul believe fhe had raifed Samuel, why fhould
fhe *pretend* to be frighted at the fight of him ? at the fight of
the perfon whom Saul defired, and fhe undertook to raife ? I
allow, fhe did not really expect to raife Samuel ; neverthelefs,
as fhe gave Saul this expectation, why did fhe counterfeit furprize at (what it became her to appear to expect) the fuccefs
of her own art ? To me it feems moft probable, that her fur-
prife was not feigned, but real, and as fuch the hiftorian reprefents it.

|| This is fomewhat like the complaint of Atoffa in the Per-
fæ of Æfchylus, v. 683.

monition and prediction; an oath in those days being esteemed so sacred, that persons readily ventured
their lives upon its credit.

With regard to her prediction, concerning the
death of Saul and his sons, and the defeat of his army on *the morrow;* it has been affirmed by some,
that it was not punctually accomplished; there being
(in their opinion) more than a day from the time of
its delivery to Saul's engaging the Philistines. And
if by *to-morrow* *, the pythoness meant *the time to
come;* the prophecy was vague and indeterminate,
and justly liable to the suspicion of imposture. She
knew the situation of public affairs, and that the ar-
mies of the Philistines and Israelites were ready to
engage; she clearly inferred the issue, from the superior numbers of the enemy, from the despondency
of Saul, and his rejection by God, and from the appointment of David to succeed him †. It seemed
                                                        most

---

* The original word, *machar*, signifies ' the next day,' in
the following passages, Exod. xvi. 23. ch. xxxii. 5. 1 Sam.
ix. 16. ch. xix. 4. 1 Kings xix. 2. ch. xx. 6. 2 Kings vii. 1,
18. ch. x. 6. It means ' the time to come,' indefinitely, in
Gen. xxx. 33. Exod. xiii. 14. Deut. vi. 20. Josh. xxii. 24,
27, 28. compare Mat. vi. 34. The occasion therefore on
which this word is used must determine the meaning of it.
And on this occasion it must mean ' the next day,' or ' very
shortly;' otherwise Samuel only affirms, that Saul and his sons
would ' in some future time' be numbered amongst the dead.
Compare 1 Sam. xi. 9, 10. And if the prophecy was not accomplished in this sense, it was not delivered by the real Samuel, but one who personated him.

† 1 Sam. xv. 28. ch. xxiv. 21. ch. xxvi. 25.

moſt probable to her, that Saul and his ſons would not ſtain their charaＣters by cowardice, and ſave their lives by a ſhameful flight. She might be diſ-appointed; but ſhe knew how to recover her credit in caſe ſhe loſt any, by imputing her deception to the omiſſion of ſome neceſſary ceremony or incantation. By the event it appeared, that ſhe was uncommonly fortunate in her conjeＣtures. And the ſacred hiſto-rian ſaw fit to record this very remarkable caſe, part-ly to ſhew how deſervedly Saul was rejeＣted by God, and partly to guard the Iſraelites from giving too ea-ſy credit to the prophecies of Pagan diviners. This opinion, however, like the immediately foregoing one, contradiＣts the ſacred hiſtorian, who not only repreſents the pythoneſs as affirming, but himſelf af-firms *, that *ſhe ſaw Samuel*, and that *Samuel ſpoke to Saul;* nor has he dropt the leaſt hint, that it was not the real Samuel of whom he was ſpeaking. I add, therefore,

IV. That there is an opinion concerning this mat-ter different from the foregoing: and it is this, that the appearance of Samuel to Saul was a divine mira-cle; (though whether the miracle conſiſted in raiſ-

ing

---

* "And the woman ſaw Samuel," 1 Sam. xxviii. 12. "Samuel ſaid to Saul," v. 15. "Then ſaid Samuel," v. 16. Perhaps it may be objeＣted, that the hiſtorian does not himſelf affirm, that the woman ſaw Samuel; and deſigned only to relate the account given by her, though he himſelf believed it to be falſe. But in this caſe, ought he not to have ſaid, *the woman pretended* to ſee Samuel? and that the *pretended* Samuel ſpoke to Saul?

ing Samuel, or in prefenting an image or reprefentation of him before Saul, it is not neceffary to determine.)   It feems to have been the opinion of the antient Jews *, that Samuel now appeared to Saul.
And if this was the real cafe; the apparition muft
be afcribed, not to the power of inchantment, but to
the immediate appointment of God †, as a rebuke
and punifhment to Saul.

In fupport of this opinion, it may be obferved,
that Saul came to the woman by night, when fhe
did not expect him, and was unprepared; and yet
no fooner had fhe obtained from him a promife of
fafety, and learnt who the perfon was he wanted her
to raife, than Samuel appeared; before fhe had any
time for juggle or artifice, or for the performance of
the

---

* The author of the book of Ecclefiafticus, ch. xlvi. 20,
fays, " After his death Samuel prophecied, and fhewed the
king his end."   And the LXX, after relating the death of
Saul for confulting the witch, add, " and the prophet Samuel
anfwered him," 1 Chron. x. 13.   Jofephus likewife was in
the fame fentiment, Antiq. l. 6. c. 14. fect. 2.

† This opinion is maintained by Dr. Waterland, in his fer-
mons, V. 2. p. 267. and defended by Dr. Delany in his Life
of David.   The fucceeding writer of the fame life, the learned Dr. Chandler, has combated this opinion, and given new
ftrength to thofe objections which had been raifed againft it.
I have attempted to anfwer or obviate thofe objections, except
fuch as do not affect the Scripture hiftory of this matter; for
the doctor lays a ftrefs on fuch, and particularly on Samuel's
concealing himfelf " in a dark underground magic chamber of
" a witch.   But" (as the doctor obferves on another occafion)
" this is not the hiftory, but an addition to it."

the neceffary facrifices and incantations. " Saul faid,
" Bring me up Samuel. And the woman faw Sa-
" muel, and cried *." The hiftorian here affirms,
" that the woman faw Samuel," not that fhe *pretend-*
ed to fee him, much lefs that fhe *raifed* him. And
the language plainly implies, that fhe faw him *imme-*
diately † after Saul's requeft. At this fight, the text
fays, " fhe cried with a loud voice," in the utmoft
furprize and terror ‡, having no expectation of feeing Samuel, and having no pretence for afcribing his
appearance to her own art, which fhe had not fo
much as exerted. This (as a juftly celebrated cri-

Y   tic

---

* 1 Sam. xxviii. 11, 12.

† This is an important circumftance. It is generally fuppofed, that fome fpace of time intervened between the requeft
of Saul, and the appearance of Samuel, fo as to leave room
for the ufe of magical rites ; and that it was in the ufe of thefe
rites that Samuel was raifed. The Englifh tranflation favours
this fuppofition, and Dr. Chandler all along argues upon it.
And it is acknowleged, that he very fuccefsfully fhews, that
it is very improbable, either that the witch fhould raife up Samuel by the power of magic, or that God himfelf fhould raife
him up in her ufe of the magic art, efpecially as Samuel did
not exprefsly inform Saul, that his appearing to him was not
owing to her, but God. But this reafoning proceeds on a fuppofition wholly groundlefs ; it does not appear that any magical rites were ufed, or that a moment's time intervened between Saul's requeft and Samuel's appearance. The Englifh
tranflators have inferted the particle *when,* (" And when the
woman faw Samuel,") without any authority from the original,
and merely to favour their own prejudices.

‡ See above, p. 333. note ‡.

tic* obſerves) " ſeems to be a plain evidence that her *art*
was a cheat; and that the reality, (which he calls *a
likeneſs of Samuel,*) unexpected to *her*, was God's own
extraordinary interpoſition." The ſorcereſs believing
that Samuel could be ſent to no leſs a perſon than
Saul; from the appearance of the former, ſhe concluded the latter was now preſent in diſguiſe: which
naturally made her very uneaſy; as Saul had formerly cut off all thoſe of her profeſſion, and would now,
ſhe feared, be excited by Samuel to renew his former
ſeverity †. The king bade her not be afraid, and aſked what ſhe ſaw ? It muſt be acknowleged, that this
queſtion is a proof, that Saul did not himſelf ſee Samuel at firſt; but it ſeems pretty evident from the
hiſtory, that he ſaw him afterwards. To Saul's queſtion the woman replied, *I ſaw gods* ‡, or *a god*, a perſon of a majeſtic form, or one in the habit of a judge
or magiſtrate ‖, *aſcending out of the earth.* The dead
were

---

* Dr. Clarke, V. 2. p. 361. fol.

† " But why ſhould the witch be frightened, if ſhe had not
uſed her magic arts?" She had acknowleged herſelf to be
one that had a familiar ſpirit, and at Saul's deſire had actually
engaged to raiſe up Samuel. And it is in this ſenſe ſhe ſays,
ſhe had " obeyed Saul, and put her life into his hand." 1 Sam.
xxviii. 21.

‡ 1 Sam. xxviii. 13.

‖ That the word *elohim* is applied to judges and magiſtrates,
cannot be denied. See Exod. xxii. 8, 9, 28. Pſ. lxxxii. 1, 6.
Le Clerc and Patrick on 1 Sam. xxviii. 13. Dr. Chandler,
(in his Life of David, p. 239.) objects to the application of
this

were thought to fpeak out of the earth *, but Samuel
afcended and ftood upon its furface in full view. Saul
farther inquired, " What form is he of?" The woman replied, " An old man cometh up, and he is
covered with a mantle." What witches undertook
to raife, was, the ghofts of the dead; but the prefent
appearance did not refemble a mere ghoft or fhadow,
and agrees beft with the fuppofition of its being Samuel himfelf, or a miraculous reprefention of his perfon and habit. It is obfervable, that Samuel was
now covered with *a mantle*, the very habit in which
he was clad, when he denounced † that fentence upon
Saul, which he came now to confirm. While the woman was giving Saul this defcription of the apparition, Samuel feems to have advanced forward within
his fight. For it is added, " And Saul perceived that
it was Samuel himfelf‡," not merely from the defcrip-

Y 2   tion

---

this plural term to a fingle perfon; yet this term is applied to
Mofes, Exod. vii. 1. as was obferved above, p. 330. And it
is certain that Saul did not underftand the witch as fpeaking
of more than one perfon, for he afks, " What is his form?"
And fhe explains her own meaning in the anfwer fhe returns
to this queftion, " An old man arifeth."

* If. xxix. 4. ch. viii. 19.

† 1 Sam. xv. 27.

‡ The Englifh tranflators, in order to favour the vulgar fuperftition concerning the power of witches to raife ghofts and
fpectres, have in this paffage funk the word, *himfelf*; which
feems to have been inferted in the original, on purpofe to diftinguifh this appearance or reprefentation of Samuel, from his
ghoft or fhadow, over which alone the pythonefs pretended to
have any power.

tion given of him by the woman, and from the cir-
cumſtance of his appearing without her intervention,
but by the evidence of his own ſenſes; otherwiſe why
are we told, that " he ſtooped with his face to the
ground, and bowed himſelf?" Is not this equivalent
to telling us he ſaw Samuel * ? Beſides, the converſation between Saul and Samuel is itſelf a ſtrong pre-
ſumption, that they were now in the preſence of each
other.

This converſation was carried on in the abſence
of the pythoneſs, who withdrew from a preſence ſhe
little expected ; for after the departure of Samuel,
" the woman came to Saul †." The behaviour of
Samuel agrees well with the ſuppoſition of there being, purſuant to a divine command, either a real appearance or miraculous repreſentation of this prophet
of God. He begins with a ſevere reproof of Saul,
" Why haſt thou *provoked* ‡ me, to make (occaſion)
me

---

* When David bowed to Jonathan, 1 Sam. xx. 41. and
the man from Saul's camp bowed to David, 2 Sam. i. 2. ; is it
not hereby implied, that each ſaw the perſon who ſpoke to
him ? and yet this is not aſſerted in the text. Now, if it be allowed, that Saul ſaw the perſon who ſpoke to him ; it will be
impoſſible to deny the reality of Samuel's appearance, or of
ſome miraculous repreſentation of him : ſo well known was he
to Saul by his voice, lineaments, and ſtature.

† 1 Sam. xxviii. 21.

‡ This is the true rendering of the original word, which is
derived from רגז. A very learned critic (Dr. Chandler, in his
Life of David, p. 249.) is miſtaken in aſſerting, that " it never denotes *to provoke*, but to move and diſturb *by violence.*"
It

me to rife up?" Here his rifing up is not afcribed
to the pythonefs, or to her magic art; nor ſtrictly
and properly to Saul, it being cuſtomary with the
Hebrews to exprefs the *intention* by the *effect* *;) but
to the prophet's *indignation* conceived againſt the king
on account of his inquiring what to do, in a way
fo exprefsly forbidden by God; to the impoſſibility
(as it were) of God's paſſing over fo great an offence
in filence. Accordingly, Saul's anfwer is manifeſt-
ly an apology, and ſhews that he underſtood the prophet as reproving him, " I am fore diſtreſſed; for
" the Philiſtines make war againſt me, and God is
" departed from me, and anfwereth me no more,
" neither by prophets, nor by dreams: therefore
" have I called thee †, that thou mayeſt make known
" unto me what I ſhall do ‡."

Y 3   Samuel,

It is ufed to defcribe any violent commotion or concuſſion;
(Job. ix. 6. ch. xxxvii. 2. Iſ. v. 25. Amos viii. 8. Hab. iii.
7.) and hence is applied to the violent agitation of any paffion, and of anger in particular. In Prov. xxix. 9. it is rendered, ' to rage;' in Ezek. xvi. 43. ' to fret;' (where the
context requires a much ſtronger word, ' to provoke even to
fury;') in Iſ. xxviii. 21, ' to be wroth;' in Job xii. 6. ' to
provoke.' See likewife Hab. iii. 2. Iſ. xxxvii. 28, 29. Job
xxxix. 24. where the noun derived from this verb is tranſlated
rage. It cannot therefore be inferred from the ufe of this
word, that Samuel was *forcibly compelled* to appear on this occafion.

* See above, ch. 4. ſect. i. p. 312. note ||.

† This language of Saul does not imply, that he had invoked Samuel; it expreſſes only his defign in applying to the
witch.

‡ 1 Sam. xxviii. 15.

Samuel, in his reply, firſt of all expoſes the abſurdity of Saul's conduct in applying to him, when he
found himſelf abandoned by God ; then explains to
him the true grounds of his deſertion, and of the
preſent diſtreſſed ſituation of his affairs ; and laſtly
denounces farther judgments againſt him, as a puniſhment of the guilt he was at that very time contracting. " Wherefore then doeſt thou aſk" (direction and aſſiſtance) " of me, ſeeing Jehovah is
" departed from thee, and is become thine enemy,
" or, is with thine enemy *? And Jehovah hath
" done (or, *will do*) to him, (viz. Saul's rival or
" enemy) as he ſpake by me :" that is, " prone
" as you were to doubt of the truth of thoſe threat-
" nings which God uttered againſt you by my mouth,
" they are now ready to be accompliſhed : for Je-
" hovah has rent the kingdom out of thine hand,
" and given it to thy neighbour, even David : be-
" cauſe thou obeyedſt not the voice of Jehovah, nor
" executed his fierce wrath upon Amalek, therefore
" has Jehovah done this thing unto thee this day.
" Moreover, Jehovah will alſo deliver Iſrael, with
" thee, into the hands of the Philiſtines : and to-
" morrow ſhalt thou and thy ſons be with me," (in
the ſtate of death, or of ſeparate ſpirits †.) " Jehovah
" ſhall

---

* Thus the laſt clauſe of the 16th verſe may be rendered ;
and the meaning is, as Vatablus obſerves, " Jehovah favours
thine enemy." This gives an eaſy ſenſe to the firſt clauſe of
the 17th verſe, " And Jehovah has done" (or will do) " to
him," viz. to thine enemy, &c.

† Probably this is all that Samuel meant by telling Saul,
" he

" fhall alfo deliver the hoft of Ifrael into the hands
" of the Philiftines." Is this the language of an artful impoftor, whofe bufinefs it was to flatter and delude the king, to foothe his diftrefs, and gain his favour, and thereby procure from him a larger gratui-
ty ? Or if, from a regard to the credit of her art, fhe
did not chufe to raife his hopes; why did fhe ftrive
to provoke his refentment, by the freedom of her re-
proofs, and the denunciation of the moft dreadful
judgments? There is a *keennefs* and *afperity* in this
anfwer, abfolutely inconfiftent with the leaft regard
to her own intereft or fafety ; and not to be accounted for on the fuppofition of its proceeding from a
perfon of art and addrefs under the circumftances of
this forcerefs. Indeed the very foul of Samuel feems
to breathe in thefe expreffions of difpleafure againft
the difobedience and wickednefs of Saul.

But it is objected, " that this could not be the
" language of the real Samuel, becaufe he has not
" expreffed any difapprobation of Saul for having
" recourfe to the arts of divination, which were fo
" offenfive to God : and that it was unworthy of
" God to raife up Samuel from the dead, only to
" confirm a former fentence againft Saul, which
" was declared irrevocable." The former fentence

Y 4   againft

" he fhould be with him." So that there is here no neceffary
reference to the antient opinion of the Pagans, that the fhades
dwelt together according to their tribes and families; Homer.
Odyff. A ; nor any affurance given him of happinefs in a future
ftate, though fome who fuffer the judgments of God in this
world, are objects of his forgivenefs in the next ; 1 Cor. xi. 32.

againft Saul did not affect his life, but his crown only ; nor was the time fixed for the execution of this
fentence.   Saul was fpared, and even permitted to
reign over Ifrael, till the commiffion of this new
crime of confulting the witch ; which the author of
the book of Chronicles affigns particularly as the
ground of his death, though not exclufively of his
former difobedience : " So Saul died for his tranf-
" greffion which he committed againft the Lord,
" even againft the word of the Lord, which he kept
" not ; and alfo for afking counfel of one that had a
" familiar fpirit, to inquire of it *."   And it is evident from the language of Samuel, that, befides confirming the former fentence, he denounced new and
moft terrible judgments againft Saul, and againft his
family and forces ; and for no other reafon that appears, but the crime he was at this time committing.
It is farther objected, " that Samuel dexteroufly a-
" voided an anfwer to Saul's principal inquiry," and
that his language " has all the air of evafion and artifice †."   Saul wanted to be informed by Samuel,
how he was to act in his prefent critical fituation, or
how he might extricate himfelf from the danger which
then threatened him. And Samuel, inftead of having
recourfe to any evafion or artifice " to extricate himfelf from the" (pretended) " difficulty and neceffity
of giving Saul the advice he wanted ;" gave him
plainly to underftand, that it was too late to apply
                                                    for

---

* 1 Chron. x. 13.

† Dr. Chandler's Life of David, V. 1. p. 251, 252.

for any fuch advice as he afked; his doom being already fealed, 'and his fentence on the point of being
carried into execution.

Though Samuel's prophecy is called by fome an
eafy conjecture; yet it feems to argue a forefight
more than human. Samuel diftinctly foretold the
following remarkable particulars. Firft of all, the
death of Saul. And, was it certain that Saul would
not fhun an engagement, when he was fo dejected,
and had been in fo remarkable a manner fore-warned
of his danger? and that he would even rufh on his
deftruction? Secondly, Samuel farther foretold the
death of Saul's *fons.* And who but God could certainly forefee that Saul's three fons, who endeavoured
to fave themfelves by flight, fhould neverthelefs pe-
rifh by the fword of the enemy? Thirdly, Samuel
foretold, that, together with Saul, God would deliver up Ifrael, the army and people of Ifrael, into the
power of their enemies, and that their camp fhould
be taken, which made it the more difficult to bring a
new army into the field, and expofed their country to
the inroads of the Philiftines *. Laftly, the exact
time

---

* The laft claufe of the 19th verfe is not, what it is commonly made to be, a bare repetition of the firft claufe. By
Ifrael in the firft claufe, we are to underftand the army (including the people) of Ifrael; (compare v. 4. and ch. xxxi. 1.)
and by the *hoft* of Ifrael in the laft claufe, is meant more efpecially their *camp;* the lofs of which preventing them from
bringing a new army into the field, " the Philiftines came and
dwelt in" feveral of " the cities" which belonged to the Ifraelites. 1 Sam. xxxi. 7.

time is determined, when these events were to happen, which was the very next day. Accordingly,
within this space of time, the several parts of this
prediction received a punctual accomplishment. The
prophecy therefore seems to argue an unerring and
divine prescience.*.

But here it may be asked, " Is it likely, that God
" should refuse to answer Saul, when he consulted
" him in ways appointed by himself, and yet should
" answer him in a forbidden way; and hereby fa-
" vour and encourage necromantic divinations, when
" he had expressly ordered those who practised them
" to be punished with death?" Saul having been rejected by God for his stubborn disobedience to the divine orders, had no right to ask or expect his *direction*
and *preservation* in his present danger; nor could God
have granted it, consistently with his design of pre-
paring the way for the advancement of David to the
throne of Israel. For this reason, God did not answer

---

* Those, instead of falsifying, do really confirm the truth
of this prediction, who object, " that Saul hardly returned
" to his camp early enough in the morning after he had con-
" sulted the witch, or in sufficient spirits to prepare for the
" battle that day, which therefore must have been fought the
" day after." For what would be with us the *second* day after
the night in which Saul consulted the witch, was the morrow
or *next* day with the Jews, who reckoned from sun-set to sun-
set; and consequently included what we should call the next
day, in the natural day on which he was at Endor. Nay, if
the prophecy was not delivered till after midnight, *we* should
not understand by to-morrow any part of the day which was
begun.

fwer him in ways of his own appointment. Nor did he afterwards anfwer him in a forbidden way; but (if the explication here given of this hiftory be juft) interpofed previoufly to the ufe of magic rites, and on purpofe to reprove Saul for having recourfe to them, and to pronounce upon him the fentence of death for this very crime at the inftant he was committing it; and thus to teftify the divine difpleafure againft it. How this could encourage the ufe of necromancy, or indeed how God could more effeƐtually difcourage that moft deteftable art; I am not able to conceive. The method of God's proceeding on this occafion, feems very conformable to what he had been pleafed to do before, in other cafes of a like nature. When the king of Moab had recourfe to forceries, God himfelf interpofed, and fo over-ruled the mind of Balaam, that he was compelled to blefs thofe whom Balak wanted him to curfe *. And when king Ahaziah fent to confult Baalzebub about his recovery, God by his prophet Elijah ftopt his meffengers, reproved their mafter, and denounced his death †. And why might not God in like manner interpofe in the cafe of Saul, in order to difappoint his hopes of divine proteƐion, and to denounce his doom; the foreknowlege of which had fo great an effeƐ upon him, that he inftantly fell down into a fwoon, and could no longer bear up againft the bitter agonies of his mind? What is there in this conduƐ,

* Numb. xxiii.

† 2 Kings i. 2—4.

duct inconfiftent with the juftice or fanctity of the
great Governor of the world? Could Saul complain
of being fentenced to die for having recourfe to thofe
impious arts, the exercife of which he himfelf had
heretofore punifhed with death? How proper was
it, that his death fhould *appear* to be the punifhment
of his guilt? His death, if it had not been foretold,
would have been confidered as a common event, rather than as the execution of the divine difpleafure.
He had certainly difregarded the threatenings of God
to depofe him, and to appoint David in his ftead;
and very probably he had taken occafion from his
fufpending their execution, to turn them into ridi-
cule. Finding that he continued in the full poffeffion of his kingdom, many years after Samuel had
foretold it fhould be taken from him; he might afcribe
the prediction to the difaffection and enmity of the
prophet, and his attachment to David. To clear the
character of Samuel from all fufpicion, and vindicate
the credit of his predictions; to evidence the divine
defignation of David to the throne of Ifrael; and in
the moft affecting manner to difplay the righteous
vengeance of God againft the practice of necromantic divinations, by which Saul had now filled up the
meafure of his guilt; feems to have been the defign
of God in this miraculous appearance of his prophet.

I have now laid before the reader, what occurred
to me upon this difficult fubject; and fupported in
the ftrongeft manner I was able, from the reafonings
of others, and my own reflections, the two different
explications of it which carry with them the greateft

appearance

appearance of probability. I pretend not to decide which explication is true. Neither of them countenances the opinion, that miracles are performed by evil fpirits; which is all I contend for. That which was propofed laft, feems to me the beft fupported; though on this, as on every other point, I leave every one to form his own judgment.

The cafe of the devil's appearing to our Saviour in the wildernefs, and tranfporting or accompanying him from one place to another, and fhewing him all the kingdoms of the world; would naturally fall next under our confideration. But if the explication I have elfewhere given of this hiftory, be juft; it is no exception to the principle we have hitherto been endeavouring to eftablifh. In confirmation of that explication, I would obferve, that if it be true, that the Scripture appropriates all miracles to God; then the common interpretation of our Saviour's temptations, which afcribes fo many miracles to the devil, muft be falfe.

We have now examined the fenfe of revelation concerning the author of miracles; produced many arguments to fhew, that the Scriptures reprefent them as works peculiar to God, and attempted to folve the feveral objections againft this account. The number and eminence of thofe Chriftian writers, who have taught, that the Scriptures allow to evil fpirits a miraculous power, and the ufe made of that doctrine by unbelievers, in fapping the foundation of the Jewifh and Chriftian revelations, together with the nature and importance of the fubject itfelf, will excufe the

compafs

compafs with which it has been treated. I will add, that deifts fhould not avail themfelves of the errors of Chriftians, which are arguments only againft the perfons who advance them, not againft their religion. And even for them much allowance will be made by thofe, who confider, that the opinion entertained at prefent concerning the miraculous power of evil fpirits, prevailed very generally amongft the ancient Heathens and Jews; was early engrafted into the Scriptures themfelves, by falfe tranflations of them; and during the triumph of popery was deemed an effential article of the Chriftian faith. For how many ages were men prevented, by their prejudices, from underftanding the volume of nature, as well as that of revelation? At the revival of learning, and the glorious era of the Reformation, when men began to recover the ufe of their underftandings, and to apply the true rules of criticifm to the ftudy of the Scriptures; they at the fame time began to call in queftion the empire of Satan over the natural world. Luther abolifhed the practice of exorcifms, and many others no longer gave credit to idle ftories of fafcinations and magic. Much was then done to clear revelation from various corruptions which had been introduced into it. " And much" (fays one of the moft capable judges * of the fubject) " ftill remains to be done." No empire fo durable as that of error

and

* Dr. Lowth, bifhop of Oxford, in his fermon at the vifitation of the bifhop of Durham, p. 24.

and prejudice over the human mind ; and it may ſtill require a length of ages totally to ſubvert it.   In the mean time, no one can complain of the obſcurity of the Scriptures, in any neceſſary article of faith or practice.

.   C H A P.

CHAP. V.

SHEWING THAT MIRACLES, CONSIDERED AS DI-
VINE INTERPOSITIONS, ARE A CERTAIN PROOF
OF THE DIVINITY OF THE MISSION AND DOC-
TRINE OF A PROPHET.   THE ADVANTAGES AND
NECESSITY OF THIS PROOF IN CONFIRMING AND
PROPAGATING A NEW REVELATION.   MIRACLES
USEFUL IN REVIVING AND ESTABLISHING THE
PRINCIPLES OF NATURAL RELIGION.

HITHERTO we have been endeavouring to
prove, that miracles require an immediate
act or order of God, and are his peculiar works.
We are now to shew, what is a neceffary confequence
from this principle, that thefe works, when properly
applied, are a divine teftimony to the perfon on
whofe account they are wrought, and to that doctrine
or meffage which he delivers in the name of God.
It was for the fake of this important conclufion, that
we undertook to prove in the preceding chapters, by
arguments drawn both from reafon and revelation,
that miracles are divine interpofitions.

Miracles may be performed by God, without the
intervention of men; and for other purpofes, befides
that of attefting the miffion of a prophet.   Nor can
they ferve as teftimonials to a prophet, but under fuch
circumftances, as point out a relation between thofe
                                        works

works and his miffion. If it does not clearly appear, that they are wrought at his inftance, or in his favour; they will not be known to bear any more relation to him, than to any other perfon. Equally neceffary is it, that the prophet fhould exprefsly affert his miffion front God, explain its purport, and allege his miracles in proof of it; that their true intention may neither be overlooked nor miftaken, as the miracle of St. Paul at Lyftra was at firft by the Lycaonians *, through their inattention to the doctrine which he preached. If miracles are not declared to be figns of a divine miffion; they cannot be intended, nor ought to be regarded as fuch. It feems likewife to be farther requifite, that the perfon who claims a divine commiffion, and appeals to miracles in proof of it, fhould explain this commiffion, and deliver his meffage, when going to perform his miracles, or while he continues to perform them; that he may not apply them, nor be fufpected of applying them to a wrong purpofe; and that the connexion between them, and the point to be proved by them, may be the more readily difcerned, and fenfibly felt.

But miracles, if they argue a divine interpofition, muft be efteemed divine credentials, under the following circumftances: when it clearly appears, that they are wrought at the inftance, or in favour, of a perfon, who claims a miffion from God, delivers a meffage in his name, and appeals to thefe works, before or during the time of their performance, in proof of the divinity of his miffion and doctrine. The works

Z   having

* Acts xiv. 11.

having God for their author, muſt, in this caſe, be
conſidered as a declaration of his will, as his immediate anſwer to the appeal that had been made to him,
as the ſigns or teſtimonies of his approbation of the
perſon claiming a miſſion from him, and profeſſing
to reveal his will. In this method God may be ſaid
to ſeal his commiſſion, and to teſtify his approbation
of the purport of it ; juſt as we teſtify our aſſent to
what another ſpeaks in our name, by ſome particular
token ; or make what is contained in a writing,
though not drawn up by ourſelves, our own act and
deed, by ſetting our hand and ſeal to it. It is evident, that miracles, in the caſe here ſuppoſed, prove
the divinity of *the doctrine*, as well as of the miſſion
of the perſon employed in publiſhing it to the world ;
or God's approbation of him, both in aſſerting and
executing his commiſſion. It is ſcarce neceſſary to
add, that if divine interpoſitions in favour of a perſon claiming a commiſſion from God, prove the *divinity* of his doctrine, they likewiſe prove its *truth* *.
For it is impoſſible, as all men will allow, that God
ſhould affix his ſeal to a lie † ; or bear an immediate
teſtimony

---

* To the prophet who had raiſed up her ſon to life, the woman of Sarepta ſaid, " Now by this I know thou art a man of
" God, and that the word of the Lord by thy mouth is truth."
1 Kings xvii. 24. This is the language of nature and common ſenſe.

† Κομιδῇ ἄρα ὁ Θεὸς ἁπλοῦν ϗ ἀληθὲς, ἔν τε ἔργῳ ϗ ἐν λόγῳ. Καὶ
οὔτε αὐτὸς μεθίςαται, οὔτε ἄλλους ἐξαπατᾷ, οὔτε κατὰ φαντασίας, οὔτε
κατὰ λόγους, οὔτε κατὰ σημείων πομπὰς, οὐδ' ὕπαρ οὐδ' ὄναρ. Plat.
Republ. l. 2. p. 431. ed. Ficini.

teftimony in favour of one, who either falfely claims
a divine commiffion, or is unfaithful in the execution
of it. God is too wife to be deceived himfelf, too
juft and too good to deceive his creatures.

This is the manner in which miracles, fuppofing
them to be divine interpofitions, furnifh out a conclufive proof of the truth and divine original of a
fupernatural revelation. Before we proceed to confider the advantages of this proof, it will be neceffary to take notice of the different manner in which
the argument is ftated by other writers.

1. By the adverfaries of revelation it has been afferted, " that miracles, of themfelves, are proofs only
" of *power*, without having any relation to the *doc-*
" *trine* of the performer." ·Nay, the advocates of
revelation *, though they think " that miracles di-
" rectly prove the *commiffion* of the perfon who does
" them to proceed from him, by whofe power alone
" they could be performed;" yet maintain, " that
" miracles cannot prove *the truth* of any doctrine,"
and that " there is *no connexion* between any miracles
" and doctrines." If miracles, in themfelves, prove
only the interpofition of fome fuperior being; it muft
be difficult, we allow, to difcern any connexion between thefe works and the truth of doctrines. But
it has been fhewn, that thefe works are proofs of a
divine power and interpofition; and therefore, under
proper circumftances, divine teftimonials to a pro-

Z 2   phet;

---

* See Bp. Sherlock's Difcourfes, V. 1. p. 289, 290. and
V. 2. p. 10.

phet; teftimonials to his doctrine as well as to his miffion. If he declares himfelf to be fent from God, to deliver a meffage in his name, or to teach a new doctrine; and performs and appeals to miracles in proof both of his miffion and doctrine; will not the miracles (fuppofing them to be divinè works) equally prove the divinity of both? Indeed, his doctrine is included in his commiffion, and what God principally intended to atteft. And if the miracles prove the *divinity* of his doctrine, they muft prove its *truth;* unlefs proving it to be from God, be no proof that it is true. According to this ftate of the cafe, there is a very ftrict connexion between miracles, and the truth of doctrines *. Agreeably hereto, we find that the prophets of God, both under the Old Teftament and the New, at the fame time that they afferted their divine miffion, explained the particular object of it, or the purpofe for which they were fent: and that they urged their miracles as immediate divine teftimonies to their meffage or doctrine †, as well as to their miffion. Nor can we have any higher evidence of the truth and certainty of any doctrine, than the immediate atteftation of God to it.——If

fome ·

---

* It might have been added, that miracles may be of fuch a nature as to exemplify, as well as to atteft, the doctrine of a prophet. But this connexion between doctrines and fuch miracles as are proper famples of thofe doctrines, could not be taken notice of here; as we are now confidering miracles only in their moft general view, as divine interpofitions.

† John xiv. 10, 11. Mark xvi. 20. Acts xiv. 3. See above, ch. 3. fect. 6. p. 266.

fome have contracted the ufe of miracles within too narrow limits; others, running into the oppofite extreme, have ftretched it too far. For,

2. Miracles have been urged, to prove the univerfal and perpetual infpiration of the perfons who performed them. By fome learned writers it has been afferted *, that " we may be rationally affured, that " a prophet is fent of God; BEFORE we have " heard one word of his doctrine;" and fuppofed †, that all the miracles of a prophet may be performed firft, and his doctrine be delivered afterwards. In proof of this point, they appeal firft to the miracles of Mofes in Egypt, and at the Red Sea; which they allege, proved Mofes to be *an oracle*, and would have proved the divinity of all the doctrines and precepts he afterwards delivered, even if Mofes had performed no other miracles ‡. · Whereas the ends propofed, or the doctrines to be proved by the miracles of Mofes in Egypt, were diftinctly ftated *before* ‖ the works were performed. Thofe ends were, not the proving Mofes to be an oracle, or a divine lawgiver to the Ifrael-

Z 3 ites,

---

* By Mr. Hallet on miracles, p. 57, 61, 63. and Dr. Benfon, in his life of Chrift, ch. 6. fect. 6. p. 224.

† Dr. Benfon, p. 225, 228, &c. .

‡ P. 229.

‖ " Aaron fpake all the words which Jehovah had fpoken " unto Mofes, and (then) did the figns in the fight of the " people." Exod. iv. 29, 30. In like manner Mofes and Aaron delivered their meffage to Phaorah, before they proved their miffion by miracles. Exod. v. 1.

ites, but the effecting their deliverance out of Egypt, the exemplary punishment of oppression and idolatry, and the manifestation of the true God to the world *. Nor was it upon this evidence, but upon the evidence of the miracles wrought afterwards in the wilderness, that the Israelites received Moses as a divine lawgiver, whose authority God continued to support by a series of miracles, even after all his doctrines and precepts were delivered.   The learned writers † next appeal to the miracles wrought by St. Paul at Philippi; though we read of his *preaching* ‡ there some considerable time before we have any account of his working miracles.   These ingenious gentlemen all along argue on the supposition, that the miracles of a prophet are a general assurance, that we may safely trust him as an oracle ‖, and depend upon all he says as long as he lives §: a supposition altogether groundless, and of a like nature with that on which the unhappy man seems to have proceeded, who was slain by a lion, for giving too hasty credit to a prophet ¶.

Hardly any thing has done more prejudice to revelation, than the misapplication of its miracles to purposes they were never intended to answer.   What

has

* See above, ch. iii. sect. 5.

† Dr. Benson, p. 230.   Mr. Hallet, p. 63.

‡ Acts xvi. 14—18.

‖ Mr. Hallet, p. 41, &c.

§ Dr. Benson, p. 224, 230.

¶ 1 Kings xiii.

has furnifhed infidelity with more objections *, and
occafioned fo much perplexity to fincere Chriftians ; as
mens maintaining that a prophet who has once performed miracles, is thereby rendered for ever incapable of error and vice †; and their building articles
of faith on his private opinions with refpect to fub-

Z 4   jects

* Mr. Voltaire, in his Treatife on Toleration, fays, " that
" Jephtha's declaration, (Judges xi. 24.) who was infpired by
" God, is at leaft an evident proof; that God permitted the
" worfhip of Chemofh." But this writer mifreprefents the
meaning of Jephtha, who is only arguing with idolaters upon
their own principle, that all nations had a right to keep what
their gods had enabled them to poffefs : which is very different
from allowing the divinity and worfhip of Chemofh. Nor was
Jephtha infpired when he fpoke the words here referred to.
" The Spirit of the LORD came upon him" afterwards,
(Judges xi. 29.) inciting him to undertake, and enabling him
to accomplifh, the deliverance of the Ifraelites. Can it be inferred from hence, that whenever he fpoke it was by divine
infpiration ?

† An opinion repugnant to the exprefs declarations of revelation. Mat. vii. 22, 23. Heb. vi. 4, 5, 6. See alfo Acts
xxiii. 5. ch. xv. 12, 39. Gal. ii. 11, 14. When our Saviour
fays, Mark ix. 39. " No man, who fhall do a miracle in my
" name, can lightly (ταχὺ, quickly) fpeak evil of me ;" he
means, that it ought not to be fuppofed concerning any perfon,
who had fo great faith in him, as to undertake and perform
miracles in a dependance upon his divine power, that he was
at that time difpofed to revile and blafpheme him. This faith,
however, did not always govern mens lives. For to fome,
" who did many wonderful works in the name of Chrift, he
" will fay, I never knew (or approved) you." The eleven
apoftles, while their minds were darkened by many prejudices,
and even Judas, wrought miracles.

jeċts not included in his commiſſion, and with regard to which he might think and ſpeak like all other
men ?

All the prophets of God did not perform their miracles with one view, nor were their commiſſions of
the ſame extent. The commiſſion of ſome was limited to one particular purpoſe or ſeaſon; that of
others was more general and laſting. Each clearly
ſtated the diſtinct and ſpecial purpoſes of his own
miſſion and miracles; and *always* declared what thoſe
purpoſes were, *before* he performed his miracles, or
(which is the ſame thing) before he ceaſed to perform
miracles. And the miracles were deſigned to atteſt
his commiſſion, and the purpoſes of it, in their juſt
extent, as explained by the prophet himſelf, during
the time that the miraculous teſtimony was borne to
him. On this plan, no inconvenience could poſſibly
enſue from the errors of a prophet, on ſubjects foreign
to his commiſſion; nor even from his acting afterwards contrary to his own convictions, with reſpect
to the ſubject of his commiſſion; or on any other
occaſion. The evidence of Chriſt's divine authority,
ariſing from miracles performed by thoſe who afterwards revolted from the faith or practice of Chriſtianity, was not impaired by that revolt. Nor did the
culpable timidity of Peter, in withdrawing himſelf
from the ſociety of the Gentile Chriſtians, that he
might not give offence to the Jews, weaken thoſe
proofs of the exemption of the former from the obligation of circumciſion, which aroſe from the ſpecial
miracles by which it was confirmed, in the caſe of
Cornelius and other uncircumciſed Gentiles. In a
word,

word, miracles muft not be extended beyond their
proper ufe, nor applied to any other purpofes, than
what the nature of the works themfelves, or the declarations of the performer, will warrant. Miracles
are the teftimony of God himfelf, to a perfon profeffing to deliver a meffage from him; a proof of the
divine original of his miffion and doctrine. But we
are to receive as divine upon this evidence, no other
doctrines, than thofe it was defigned to confirm.

Having attempted to fhew, under what circumftances miracles, confidered as divine interpofitions,
are a certain proof of doctrines; I proceed to point
out the advantages of this proof, particularly in introducing and eftablifhing a revelation from God.
We fhall ftill argue on the fuppofition of miracles
being divine works; though, after what has been
urged above, it muft be unneceffary at every turn to
fhew, that the argument concludes only on this fuppofition.

I. The proof from miracles of the divine commiffion and doctrine of a prophet, is, in itfelf, decifive
and *abfolute.* What reafoning can be more conclufive than this, " He that does fuch works as no man
" can do, unlefs God be with him, muft be fent of
" God, and faithfully publifh his will to the world ?"
The God of truth cannot bear an immediate teftimony to any one as a divine meffenger, whom he has
not fent, or who publifhes his own inventions as the
oracles of heaven. No man was ever fo abfurd as to
maintain, that atteftations properly divine can deceive us, or that God would immediately interpofe
in fupport of falfe claims. And this proof of a divine

vine commiffion from the credentials we are now
fpeaking of, is full and fufficient, without taking into
confideration the doctrine. they atteft. The proof
arifes out of the nature of the miracles, independent
of every thing elfe. This fully vindicates the conduct of the prophets of God, who, as was fhewn
above *, demanded the immediate affent and regard
of mankind to their divine commiffion, upon the fole
evidence of their miracles, and prior to all reafonings
concerning the natural propriety and fitnefs of their
doctrine. It was only by fuch works, as were fure
tokens of a divine miffion, that it was poffible for
them to overcome the objections and corrupt prejudices of mankind againft their meffage. Had Mofes told
Pharaoh, or Chrift the Jews †, " that before the evi-
" dence of miracles was admitted, as a proof of a di-
" vine commiffion, the *matter* of that commiffion
" muft be examined by mens natural notions, and
" be made appear to be conformable to them ;" the
miracles of thefe divine prophets would have produced only endlefs debates, inftead of conviction. But
the evidence of their miffions from thefe works, was
in itfelf (as it was neceffary it fhould be) decifive and
abfolute.

To what is here advanced, fome may object, " that
" if doctrines are to be received as coming from
" God, upon the bare atteftation of miracles, with-
" out regard to the nature of the doctrines them-
                                        " felves;

* Ch. 3. fect. 6.

† See p. 396.

" felves; we may then be obliged, under the fanc-
" tion of thefe works, to receive the moſt abſurd and
" immoral doctrines, and there can be no poſſible
" guard againſt impoſture." This objection ſuppoſes,
that doctrines immoral and abſurd may receive the
ſanction of miracles : a ſuppoſition which ought not to
be made; becauſe miracles are works peculiar to God,
and it is impoſſible for God to lie. The principle on
which we here argue, that miracles are immediately
to be referred to God, is ſo far from leaving us open
to deluſion and impoſture, that it contains our great-
eſt ſecurity from it; it furniſhes us with all the evidence we can derive from the wiſdom, veracity, and
perfect rectitude of the divine Being, that the atteſtation of miracles cannot accompany any falſe doctrines. It has never been ſhewn, that ſuch doctrines
ever have received * the atteſtation of miracles : and
inaſmuch as miracles are works appropriate to God,
it is impoſſible that ſuch doctrines ever ſhould receive
this atteſtation. Whenever therefore the miracle is
apparent, (there being either ocular demonſtration,
or other certain evidence of its truth;) it is not neceſſary to enquire, whether the doctrine be ſuch as
may come from God, or *may* be true: for the miracle (being divine) does alone aſſure us, previous to
ſuch enquiry, that it *did* come from God, and therefore that it *is* true; nay, that it is as impoſſible it
ſhould be falſe or immoral, or abſurd, as it is that God
ſhould act contrary to his own perfections. If the
miracle be of *dubious* evidence, and the doctrine ſuch

as

* See above, ch. 2. ſect. 2.

as could not proceed from God; the proper inference will be, not that the miracle was performed by
wicked fpirits, but that it was invented by wicked
men.   The confideration of the doctrine may ferve,
in this cafe, to detect the falfehood of miracles; but
is never neceffary to eftablifh the divinity of thefe
works, or the truth and divinity of the doctrine itfelf
which they are wrought to confirm : the latter muft
be true and divine, becaufe the former can have no
other author but God.   The objection therefore puts
a cafe which can never poffibly happen : it fuppofes
that God may publifh and atteft a falfehood to the
world.

   II. The proof of a divine miffion and doctrine
from miracles, is the moft *natural* and *agreeable to*
the common fenfe of mankind in all ages.   The works
of creation are ftanding evidences of the exiftence
and attributes of God.   The continued order of the
univerfe is a fure demonftration of his conftant providence.   It is upon the theatre of nature, that God
is continually manifefting himfelf to mankind.   Here,
therefore, it is moft natural to fuppofe, he will difplay his power, and fignify his pleafure; fhould he
fee fit to make any new difcoveries of his will.   If
he would evidence to his creatures the interpofition
of the Lord of nature; in what other method can
this be fo fuitably done, as by controuling the laws
of nature?   And when he does this in anfwer to an
immediate appeal to him, made by one who claims a
miffion from him; does he not declare in the moft
proper and expreffive language, that it is his will,
that that claim fhould be received and admitted?
                                                  This

This appears to have been the general fenfe of mankind in all ages, concerning genuine miracles; as we have had occafion to fhew *.

The natural fenfe of mankind with regard to this, as well as other fubjects, may, no doubt, be in fome meafure perverted by fophiftry and fuperftition. And it has been by fome affirmed, that in the age in which the Gofpel was publifhed, both Jews and Gentiles entertained a very *low opinion* of miracles in general. From hence others have been forward to conclude, that they were not a very proper means of recommending the Gofpel to the regard of mankind. It is not true, however, that genuine and inconteftable miracles were held in difefteem at the commencement of the Chriftian era. The Jews indeed objected to Chrift, that he difpoffeffed demoniacs by the affiftance of the prince of demons; but it has been fhewn †, that they did not, and could not, pafs the like judgments on his other miraculous works. Their own religion being grounded upon miracles; they were not fo abfurd as to deny their being proper proofs of a divine miffion. Miracles were not only an evidence, by which they were determined, but which they preferred to any other : " The Jews require a fign ‡."

With

* Ch. 2. fect. 5.

† Ch. 3. fect. 6. p. 270. Mr. Bifcoe, after others, afferts, that both Jews and Heathens afcribed the miracles both of Chrift and his apoftles to the power of magic. Sermons at Boyle's Lecture, p. 293. But his authorfles will not fupport his affertion, in this large extent.

‡ 1 Cor. i. 22.

With refpect to the Greeks or Gentiles, the learned amongſt them, it is acknowleged, *ſought after wiſdom,* were captivated with curious ſpeculations, ſet off with the charms of eloquence; and may in ſome ſenſe be ſaid to have held miracles in contempt *, that is, *ſuch* events as were by them commonly deſcribed by this term. Theſe were of two ſorts. Some of them, though eſteemed miracles by the vulgar, were not really ſuch, but mere natural events; inundations, prodigies, monſters, together with all the feats of ſorcery and magic : and theſe might very reaſonably be rejected by all who were acquainted with the powers of nature † and art. Others were events truly ſupernatural; but they were conſidered as groſs impoſtures. They were not only ſo ill atteſted, but ſo incredible in themſelves, ſo deſtitute of all rational intention and wiſe contrivance, ſo viſibly calculated to ſerve ſome political purpoſe, ſo trifling, or ridiculous, or abſurd in their own nature; that it cannot be matter of wonder, that the wiſer Heathens rejected them with diſdain. Marcus Antoninus in particular deſpiſed all the ſtories of them, under the notion of their being mere fables. His words are, " I have " learnt not to believe thoſe things which are re- " ported concerning wonder-workers, or jugglers and " magicians, in relation to their charms, and expul-

" ſion

---

* Somnia, terrores magicos, miracula, ſagas,
   Nocturnos lemures, portentaque Theſſala rides? Hor.

† Vid. Tacit. Hiſt. l. 1. c. 86. & l. 2. c. 1.

" fion of demons, and the like *." The followers
of Epicurus were under a neceffity of rejecting every
hiftory of miracles; becaufe they denied a providence, and thought the gods did not intereft themfelves in the affairs of mankind †. But this very reafoning fhews, that they confidered miracles as divine
operations, and therefore were not difpofed to deride
the works themfelves, had they been convinced that
any fuch works had been truly performed.

The proof of revelation therefore from real and
unfufpected miracles, was not improper to be propofed to the Heathen world : for it is one thing to fuf-
pect or deny the *truth* of miracles ; and quite another, when we allow their truth, to difpute their authority ‡. How well this evidence was adapted to
the

---

* Marc. Anton. l. i. § 6. Plutarch likewife (de Superftit.
p. 171.) ranks γοιτειαι and μαγειαι amongft the moft ridiculous
parts of Pagan fuperftition. Θαυματα μωροις, might well grow
into a proverb, with refpect to fuch miracles ; which were fit
only to produce the fcorn and averfion which Horace expreffes,

Aut in avem Progne vertatur, Cadmus in anguem.
Quodcunque oftendis mihi fic, incredulus odi.
De Art. Poet. l. 187.

† ——————— Credat Judæus Apella,
Non ego ; namque deos didici fecurum agere ævum.
Horat. Sat. l. 1. Sat. 5. l. 100.

‡ It may here be objected, that thofe Heathens who believed a providence, afcribed miracles to demons. But it will
not follow from hence, that they believed that demons wrought
miracles in oppofition to heaven, and in confirmation of falfehood. Παντη αρα αψευδες το δαιμονιοντε κ᾽ το θειον. Plat. de Re-
pub. l. 2. p. 431. ed. Ficini. Should any afk, How came it
to

the ftate of the Heathens, appears from its great fuccefs, in converting them from atheifm and idolatry to the Chriftian faith.   And this fuccefs would have been ftill greater, had there been no more objection to the *doctrine*, than there was to. the *miracles* of Chriftianity: for thefe works immediately difgraced all the artifices of impofture *, and bore upon themfelves fuch characters of divinity, that the Heathens regarded the performers of them as *gods*, and were with difficulty reftrained from paying them divine honours †.   From what has been advanced under this head, it in fome meafure appears, that,

III. Miracles form the moft *eafy* and *compendious* proof of a new revelation; fuch as lies level to the capacities of all mankind, even of thofe who have little leifure or ability for deep refearches after truth. That *the bulk of mankind* are not endowed with faculties to apprehend the force of long and intricate reafonings; and that the neceffary duties of their ftation engrofs almoft all their attention; are facts too plain to be difputed.   And to thofe who are at all acquainted with the writings of *the learned*, it is as evident, that thofe abftract reafonings which are above the capacity of the vulgar, are often unfatisfactory to

perfons

---

to pafs that the Heathens did not pay more regard to the miracles of Chriftianity? I would refer them for fatisfaction to Dr. Law's " Confiderations," &c. p. 121. note e. 3d ed. who treats this fubject with his ufual candour and judgment.

* See Acts viii. 9—24. ch. xiii. 8—11. ch. xix. 19.

† Acts xiv. 11—13.

perfons of judgment; and may generally be oppofed by arguments fo probable, as to caufe perfons of
the beft abilities to doubt on which fide truth is
to be found. The fpeculations which have had the
fanction of one age, have been exploded in the next;
nay, thofe which have reigned abfolute ovet all the
cultivated parts of the world, for many ages together, are now funk into contempt. And the new
opinions which are fubftituted in the room of the
former exploded ones, may hereafter undergo the
fame fate with them. For there is very little certainty in any fcience, (except mathematical,) any
farther than the reafoning is grounded upon *facts*.
God therefore intending the Chriftian revelation for
the benefit of all, founded it upon an evidence adapted to the capacities of all; upon fuch *facts* as clearly
demonftrated his own interpofition and countenance;
and exhibited to the very fenfes, as well as to the underftandings of mankind, the doctrines they were defigned to atteft, the miracles being fpecimens or famples of thofe doctrines. This teftimony which God
bore to his Son, was equally fitted to convince the
learned and illiterate; the force of it was eafily and
immediately apprehended, by all who were willing to
open their eyes, and fee the light. Had it been neceffary, that mankind fhould have been made *philofophers*, before they became *Chriftians;* how fmall,
and how flow a progrefs would the Gofpel have
made; efpecially as it was to be publifhed to thofe,
who had the greateft need of fupernatural affiftance,
whofe underftandings had been debafed by fuperftition and idolatry, and whofe minds were inflamed by

A a   prejudices

prejudices and bigotry, as well as undifciplined to thought and reflection, and employed about the cares of life? But the Gofpel, by being accompanied with a proof of its divinity, that was plain and eafy, and carried inftant conviction, did in a fhort time eftablifh itfelf in every part of the earth. This divine light, like that of the fun, enlightens every man without any diftinction, and in a moment darts its beams from one end of the world to the other.

IV. Miracles are a very *powerful* method of conviction, making a ftrong impreffion upon *the heart*, at the fame time that they carry light to the underftanding. Such fenfible and unufual effects, pointing out the immediate hand of God in producing them, arreft the attention, roufe the mind from the fupine ftate into which it was funk, ftrike it with an awe of God, imprefs the conviction of his peculiar prefence, and carry with them an obligation to receive and obey the truths which they confirm. They add weight and energy to thofe truths, whofe importance thus interefts heaven in their behalf. Every one who confiders the wifdom and majefty of the divine Being, muft be fenfible, that no trivial occafion, that nothing but the execution of fome defign of the higheft importance, can induce him in any inftance to fufpend his own laws, and produce events quite out of the fettled order of his government. I add, that miracles, when they are not related, but *feen;* and when they are performed in our prefence in a manner worthy of the Divinity; make a very peculiar impreffion; they muft ftrike the mind much more powerfully, than any hiftory (whatever credit

we

we give it) can do. So that in thefe circumftances, no man can refift their efficacy, without contracting a peculiar guilt, and incurring an high degree of the divine difpleafure; which was accordingly denounced by Chrift and his apoftles, againft fuch as withftood the conviction of thofe mighty works, by which the Gofpel was confirmed *.

V. Powerful as thefe means of conviction may be, they are *not violent and compulfive;* nor do they produce their full effect, in engaging men to receive and obey a new revelation, without the exercife of right difpofitions of mind. Whatever fome have fuggefted to the contrary, by miracles God appeals to our *reafon,* to judge whether they are operations of his power, and evidences of his will; and whether thofe at whofe inftance they are performed, are commiffioned to deliver it. And when the underftanding is convinced, that the miffion is divine, our compliance with the meffage is an act of the will. Miracles are the fame method of addrefs to mankind, as the works of nature, confidered as the effects of God's power, and the fignifications of his will, which neither produce a full conviction without fome attention and reflection, nor obedience without a becoming reverence of God.

Miracles, it may be faid, neceffarily ftrike the mind with aftonifhment; but fo likewife do the wonders of nature, while they are new: and this, in either

A a 2 cafe,

---

* John xv. 24. Mat. xi. 21. ch. xii. 31, 32. Heb. vi. 4, &c. ch. x. 29.

cafe, (ufeful as it may prove to fome,) is of little
ufe to thofe, who ftudioufly divert their thoughts
from the operations of the divine hand, and are only
looking out for matter of cavil againft them. Miracles
are no remedy for obftinacy; nor can the brighteft
manifeftations of the Divinity open thofe eyes which
are wilfully clofed. Signs of an extraordinary divine
interpofition will attract the readieft regard from
thofe, who have cultivated right fentiments towards
God, and are previoufly prepared to obey his will.
So that the evidence of miracles is not unfuitable to
the nature of religion, as a reafonable and voluntary
fervice; nor to the nature of man, as a moral agent;
and at the fame time it is peculiarly adapted to gain
thofe over to the faith of the Chriftian revelation,
who are beft difpofed to comply with its defign *.

VI. The *neceffity* of miracles is no lefs evident,
than their propriety and advantage, in attefting a
divine commiffion, and propagating a new revelation. For how can God give any evidence of his
will, but by the operations of his power, or the effects of his omnifcience? By what but the outward
and fenfible difplays of both, can he bear a public
teftimony to an extraordinary meffenger from heaven? The general laws of nature and providence
anfwer the end for which they were defigned; but
cannot

* This account of miracles is confirmed, by the effects
which thofe of the Gofpel produced. Some rejected this evidence, others were convinced, but not laftingly reformed by
it, (Mat. vii. 22, 23.) on others it had a perfect and permanent influence; according to their refpective difpofitions.

cannot ferve the purpofe of a peculiar atteftation to a prophet of God. Nor can the excellent tendency of the doctrine, feparately confidered, prove that it came from God. Had Chriftianity been only a republication of the law of nature, or a revival of certain principles obfcured by fuperftition, but demonftrable by reafon, when awakened into exercife; even then miracles would have been *ufeful* to excite the attention of the world to thofe principles, and to give them new evidence and certainty; nay, *neceffary*, though not to eftablifh their *truth*, yet to prove a particular *divine commiffion*, to revive the knowlege of them, and thereby to give the publifhers of them the greater authority to reform the world, and procure them a more fpeedy fuccefs. But when a new religion is (like that of the Gofpel) the free refult of the divine wifdom for the falvation of finful men, and contains brighter difplays of the divine philanthropy, than natural reafon is acquainted with; how can the divine original of fuch a new religion be eftablifhed, if no fupernatural teftimony be borne to it by God?

The more immediate defign of the miracles of the Gofpel, was, to prove the divine commiffion of the firft publifhers of it, and to engage men to receive it as an immediate meffage from God. They were more efpecially intended to demonftrate Jefus of Nazareth to be the Meffiah, the divinely appointed prince and faviour: a claim that could not be fupported, but by the divine teftimony of prophecies and miracles. Chrift not only affumed the honour of a prophet of God, but a far fuperior dignity and authority to any of the prophets; he fpoke of him-

felf

felf as the Son of God, in a fenfe peculiar and tran-
fcendent; as one appointed to govern the church,
and to judge the world. Now, the more extraordinary his claims were, fo much the more neceffary
was it to confirm them by adequate miracles. Had
Chrift reafoned like a philofopher, he might have
been efteemed as fuch ; but, without producing proper credentials of a divine miffion * and authority,
he could not have enforced his inftructions upon the
confcience, as the immediate dictates and oracles of
the Divinity; nor have been received by the world
under his proper character, as the Son of God, the
Saviour, Sovereign, and Judge of mankind. Chrift
had fuffered death, as a malefactor. His apoftles affirmed, that God had raifed him up again, advanced
him to a ftate of the higheft dignity and authority in
his prefence and kingdom, and invefted him with
power to beftow immortality on his followers. But,
who ought or could give credit to their doctrine and
teftimony, if it had not been confirmed by God himfelf, on whofe good pleafure alone the conftitution
of the Gofpel was founded? It was impoffible by
reafon, to prove the antecedent propriety and neceffity of fuch a conftitution. If any thing can render
the neceffity of miracles to confirm and propagate the
Gofpel, ftill more apparent; it is the confideration of
the

* This argument might receive large illuftration from the
cafe of Mofes, both as a divine ambaffador to Pharaoh, and
a divine legiflator to the Ifraelites. Even his main doctrine,
viz. that the God of the Hebrews was the only true God, as
well as his commiffion, could be eftablifhed only by miracles.

the great corruption * of the world, at the time of
Chrift's appearance in it, creating in men a difaffection to the purity of this new revelation; the difgrace
and danger that attended the public profeffion of it;
the violent prejudices entertained both by Jews and
Gentiles againft the doctrine of the crofs; the Gofpel's fuperfeding the neceffity of the Jewifh revelation, and eftablifhing itfelf upon the ruins of Pagan
idolatry; and the confequent oppofition it met with
from all the powers of the world. Thefe difficulties
and obftructions could not have been furmounted, if
the Gofpel had not been fupported and recommended
by the moft unqueftionable operations of God's
power, and the plaineft teftimonies of his approbation.

VII. Miracles, while they are more immediately
and directly employed in introducing and eftablifhing a new revelation, may ferve to revive and confirm the principles of natural religion, and to recover
men from thofe two oppofite extremes of atheifm and
idolatry. Into the one or other of thefe extremes,
the world was very generally fallen, in the age of the
Gofpel. Perfons in the higher ranks of life, were
infected with atheifm; thofe in the lower, were quite

A a 4 over-run

* See what was urged above, to fhew the neceffity of confirming the Gofpel by miracles, and of confidering thefe works
as in themfelves certain evidences of a divine interpofition, from
the confideration of the ftrong prejudices both of Jews and
Gentiles againft the claims of Chrift, and from the great corruption of the age in which the Gofpel was publifhed, ch. 3,
fect. 6.

over-run with idolatry. Now, no properer cure of both thefe evils could be prefcribed, than miracles.

1. Thefe works confute the pretences of *atheifm*, and afford new evidence of thofe firft principles of all religion, the being and providence of God. It has, indeed, been often affirmed, that miracles offered in fupport of a miffion from God, do only fuppofe, and cannot demonftrate, his exiftence. Neverthelefs, if they are his immediate acts, and prove a divine mif-fion ; they muft prove that there is a God, from whom the miffionary comes, and by whofe authority he acts. Supernatural figns and wonders demonftrate his ex-iftence, in the fame way of reafoning as the works of nature do. In both cafes we proceed on one com-mon principle, that every effect muft have fome caufe; and argue from the vifible effects, to an invifible caufe, by which they were produced. If you confi-der only the grandeur of the works, the exiftence of the world (fo replete with wonders!) bears a more ample teftimony to the being of a God, than all the miracles of the Jewifh and Chriftian difpenfations. Neverthelefs, *occafional* and *uncommon* operations of the divine power have this peculiar advantage to re-commend them, that they ftrike our attention more forcibly, than that fettled courfe of things, which falls under our conftant obfervation.

Miracles not only contain a new demonftration of God's exiftence, but ftrengthen the proofs of it drawn from the frame of the world, and clear them from the two principal objections of atheifm, viz. either that the world is eternal, or elfe owed its exiftence to the fortuitous concourfe of atoms. Sometimes the

the atheift affirms, that the world was never made at all, but has exifted from eternity juft as it is at pre- fent; and is fubject to fate or neceffity: and thus he endeavours to evade the argument drawn from na- ture, to prove the exiftence of its Creator and Lord. But the fupernatural proof of this important point is not liable to the fame objection, and is even fer vice- able in removing it. No one affirms, that miracles exifted from eternity; and if they are really effected, they muft have a caufe. If they are effected at the interceffion of a prophet, and in atteftation of his commiffion, they muft have a voluntary defigning caufe; and cannot be afcribed either to neceffity or fate. And inafmuch as they controul or fuperfede the laws of nature; their efficient caufe muft be dif- tinct from nature, and fuperior to it; and can be no other than the fovereign Lord of nature, the fame whom we call God. Not to add, that had the world been eternal, the courfe of nature would have conti- nued the fame without any interruption. Nor can vifible figns of an invifible power that commands na- ture, be any more reconciled with the formation of the world by the fortuitous concourfe of atoms, than with the notion of its eternal neceffary exiftence. In oppofition to both thefe pleas, they prove the world to be.the work of a free and almighty Agent *. For who can controul the fettled courfe of nature, but that

---

* So that whether the apoftle confidered *the declaration* of Mofes, Gen. i. 1. as that of a prophet, or the *credentials* of his miffion; he might fay, " By faith we know that the worlds were framed by the word of God," Heb. xi. 3. Faith fup- plies us with new evidence of this truth, without weakening that

that great Being that eftablifhed it? If the world had no creator, it could have no lord. He alone who caufed it to be what it is, could make what changes in it he pleafed. The vifible figns of God's power do fo clearly demonftrate his exiftence, that the atheift denies there ever were any miracles, to avoid being compelled into the belief of a God.

Miracles alfo bear a noble teftimony to divine providence. They are actual exercifes of God's jurifdiction over the world, and therefore a proof of fact that he governs it, and interefts himfelf in its affairs. Prophecies likewife are a farther illuftration and evidence of this important truth. When they defcribe the moft contingent events, the actions of free agents; comprehend the fates of various nations and perfons; and reach through a great length of ages; they afford a moft fenfible proof of the univerfal and perpetual fuperintendency of an unerring providence. Thefe miraculous effects of the divine power and knowlege, are a very valuable *addition* to that evidence of God's exiftence and government, which arifes from the order of nature; and ferve to vindicate and confirm it.

2. Miracles are a remedy againft the evil of *idolatry*, as well as that of atheifm. In the opinion of idolaters themfelves, thefe works are a demonftration of a divine power *. And when they are performed

---

that of reafon. And Mofes might clearly and certainly infer from his miracles, even without an immediate revelation, that, :' In the beginning God created the heaven and the earth."

* Acts xiv. 11.

formed in the name of Jehovah, under the character of the only living and true God, in direct oppofition to all the claims of idolatry; they equally eftablifh the divinity of Jehovah, and confute the pretenfions of all his rivals and oppofers. The truth of his claims neceffarily infers the falfehood of theirs. Miracles, being in themfelves exercifes of God's fovereign dominion over the powers of nature, which were the principal gods of Paganifm, and from whom the inferior deities were fuppofed to derive all their authority; overturn the very foundation of the Pagan idolatry, and bring men to the knowlege of the true God *.

This

---

* 1 Theff. i. 9, 10. 1 Pet. i. 21. 1 Cor. xii. 2. Acts xiv. 15. Mr. Voltaire (in his Dictionaire Philofophique, p. 268.) feems to approve of the philofopher, who faid, that the fight of miracles would convince him of the exiftence of two oppofite principles, one of whom undoes what the other had been doing. This objection proceeds on the falfe fuppofition, that miracles contradict or defeat the intention of the laws of nature : whereas they only aim at an end, which could not be anfwered by the regular operation of thofe laws; (as was fhewn above, p. 21.) And it is evident, that, when they are performed in the name of the true God, and in proof of his fole dominion over nature, or (which is the fame thing in effect) in proof of a miffion from him, under the character of the fole author and fovereign of the world, and are not (as they never can be) controuled by oppofite miracles; inftead of eftablifhing, they directly confute the doctrine of two or more rival deities. Accordingly, the miracles of the Jewifh and Chriftian revelations were the means of converting men from polytheifm, to the faith and worfhip of the true God. " By him (Chrift) ye believe in God, that raifed him from " the dead, and gave him glory, that your faith and hope " might be in God." 1 Pet. i. 21.

This argument might receive large illuſtration
from the *peculiar nature* of the Scripture miracles,
were this the proper place for entering on the examination of them.   But we are here only ſhewing the
uſe of miracles in general, in bearing teſtimony to
the exiſtence, unity, and providence of God; and
confidering theſe works in their moſt general view,
as divine operations.

For this reafon, we forbear likewiſe to ſhew, that
when miracles are in their own nature, diſplays of
the beneficence and rectitude of the divine Being,
inſtances of his favour or diſpleaſure, according to
mens different characters; and are likewiſe fubfervient to a ſcheme calculated to recover men to piery
and virtue; they are then a new confirmation of
God's *moral* perfections and providence, fuch as may
ferve for the conviction of all who call them into
queſtion, and be of fingular uſe to thoſe who worſhip gods of the moſt flagitious characters, and do it
by acts of wickednefs fuitable to their apprehended
natures.   Thus the antient Heathens did; who neverthelefs were recovered by fuch miracles as are here
defcribed, to the knowledge and adoration of the Holy
One of Ifrael.

The foregoing obfervations are, I hope, fufficient
to ſhew, that how low an opinion foever thoſe may
entertain of miracles, who will not allow them to be
the immediate operation of God; yet when confidered in this their true light, their uſe, importance, and
neceffity in introducing and eſtabliſhing a new revelation, is clearly difcerned; and that, while they give
authority to a prophet to reveal the divine will to
                                              mankind,

mankind, they bear a ſtriking teſtimony to the exiſtence and providence of God, and are highly uſeful,
if not neceſſary, for the conviction of mankind, when
funk into atheiſm and idolatry. They have actually
anſwered this end, when all the works of nature
failed of their effect. I would only obſerve farther,

VIII. That the evidence of miracles (whether of
power or knowlege) is the fitteſt to accompany a
ſtanding revelation ; becauſe it is not confined to one
age or nation, but may be extended over the whole
globe, and conveyed to the moſt diſtant generations.
Miracles of *power* carry inſtant conviction, procure
preſent credit to a prophet ; and muſt make a very
peculiar impreſſion on the ſpectators. Nevertheleſs,
their uſe is not confined to them ; for they may be
ſo credible in themſelves, ſo ſtrongly atteſted, ſo faithfully recorded, and ſo neceſſarily connected with
other ſubſequent facts, not to be diſputed, nor accounted for in a natural way, as to leave no room
for thoſe to doubt of their reality, who had not the
advantage of ſeeing them performed. With reſpect
to miracles of *knowledge ;* they ſerve in ſome inſtances
for immediate uſe, particularly the diſcoveries of
diſtant and hidden tranſactions, and of the ſecrets of
the human heart. There are other inſtances of ſupernatural knowlege, the predictions of future events,
which are deſigned to carry conviction in ſome diſtant period. The diſtances between the delivery of
the prophecies and their accompliſhment may be very
different : ſome prophecies may receive a ſpeedy
completion; others may be gradually accompliſhing
through many ſucceeding ages, to the very end of
time ;

time; and hereby furnifh ' evidence to the world, through all thefe different periods. Such prophecies are a *ftanding* and *perpetual* evidence of the miffion of a prophet; always lying *open* to the view and examination of the world. They give credibility to the hiftory of his other miracles, being themfelves one fpecies of miracles, fuch as neceffarily argue a fpecial divine interpofition. And the evidence arifing from them, inftead of being diminifhed, will be increafed by their diftance from the time of their delivery, as the events foretold fucceffively happen.

From the whole of what has been offered, in this and the feveral foregoing chapters, it appears, I hope, that it can be no objection againft the Jewifh and Chriftian revelations, that they reft upon the bafis of miracles.

THE END.